reached out and caught at his hands, trapped the fingers in his own, and Kellin's speech was banished.

This time there were no gods to invoke. The words spilled free of the stranger's mouth as if he could not stop them. *"He is the sword,"* the hissing voice whispered. *"The sword and the bow and the knife. He is the weapon of every man who uses him for ill, and the strength of every man who uses him for good. Child of darkness, child of light; of like breeding with like, until the blood is one again. He is Cynric: the sword and the bow and the knife, and all men shall name him evil until Man is made whole again."*

The voice stopped. Kellin stared, struggling to make an answer, any sort of answer, but the sound began again.

"The lion shall lie down with the witch; out of darkness shall come light; out of death: life; out of the old: the new. The lion shall lie down with the witch, and the witch-child born to rule what the lion must swallow. The lion shall devour the House of Homana and all of her children, so the newborn child shall sit upon the throne and know himself lord of all."

A shudder wracked Kellin from head to toe, and then he cried out and snatched his hands away.

He scrambled to his feet even as the guardsmen shredded canvas with steel to enter the tent. He saw their faces, saw their intent. One of the guards put his hand upon his prince's rigid shoulder, but Kellin did not feel it.

The Lion. The LION.

None of them understood. No one at all knew him for what he was. They saw only the boy . . .

But the Lion wanted him.

CHRONICLES OF THE CHEYSULI: BOOK EIGHT

A TAPESTRY OF LIONS

JENNIFER ROBERSON

DAW BOOKS, INC.

DONALD A. WOLLHEIM, FOUNDER

375 Hudson Street, New York, NY 10014

ELIZABETH R. WOLLHEIM
SHEILA E. GILBERT
PUBLISHERS

This novel is dedicated to the readers.
Leijhana tu'sai.

the Tuhle Ocean
Valgaard
Atvia
Andemir
Rondule
Kilore
Homana
Erinn
Mujhara
Lestra
the Idrian Ocean
Solinde
Hondarth
the Crystal Isle
©Danforth 1984

The Chronicles of the Cheysuli: An Overview

THE PROPHECY OF THE FIRSTBORN:
"One day a man of all blood shall unite, in peace, four warring realms and two magical races.

Originally a race of shapechangers known as the Cheysuli, descendants of the Firstborn, Homana's original race, held the Lion Throne, but increasing unrest on the part of the Homanans, who lacked magical powers and therefore feared the Cheysuli, threatened to tear the realm apart. The Cheysuli royal dynast voluntarily gave up the Lion Throne so that Homanans could rule Homana, thereby avoiding fullblown internecine war.

The clans withdrew altogether from Homanan society save for one remaining and binding tradition: each Homanan king, called a Mujhar, must have a Cheysuli liege man as bodyguard, councillor, companion, dedicated to serving the throne and protecting the Mujhar, until such a time as the prophecy is fulfilled and the Firstborn rule again.

This tradition was adhered to without incident for nearly four centuries, until Lindir, the only daughter of Shaine the Mujhar, jilted her prospective bridegroom to elope with Hale, her father's Cheysuli liege man. Because the jilted bridegroom was the heir of a neighboring king, Bellam of Solinde, and because the marriage was meant to seal an alliance after years of bloody war, the elopement resulted in tragic consequences. Shaine concocted a web of lies to salve his obsessive pride, and in so doing laid the groundwork for the annihilation of a race.

Declared sorcerers and demons dedicated to the downfall of the Homanan throne, the Cheysuli were summarily outlawed and sentenced to immediate execution if found within Homanan borders.

Shapechangers begins the "Chronicles of the Cheysuli," telling the tale of Alix, daughter of Lindir, once Princess of Homana, and Hale, once Cheysuli liege man to Shaine. Alix is an unknown catalyst bearing the Old Blood of the Firstborn, which gives her the ability to link with all *lir* and assume any animal shape at will. But Alix is raised by a Homanan and has no knowledge of her abilities, until she is kidnapped by Finn, a Cheysuli warrior who is Hale's son by his Cheysuli wife, and therefore Alix's half-brother. Kidnapped with her is Carillon, Prince of Homana. Alix learns the true power in her gifts, the nature of the prophecy which rules all Cheysuli, and eventually marries a warrior, Duncan, to whom she bears a son, Donal, and, much later, a daughter, Bronwyn. But Homana's internal strife weakens her defenses. Bellam of Solinde, with his sorcerous aide, Tynstar the Ihlini, conquers Homana and assumes the Lion Throne.

In *The Song of Homana*, Carillon returns from a five-year exile, faced with the difficult task of gathering an army capable of overcoming Bellam. He is accompanied by Finn, who has assumed the traditional role of liege man. Aided by Cheysuli magic and his own brand of personal power, Carillon is able to win back his realm and restore the Cheysuli to their homeland by ending the purge begun by his uncle, Shaine, Alix's grandfather. He marries Bellam's daughter to seal peace between the lands, but Electra has already cast her lot with Tynstar the Ihlini, and works against her Homanan husband. Carillon's failure to father a son forces him to betroth his only daughter, Aislinn, to Donal, Alix's son, whom he names Prince of Homana. This public approbation of a Cheysuli warrior is the first step in restoring the Lion Throne to the sovereignty of the Cheysuli, required by the prophecy, and sows the seeds of civil unrest.

Legacy of the Sword focuses on Donal's slow assumption of power within Homana, and his personal assumption of his role in the prophecy. Because by clan custom a warrior is free to take both wife and mistress, Donal has started a Cheysuli family even though he will one day have to marry Carillon's daughter to cement his right to the Lion Throne. By his Cheysuli mistress he has two children, Ian and Isolde; by Aislinn, Carillon's daughter, he eventually sires a son who will become his heir. But the marriage is rocky immediately; in addition to the problems caused by a second family, Donal's Homanan wife is also under the magical influence of her mother, Electra, who is mistress to Tynstar. Problems are compounded by the son of Tynstar and Electra, Strahan, who has his father's powers in full measure. On Carillon's death Donal inherits the Lion, naming his legitimate son, Niall, to succeed him. But to further the prophecy he marries his sister, Bronwyn, to Alaric of Atvia, lord of an island kingdom. Bronwyn is later killed by Alaric accidentally while in *lir*-shape, but lives long enough to give birth to a daughter, Gisella, who is mad.

In *Track of the White Wolf*, Donal's son Niall is a young man caught between two worlds. To the Homanans, fearful of Cheysuli power and intentions, he is worthy only of distrust, the focus of

their discontent. To the Cheysuli he is an "unblessed" man, because even though far past the
age for it, Niall has not linked with his animal.
He is therfore a *lirless* man, a warrior with no
power, and such a man has no place within the
clans. His Cheysuli half-brother is his liege man,
fully "blessed," and Ian's abilities serve to add to
Niall's feelings of inferiority.

Niall is meant to marry his half-Atvian cousin,
Gisella, but falls in love with the princess of a
neighboring kingdom, Deirdre of Erinn. *Lirless*,
and with Gisella under the influence of Tynstar's
Ihlini daughter, Lillith, Niall falls prey to sorcery.
Eventually he links with his *lir* and assumes the
full range of Cheysuli powers, but he pays for it
with an eye. His marriage to Gisella is disastrous,
but two sets of twins are born—Brennan and Hart,
Corin and Keely—which gives Niall the opportunity to extend his range of influence via betrothal
alliances. He banishes Gisella to Atvia after he
foils an Ihlini plot involving her, and then settles
into life with his mistress, Deirdre of Erinn, who
has already borne Maeve, his illegitimate
daughter.

A Pride of Princes tells the story of each of Niall's
three sons. Brennan, the eldest, will inherit Homana and has been betrothed to Aileen, Deirdre's
niece, to add a heretofore unknown bloodline to
the prophecy. Brennan's twin, Hart, is Prince of
Solinde, a compulsive gambler whose addiction
results in a tragic accident involving all three of
Niall's sons. Hart is banished to Solinde for a year,
and the rebellious youngest son, Corin, to Atvia.
Brennan is tricked into siring a child on an Ihlini-
Cheysuli woman; Hart loses a hand and nearly his
life in a Solindish plot; in Erinn, Corin falls in
love with Brennan's bride, Aileen, before going to
Atvia. One by one each is captured by Strahan,

Tynstar's son, who intends to turn Niall's sons into puppet-kings so he can rule through them. All three manage to escape, but not until after each has been made to recognize particular strengths and weaknesses.

For Keely, sister of Niall's sons, things are different. In *Daughter of the Lion*, Keely herself is caught up in the machinations of politics, evil sorcery, and her own volatile emotions. Trained from childhood in masculine pursuits such as weaponry, Keely prefers the freedom of choice and lifestyle, and as both are threatened by the imminent arrival of her betrothed, Sean of Erinn, she fights to maintain her sense of self in a world ruled by men. She is therefore ripe for rebellion when a strong-minded, powerful Erinnish brigand—and possible murderer—enters her life.

But Keely's battles are increased tenfold when Strahan chooses her as his next target. Betrayed, trapped, and imprisoned on the Crystal Isle, Keely is forced through sorcery into a liaison with the Ihlini that results in pregnancy. But before the child can be born, Keely escapes with the aid of the Ihlini bard, Taliesin. On her way home she meets the man believed to be her betrothed, and realizes not only must she somehow rid herself of the unwanted child, but must also decide which man she will have—thief or prince—in order to be a true Cheysuli in service to the prophecy.

Flight of the Raven is the story of Aidan, only son of Brennan and Aileen. Hounded in childhood by nightmares, Aidan grows to adulthood convinced he is not meant to hold the Lion Throne after all, but is intended to follow a different path. This path becomes more evident as he sets out to visit his kin in Solinde and Erinn in order to find a bride; very quickly it becomes apparent that Aidan has been singled out by the Cheysuli gods to complete a quest for golden links personifying specific Mujhars. In pursuing his quest, Aidan becomes the target of Lochiel the Ihlini, Strahan's son.

Bound by their mutual Erinnish gift of *kivarna*, a strong empathy, Aidan and Shona of Erinn marry. The child of this union will bring the Cheysuli one step closer to completion of the prophecy, and is therefore a grave threat to Lochiel. The Ihlini attacks Clankeep, kills Shona, and cuts the child from her belly. Aidan, seriously wounded, falls victim to epilepsy; in his "fits" he prophesies of the coming of Cynric, the Firstborn. To get back his stolen child, Aidan conquers his weakness to confront Lochiel in Valgaard itself, where he wins back his son. But Aidan realizes he is not meant for thrones and titles; he renounces his rank, gives his son, Kellin, into the keeping of Aileen and Brennan, and takes up residence as a *shar tahl* on the Crystal Isle, where he begins to prepare the way for the coming of the Firstborn.

Prologue

In thread, on cloth, against a rose-red stone wall gilt-washed by early light: Lions. Mujhars, Cheysuli, and Homanan; and the makings of the world in which the boy and his grand-uncle lived.

"Magic," the boy declared solemnly, more intent upon his declaration than most eight-year-olds; but then most eight-year-old boys do not discover magic within the walls of their homes.

The old man agreed easily without the hesitation of those who doubted, or wished to doubt, put off by magic's power; magic was no more alien to him than to the boy, in whose blood it lived as it lived in his own, and in others Cheysuli-born.

"Woman's magic," he said, "conjured from head and hands." His own long-fingered left hand, once darkly supple and eloquent, now stiffened bone beneath wrinkled, yellowing flesh, traced out the intricate stitchwork patterns of the massive embroidered arras hung behind the Lion Throne. "Do you see, Kellin? This is Shaine, whom the Homanans would call your five times great-grandfather. Cheysuli would call him *hosa'ana.*"

It was mid-morning in Shaine's own Great Hall. Moted light sliced through stained glass casements to paint the hall all colors, illuminating the vast expanse of ancient architecture that had housed a hundred kings long before Kellin—or Ian—was born.

The boy, undaunted by the immensity of history or the richness of the hammer-beamed hall and its multitude of trappings, nodded crisply, a little impatient, black brows drawn together in a frown old for his years; as if Kellin, Prince of Homana, knew very well who Shaine was, but did not count him important.

Ian smiled. *And well he might not; his history is more recent, and his youth concerned with now, not yesterday's old Mujhars.*

"Who is this?" A finger, too slender for the characteristic incomplete stubbiness of youth—Cheysuli hands, despite the other houses thickening his blood—transfixed a stitchwork lion made static by the precise skill of a woman's hands. "Is *this* my father?"

"No." The old man's lean, creased-leather face gave away nothing of his thoughts, nothing of his feelings, as he answered the poorly concealed hope in the boy's tone. "No, Kellin. This tapestry was completed before your father was born. It stops here—you see?—" he touched thread, "—with your grandsire."

A dirt-rimmed fingernail bitten off crookedly inserted itself imperatively between dusty threads, once-brilliant colors muted by time and long-set sunlight. "But he should be here. My father. *Somewhere.*"

The expression was abruptly fierce, no longer hopeful, no longer clay as yet unworked, but the taut arrogance of a young warrior as he looked up at the old man, who knew more than the boy what it was to be a warrior; he had even *been* in true war, and was not merely a construct of aging tales.

Ian smiled, new wrinkles replacing old between the thick curtains of snowy hair. "And so he would be, had it taken longer for Deirdre and her women

to complete the Tapestry of Lions. Perhaps someday another woman will begin a new tapestry and
put you and your father and *your* heir in it."

"Mujhars," Kellin said consideringly. "That's
what all of them were." He glanced back at the
huge tapestry filling the wall behind the dais, fixing a dispassionate gaze upon it. The murmured
names were a litany as he moved his finger from
one lion to another: "Shaine, Carillon, Donal,
Niall, Brennan . . ." Abruptly the boy broke off and
took his finger from the stitching. "But my father
isn't Mujhar and never will be." He stared hard
at the old man as if he longed to challenge but
did not know how. "Never *will* be."

It did not discomfit Ian, who had heard it
phrased one way or another for several years. The
intent was identical despite differences in phrase-
ology: Kellin desperately wanted his father, Aidan,
whom he had never met. "No," Ian agreed. "You
are next, after Brennan . . . they have told you
why."

The boy nodded. "Because he left." He meant to
sound matter-of-fact, but did not; the unexpected
shine of tears in clear green eyes dissipated former
fierceness. "He ran *away*!"

Ian tensed. *It would come, one day; now I must
drive it back.* "No." He reached and caught one
slight shoulder, squeezing slightly as he felt the
suppressed, minute trembling. "Kellin—who said
such a monstrous thing? It is not true, as you well
know . . . your father ran from nothing, but *to* his
tahlmorra—"

"They said—" Kellin's lips were white as he
compressed them. "They said he left because he
hated me."

"*Who* said this?"

Kellin bit into his bottom lip. "They said I
wasn't the son he wanted."

"Kellin—"

It was very nearly a wail though he worked to choke it off. "What did I do to make him *hate* me so?"

"Your *jehan* does not hate you."

"Then why isn't he *here*? Why can't he come? Why can't I go *there*?" Green eyes burned fiercely. "Have I done something wrong?"

"No. No, Kellin—you have done nothing wrong."

The small face was pale. "Sometimes I think I must be a bad son."

"In *no way*, Kellin—"

"Then, why?" he asked desperately. "Why can't he come?"

Why indeed? Ian asked himself. He did not in the least blame the boy for voicing what all of them wondered, but Aidan was intransigent. The boy was not to come until he was summoned. Nor would Aidan visit unless the gods indicated it was the proper time. *But will it ever be the proper time?*

He looked at the boy, who tried so hard to give away none of his anguish, to hide the blazing pain. *Homana-Mujhar begins to put jesses on the fledgling.*

Strength waned. Ian desired to sit down upon the dais so as to be on the boy's level and discuss things more equally, but he was old, stiff, and weary; rising again would prove difficult. There was so much he wanted to say that little of it suggested a way *to* be said. Instead, he settled for a simple wisdom. "I think perhaps you have spent too much time of late with the castle boys. You should ask to go to Clankeep. The boys there know better."

It was not enough. It was no answer at all. Ian regretted it immediately when he saw Kellin's expression.

"Grandsire says I may not go. I am to stay *here*,

he says—but he won't tell me why. But I heard—I heard one of the servants say—" He broke it off.

"What?" Ian asked gently. "What have the servants said?"

"That—that even in Clankeep, the Mujhar fears for my safety. That because Lochiel went there once, he might again—and if he knew *I* was there . . ." Kellin shrugged small shoulders. "I'm to be kept here."

It is no wonder, then, he listens to castle boys. Ian sighed and attempted a smile. "There will always be boys who seek to hurt with words. You are a prince—they are not. It is resentment, Kellin. You must not put faith in what they say about your *jehan*. They none of them know what he is."

Kellin's tone was flat, utterly lifeless; his attempt to hide the hurt merely increased its poignancy. "They say he was a coward. And sick. And given to *fits*."

All this, and more . . . he has years yet before they stop, if any of them ever will stop; it may become a weapon meant to prick and goad first prince, then Mujhar. Ian felt a tightness in his chest. The winter had been cold, the coldest he recalled in several seasons, and hard on him. He had caught a cough, and it had not completely faded even with the onset of full-blown spring.

He drew in a carefully measured breath, seeking to lay waste to words meant to taunt the smallest of boys who would one day be the largest, in rank if not in height. "He is a *shar tahl*, Kellin, not a madman. Those who say so are ignorant, with no respect for Cheysuli customs." Inwardly he chided himself for speaking so baldly of Homanans to a young, impressionable boy, but Ian saw no reason to lie. Ignorance was ignorance regardless of its racial origins; he knew his share of stubborn Chey-

suli, too. "We have explained many times why he
went to the Crystal Isle."

"Can't he come to *visit*? That's all I want. Just
a visit." The chin that promised adult intransigence was no less tolerant now. "Or can't I go
there? Wouldn't I be safe *there*, with him?"

Ian coughed, pressing determinedly against the
sunken breastbone hidden beneath Cheysuli jerkin
as if to squeeze his lungs into compliance. "A *shar
tahl* is not like everyone else, Kellin. He serves the
gods . . . he cannot be expected to conduct himself
according to the whims and desires of others." It
was the simple truth, Ian knew, but doubted it
offered enough weight to crush a boy's pain. "He
answers to neither Mujhar nor clan-leader, but to
the gods themselves. If you are to see your *jehan*,
he will send for you."

"It isn't fair," Kellin blurted in newborn bitterness. "Everyone else has a father!"

"Everyone else does *not* have a father." Ian
knew of several boys in Homana-Mujhar and Clankeep who lacked one or both parents. "*Jehans* and
jehanas die, leaving children behind."

"My mother died." His face spasmed briefly.
"They said I killed her."

"No—" No, Kellin had not killed Shona; Lochiel
had. But the boy no longer listened.

"*She's* dead—but my father is *alive*! Can't he
come?"

The cough broke free of Ian's wishes, wracking
lungs and throat. He wanted very much to answer
the boy, his long-dead brother's great-grandson,
but he lacked the breath for it. "—Kellin—"

At last the boy was alarmed. "*Su'fali?*" Ian was
many generations beyond uncle, but it was the
Cheysuli term used in place of a more complex
one involving multiple generations. "Are you sick
still?"

"Winter lingers." He grinned briefly. "The bite of the Lion . . ."

"The Lion is *biting* you?" Kellin's eyes were enormous; clearly he believed there was truth in the imagery.

"No." Ian bent, trying to keep the pain from the boy. It felt as if a burning brand had been thrust deep into his chest. "Here—help me to sit . . ."

"Not there, not on the *Lion*—" Kellin grasped a trembling arm. "I won't let him bite you, *su'fali*."

The breath of laughter wisped into wheezing. "Kellin—"

But the boy chattered on of a Cheysuli warrior's protection, far superior to that offered by others unblessed by *lir* or shapechanging arts and the earth magic, and guided Ian down toward the step. The throne's cushion would soften the harshness of old wood, but clearly the brief mention of the Lion had burned itself into Kellin's brain; the boy would not allow him to sit in the throne now, even now, and Ian had no strength to dissuade him of his false conviction.

"Here, *su'fali*." The small, piquant face was a warrior's again, fierce and determined. The boy cast a sharp glance over his shoulder, as if to ward away the beast.

"Kellin—" But it hurt very badly to talk through the pain in his chest. His left arm felt tired and weak. Breathing was difficult. *Lir* . . . It was imperative, instinctive; through the *lir*-link Ian summoned Tasha from his chambers, where she lazed in a shaft of spring sunlight across the middlemost part of his bed. *Forgive my waking you*—

But the mountain cat was quite awake and moving, answering what she sensed more clearly than what she heard.

And more— With the boy's help Ian lowered himself to the top step of the dais, then bit back a grimace. Breathlessly, he said, "Kellin—fetch your grandsire."

The boy was all Cheysuli save for lighter-hued flesh and Erinnish eyes, wide-sprung eyes: dead Deirdre's eyes, who had begun the tapestry for her husband, Niall, Ian's half-brother, decades before ... —*green as Aileen's eyes*— ... the Queen of Homana, grandmother to the boy; sister to Sean of Erinn, married to Keely, mother of Kellin's dead mother. *So many bloodlines now ... have we pleased the gods and the prophecy?*

The flesh of Kellin's Cheysuli face was pinched Homanan-pale beneath thick black hair. *"Su'fali—"*

Ian twitched a trembling finger in the direction of the massive silver doors gleaming dully at the far end of the Great Hall. "Do me this service, Kellin—"

And as the boy hastened away, crying out loudly of deadly lions, the dying Cheysuli warrior bid his mountain cat to run.

PART I

One

"Summerfair," Kellin whispered in his bed-chamber, testing the sound of the word and all its implications. Then, in exultation, "*Summer*fair!"

He threw back the lid of a clothing trunk and fetched out an array of velvets and brocades, tossing all aside in favor of quieter leathers. He desired to present himself properly but without Homanan pretension, which he disliked, putting into its place the dignity of a Cheysuli.

Summerfair. He was to go, this year. Last year it had been forbidden, punishment as much for his stubborn insistence that he had been right as for the transgression itself, which he *still* believed necessary. They had misunderstood, his grandsire and granddame, and all the castle servants; they had *all* misunderstood, each and every one, regardless of rank, birth, or race.

Ian would have understood, but Kellin's *harani* was two years' dead. And it was *because* of Ian's death—and the means by which that death was delivered—that Kellin sought to destroy what he viewed as further threat to those he loved.

None of them understood. But his mind jumped ahead rapidly, discarding the painful memories of that unfortunate time as he dragged forth from the trunk a proper set of Cheysuli leathers: soft-tanned, russet jerkin with matching leggings; a

25

belt fastened with onyx and worked gold; soft, droopy boots with soles made for leaf-carpeted forest, not the hard bricks of the city.

"—still fit—?" Kellin dragged on one boot and discovered that no, it did not fit, which meant the other didn't either; which meant he had grown again and was likely in need of attention from Aileen's sempstresses with regard to Homanan clothing . . . He grimaced. He intensely disliked such attention. Perhaps he could put on the Cheysuli leathers and wear new Homanan boots; or was that sacrilege?

He stripped free of Homanan tunic and breeches and replaced them with preferred Cheysuli garb, discovering the leggings had shrunk; no, his legs had *lengthened*, which Kellin found pleasing. For a time he had been small, but it seemed he was at last making up for it. Perhaps now no one would believe him a mere eight-year-old, but would understand the increased maturity ten years brought.

Kellin sorted out the fit of his clothing and clasped the belt around slender hips, then turned to survey himself critically in the polished bronze plate hung upon the wall. Newly-washed hair was drying into accustomed curls—Kellin, frowning, instantly tried to mash them away—but his chin was smooth and childish, unmarred by the disfiguring hair Homanans called a beard. Such a thing marked a man less than Cheysuli, Kellin felt, for Cheysuli could not ordinarily grow beards—although some mixed-blood Cheysuli not only could but *did;* it was said Corin, in distant Atvia, wore a beard, as did Kellin's own Errinish grandfather, Sean—but *he* would never do so. Kellin would never subscribe to a fashion that hid a man's heritage behind the hair on his face.

Kellin examined his hairless chin, then ran a finger up one soft-fleshed cheek, across to his nose, and explored the curve of immature browbone above his eyes. Everyone *said* he was a true Chey-suli, save for his eyes—and skin tinted halfway between bronze and fair; though in summer he tanned dark enough to pass as a trueblood—but he could not replace his eyes, and his prayers in childhood that the gods do so had eventually been usurped by a growing determination to overlook the improper color of his eyes and concentrate on other matters, such as warrior skills, which he practiced diligently so as not to dishonor his heri-tage. And anyway, he was *not* solely Cheysuli; had they not, all of them, told him repeatedly he was a mixture of nearly every bloodline there was—or of every one that *counted*—and that he alone could advance the prophecy of the Firstborn one step closer to completion?

They had. Kellin understood. He was Cheysuli, but also Homanan, Solindish, Atvian, and Erin-nish. He was needed, he was important, he was *necessary*.

But sometimes he wondered if he himself, Kel-lin, were not so necessary as his blood. If he cut himself, and spilled it, would that satisfy them—and then make him unimportant?

Kellin grimaced at his reflection. "Sometimes they treat me like Gareth's prize stallion ... I think he forgets what it is to be a *horse*, the way they all treat him. . . ." But Kellin let it go. The image in the polished plate stared back, green eyes transmuted by bronze to dark hazel. The familiar-ity of his features was momentarily blurred by imagination, and he became another boy, a strange boy, a boy with different powers promised one day.

"Ihlini," Kellin whispered. "What are you *really* like? Do you look like demons?"

"I think that unlikely," said a voice from the

doorway: Rogan, his tutor. "I think they probably resemble you and me, rather than horrid specters of the netherworld. You've heard stories of Strahan and Lochiel. They look like everyone else."

Kellin could see Rogan's distorted reflection in the bronze. "Could *you* be Ihlini?"

"Certainly," Rogan replied. "I am an evil sorcerer sent here from Lochiel himself, to take you prisoner and carry you away to Valgaard, where you will doubtlessly be tortured and slain, then given over to Asar-Suti, the Seker—"

Kellin took it up with appropriate melodrama: "—the god of the netherworld, who made and dwells in darkness, and—"

"—who clothes himself in the noxious fumes of his slain victims," Rogan finished.

Kellin grinned his delight; it was an old game. "Grandsire would protect me."

"Aye, he would. That is what a Mujhar is for. He would never allow anyone, sorcerer or not, to steal his favorite grandson."

"I am his *only* grandson."

"And therefore all the more valuable." Rogan's reflection sighed. "I know it has been very difficult for you, being mewed up in Homana-Mujhar for so many years, but it was necessary. You know why."

Kellin knew why, but he did not entirely understand. Punishment had kept him from attending Summerfair for two years, but there was much more to it than that. He had *never* known any freedom to visit Mujhara as others did, or even Clankeep without constant protection.

Kellin turned from the polished plate and looked at Rogan. The Homanan was very tall and thin and was inclined to stoop when he was tired, as he stooped just now. His graying brown hair was damp from recent washing, and he had put on what Kellin called his "medium" clothes: not as plain as his usual somber apparel, but not so fine as those he wore when summoned to sup in the Great Hall with the family, as occasionally happened. Plain black breeches and gray wool tunic over linen shirt, belted and clasped with bronze, replaced his customary attire.

"Why?" Kellin blurted. "Why do they let me go *now*? I heard some of the servants talking. They said grandsire and granddame were too frightened to let me go out."

The lines in Rogan's face etched themselves a little more deeply. "Even they understand they cannot keep you in jesses forever. You must be permitted to weather outside like a hawk on the blocks, or be unfit for the task. And so they have decided you may go this year, as you have improved your manners—and because it is time. I am put in charge . . . but there will be guards also."

Kellin nodded; there were always guards. "Because I'm Aidan's only son, and the only heir." He did not understand all of it. "Because—because if Lochiel killed me, there would be no more threat." He lifted his chin. "That's what they say in the baileys and kitchens."

Rogan's eyes flinched. "You listen entirely too much to gossip—but I suppose it is to be expected. Aye, you are a threat to the Ihlini. And that is why you are so closely guarded. With so many Cheysuli here Lochiel's sorcery cannot reach you, and so you are closely kept—but there *are* other ways, ways involving nothing so much as a greedy cook desiring Ihlini gold—" But Rogan waved it away with a sharply dismissive gesture. "Enough of a sad topic. There will be guards, as always, but your grandsire has decided to allow you this small freedom."

Summerfair was more than a freedom. It was renewal. Kellin forgot all about rumor and gossip. Grinning, he pointed at the purse depending from the belt. His grandfather had given Rogan coin for Summerfair. "Can we go? Now?"

"We can go. Now."

"Then put on your Summerfair face," Kellin ordered sternly. Rogan was a plain, soft-spoken man in his mid-forties only rarely given to laughter, but Kellin had always known a quiet, steady warmth from the Homanan. He enjoyed teasing Rogan out of his melancholy moods, and today was not a day for sad faces. "You will scare away the ladies with that sad scowl."

"What does my face have to do with the ladies?" Rogan asked suspiciously.

"It's *Summerfair*," Kellin declared. "Everyone will be happier than usual because of Summerfair. Even *you* will attract the ladies ... if you put away that scowl."

"I am not scowling, and what do you know about ladies?"

"Enough," Kellin said airily, and strode out of the room.

Rogan followed. "How much is enough, my young lord?"

"*You* know." Kellin stopped in the corridor. "I heard Melora. She was talking to Belinda, who said it had been too long since you'd had a good woman in your bed." Rogan's face reddened immediately. It was the first time any of Kellin's sallies had provoked such a personal reaction, and the boy was fascinated. "Has it been?"

The man rubbed wearily at his scalp. "Aye, well, perhaps. Had I known Belinda and Melora were so concerned about it, I might have asked them for advice on how to change matters." He eyed his charge closely. "How much do you know about men and women?"

"Oh, everything. I know all about them." Kellin set off down the corridor with Rogan matching his longer strides to the boy's. "I was hoping I might find a likely lady during Summerfair."

A large hand descended upon Kellin's shoulder and stopped him in his tracks. "My lord," Rogan said formally, "would you be so good as to tell your ignorant tutor precisely what you are talking about?"

"If you mean how much do I know," Kellin began, "I *know*. I learned all about it last year. And now I would like to try it for myself."

"At ten?" Rogan murmured, as much for himself as for Kellin.

"How old were *you*?"

Rogan looked thoughtful. "They say Cheysuli grow up quickly, and there are stories about your grandsire and his brothers. . . ."

Kellin grinned. "This might be the best Summerfair of all."

"Better than last year, certainly." The understated amusement faded from Rogan's tone. "You do recall why you were refused permission to go."

Kellin shrugged it away. "Punishment."

"And why were you punished?"

Kellin sighed; it was very like Rogan to impose lessons upon a holiday, and reminders of other lessons. "Because I set fire to the tapestry."

"And the year before that?"

"Tried to chop the Lion to bits." Kellin nodded matter-of-factly. "I had to do it, Rogan. It was the Lion who killed Ian."

"Kellin—"

"It came alive, and it bit him. My *harani* said so."

Rogan was patient. "Then why did you try to burn down the tapestry?"

"Because *it's* made of lions, too. You know that." Kellin firmed his mouth; none of them understood, even when he explained. "I have to kill all the lions before they kill me."

Summer was Kellin's favorite season, and the fair the best part of it. Never searingly hot, Homana nonetheless warmed considerably during midsummer, and the freedom everyone felt was reflected in high spirits, habits, and clothing. Banished were the leathers and furs and coarse woolens of winter, replaced by linens and cambrics and silks, unless one was determinedly Cheysuli in habits at all times, as was Kellin, who wore jerkin and leggings whenever he could. Everyone put on Summerfair clothing, brightly dyed and embroidered, and went out into the streets to celebrate the season.

Doors stood open and families gathered before dwellings, trading news and stories, sharing food and drink. In Market Square Mujharan merchants and foreign traders gathered to hawk wares. The streets were choked with the music of laughter, jokes, tambors, pipes and lutes, and the chime of coin exchanged. The air carried the aromas of spices and sweetmeats, and the tang of roasting beef, pork, mutton, and various delicacies.

"Sausage!" Kellin cried. Then, correcting himself—he had taken pains to learn the proper foreign word: "*Suhoqla!* Hurry, Rogan!"

Kellin's nose led him directly to the wagons at the outermost edge of Market Square, conspicuously far from the worst of the tangle in the center of the square. Already a small crowd gathered, Homanans nudging one another with elbows and murmuring pointed comments about the foreigners and foreign ways. That other traders were as foreign did not seem to occur to them; *these* foreigners were rarely seen, and therefore all the more fascinating.

Kellin did not care that they were foreign, save their foreignness promised *suhoqla*, which he adored, and other things as intriguing.

Rogan's voice was stern. "A more deliberate pace, if you please—no darting through the crowd. You make it difficult for the guard to keep up in such crowded streets—and if we lose them, we must return to the palace at once. Is that what you wish to risk?"

Kellin glanced around. There they were, the guard: four men of the Mujharan Guard, handpicked to protect the Prince of Homana. They were unobtrusive in habits and clothing generally, except now they wore the crimson tabards of their station to mark them for what they were: bodyguards to the boy in whom the future of the Cheysuli—and Homana herself—resided.

"But it's *suhoqla* . . . you know how I love it, Rogan."

"Indeed, so you have said many times."

"And I haven't had it for almost two years!"

"Then by all means have some now. All I ask is that you recall I am almost four decades older than you. Old men cannot keep up with small—" he altered it in midsentence, "—young men."

Kellin grinned up at him. "A man as tall as you need only stretch out prodigious legs, and he is in Ellas."

Rogan smiled faintly. "So I have often been told," he looked beyond Kellin to the wagon. "*Suhoqla* it is, then. Though how your belly can abide it . . ." He shook his head in despair. "You will have none left by the time you are my great age."

"It isn't my belly I care about, it's my mouth."

Kellin edged his way more slowly through the throng with Rogan and the watchdogs following closely. "By the time it gets to my belly, it's tamed."

"Ah. Well, here you are."

Here he was. Kellin stared at the three women kneeling around the bowl-shaped frying surface. They had dug a hollow in the sand, placed heated stones in the bottom, then the clay plank atop the stones. The curling links of sausage were cooked slowly in their own grease, absorbing spiced oil.

The women were black-haired and black-eyed, with skins the color of old ivory. Two of them were little more than crones, but the third was much younger. Her eyes, tilted in an oval face, were bright and curious as she flicked a quick assessive glance across the crowd, but only rarely did she look anyone in the eye. She and her companions wore shapeless dark robes and bone jewelry— necklaces, earrings, and bracelets. The old women wore cloth head-coverings; the youngest had pulled her hair up high on the back of her head, tying it so that it hung down her back in a series of tight braids. Two yellow feathers fluttered from one braid as she moved.

"A harsh place, the Steppes," Rogan murmured. "You can see it in their faces."

"Not in *hers*," Kellin declared.

"She is young," Rogan said sadly. "In time, she'll grow to look like the others."

Kellin didn't like to think so, but filling his mouth was more important than concerning himself with a woman's vanishing youth. "Buy me some, Rogan, if you please."

Obligingly Rogan fished a coin out of the purse provided by the Mujhar, and handed it to one of the old women. The young one speared two links with a sharpened stick, then held it out to Kellin.

"Ah," Rogan said, looking beyond. "It isn't merely the women, after all, that attract so many . . . Kellin, do you see the warrior?"

Tentatively testing the heat of the spiced sausages, Kellin peered beyond the women and saw the man Rogan indicated. He forgot his *suhoqla* almost at once; Steppes warriors only rarely showed themselves in Mujhara, preferring to watch their womenfolk from the wagons. This one had altered custom to present himself in the flesh.

The warrior was nearly naked, clad only in a brief leather loin-kilt, an abundance of knives, and scars. He was not tall, but compactly muscled. Black hair was clubbed back and greased, with a straight fringe cut across his brow. He wore a plug of ivory on one nostril, and twin scars bisected each cheek, ridged and black, standing up like ropes from butter-smooth flesh.

Kellin lost count of the scars on the warrior's body; by their patterns and numbers, he began to wonder if perhaps they were to the Steppes warriors as much a badge of honor and manhood as *lir*-gold to a Cheysuli.

At the warrior's waist were belted three knives of differing lengths, and he wore another on his right forearm while yet another was hung about his throat. It depended from a narrow leather thong, sheathed, its greenish hilt glinting oddly in the sunlight of a Homanan summer. The warrior stood spread-legged, arms folded, seemingly deaf and blind to those who gaped and commented, but Kellin knew instinctively the Steppesman was prepared to defend the women—the young one, perhaps?—at a moment's notice.

Kellin looked up at his tutor. "Homana has never fought the Steppes, has she?"

Rogan sighed. "You recall your history, I see. No, Kellin, she has not. Homana has nothing to do with the Steppes, no treaties, no alliances, nothing at all. A few warriors and woman come occasionally to Summerfair, that is all."

"But—I remember *something*—"

"That speaks well of your learning," Rogan said dryly. "What you recall, I believe, is that one of your ancestors, exiled from Homana, went into the service of Caledon and fought against Steppes border raiders."

"Carillon." Kellin nodded. "And Finn, his Cheysuli liege man." He grinned. "I am kin to both."

"So you are." Rogan looked again at the scarred warrior. "A formidable foe, but then Carillon himself was a gifted soldier—"

"—and Finn was *Cheysuli*." Kellin's tone was definitive; nothing more need be said.

"Aye." Rogan was resigned. "Finn was indeed Cheysuli."

Kellin stared hard at the Steppes warrior. The forgotten *suhogla* dripped spiced grease down the front of his jerkin. It was in his mind to make the warrior acknowledge the preeminence of the Cheysuli, to mark the presence of superiority; he wanted badly for the fierceness of the scarred man to pale to insignificance beside the power of his own race, men—and some women—who could assume the shape of animals at will. It was important that the man be made to look at him, to *see* him, to know he was Cheysuli, as was Finn, who had battled Steppes raiders a hundred years before.

At last the black, slanting eyes deigned to glance in his direction. Instinctively, Kellin raised his chin in challenge. "I am Cheysuli."

Rogan grunted. "I doubt he speaks Homanan."

"Then how does he know what anyone says?"

The young woman moved slightly, eyes downcast. "I speak." Her voice was very soft, the Homanan words heavily accented. "I speak, tell Tuqhoc what is said, Tuqhoc decides if speaker lives."

Kellin stared at her in astonishment. "*He* decides!"

"If insult is given, speaker must die." The young woman glanced at the warrior, Tuqhoc, whose eyes had lost their impassivity, and spoke rapidly in a strange tongue.

Kellin felt a foolhardy courage fill up his chest, driving him to further challenge. "Is he going to kill me now?"

The young woman's eyes remained downcast. "I told him you understand the custom."

"And if I insulted you?"

"Kellin," Rogan warned. "Play at no semantics with these people; such folly promises danger."

The young woman was matter-of-fact. "He would choose a knife, and you would die."

Kellin stared at the array of knives strapped against scarred flesh. "Which one?"

She considered it seriously a moment. "The king-knife. That one, one around his neck."

"That one?" Kellin looked at it. "Why?"

Her smile was fleeting, and aimed at the ground. "A king-knife for a king—or a king's son."

It was utterly unexpected. Heat filled Kellin's face. Everyone else *knew;* he was no longer required to explain. He had set aside such explanations years before. But now the young woman had stirred up the emotions again, and he found the words difficult. "My father is not a king."

"You walk with dogs."

"Dogs?" Baffled, Kellin glanced up at Rogan. "He is my tutor, not a dog. He teaches me things."

"I try to," Rogan remarked dryly.

She was undeterred by the irony. "Them." Her glance indicated the alerted Mujharan Guard,

moving closer now that their charge conversed
with strangers from the Steppes.

Kellin saw her gaze, saw her expression, and
imagined what she thought. It diminished him. In
her eyes, he was a boy guarded by dogs; in his,
the son of a man who had renounced his rank and
legacy, as well as the seed of his loins. In that
moment Kellin lost his identity, stripped of it by
foreigners, and it infuriated him.

He stared a challenge at the warrior. "Show
me."

Rogan's hand came down on Kellin's shoulder.
Fingers gripped firmly, pressing him to turn. "This
is quite enough."

Kellin was wholly focused on the warrior as he
twisted free of the tutor's grip. "*Show* me."

Rogan's voice was clipped. "Kellin, I said it was
enough."

The watchdogs were there, *right* there, so close
they blocked the sun. But Kellin ignored them. He
stared at the young woman. "Tell him to show
me. Now!"

The ivory-dark faced paled. "Tuqhoc never
shows—Tuqhoc *does*."

Kellin did not so much as blink even as the
watchdogs crowded him. He pulled free of a hand:
Rogan's. "Tell him what I said."

Tuqhoc, clearly disturbed by the change in tone
and stance—and the free use of his own name—
barked out a clipped question. The young woman
answered reluctantly. Tuqhoc repeated himself, as
if disbelieving, then laughed. For the first time
emotion glinted in his eyes. Tuqhoc smiled at Kellin and made a declaration in the Steppes tongue.

Rogan's hands closed on both shoulders deci-
sively. "We are leaving. I warned you, my lord."

"No," Kellin declared. To the young woman:
"What did he say?"

"Tuqhoc says, if he shows, you die."

"Only a fool taunts a Steppes warrior—I thought you knew better." Rogan's hands forced Kellin to turn. "Away. Now."

Kellin tore free. "*Show* me!" Even as Rogan blurted an order, the watchdogs closed on the warrior, drawing swords. Kellin ducked around one man, then slid through two others. The dark Steppes eyes were fixed on the approaching men in fierce challenge. Kellin desperately wanted to regain that attention for himself. "Show me!" he shouted.

Tuqhoc slipped the guard easily, *so* easily—even as the challenge was accepted. In one quick, effortless motion Tuqhoc plucked the knife from the thong around his neck and threw.

For Kellin, the knife was all. He was only peripherally aware of the women crying out, the guttural invective of the warrior as the watchdogs pressed steel against his flesh.

Rogan reached for him—

Too late. The knife was in the air. And even as Rogan twisted, intending to protect his charge by using his own body as shield, Kellin stepped nimbly aside. *For ME*—

He saw the blade, watched it, judged its arc, its angle, anticipated its path. Then he reached out and slapped the blade to the ground.

"By the gods—" Rogan caught his shoulders and jerked him aside. "Have you any idea—?"

Kellin did. He could not help it. He stared at the warrior, at the Steppes women, at the knife in the street. He knew precisely what he had done, and why.

He wanted to shout his exultation, but knew better. He looked at the watchdogs and saw the fixed, almost feral set of jaws; the grimness in their faces; the acknowledgment in their eyes as they caged the Steppesman with steel.

It was not his place to gloat; Cheysuli warriors did not lower themselves to such unnecessary displays.

Kellin bent and picked up the knife. He noted the odd greenish color and oily texture of the blade. He looked at Rogan, then at the young woman whose eyes were astonished.

As much as for his tutor's benefit as for hers, Kellin said: "Tell Tuqhoc that I am Cheysuli."

Two

Rogan's hand shut more firmly on Kellin's shoulder and guided him away despite his burgeoning protest. Kellin was aware of the Mujharan Guard speaking to Tuqhoc and the young woman, of the tension in Rogan's body, and of the startled murmuring of the crowd.

"Wait—" He wanted to twist away from Rogan's grasp, to confront Tuqhoc of the Steppes and see the acknowledgment in *his* eyes, as it was in the woman's, that a Cheysuli, regardless of youth and size, was someone to be respected. But Rogan permitted no movement save that engineered by himself. *Doesn't he understand? Doesn't he know?*

Unerringly—and unsparing of his firmness—the Homanan guided Kellin away from the wagons to a quieter pocket in the square some distance away. His tone was flat, as if he squeezed out all emotion for fear of showing too much. "Let me see your hand."

Now that the moment had passed and he could no longer see the Steppes warrior, Kellin's elation died. He felt listless, robbed of his victory. Sullenly he extended his hand, allowing Rogan to see the slice across the fleshy part of three fingers and the blood running down his palm.

Tight-mouthed, Rogan muttered something about childish fancies; Kellin promptly snatched back his bleeding hand and pressed it against the

41

sausage-stained jerkin. The uneaten *suhoqla* grasped in his other hand grew colder by the moment.

Rogan said crisply, "I will find something with which to bind these cuts."

Blood mingled with sausage grease as Kellin pressed the fingers against his jerkin. It stung badly enough to make the corners of his mouth crimp, but he would not speak of it. He would give away nothing. "Leave it be. It has already stopped." He fisted his hand so hard the knuckles turned white, then displayed it to Rogan. "You see?"

The tutor shook his head slowly, but he gave the hand only the merest contemplation; he looked mostly at Kellin's face, as if judging him.

I won't let him know. Kellin put up his chin. "I am a warrior. Such things do not trouble warriors."

Rogan shook his head again. Something broke in his eyes: an odd, twisted anguish. His breath hissed between white teeth. "While you are fixed wholly on comporting yourself as a warrior, neglecting to recall you are still but a *boy*—I realize it will do little if any good to point out that the knife could have *killed you.*" The teeth clamped themselves shut. "But I'll wager that was part of the reason you challenged him. Yet you should know that such folly could result in serious repercussions."

"But I could *see*—"

Rogan cut off the protest. "If not for yourself, for me and the guard! Do you realize what would become of us if you came to harm?"

Kellin had not considered that. He looked at Rogan more closely and saw the very real fear in his tutor's eyes. Shame goaded. "No," he admitted, then anxiousness usurped it, and the need to explain. "But I needed him to see. To *know*—"

"Know what? That you are a boy too accustomed to having his own way?"

"That I am Cheysuli." Kellin squeezed his cut hand more tightly closed. "I want them *all* to know. They have to know—they have to understand that I am not *he*—"

"Kellin—"

"Don't you see? I have to prove I am a *true* man, not a coward—that I will not turn my back on duty and my people—and—and—" he swallowed painfully, finishing his explanation quickly, unevenly, "—any sons *I* might sire."

Rogan's mouth loosened. After a moment it tightened again, and the muscles of his jaw rolled briefly. Quietly, he said, "Promise me *never* to do such a thoughtless thing again."

Feeling small, Kellin nodded, then essayed a final attempt at explanation. "I watched his eyes. Tuqhoc's. I knew when he would throw, and how, and what the knife would do. I had only to put out my hand, and the knife was *there*." He shrugged self-consciously, seeing the arrested expression in Rogan's eyes. "I just knew. I *saw*." Dismayed, he observed his congealing sausage as Rogan fixed him with a more penetrating assessment. Kellin extended the stick with its weight of greasy *suhqla*. "Do you want this?"

The Homanan grimaced. "I cannot abide the foul taste of those things. *You* wanted it—eat it."

But Kellin's appetite was banished by aftermath. "It's cold." He glanced around, spied a likely looking dog, and approached to offer the sausage. The mongrel investigated the meat, wrinkled its nose and sneezed, then departed speedily.

"*That* says something for your taste," Rogan remarked dryly. He drew his own knife, cut a strip of fabric from the hem of his tunic, motioned a passing water-seller over and bought a cup. He dipped the cloth into the water and began to wipe the cut clean. "By the gods, the Queen will have my hide for this . . . you are covered with grease and blood."

Rogan's ministrations hurt. No longer hungry, Kellin discarded the *suhoqla*. He bit into his lip as the watchdogs came up and resumed their places, though the distance between their charge and their persons was much smaller now.

Humiliation scorched his face; warriors did not, he believed, submit so easily to public nursing. "I want to see the market."

Rogan looped the fabric around the fingers and palm to make a bandage, then tied it off. "We are *in* the market; look around, and you will see it." He tightened the knot. "There. It will do until we return to the palace."

Kellin's mind was no longer on the stinging cut or its makeshift bandage. He frowned as a young boy passed by, calling out in singsong Homanan. "A fortune-teller!"

"No," Rogan said promptly.

"But *Rogan*—"

"Such things are a waste of good coin." Rogan shrugged. "You are Cheysuli. You already know your *tahlmorra*."

"But you don't yet know yours." Grinning anticipation, Kellin locked his bandaged hand over Rogan's wrist. "Don't you want to find out if you'll share your bed with Melora or Belinda?"

Rogan coughed a laugh, glancing sidelong at the guards. "No mere fortune-teller can predict *that*. Women do what they choose to do; they do not depend on fate."

Kellin tugged his tutor in the direction the passing boy had indicated. "Let us go, Rogan. That boy says the fortune-teller can predict what becomes of me."

"That boy is a shill. He says what he's told to say, and the fortune-teller says what he's *paid* to say."

"*Ro*-gan!"

Rogan sighed. "If you desire it so much—"

"Aye!" Kellin tugged him on until they stood before a tent slumped halfheartedly against a wall. A black cat, small version of the Mujhar's *lir*, Sleeta, lay stretched out on a faded rug before the entrance, idly licking one paw; beside him curled a half-grown fawn-hued dog who barely lifted an eyelid. The tent itself was small, its once-glorious stripes faded gold against pale brown, so that it merged into the wall. "My grandsire gave you coin for such things," Kellin reminded his tutor. "Surely he could not count it ill-spent if we *enjoyed* it!"

Graying eyebrows arched. "A sound point. That much you have mastered, if not your history." Rogan gestured for the guardsmen to precede them into the tent.

"No!" Kellin cried.

"They must, Kellin. The Mujhar has given orders. And after what you provoked in the Steppes warrior, I *should* take you home immediately."

Kellin compromised immediately. "They may come wait *here*." His gesture encompassed the rug and entrance. "But not inside the tent. A fortune is a private thing."

"I cannot allow the Prince of—"

"Say nothing of titles!" Kellin cried. "How will the fortune-teller give me the truth otherwise? If he knows what I am, it cheats the game."

"At least you admit it *is* a game, for which I thank the gods; you are not entirely gullible. But rules are rules; the Mujhar is my lord, not you." Rogan ordered one of the guardsmen into the tent. "He will see that it is safe."

Kellin waited impatiently until the guardsman

came out again. When the man nodded his head, Rogan had him and his companions assume posts just outside the tent.

"Now?" Kellin asked, and as Rogan nodded he slipped through the doorflap.

Inside the tent, Kellin found the shadows stuffy and redolent of an acrid, spice-laden smoke that set his eyes to watering. He wiped at them hastily, wrinkling his nose at the smell very much as the street dog did to the *suhoqla*, and squinted to peer through the thready haze. A gauzy dark curtain merged with shadow to hide a portion of the tent; he and Rogan stood in what a castle-raised boy would call an antechamber, though the walls were fabric in place of stone.

Rogan bent slightly, resting a hand on Kellin's shoulder as he spoke in a low tone. "You must recall that he works for *coin*, Kellin. Put no faith in his words."

Kellin frowned. "Don't spoil it."

"I merely forewarn that what he says—"

"Don't *spoil* it!"

The gauzy curtain was parted. The fortune-teller was a nondescript, colorless foreign man of indeterminate features, wearing baggy saffron pantaloons and three silk vests over a plain tunic: one dyed blue, the next red, the third bright green. "Forgive an old man his vice: I smoke *husath*, which is not suitable for guests unless they also share the vice." He moved out of the shadowed curtain, bringing the sweet-sour aroma with him. "I do not believe either of you would care for it."

"What is it?" Kellin was fascinated.

Rogan stirred slightly. "Indeed, a vice. It puts dreams in a man's head."

Kellin shrugged. "Dreams are not so bad. I dream every night."

"*Husath* dreams are different. They can be dangerous when they make a man forget to eat or drink." Rogan stared hard at the man. "The boy wants his fortune told, nothing more. You need not initiate him into a curiosity that may prove dangerous."

"Of course." The man smiled faintly and gestured to a rug spread across the floor. "Be in comfort, and I will share with you your future, and a little of your past."

"He is all of ten; his past is short," Rogan said dryly. "This shouldn't take long."

"It will take as long as it must." The fortune-teller gestured again. "I promise you no tricks, no *husath*, no nonsense, only the truth."

Kellin turned and gazed up at Rogan. "You first."

The brows arched again. "We came for *you*."

"You *first*."

Rogan considered it, then surrendered gracefully, folding long legs to seat himself upon the rug just opposite the fortune-teller. "For the boy's sake, then."

"And nothing for yourself?" The fortune-teller's teeth were stained pale yellow. "Give me your hands."

Kellin dropped to his knees and waited eagerly. "Go on, Rogan. Give him your hands."

With a small, ironic smile, Rogan acquiesced. The fortune-teller merely looked at the tutor's hands for a long moment, examining the minute whorls and scars in his flesh, the length of fingers, the fit of nails, the color of the skin. Then he linked his fingers with Rogan's, held them lightly, and began to murmur steadily as if invoking the gods.

"No tricks," Rogan reminded.

"Shhh," Kellin said. "Don't spoil the magic."

"This isn't magic, Kellin ... this is merely entertainment."

But the fortune-teller's tone altered, interrupting the debate. His voice dropped low into a singsong cadence that made the hair rise up on the back of Kellin's neck: *"Alone in the midst of many, even those whom you love . . . apart and separate, consumed by grief. She lives within you when she is dead, and you live through her, seeing her face when you sleep and wake, longing for the love she cannot offer. You live in the pasts of kings and queens and those who have gone before you, but you thrive upon your own. Your past is your present and will be your future, until you summon the strength to give her life again. Offered and spurned, it is offered again; spurned and offered a third time until, accepting, you free yourself from the misery of what is lost to you, and then live in the misery of what you have done. You will die knowing what you have done, and why, and the price of your reward. You will use and be used in turn, discarded at last when your use is passed."*

Rogan jerked his hands away with a choked, inarticulate protest. Kellin, astonished, stared at his tutor; what he saw made him afraid. The man's face was ashen, devoid of life, and his eyes swam with tears.

"Rogan?" Apprehension seized his bones and washed his flesh ice-cold. *"Rogan!"*

But Rogan offered no answer. He sat upon the rug and stared at nothingness as tears ran down his face.

"A harsh truth," the fortune-teller said quietly, exhaling *husath* fumes. "I promise no happiness."

"Rogan—" Kellin began, and then the fortune-teller reached out and caught at *his* hands, trapped the fingers in his own, and Kellin's speech was banished.

This time there were no gods to invoke. The words spilled free of the stranger's mouth as if he could not stop them. *"He is the sword,"* the hissing voice whispered. *"The sword and the bow and the knife. He is the weapon of every man who uses him for ill, and the strength of every man who uses him for good. Child of darkness, child of light; of like breeding with like, until the blood is one again. He is Cynric, he is Cynric: the sword and the bow and the knife, and all men shall name him evil until Man is made whole again."*

The voice stopped. Kellin stared, struggling to make an answer, any sort of answer, but the sound began again.

"The lion shall lie down with the witch; out of darkness shall come light; out of death: life; out of the old: the new. The lion shall lie down with the witch, and the witch-child born to rule what the lion must swallow. The lion shall devour the House of Homana and all of her children, so the newborn child shall sit upon the throne and know himself lord of all."

A shudder wracked Kellin from head to toe, and then he cried out and snatched his hands away. "The Lion!" he cried. "The Lion *will* eat me!"

He scrambled to his feet even as the guardsmen shredded canvas with steel to enter the tent. He saw their faces, saw their intent; he saw Rogan's tear-streaked face turning to him. Rogan's mouth moved, but Kellin heard nothing. One of the guards put his hand upon his prince's rigid shoulder, but Kellin did not feel it.

The Lion. The LION.

He knew in that instant they were unprepared, just as the Steppes warrior had been unprepared. *None* of them understood. No one at all knew him for what he was. They saw only the boy, the deserted son, and judged him worthless.

Aren't I worthless?

But the Lion wanted him.

Kellin caught his breath. *Would the Lion want to eat a worthless boy?*

Perhaps he *was* worthless, and that fact alone was why the Lion might want to eat him.

To save Homana from a worthless Mujhar.

With an inarticulate cry, Kellin tore free of the guardsman's hand and ran headlong from the tent. He ignored the shouts of the Mujharan guard and the blurted outcry of his tutor. He tore free of them all, even of the tent, and clawed his way out of pale shadow into the brilliance of the day.

"Lion—" Kellin blurted, then darted into the crowd even as the man came after him.

Run—
He ran.
Where—?
He did not know.
Away from the Lion—
Away.
—won't let the Lion eat me— He tripped and fell, facedown, banging his chin into a cobble hard enough to make himself bite his lip. Blood filled his mouth; Kellin spat, lurched up to hands and knees, then pressed the back of one hand against his lower lip to stanch the bleeding. The hand bled, too; Rogan's bandage had come off. The cut palm and his cut mouth stung.

It smells— It did. He had landed full-force in a puddle of horse urine. His jerkin was soaked with it; the knees of his leggings, ground into cobbles as well, displayed the telltale color and damp texture of compressed horse droppings.

Aghast, Kellin scrambled to his feet. He was *filthy*. In addition to urine and droppings weighting his leathers, there was mud, grease, and blood; and he had lost his belt entirely somewhere in his mad rush to escape the Lion. No one, seeing him now, would predict his heritage or House.

"Rogan?" He turned, thinking of his tutor instead of the Lion; recalled the fortune-teller's words, and how Rogan had reacted. And the watchdogs; where were they? Had he left everyone behind? *Where am—*

Someone laughed. "Poor boy," said a woman's voice, "have you spoiled all your Summerfair finery?"

Startled, he gaped at her. She was blonde and pretty, in a coarse sort of way, overblown and overpainted. Blue eyes sparkled with laughter; a smile displayed crooked teeth.

Humiliated, Kellin stared hard at the ground and tried to uncurl his toes. *I don't want to be here. I want to go HOME.*

"What a pretty blush; as well as I could do, once." Skirts rustled faintly. "Come here."

Reluctantly Kellin glanced up slantwise, marking the garish colors of her multiple skirts. One hand beckoned. He ignored it, thinking to turn his back on her, to leave the woman behind, but the laughter now was muted, replaced with a gentler facade.

"Come," she said. "Has happened to others, too."

She wasn't his granddame, who welcomed him into her arms when he needed a woman's comfort, but she *was* a woman, and she spoke kindly enough now. This time when she beckoned, he answered. She slipped a hand beneath his bloodied chin, forcing him to look up into her own face. At closer range her age increased, yet her eyes seemed kind enough in an assessive sort of way. Her hair was not really blonde, he discovered by staring at exposed roots, and the faintest hint of dark fuzz smudged her upper lip.

The woman laughed. "Don't blush *quite* so much, boy. You'll have me thinking you've never seen a whore before."

He gaped. "You are a light woman?"

"A *light*—" She broke off, brows lifting. "Is that the genuine accent of aristrocracy?" She leaned closer, enveloping him in a powerful, musky scent. "Or are you like me: a very good mimic?"

She is NOT like granddame after all. Kellin tugged at his ruined jerkin, than blotted again at his split lip. She watched him do it, her smile less barbed, and at last she took her hand from his chin, which relieved him immeasurably. "Lady—"

"No, not that. Never that." Her hand strayed into his hair, lingered in languourous familiarity. Her touch did not now *in the least* remind him of his grandmother's. "Why is it," the woman began, "that boys and men have thicker hair and longer lashes? The gods have truly blessed you, my green-eyed little man." The other hand touched his leggings. "And how little *are* we in things that really matter?"

Kellin nearly squirmed. "I—I must go."

"Not so soon, I pray you." She mocked the elaborate speech of highborn Homanans. "We hardly know one another."

That much Kellin knew; he'd heard the horse-boys speaking of whores. "I have no money." Rogan had plenty, but he doubted the Mujhar would approve of it being spent on women.

The whore laughed. "Well, then, what *have* you? Youth. Spirit. Pretty eyes, and a prettier face— you'll have women killing over you, when you're grown." Her eyes lost their laughter. "Men would kill for you now." The smile fell off her face. "And innocence, which is something everyone in the Midden has lost. If I could get some back, *steal* it back, somehow—"

Kellin took a single step backward. Her hand latched itself into his filthy jerkin; she did not seem to notice her hand now was also soiled. "I must go," he tried again.

"No," she said intently. "No. Stay a while. Share with me youth and innocence—"

Kellin wrenched away from her. As he ran, he heard her curse.

This time when he fell, Kellin managed to avoid urine and droppings, landing instead against hard stone cobbles after his collision with a woman carrying a basket. He feared at first she might also be a whore, but she had none of the ways or coarse speech. She was angry, aye, because he had upset her basket; and then she was screaming something about a thief—

"No!" Kellin cried, thinking he could explain and set everything to rights—the Prince of Homana, a *thief*?—but the woman kept on shrieking, ignoring his denials, and he saw the men, big men all, hastening toward him.

He ran again, and was caught. The man grabbed him by one arm and hoisted him into the air so that one boot toe barely scraped the cobblestones. "Give over, boy. No more kicking and biting."

Kellin, who had not thought to bite, squirmed in the tight grasp. He intensely disliked being hung by one wrist like a side of venison. "I am not a boy, I'm a *prince*—"

"And I'm the Mujhar of Homana." The man waited until Kellin's struggles subsided. "Done, are we?"

"Let me *go*!"

"Not until I have the ropes on you."

Kellin stiffened. "Ropes!"

"I and others like me are sworn to keep the rabble off the streets during Summerfair," the big man explained. "That includes catching all the little thieves who prey on innocent people."

"I'm not a thief, you *ku'reshtin*—"

The big hand closed more tightly. "Round speech for a boy, by your tone."

"I am the Prince of Homana!"

The man sighed. He was very large, and red-haired; he was also patently unimpressed by Kellin's protests. "Save your breath, boy. It only means a night under a decent roof, instead of some alley or doorway. And you'll be fed, so don't be complaining so much when you're better off now than you were."

"But I'm—" Kellin broke off in astonishment as the men looped a rope around one wrist, then the other. Prince or no, he was snugged tight as a gamebird. "Wait!"

The man nodded patiently. "Come along, then, and I'll see to it you have a decent meal and a place to sleep. I'll free you first thing in the morning if anyone comes to fetch you."

The furious challenge was immediate. "If I had a *lir*—"

"What? Cheysuli, too?" The giant laughed, though not unkindly. "Well, I'm thinking not. I've never yet seen one with green eyes, nor leathers *quite* so filthy."

Three

Kellin did not know Mujhara well. In fact, he knew very little about the city he would one day rule, other than the historical implications Rogan had discussed so often; and even then he was ignorant of details because he had not listened well. He wanted to do something much more exciting than spend his days speaking of the past. The future attracted him more, even though Rogan explained again and again that the past affected that future; that a man learning from the past often avoided future difficulties.

Because he was so closely accompanied each time he left Homana-Mujhar, Kellin had come to rely on others to direct him. Left to his own devices, he would have been lost in a moment as he was lost now. The big red-haired man led him like a leashed dog through the winding closes, alleys, and streets, turning this way and that, until Kellin could not so much as tell which direction was which.

He felt the heat of shame as he was led unrelentingly. *Don't look at me—* But they did, all the people, the Summerfair crowds thronging the closes, alleys, and streets. Kellin thought at first if he called out to them and told them who he was, if he asked for their support, they would give it gladly. But the first time he tried, a man laughed at him and called him a fool for thinking they would believe such a lie; would the Prince of Homana wear horse piss on his clothing?

Don't look at me. But they looked. Inwardly, Kellin died a small, quiet death, the death of dignity. *I just want to go home.*

"Here," his captor said. "You'll spend the night inside." The giant opened the door, took Kellin inside, then handed over the "leash" to another man, this one brown-haired and brown-eyed, showing missing teeth. "Tried to steal a goodwife's basket of ribbons."

"No!" Kellin cried. "I did *not*. I fell against her, no more, and knocked it out of her hands. What would I want with ribbons?"

The gap-toothed man grinned. "To sell them, most like. At a profit, since you paid nothing for them in the first place."

Kellin was outraged. "I did not steal her ribbons!"

"Had no chance to," the redhead laughed. "She saw to that, with her shrieking."

Kellin drew himself up, depending on offended dignity and superior comportment to put an end to the intolerable situation. Plainly he declared, "I am the Prince of Homana."

He expected apologies, respect, and got neither. The two men exchanged amused glances. The gap-toothed Homanan nodded. "As good a liar as a thief, isn't he? Only that's not so good, is it, since you're *here*?"

Courage wavered; Kellin shored it up with a desperate condescension. "I am here with my tutor and four guardsman, four of the *Mujharan Guard*." He hoped it would make a suitable impression, invoking his grandfather's personal company. "Go and ask *them;* they will tell you."

"Wild goose chase," said the redhead. "Waste of time."

Desperation nearly engulfed injured pride. "Go

and *ask*," Kellin directed. "Go to Homana-Mujhar. My grandsire will tell you the truth."

"Your grandsire. The Mujhar?" Gap-tooth laughed, slanting a bright glance at the giant.

Kellin bared his teeth, desiring very badly to prove the truth of his claims. But his leathers were smeared with filth, his bottom lip swollen, and his face, no doubt, as dirty. "My boots," he said sharply, sticking out one foot. "Would a thief have boots like these?"

The redhead grinned. "If he stole them."

"But they *fit*. Stolen boots would not fit."

Gap-tooth sighed. "Enough of your jabber, brat. You'll not be harmed, just kept until someone comes to fetch you."

"But no one knows where I am! How can they come?"

"If you're the Prince of Homana, they'll know." The giant's eyes were bright. "D'ye think I'm a fool? You've *my* eyes, boy, plain Homanan green, not the yellow of a Cheysuli. Next time you want to claim yourself royalty, you'd best think better of it."

Kellin gaped. "My granddame is Erinnish, with hair red as yours—redder! I have *her* eyes—"

"Your granddame—and your mother to boot—was likely a street whore, brat . . . no more chatter from you. Into the room. We're not here to harm you, just *keep* you." The red-haired giant pushed Kellin through another door as Gap-tooth unlocked it. He was dumped unceremoniously onto a thin pallet in a small, stuffy room, then the door was locked.

For a moment Kellin lay sprawled in shock, speechless in disbelief. Then he realized they'd stripped the rope from his wrists. He scrambled up and hammered at the door.

"They won't open it. They won't."

Kellin jerked around, seeing the boy in the corner for the first time. The light was poor, admitted only through a few holes high up in the walls. The boy slumped against the wall with the insouciance of a longtime scofflaw. His face was thin, grimy, and bruised. Lank blond hair hung into his eyes, but his grin was undiminished by Kellin's blatant surprise.

"Urchin," the boy said cheerfully, answering the unasked question.

Kellin was distracted by newborn pain in his cut hand, which now lacked Rogan's bandage. He frowned to see the slices were packed with dirt and other filth; wiping it against his jerkin merely caused the slices to sting worse. Scowling, he asked, "What kind of a name is that?"

"Isn't a name. Haven't got one. That's what they call me, *when* they call me." The boy shoved a wrist through his hair. His eyes were assessive far beyond his years. "Good leathers, beneath the dirt . . . good boots, too. No thief, are ye?"

Kellin spat on the cuts and wiped them again against his jerkin. "Tell *them* that."

Urchin grinned. "Won't listen. All they want is the copper."

"Copper?"

"Copper a head for all the thieves they catch."

Kellin frowned, giving up on his sore hand. "Who pays it?"

Urchin shrugged. "People. They're fed up wi' getting their belt-purses stolen and pockets picked." He waggled fingers. "Some o' them took up a collection, like . . . for each thief caught during Summerfair, they pay a copper a head. Keeps the streets clean of us, y'see, and *they* can walk out without fearing for pockets and purses." Urchin grinned. "But if you're good enough, nobody catches you."

"*You* got caught."

"Couldn't run fast enough with this." Urchin extended a swollen, discolored foot and puffy ankle. "Dog set on me." He was patently unconcerned by the condition of foot and ankle. "If you're not a thief, why're you here?"

Kellin grimaced. "I was running. They thought it was because I was stealing."

"Never run in Mujhara," the boy advised solemnly, then reconsidered. "Unless you be a fine Homanan lord, and then no one will bother you no matter *what* you do."

Kellin glanced around. On closer inspection, the room was no better than his first impression, a small imprisonment, empty save for them. "Not so many copper pieces today."

Urchin shrugged. "The other room is full. They'll put the new catches in here. You're the first, after me."

Kellin peeled a crust of blood from his chin. "How do we get out?"

"Wait till someone pays your copper. Otherwise we stay here till Summerfair is over, because then it won't matter."

"That's three days from now!"

Urchin shrugged, surveying his injured foot. "Be hard to steal with this."

Kellin stared at the swollen limb, marking the angry discoloration and the streaks beginning to make their way up Urchin's leg. It was a far worse injury than the few slices in his hand. "You need that healed."

Urchin's mouth hooked down. "Leeches cost coin."

Morbidly fascinated by the infected limb, Kellin knelt down to look more closely. "A Cheysuli could heal this, and he would cost nothing."

Urchin snorted.

"He *could*," Kellin insisted. "*I* could, had I a *lir*."

Urchin's eyes widened. "You say *you're* Cheysuli?"

"I am. But I can't heal yet." Kellin shrugged a little. "Until I have a *lir*, I'm just like you." The wound stank of early putrefaction. "My grandsire will heal you. He has a *lir*; he can." *And he will heal my wounds, too.*

Urchin grunted. "Will he come here to pay your copper?"

Kellin considered it. "No," he said finally, feeling small inside. "I think Rogan will do that, and I doubt he will like it."

"Few men like parting with coin."

"Oh, it is not the coin. He will not like *why* he has to do it, and it will give him fuel to use against me for months." Kellin cast a glance around the gloomy room. "He would say I deserved this, to teach me a lesson. But it was the *Lion*—" He looked quickly at Urchin, breaking off.

The Homanan boy frowned. "What lion?"

"Nothing." Kellin left Urchin's side and retreated to a pallet near the door. He pressed shoulder blades into the wall. "He will come for me."

"That tutor?" Urchin's mouth twisted. "I had a tutor, once. He taught me how to steal."

Kellin shrugged. "Then stop."

"Stop." Urchin stared. "D'ye think it's so easy? D'ye think I asked the gods for this life?"

"No one would ask it. But why do you stay *in* it?"

"No choice." Urchin picked at his threadbare tunic. His thin face was pinched as if his leg pained him. "No mother, no father, no kin." His expression hardened. "I'm a thief, and a good one." He looked at his swollen ankle. "Sometimes."

Kellin nodded. "Then I will have Rogan pay

your copper, too, and you will come back with me."

Urchin's dirt-mottled face mocked. "With you."

"To Homana-Mujhar."

"Liar."

Kellin laughed. "As good a liar as a thief."

Urchin turned his shoulder: eloquent dismissal.

With his pallet nearest the door, Kellin awoke each time a new arrival was pushed into the room throughout the night. At first he had been intrigued by the number and their disparate "crimes," but soon enough boredom set in, and later weariness; he fell asleep not long after a plain supper of bread and thin gravy was served, and slept with many interruptions until dawn.

The commotion was distant at first, interesting only the few recently imprisoned souls who hoped for early release. That hope had faded in Kellin, who found himself reiterating to a dubious Urchin that indeed he *was* who he said he was, and was restored only when he heard the voice through the door: the red-haired man, clearly frightened as well as astonished.

Kellin grinned at the young thief through pale dawn. "Rogan. I *told* you, Urchin."

The door was opened and a man came in. It wasn't Rogan at all, but the Mujhar himself, followed by the giant.

Kellin scrambled hastily to his feet. "Grandsire! You?"

The giant was very pale. "My lord, how could we know? *Had* we known—"

Stung by the outrage, Kellin turned on the man. "You knew," he declared. "I told you. You just didn't *believe* me." He looked at his grandfather. "None of them believed me."

"Nor would I," Brennan said calmly. He arched

a single eloquent brow. "Have you taken to swimming in the midden?" Yellow eyes brightened faintly, dispelling the barb. "Or was it an entirely *different* kind of Midden?"

Kellin recalled then the whore's words, her mention of the Midden. It basted his face with heat. Such *shame* before his grandsire! "My lord Mujhar ..." He let it trail off. Part of him was overwhelmed to be safe at last, while the other part was mortified that his grandsire should see him so. "No," he said softly, squirming inside filthy leathers. "I fell ... I did not mean to get so dirty."

"Nor so smelly." Brennan's gaze was steady. "Explain yourself, if you please."

Kellin looked at the giant. "Didn't *he* tell you?"

"He told me. So did the other man. Now it is for you."

Kellin was hideously aware of everyone else in the room, but especially of his grandfather, his tall, strong, *Cheysuli* grandfather, whose dignity, purpose, and sense of self was so powerful as to flatten everyone else, certainly a ten-year-old grandson. The Mujhar *himself*, not Rogan, standing in the doorway with the sunrise on his back, *lir*-gold gleaming brightly, silver in his hair, stern face even sterner. The wealth on his arms alone would keep Urchin and others like him alive for years.

In a small voice, Kellin suggested, "It would be better done in private."

"No doubt. I want it done here."

Kellin swallowed heavily. He told his grandsire the whole of it, even to the woman.

Brennan did not smile, but his mouth relaxed. Tension Kellin had been unaware of until that moment left the Mujhar's body. "And what have you learned from this?"

Kellin looked straight back. "Not to run in Mujhara."

After a moment of startled silence, the Mujhar laughed aloud, folding bare bronzed arms across his chest with no pretensions at maintaining a stern facade, even before the others. Kellin gaped in surprise; what was so amusing, that his grandsire would sacrifice his dignity before the others without hesitation?

"I had expected something else entirely," Brennan said at last, "but I cannot fault your statement. There is truth in it." Amusement faded. "But there is also Rogan."

Kellin's belly clenched. He nodded and stared at his boot toes. "Rogan," he echoed. "I meant not to make him worry."

"Tell him that."

"I will."

"Now."

Kellin looked up from the ground and saw Rogan in the doorway just behind his grandsire. The man's face was haggard and gray, his eyes reddened from sleeplessness. Kellin thought then of the aforementioned repercussions, Rogan's own question regarding what would become of him and the Mujharan Guard if harm came to Kellin.

"I am unharmed," Kellin said quickly, grasping the repercussions as he never had before. "I am whole, save for my lip, and that I got myself when I fell down."

"And your cut hand; Rogan told me." Brennan extended his own. "Let me see."

Kellin held out his hand and allowed his grandsire to examine the cuts. "Filthy," the Mujhar commented. "It will want a good cleaning when we return, but will heal of its own." His yellow eyes burned fiercely. "You must know not to test others, Kellin. No matter the provocation. If you had not been so quick—"

"But I knew I *was*," Kellin insisted; couldn't any of them see? "I watched him. I watched the knife. I *knew* what it would do."

Brennan's mouth crimped. "We will speak of this another time. For now, I charge you to recall that for such a serious transgression as this one, you endanger others as well as yourself."

Kellin looked again at Rogan. He tugged ineffectually at his ruined jerkin. "I am sorry."

The tutor nodded mutely, seemingly diminished by the tension of the night. Or was it the Lion, biting now at Rogan?

"Well." The Mujhar cast a glance around the room. "It is to be expected that you smell like the Midden, or *a* midden—though I suppose it is less your own contribution than that of everyone else."

Kellin nodded, scratching at the fleas that had vacated his pallet to take up residence in his clothing.

Brennan considered him. "I begin to think you are more like my *rujholli* than I had believed possible."

It astonished Kellin, who had never thought of such a thing. "I am?"

"Aye. Hart and Corin would have gotten themselves thrown into a room just like this, or worse, for about the same reason—or perhaps for a crime even worse than thievery—and then waited for me to fetch them out." He looked his grandson up and down. "Are you not young to begin?"

Ashamed again, Kellin stared hard at the ground. Softly, he said, "I did not expect *you* to come."

"Hart and Corin did. And they were right; I always came." Brennan sighed. "You did expect someone."

"What else?" It startled Kellin. "You would not *leave* me here!"

Brennan eyed him consideringly. "I did leave you here. I knew where you were last night."

"Last *night*!" It was preposterous. "You left me here all night?"

Brennan exchanged a glance with Rogan. "In hopes you might profit from it, albeit there were guardsmen—and a Cheysuli—just across the street." His eyes narrowed. "You said you have learned not to run in Mujhara ... well, I suppose that is something." His tone was ironic. "Surely more than Hart or Corin learned."

"Grandsire—"

"But whether you learned anything is beside the point. Your granddame made it clear to me that if I did not fetch you out *at once* come dawn, she would have my head." He smiled slightly. "As you see, it is still attached."

Kellin nodded, not doubting that it was; nor his granddame's fiery Erinnish temper.

"So Rogan and I are here to fetch you, very much as you expected, and will now take you back to Homana-Mujhar, where I shall myself personally supervise the bath just to make certain the body in it *is* that of my grandson, and not some filthy street urchin masquerading as the Prince of Homana."

"Urchin!" Kellin cried, turning. "We have to take him with us!"

"Who?"

"Urchin. Him." Kellin pointed to the astonished boy. "I told him you would pay his copper and bring him with us—well, I said *Rogan* would—" Kellin cast a glance at his tutor, "—so you could heal him."

"Volunteering my services, are you, you little wretch?" But Brennan crossed the room and knelt

down by the boy thief. "How are you hurt? Ah, so
I see. Here—"

"No!" Urchin jerked away the infected foot.

"There is no need to fear me," Brennan said quietly. "I will look, no more; if you are in need of
healing, it shall be done in Homana-Mujhar."

"I can't go *there!*"

"Why not?" Brennan examined the infected
bite. "Walls and a roof, no more . . . you are as
welcome as Kellin."

"I am?"

"For now. Come. Trust me."

Kellin looked at his grandfather through Urchin's eyes: tall, dark warrior with silvered hair;
yellow eyes clear and unwavering as a wolf's, with
the same promised fierceness; *lir*-gold banding
bared arms; the soft, black-dyed leathers clothing
a powerful body. He was old in years to Kellin,
but age sat lightly on Cheysuli; Brennan was still
fit and graceful, with a cat's eloquent ease of
movement.

"He won't hurt you," Kellin explained matter-
of-factly. "He is my grandsire."

Brennan smiled. "The highest of compliments,
and surety of my goodwill."

Urchin's eyes were wide. "But—I'm a *thief.*"

"Former thief, I should hope. Come with me to
Homana-Mujhar, and you need never steal again."
The Mujhar grinned. "Where you may also shed
forty layers of dirt, ten years' worth of fleas, and
fill that hollow belly."

"No!" Urchin cried as Brennan made to pick
him up. "You'll catch my fleas!"

"Then I shall bathe also."

"I am too heavy!"

"You are not heavy at all." Brennan turned
toward the door, toward the red-haired giant. "I
will have the fines paid for everyone in this room,

and the other; you will see to it they are released at once. But I sympathize with those who fear for their purses; if any of these are caught again, keep them here till Summerfair is ended: in the name of the Mujhar." He smiled briefly at Kellin, slipping into the Old Tongue. *"Tu'halla dei."* He cast a glance at gape-mouthed faces, then settled Urchin more firmly against his chest. "The Guard has horses waiting. You'll ride behind me."

"My lord," Rogan said quietly, following his lord from the room as Kellin slipped out. "There is the matter of the fortune-teller."

"Ah." Brennan's face assumed a grim mask. He glanced down at Kellin as he carried Urchin into the street. "What did he say to you, Kellin?"

Kellin shrugged. "I couldn't understand it all. They were just—*words.*"

"Tell me the words anyway."

Kellin squirmed self-consciously; he did not want to admit to his fear of the Lion. "Cynric."

Brennan's mask slipped, baring naked shock beneath. "Cynric? He said *that?*"

"A name." Kellin frowned. "And a sword, and a bow, and a—knife?"

"Gods," Brennan whispered. "Not my grandson, *too.*"

It terrified Kellin to see his grandfather so stricken. "Not me?" he asked. "Why do you say that? Grandsire—what does it *mean?*"

"It means—" Brennan's mouth tightened into a thin, flat line. "It means we will go visit your fortune-teller—who speaks to you of Cynric—before we go home."

"Why? What did he mean?" Desperation crept in; did it have to do with the Lion? "What does 'Cynric' mean?"

" 'Cynric'?" The Mujhar sighed as he handed Urchin to a guardsman and ordered him put up on his own mount. "It is a name, Kellin . . . an old, familiar name I have not heard in ten years. Since your *jehan* first brought you to us—"

"Before he left." Kellin blurted it out all at once; bitterness encased it. "Before he *left*!"

"Aye." Brennan rubbed absently at the flesh of a face suddenly grown old. "Before he left." He looked at Rogan. "Can you direct us?"

Rogan glanced very briefly at Kellin before looking back to the Mujhar: a subtle question to which the boy was not blind, though adults believed he was. "My lord, perhaps later would be better."

"No." Brennan threaded reins through his hand, turning toward his mount. "No, I think *now*. He has spoken the name to Kellin without knowing who he was—or so you would have me believe. . . ." He patted Urchin's stiff thigh, then climbed up easily. "And even if he *did* know who Kellin was, he also knew the name. I want to ask him how he came by it, and why he speaks of it now to a ten-year-old boy."

"Aye." Rogan moved like an old man toward his own mount. "Of course, my lord, I can direct you to him at once. Although I must warn you—" the tutor mounted with effort, as if his bones hurt, "—he smokes *husath*. It is possible . . ." He made a gesture with one hand that suggested such a man was unpredictable, and his employment.

Brennan's face was grim. "Aidan never did. But he knew the name, also."

"Grandsire?" Kellin stood in the street, staring up. It seemed to him Urchin had usurped his place. "Is there a horse for me?"

"Rogan's," his grandfather told him, "so you may say more privately how sorry you are for the worry you caused."

Ashamed, Kellin nodded. "Aye, grandsire. I will."

*   *   *

Summerfair revelers still gathered in the streets, making it difficult for a mounted party to pass through; Brennan gave orders that his presence not be cried, since he wanted to come upon the fortune-teller unaware, and so the Mujharan Guard merely *suggested* people move, rather than forcing it. The journey took longer than Kellin recalled to reach the faded, striped tent, but then he could not remember for how long he had run.

"Here," Rogan murmured.

The cat and the dog were gone. Flies sheathed the doorflap. "My lord." One of the guardsmen swung down and then another. Kellin watched as two of the crimson-tabarded men entered the tent while the other two stood very close to the Mujhar and his heir.

One of the men was back almost immediately, face set grimly. "My lord."

Brennan hooked his leg frontwise over the pommel to avoid Urchin and slid off, throwing glittering, gold-banded reins to Rogan. "Stay here with Kellin."

"Grandsire!"

The Mujhar spared barely a glance. "Stay here, Kellin."

It burst from Kellin's throat: *"Don't let the Lion eat you!"*

Brennan, at the doorflap, turned sharply. "What do you mean?"

Oh, gods, now it was too late; he had let it slip; he had *said* it; and his grandsire would laugh; *all* of them would laugh—

"Kellin."

Kellin pressed himself against Rogan's back. "Nothing," he whispered.

Rogan stirred. "A childhood tale, my lord. Nothing more."

Brennan nodded after a moment's hesitation, then went into the tent.

Don't let the Lion eat him—

"Kellin." Rogan's voice, very soft. "What is this lion?"

"Just—the Lion. You know. I told you."

"There is no lion in there."

"You don't *know* that. The fortune-teller said—"

"—too much," Rogan declared. "Entirely too much."

"Aye, but . . . Rogan, there really is a lion. The *Lion*—he wants to eat Homana."

"A dog bit my ankle," Urchin offered. "But that's not the same as a *lion* biting it."

Kellin stared at him. "The Lion bit my *harani*. And he died."

Rogan began quietly, "Kellin, I think—"

But he never finished because the Mujhar came out again, yellow eyes oddly feral as he stared at his grandson. "Kellin, you must tell me what the fortune-teller said. Everything."

"About Cynric?"

"Everything." The Mujhar's mouth was crimped tight at the corners. "About the lions, too."

It alarmed Kellin. "Why? *Was* it the Lion? Did it eat the fortune-teller?"

"Kellin—*wait*—"

But Kellin slid off over the horse's rump and darted between his grandfather and the doorflap. He stumbled over a rucked-up rug just inside, caught his precarious balance, then stopped short.

Sprawled on his back amid blood-soaked cushions and carpets lay the fortune-teller. A gaping, ragged hole usurped the place his throat had been.

Four

Torches illuminated the corridor. Kellin crept through it silently, taking care to make no sound; he wanted no one to discover him in the middle of the night, lest they send him off to bed before his task could be accomplished.

Ahead— He drew in a deep breath to fill his hollow chest, then turned the corner. Massive silver doors threw back redoubled torchlight, so bright he nearly squinted. *They must have polished them today*. But that was not important. Importance lay beyond, within the Great Hall itself.

Ten more steps, and he was there. Kellin filled his chest with air again, then leaned with all his weight against the nearest door. *Hinges oiled, too.* It cracked open mutely, then gave as he leaned harder, until he could slide through the space into the dimness of the Great Hall.

He paused there, just inside, and stared hard into darkness. Moonlight slanted through stained glass casements, providing dim but multicolored illumination. Kellin used it in place of torchlight, fixing his gaze upon the beast.

There— And it was, as always: crouched upon the dais as if in attack, rampant wood upon gold-veined marble, teeth bared in ferocity, gilt gleaming in mouth and eyes.

There— And him *here*, pressed against the silver doors, shoulder blades scraping.

Twice he had come, since Ian had died. First, to chop the Lion into bits; again to burn the tapestry hanging just behind, lest the Lion summon confederates in his bid to devour the Mujhar, the queen, and perhaps Kellin himself.

The fortune-teller said so— Kellin shivered. He came now with no ax, no torch to set flame to tapestry, but alone and unweaponed, intending no harm at all this time but warning in harm's place, to make the Lion *know.*

He sucked in a noisy breath, then set out on the long journey. Step by step by step, pacing out the firepit, until he reached the dais. Until he faced the beast.

Kellin balanced lightly, distributing weight as he had been taught: upon the balls of his feet, knees slightly bent, arms loose at his sides, so he could flee if required, or fight.

"You," he exhaled. "Lion."

The throne offered no answer. Kellin swallowed heavily, staring fixedly at the shadow-shrouded beast.

"Do you hear?" he asked. He disliked the quaver in his tone and altered it, improving volume also. "It is I: Kellin, who will be Mujhar one day. Kellin of Homana." He leaned forward slightly, to make certain the Lion heard. "I am not alone anymore."

Still there was no answer.

Kellin wet his lips, then expelled the final warning: "I have a *friend.*"

"Kellin?"

He twitched; was it the Lion? *No—* He spun. "Urchin!"

The Homanan boy squeezed his way through the doors just as Kellin had done. "Why are you—" He broke it off, staring beyond Kellin. "Is that the Lion Throne?"

Kellin was very aware of the weight crouched behind him. "Aye."

Urchin's steps were steady as he approached, showing no signs of limp. The Mujhar's healing a week before had proved efficient as always; once over the shock of being touched by legendary Cheysuli magic, Urchin had recovered his customary spirit. "What are you doing here? Talking to it?"

Before Urchin, Kellin did not feel defensive. "Warning it."

"About what?" Urchin arrived before the dais, brushing aside still-lank but now-clean hair. "Does it answer?"

"It eats people." Kellin slanted Urchin a glance. "It killed my *su'fali*."

"Your what?"

"*Su'fali*. Uncle—well, great-uncle. It bit him, and he died." The pain squeezed a little, aching inside his chest. "Two springs ago."

"Oh." Urchin stared at the throne: wary fascination. "You mean—it comes alive?"

It was hard to explain. Others had told him not to speak such nonsense, and he had locked it all within. Now Urchin wanted the truth. It was easier to say nothing. "It wants my grandsire next."

"It does?" After a startled reassessment, Urchin frowned. "How do you know?"

"I just know. In here." Kellin touched his chest. "And the fortune-teller said so. It ate *him*, too."

"Rogan said—"

"Rogan said what the Mujhar told him to say." Kellin scowled. "They don't want to believe me. They didn't believe me when I told them about Ian, and they don't believe me now." He looked hard at Urchin. "Do you believe me?"

Urchin blinked. "I don't know. It's *wood*—"

"It's the Lion, and it wants to eat Homana."

Kellin lifted his chin. "I told it I had a friend, now; that I wasn't alone anymore."

Urchin blinked. "You mean—me?"

"*Aren't* you my friend?"

"Well—aye. Aye, I am, but . . . you're the Prince of Homana."

"Princes need friends, too." Kellin tried to keep the plea out of his voice.

"But I'm only a *spit*-boy."

"Grandsire will give you better when you've learned things," Kellin explained. "He told me it's best if you start there, then move up, because a castle is strange to you."

"It is," Urchin agreed. He eyed the Lion again, then glanced back to Kellin. "Rogan doesn't teach the other spit-boys."

"No. I asked grandsire because I said we were friends."

Urchin nodded, looking around the massive Great Hall. "This will be yours, one day?"

"When grandsire dies."

"He's strong; he'll live a long time." Urchin slanted a sidelong glance at Kellin. "Why isn't your father here? Shouldn't he be next?"

Kellin's belly hurt, as it often did when someone mentioned his father. "He gave it up. He *renounced* his title." His spine was rigid. Words spilled out, and virulence; he had learned to say it first, before anyone else could. "He is mad. He lives on an island and talks about the gods."

Urchin blinked. "The priests do that all the time, and they're not mad."

"My father *sees* things. Visions. He has fits." Kellin shrugged, trying not to show how much it hurt. Urchin was his friend, but there were things Kellin could not share. "Grandsire says he is a *shar tahl*—that is Old Tongue for 'priest-historian'—but I say he is something else. Something *more:* part priest, part warrior, part fortune-teller—and all fool."

"He gave away *everything*?"

Kellin nodded mutely.

"He could have been Mujhar . . ." Urchin looked at the Lion again. "He could have been *Mujhar*."

"A fool," Kellin declared. "And one day I will tell him. I will go to the Crystal Isle, and find him, and *tell* him."

Urchin grinned at him. "Can I go with you?"

Kellin smiled back. "You will be my captain of the guard. Commander of the *Mujharan* Guard, and I will take you everywhere."

Urchin nodded. "Good." He stared up at the Lion, studied it, then drew himself up before it. He slanted a grin at Kellin, then turned back to the throne. "I am Urchin, Lion! In the name of Kellin, I command the Mujharan Guard! And I say to you, Lion, you shall set no teeth to his flesh, nor spill royal blood!"

It echoed in the hall. Gilt eyes glinted faintly.

Kellin stared at the Lion. "You see? I am not alone anymore."

The Queen of Homana, in her solar, approved of them both. Kellin could tell. He had pleased her by working harder at his studies, and by being altogether less obdurate about learning his duties as Prince of Homana. When she was pleased, her green eyes kindled; just now, he felt the warmth redoubled as she smiled at him and Urchin. "Rogan says both of you are doing very well."

Kellin and Urchin exchanged glances. Urchin was stiff, as he always was before the queen or the Mujhar, but his smile was relaxed and genuine. Cleaned up, he was altogether presentable, even for a spit-boy. The weeks had improved him in many ways.

"In fact," the queen went on, "he told me yesterday he was quite impressed with both of you. Urchin is yet behind you, Kellin, but 'tis to be expected. He's had no proper lessons before now." Her expression softened as she glanced at the taller boy. "You are to be commended for your diligence."

Urchin's face reddened. "Kellin helps me."

"But he learns on his own," Kellin put in quickly. "I only point out a few things here and there. He does most of it himself."

"I know." Aileen of Homana had lost none of her vividness with the passage of time, though her color had dimmed a trifle from the brilliant red of youth to a rusted silver. But she was still Erinnish, born of an island kingdom, and she still boasted the tenacity and fiery outspokenness that had nearly caused a political incident between her realm and Homana when she had professed to love Niall's third-born son in place of the prince she was meant to wed; Corin himself had prevented it by taking up his *tahlmorra* in Atvia, and Aileen had married Brennan after all. "He's as quick at his learning as he is his duties at the spit; 'twill not be long before he outgrows the kitchens and enters into more personal service."

"With me?" Kellin blurted.

Aileen laughed. "In time, Kellin—first he must learn the household. Then we'll be seeing if he's ready to become the Prince of Homana's personal squire."

"But he has to be," Kellin insisted. "I want to make him commander of the Mujharan Guard."

"Oh?" Rusty brows lifted. "I think Harlech might be wishing to keep his post."

"Oh, not *yet*." Kellin waved a hand. "When he is older. When I am Mujhar."

Aileen's mouth crimped only slightly. "Indeed."

She looked at Urchin. "Do you feel yourself fit for such duty?"

"Not yet," Urchin replied promptly. "But—I will be." He cast a sidelong glance at Kellin. "I mean to guard him against the Lion."

Aileen's smiled faded. Her glance went beyond the boys to the man in the doorway.

"The Lion," echoed the Mujhar; both boys swung at once. "The Lion is no threat, as I have said many times. It is a throne, no more. Symbolic of Homana, the Cheysuli, and our *tahlmorra*, which is of no little import—" he smiled faintly, "—but assuredly it offers nothing more than the dusty odor of history and the burdensome weight of tradition."

Kellin knew better than to protest; let them believe as they would. He *knew* better.

Now, so did Urchin.

"I, too, am pleased," the Mujhar declared. "Rogan has brought good tidings of your progress." He glanced briefly at his wife, passing a silent message, then touched each boy on the shoulder. "Now, surely you can find better ways to spend your time than with women and women's things," he grinned at the queen to show he meant no gibe, "so I suggest you be about it. Rogan has the day to himself and has gone into the city; I suggest you see if Harlech has something to teach you of a commander's duties."

Urchin bowed quick acquiesence, then followed Kellin from the chamber.

"Wait." Kellin stepped rapidly aside to the wall beside the still-open door, catching Urchin's arm to halt him. "Listen," he whispered.

Urchin's expression was dubious; blue eyes flicked in alarm toward the door. "But—"

Kellin mashed a silencing hand into his friend's mouth. He barely moved his lips. "There is something he wants to tell her . . . something I am not to hear—'' Kellin bit off his sentence as his grandmother began speaking.

" 'Tis Aidan, isn't it?'' she asked tensely in the room beyond. "You've heard.''

"A message.'' The Mujhar's tone was curiously flat, squashed all out of shape. Without seeing his grandsire, Kellin heard the layered emotions: resignation, impatience, a raw desperation. "Aidan says, 'Not yet.' ''

His granddame was not nearly so self-controlled. ."Didn't ye *tell* him, then?''

"I did. In the strongest terms possible. 'Send for your son,' I said, 'Kellin needs his father.' ''

"And?''

"And he says, 'Not yet.' ''

Urchin's breath hissed. Kellin waved him into silence.

"Gods,'' Aileen breathed. "*Has* he gone mad, as they say?''

"I—want to think not. I want to disbelieve the rumors. I want very much to *believe* there is a reason for what he does.''

"To keep himself isolate—''

"He is a *shar tahl*, Aileen. They are unlike other Cheysuli—''

Her tone was rough, as if she suppressed tears. "There's Erinnish in him, too, my braw boyo—or are you forgetting that?''

"No.'' The Mujhar sighed. "He shapes others, Aidan says, to understand the old ways must be altered by the new.''

"But to deny his own son a father—''.

"He will send for Kellin, he says, when the time is right.''

For a long moment there was silence. Then the Queen of Homana muttered an oath more appropriate to a soldier. "And when *will* it be right?

When his son is a grown man, seated upon the Lion Throne Aidan *himself* should hold?"

The Mujhar answered merely, with great weariness, "I do not know."

Tension filled the silence. Then Kellin heard a long, breathy sigh cut off awkwardly.

"Aileen, no—"

"Why not?" The voice was thick, but fierce. "He is *my son*, Brennan—I'm permitted, I'm thinking, to cry if I wish to cry."

"Aileen—"

"I miss him," she said. "Gods, but I miss him! So many years—"

"Shansu, meijhana—"

"There is no peace!" she cried. "I bore him in my body. You're not knowing what it is."

"I am bonded in my own way—"

"With a *cat*!" she said. " 'Tisn't the same, Brennan. And even if it were, you have Sleeta *here*. I have nothing. Nothing but memories of the child I bore, and the boy I raised. . . ." Her voice thickened again. " 'Tisn't fair to any of us. Not to you, to me; and certainly not to Kellin." Her voice paused. "Is there no way to *make* him come? To compel him?"

"No," Brennan said. "He is more than our son, more than a *jehan*. He is also a *shar tahl*. I will not compel a man blessed by gods to serve a mortal desire. Not for me, nor for you—"

"For *his son*?"

"No. I will not interfere."

Taut silence, as Kellin spun tightly away. Urchin hesitated only a moment, then hastened to catch up. "Kellin—"

"You heard." It took effort not to shout. "You *heard* what he said. About my father—" It filled his throat, swelling tightly, until he wanted to choke, or scream, or cry. "He doesn't want me."

"That's not what the Mujhar said. He said your father would send when the time was right."

Kellin strode on stiffly. "The time will *never* be right!"

"But you don't *know* th—"

"I do." Venomously. "He renounced the throne, and renounced me. He renounced *everything*!"

"But he's a priest. Don't priests do those things?"

"Not *shar tahls*. Not most of them. They have sons, and they love them." Kellin's tone thinned, then wavered. He clamped down on self-possession with every bit of strength he had. "Someday I will see him, whether he wants me or no, and I will tell him to his face that he is not a man."

"Kellin—"

"I *will*." Kellin stopped and stared fiercely at Urchin. "And you will come with me."

He dreamed of gods, and fathers, and islands; of demanding, impatient gods; of Lions who ate humans. He awoke with a cry as the door swung open, and moved to catch up the knife he kept on a bench beside his bed, with which he might slay lions.

"Kellin?" It was Rogan, bringing with him a cupped candle. "Are you awake?"

Kellin always woke easily, prepared for lions. "Aye." He scooched up in bed. "What is it?" His heart seized. *Not the Lion—"

There was tension in Rogan's tone as he came into the chamber, swinging shut the door behind him. He did not chide his charge for speaking of the Lion. "Kellin . . ." He came forward to the bed, bringing the light with him. It scribed deep lines in a haggard face. "There is something we must discuss."

"In the middle of the night?"

"I can think of no better time." A slight dryness

altered the tension. Rogan put the candle cup on the bench beside the knife, then sat down on the edge of the huge tester bed. "My lord, I know you are troubled. I have known for some time. Urchin came to me earlier, but do not blame him; he cares for you, and wants you content."

"Urchin?" Kellin was confused.

"He told me what you both overheard today, when you eavesdropped on the Mujhar."

"Oh." Only the faintest flicker of remorse pinched, then was consumed by remembered bitterness. "Did he tell you—"

Rogan overrode. "Aye. And after much thought, I have decided to do what no one else will do." The tutor's eyes were blackened by shadows, caved in unreadable darkness. "I offer you the opportunity to go to your father."

"To—" Kellin sat bolt upright. "You?"

Rogan nodded. His mouth was tight. "I make no attempt to explain or excuse him, my lord . . . I merely offer to escort you to the Crystal Isle, where you may ask him yourself why he has done as he has."

"My father," Kellin whispered. "*Jehan*—" He stared hard into darkness. "When?"

"In the morning."

"How?"

"We will say we are going to Clankeep. You wish to take Urchin there, do you not?"

"Aye, but—"

"I shall tell the Mujhar you wish to introduce Urchin to Clankeep and the Cheysuli. He will not refuse you that. Only we shall go to Hondarth instead."

"But—the Mujharan Guard. They'll know."

"I have prevailed upon the Mujhar to allow us to go without guards. You are Cheysuli, after all— and I know how much close confinement chafes the Mujhar. He understands the need to allow you more freedom . . . and there has been no trouble for quite some time. If Clankeep were not so close, it would be different."

"But won't he know? Won't he find out? It is two weeks' ride to Hondarth."

"It is not unusual for a Cheysuli boy, regardless of rank, to desire to spend some time among his people."

Kellin understood at once. "But we will go to the Crystal Isle while he believes we are at Clankeep!"

The tutor's silence was eloquent.

Kellin drew in a breath. "You will have to send word."

"From Hondarth. By then it will be too late for the Mujhar to stop us."

Kellin looked into the beloved face. "Why?"

Rogan's smile was ghastly. "Because it is time."

Five

They left early, very early, with only a loaf of
bread and a flagon of cider serving as breakfast.
Kellin, Urchin, and Rogan made a very small
party as they exited Homana-Mujhar before the
Mujhar and the queen were even awake.

"Where is Clankeep?" Urchin asked.

Kellin flicked a glance at Rogan, then grinned
at his Homanan friend. "We aren't going to Clankeep. We are going to the Crystal Isle. To my
jehan."

Urchin absorbed the new information. "How far
is the Crystal Isle?"

"Two weeks of riding," Kellin answered
promptly. Then, evoking his Erinnish granddame,
"And but a bit of a sail across the bay to the island." Inwardly, he said, *And to my jehan.*

"Two weeks?" Urchin scratched at his nose. "I
didn't know Homana was so big."

"Aye." Kellin grinned. "One day all of it will be
mine, and you will help me rule it."

Urchin was dubious. "I'm only a spit-boy."

"For now." Kellin looked at his tutor. "Once,
Rogan was only a man who gambled too much."

Rogan's face grayed. Even his lips went pale.
"Who told you that?"

Kellin stiffened, alarmed. "Was I not to know?"

The tutor was plainly discomfited. "You know
what you know, my lord, but it is not a past of

83

which to be proud. I thought it well behind me.
When I married—" He broke it off, abruptly, nostrils pinched and white.

Alerted, Kellin answered the scent. "You are married?"

"I was." Rogan's face was stiff, and his spine.
"She is dead. Long dead." He guided his mount
with abrupt motions, which caused the gelding to
protest the bit. "Before I married Tassia, I gambled away all my coin. She broke me of the habit,
and made me use my wits for something other
than wagering."

"And so you came to Homana-Mujhar." Kellin
nodded approvingly. "I recall the day."

"So do I, my lord." Rogan's smile was twisted.
"She was one month dead. You were all of eight,
and grieving for your great-uncle."

"The Lion bit him," Kellin muttered. "He bit
him, and Ian died."

"How far do we go today?" Urchin asked, oblivious to dead kinsmen and dead wives.

"There is a roadhouse some way out of Mujhara,
on the Hondarth road," Rogan answered. "We will
stay the night there."

The common room was dim, lighted only by a
handful of greasy tallow candles set in clay cups.
The room stank of spilled wine, skunky ale, burned
meat, and unwashed humanity. It crossed Kellin's
mind briefly, who was accustomed to better, that
the roadhouse was unworthy of them, but he
closed his mouth on a question. They were bound
for the Crystal Isle in absolute secrecy, and for a
boy to complain of his surroundings would draw
the wrong sort of attention. Instead, he breathed
through his mouth until the stench was bearable
and kept a sharp eye on the purse hanging at Ro-

gan's belt. He had learned that much from Urchin who had grown up in the streets.

"Look." Kellin leaned close to Urchin and nudged him with an elbow as they slipped into the room behind Rogan. "See the one-eyed man?"

Urchin nodded. "I see him."

"You've been places I have not—what is he doing?"

Urchin grinned. "Dicing. See the cubes? He'll toss them out of the leather cup onto the table. The highest number wins."

Rogan halted at a table near the center of the room and glanced at his two young charges. His face was arranged in a curiously blank expression. "We will sit here."

Kellin nodded, paying little attention; he watched the one-eyed man as he shook the leather cup and rolled the dice out onto the table. The man shouted, laughed, then scooped up the few coins glinting dully in wan light.

"Look at the loser," Urchin whispered as he slipped onto a stool. "D'ye see the look? He's angry."

Kellin slid a glance at the other man. The loser made no physical motion that gave away his anger, but Kellin marked the tautness of his mouth, the bunched muscles along his jaw. Deliberately the loser tossed two more coins onto the table, matched by the one-eyed man. Each man tossed dice again.

A knife appeared, glinting dully in bad light. The one-eyed man, wary of the weapon displayed specifically for his benefit, did not immediately reach to gather up his winnings.

Urchin leaned close. "He thinks the one-eyed man is cheating."

It fascinated Kellin, who had never been so close

to violence other than the Lion. "Will he kill him?"

Urchin shrugged. "I've seen men killed for less reason than a dice game."

Rogan's lips compressed. "I should not have brought you in here. We should go upstairs to our room and have a meal sent up."

"No!" Kellin said quickly. Then, as Rogan's brows arched, "I mean—should not the future Mujhar see all kinds of those he will rule?"

The taut mouth loosened a little. "Perhaps. And an astute one will recognize that to some Homanans, the man on the Lion Throne means less than nothing."

It was incomprehensible to Kellin who had been reared in a household steeped in honor and respect. "But how can they—"

A shadow fell across their table, distracting Kellin at once. A slender, well-formed hand—unlike the broad-palmed, spatulate hands of the one-eyed man and his angry companion—placed a wooden casket on the table. A subtle, muted rattle from the contents was loud in the sudden silence.

Kellin glanced up at once. The man smiled slightly, glancing at the two boys before turning his attention to Rogan. He was young, neatly dressed in good gray tunic and trews, and his blue eyes lacked the dull hostility Kellin had marked in the dicers. Shining russet hair fell in waves to his shoulders. "Will you play, sir?"

Rogan wet his lips. He moved his hands from the table top to his lap. "I—do not play."

"Ah, but it will take no time at all . . . and you may leave this table with good gold in your purse." An easy, mellifluous tone; a calm and beguiling smile.

Kellin glanced sharply at Rogan. *He would not— would he?* After all his dead wife had done?

But he could see the expression in the tutor's eyes: Rogan desired very badly to play. The older man's mouth parted slightly, then compressed again. Rogan's gaze met the stranger's. "Very well."

"But—" Kellin began.

The stranger overrode the protest easily, sliding onto a stool before Kellin could finish. "I am Corwyth, from Ellas. It is my good fortune that we are chance-met." He cast a brief glance around the room. "The others do not interest me, but you are obviously a man of good breeding." He spared a smile for Kellin and Urchin as he addressed Rogan. "Your sons?"

"Aye," Rogan said briefly; he did not so much as glance at Corwyth, but stared transfixed at the casket.

It fascinated Kellin also. A passing glance marked nothing more than plain dark wood polished smooth by time and handling, but a second glance—and a more intense examination—revealed the wood not smooth at all, but carved with a shallow frieze of intricate runes. *Inside*—? Kellin leaned forward to peer into the mouth of the casket and saw only blackness. "Where are the dice?"

Corwyth laughed softly. "Be certain they are there." He sat at Rogan's right hand, with Urchin on *his* right; Kellin's stool was directly across the table. "Have you played before?"

The Ellasian addressed him, not Rogan; he seemed to know all about Rogan. Kellin shook his head quickly, slanting a glance at his tutor. "My—father—does not allow it."

"Ah, well . . . when you are older, then." Corwyth ignored Urchin utterly as he turned his attention to Rogan. "Will you throw first, or shall I?"

Rogan's taut throat moved in a heavy swallow. "I must know the stakes first."

Corwyth's smile came easily, lighting his mobile face. "Those you know already."

A sheen of dampness filmed Rogan's brow. "Will I lose, then? Or do you play the game as if there might be a chance for me?"

The odd bitterness in the older man's tone snared Kellin's attention instantly. But Rogan said nothing more to explain himself, and Corwyth answered before Kellin could think of a proper question.

The Ellasian indicated the rune-carved casket with a flick of a fingernail. "A man makes his own fortune, regardless of the game."

Rogan scrubbed his face with a sleeve-sheathed forearm, then swore raggedly and caught up the casket. He upended it with a practiced twitch of his wrist. Six ivory cubes fell out, and six slender black sticks.

All of them were blank.

Urchin blurted surprise. Rogan stiffened on his bench, transfixed by the sticks and cubes. Breath rasped in his throat.

"Did you lose?" Kellin asked, alarmed by Rogan's glazed eyes.

Corwyth's tone was odd. "How would you like them to read?" he asked Rogan. "Tell me, and I shall do it."

Rogan's fingers gripped the edge of the table. "And if—if I requested the winning gambit?"

"Why, then I should lose." Corwyth grinned and glanced at Kellin and Urchin. "But, after all, it is my game, and I think I should still find a way to win." His gaze returned to Rogan's face. "Do you not agree?"

"Kellin—" Rogan's tone was abruptly harsh.

"Kellin, you and Urchin are to go upstairs at once."

"No," Corwyth said softly. A slender finger touched each of the blank ivory cubes and set them all to glowing with a livid purple flame.

"*Magic*—" Urchin whispered: dreadful fascination.

Kellin did not look at the cubes or the black sticks. He stared instead at Corwyth's face, into his eyes, and saw no soul.

He put out his small hand instantly and swept the cubes from the table, unheeding of the flame, then scattered all the sticks. "No," Kellin declared. "*No*."

Corwyth's smile was undiminished; if anything, it increased to one of immense satisfaction. "Perceptive, my lord. My master has indeed done well to send me for you now, while you are yet *lirless* and therefore without power. But I think for all your perception you fail to recognize the extent of *his* power, or mine—" his tone altered from conversational, "—and that the game we initiated has already been played through." Smoothly he caught Rogan's arm in one hand, and the wristbones snapped.

Rogan cried out. Sweat ran from his face. His shattered wrist remained trapped in Corwyth's hand, who appeared to exert no pressure whatsoever with anything but his will.

Kellin leapt to his feet, thinking only that somehow he must get Rogan free; he must stop Rogan's pain. But the instinct was abruptly blunted, the attempt aborted, as Corwyth shook his head. *He will injure Rogan worse.* Kellin knew it at once. Slowly he resumed his seat, aware of a minute trembling seizing all his bones. "Who?" he asked. "*Who* is your master?"

"Lochiel, of course." Corwyth smiled. His cordial attitude was undiminished by the threat he exuded without effort, which made the moment worse. "Do you know of another man who would presume to steal a prince?"

"Steal—" Kellin stiffened. *Me? He wants—me?*

Urchin stirred on his stool. His thin face was white. "Are you—Ihlini?"

The dead cubes and sticks scattered on the floor came abruptly to life again, flying from the dirt-pack to land again upon the table and commence a spinning dervish-dance across the scarred surface. Purple godfire streamed from the cubes; the black sticks glistened blood-red.

Urchin sucked in an audible breath. Kellin, infuriated by Corwyth's audacity, smashed a small fist against the table top. *"No!"*

The cubes and sticks fell at once into disarray, rattling into silence as the dance abruptly collapsed.

"Too late," Corwyth chided. "Much too late, my lord." He looked at Rogan and smiled.

The awful tension in the Homanan's body was plain to see. "No," he whispered hoarsely. "Oh, gods, I cannot—I *cannot*—"

"Too late," Corwyth repeated.

Rogan looked at Kellin. "Run!" he cried. *"Run!"*

Six

Kellin lunged to his feet, grasping for and catching a fistful of Urchin's tunic. He saw the blue blaze in Corwyth's eyes, sensed the pain radiating from Rogan's shattered wrist. *I must do something.*

"Urchin—" He tugged on the boy's tunic, who needed no urging, then together they scrabbled their way across the room, jerked open the door, and fell out into the darkness.

"Did you see—" Urchin choked.

"We have to run. Rogan said *run.*" Kellin yanked at Urchin's tunic.

Urchin was clearly terrified. "H–horses—"

"They will lie in wait for us there—we must *run,* Urchin!"

They ran away from the roadhouse, away from the road itself, making for the trees. They shared no more physical contact; Urchin had at last mastered himself. The Homanan boy, accustomed to fleeing, darted through the wood without hesitation. City-reared Kellin now was less certain of his course and followed Urchin's lead.

A branch slapped Kellin across the eyes, blurring his vision. He tasted the sourness of resin in his mouth, spat once, then forgot about it in his flight. He could see little of the ground underfoot, trusting instinctively to the balance and reflexes of youth as well as the training begun in Homana-Mujhar.

"Urchin—?"

"Here—" Ahead still, and still running, crashing through deadfall and undergrowth.

Kellin winced as another branch clawed at his tunic, digging into the flesh of bare arms. And then he saw the glint of silver in the trees and slipped down into the creek before he could halt his flight. Kellin fell forward, flailing impotently as cold water closed over his head.

He kicked, found purchase, if treacherous, not far under his feet, and thrust himself upward to the surface. Kellin choked and spat, coughing, shivering from fright and cold.

"Kellin—" It was Urchin, bankside, reaching down. Kellin caught the hand, clung, and scrabbled out onto the creek bank. Urchin's face was seamed with branch-born welts. "We can't run all night!"

Kellin tried to catch his breath. "We—have to get as far—far from them as we can—"

"There was only that one. Corwyth."

"More." Kellin sucked air, filling his chest. "Kick over one rock and find a single Ihlini . . . kick over another and find a nest." He scraped a forearm across his face, shoving soaked hair from his eyes. "That's what everyone says."

Dry, Urchin nonetheless shivered. "But if they're *sorcerers*—"

"We have to *try*—" Kellin began.

The forest around them exploded into a spectral purple glow. Out of the blinding light came two dark shadows, silhouetted against livid godfire.

Kellin grabbed at Urchin and swung him back the way they had come. "Run!"

But Corwyth himself stood on the other side of the creek. With him was Rogan.

Urchin blurted his shock even as Kellin stopped short. Breathing hard, Kellin nonetheless heard the soft susurration of men moving behind them. The hairs on the back of his neck stirred. "I taste it," he murmured blankly. "I can *taste* the magic."

Corwyth smiled. Rogan did not. The godfire painted them all an eerie lavender, but Kellin could see the pallor of his tutor's face. Rogan's eyes glistened with tears.

Pain—? Kellin wondered.

"My lord," Rogan said. "Oh, my lord . . . forgive me—"

Comprehension brought sickness. Sickness formed a stone in Kellin's belly. "Not *you!*" No, of course not; Rogan would deny it. Rogan would explain.

"My lord . . . there was nothing left for me. I had no choice."

Corwyth lifted a minatory hand. "There was choice," he reproved. "There is always choice. I may be, to you, an enemy, but I suggest you tell the truth to this boy, who is not: it was neither I nor my master who forced you to this."

Kellin's conviction was undiminished. *Rogan will deny it—he will tell me the truth.* After all, how many times had Kellin been told of the perfidiousness of Ihlini? *This is some kind of trick.* "He hurt you," Kellin declared. "He broke your wrist; what *else* can you say?"

"There was no threat," Corwyth countered quietly. "The wrist was merely to prove the need for care. I have no need of threats with Rogan. All I was required to do was promise him his dearest desire."

"Ihlini lie," Kellin declared, even as Urchin stirred in surprise beside him. "Ihlini lie all the time. You are the *enemy.*"

"To assure our survival, aye." Corwyth's young face looked older, less serene. "To Ihlini, *you* are the enemy."

It was an entirely new thought. Kellin rejected it. He looked instead at Rogan. "He's lying."

"No." Rogan's mouth warped briefly. "There was no threat, as he says. Only a promise."

It was utter betrayal. "*What* promise?" Kellin cried. "What could *he* promise you that the Mujhar could not offer?"

Rogan shut his eyes. His face was shiny with sweat.

"Tell him," Corwyth said.

"You would have me strip away *all* his innocence?"

The Ihlini shrugged. "He will lose it soon enough in Valgaard."

Urchin's face was a sickly white in fireglow. He breathed audibly. "Valgaard?"

"Rogan?" Kellin swallowed back the fear that formed a hard knot in his throat. "Rogan—this isn't *true*?"

The tutor broke. He spoke rapidly, disjointedly. "It was him . . . a year ago, he came—came and asked that I betray you to the Ihlini."

"*Me!*"

"Lochiel." Rogan shuddered. "Lochiel wants you." His entire body convulsed. "He could not reach you. He could get you no other way. Corwyth promised me you would be unharmed."

Kellin could not breathe. "You agreed?"

"My lord—if he had intended harm—"

"You *agreed*!"

"Kellin—"

It was the worst of all. "He is *Ihlini*!"

"Kellin—"

"How could you do this?" It was a refrain in Kellin's mind, in Kellin's mouth. "How could you do this?"

Rogan's face was wet with tears. "It was not—not of my devising . . . that I promise you. But *he* promised. Promised *me* . . . and I was weak, so weak. . . ."

Kellin shouted it. "*What* did he promise you?"

Rogan fell to his knees. "Forgive me—forgive—"

The stone in Kellin's belly grew. He felt it come to life. It pushed his heart aside, then squeezed up into his throat. His body was filled with it.

And the stone had a name: rage.

Kellin heard his voice—*mine?*—come from a vast distance. It was an ordinary voice, shaped by normal inflections, with no hint at all of shock, or terror, or rage. "What did he promise you?"

"My wife!" Rogan cried.

It was incomprehensible. "You said she was *dead.*" And then Kellin understood.

"My wife," the tutor whispered, hands slack upon his knees. "You are too young to understand . . . but I loved her so much I thought I would die of it, and then *she* died—she died . . . because of the child I gave her—" He broke off. His gaze was fixed on Kellin. He gathered himself visibly, attempting to master his anguish. "I refused," Rogan said quietly. "Of course I refused. Nothing could make me betray you. I would have accepted death before that."

"Why didn't you?" Kellin shouted.

"But then this man, this Ihlini, promised me my wife."

Kellin shivered. He looked at Corwyth. "You can *raise the dead*?"

The Ihlini smiled. "I am capable of many things." He extended his right hand, palm up, as if to mock the Cheysuli gesture of *tahlmorra;* then a flaring column of white light filled his hand.

"Magic," Urchin murmured.

"Tricks," Kellin declared; he could not admit the Ihlini might offer a true threat, or fear would overwhelm him.

"Is it?" The light in Corwyth's hand coalesced, then began to move, to dance, and the column resolved itself into a human shape.

A tiny, naked woman.

"*Gods*," Rogan blurted. Then, brokenly, "Tassia."

Kellin stared at the burning woman. She was a perfect embodiment of the Ihlini's power.

Corwyth smiled. The woman danced within his palm, twisting and writhing. She burned bright white and searing, spinning and spinning, so that flaming hair spun out from her body and shed brilliant sparks. Tiny breasts and slim hips were exposed, and the promise of her body.

Kellin, whose body was as yet too young to respond, looked at Rogan. The Homanan still knelt on the ground, eyes fixed in avid hunger on the tiny dancing woman.

"Do you want her?" Corwyth asked. "I did promise her to you. And I keep my promises."

"She isn't real!" Kellin cried.

"Not precisely," Corwyth agreed. "She is a summoning from my power; a conjured promise, nothing more. But I can make her real—real enough for Rogan." He smiled. "Look upon her, Kellin. Look at her perfection! It is such a simple thing to make Tassia from this."

The tiny, burning features were eloquent in their pleading. She was fully aware, Kellin saw; Tassia *knew*.

Rogan cried out. "I bargained my soul for this. Give me my payment for it!"

The light from the burning woman blanched Corwyth's face. "Your soul was mine the moment I asked for it. The promise of this woman was merely a kindness." He looked at Kellin though his words were meant for Rogan. "Speak it, prince's man. Aloud, where Kellin can hear. Renounce your service to the House of Homana.

Deny your prince as he stands here before you. Do only these two things, and you will have your payment."

Rogan shuddered.

"Speak it," Corwyth said.

"Leave him alone!" Kellin cried.

"Kellin—" Rogan's expression was wracked. "Forgive—"

"Don't say it!" Kellin shouted. "Do not give in to him!"

"Speak," Corwyth said.

Tears ran down Rogan's face. "I renounce the House of Homana."

"Rogan!"

"I renounce my prince."

"No!"

"I submit to you, Ihlini ... and now ask payment for my service!"

Corwyth smiled gently. He lifted his other hand as if in benevolent blessing. Rogan's head bowed as the hand came down, and then he was bathed in the same lurid light that shaped the tiny woman.

"Wait!" Kellin cried. "Rogan—*no*—"

Rogan's eyes stretched wide. *"This is not what you promised—"* But his body was engulfed.

Kellin fell back, coughing, even as Urchin did. The clearing was filled with smoke. Corwyth pursed his lips and blew a gentle exhalation, and the smoke dispersed completely.

"What did you do?" Kellin asked. "What did you do to Rogan?"

"I gave him what he desired, though of a decidedly different nature. He believed I intended to remake his dead wife. But even *I* cannot do that, so this will have to suffice." Corwyth's right hand supported the dancing woman, now rigidly still.

In his other hand, outstretched, burned a second tiny figure.

Urchin cried out. Kellin stared, transfixed, as he saw the formless features resolve themselves into those he knew so well. *"Rogan."*

Corwyth brought his hands together. The man and woman met, embraced, then merged into a single livid flame. "I do assure you, this was what he wanted."

Kellin was horrified. "Not like *that*!"

"Perhaps not." Corwyth grinned. "A conceit, I confess; he did not have the wit to specify how he wanted payment made."

Kellin shuddered. And then the stone in chest and throat broke free at last. He vomited violently.

"No!" Urchin cried, then screamed Rogan's name.

Corwyth knelt down beside the creek.

"Wait!" Kellin shouted.

Corwyth dipped his hands into the water. "But let it never be said I am a man who knows no mercy. Death, you might argue, is better than this."

"Rogan!"

But the flames were extinguished as water snuffed them out.

Seven

Kellin found himself on hands and knees in clammy vegetation, hunched before the creek in bizarre obeisance to the sorcerer who knelt on the bank. His belly cramped painfully. His mouth formed a single word, though the lips were warped out of shape. *Rogan.*

And then the horrible thought: *Not Rogan any more.*

A hand was on his arm, fingers digging into flesh. "Kellin—*Kellin*—" Urchin, of course; Kellin twisted his head upward and saw the pale glint of Urchin's eyes, the sweaty sheen of shock-blanched face. Ashamed of his weakness, Kellin swabbed a trembling hand across his dry mouth and climbed to his feet. *Show the Ihlini no fear.*

But he thought it was too late; surely Corwyth had seen. Surely Corwyth *knew.*

The russet-haired Ihlini rose, shaking droplets from elegant hands with negligent flicks of his fingers. "Shall you come without protest, my lord?"

Kellin whirled and stiff-armed Urchin, shoving him back a full step before the Homanan boy could speak. *"Run!"*

He darted to the left even as Urchin spun, running away from Corwyth, away from the creek, away from the horror of what he had witnessed, the terrible quenching of a *man*—

He tore headlong through limbs and leaves, shredding underbrush and vines. In huge leaps Kellin spent himself, panting through a dry throat as he ran. He fastened on one thought—*Urchin*—but the Homanan boy was making his own way, making his own future, crashing through brush only paces away. Kellin longed to call out but dared not risk it. Besides, Urchin was better suited to flight than he, growing up a boy of the streets; best Kellin tend himself.

Corwyth's voice cut through the trees like a clarion. "I require only you, Kellin. Not him. Come back, and I will spare him."

"Don't listen!" Urchin hissed as he broke through tangled foliage near Kellin. "What can he—"

The Homanan boy stopped short, fully visible in a patch of moonlight. His chest rose and fell unevenly as his breath rattled in his throat.

Kellin staggered to a stiff-limbed halt, arms outflung. His breathing was as loud. "Urchin?"

The boy's blue eyes were fixed and dilated.

"Urchin—*run*—"

Urchin's eyes bulged in their sockets.

Even as Kellin reached for him, the boy's limbs jerked. Urchin's mouth dropped open, blurting inarticulate protest. Then something pushed out against the fabric of his tunic, as if it quested for exit from the confines of his chest.

"*Ur*—" Kellin saw the blood break from Urchin's breastbone. "No!" But Urchin was down, all asprawl, face buried in leaf mold and turf. Kellin grabbed handfuls of tunic and dragged him over onto his back. "Urchin—"

Kellin recoiled. A bloodied silver wafer extruded from Urchin's breastbone, shining wetly in the moonlight.

He mouthed it: *Sorcerer's Tooth*. Kellin had heard of them. The Ihlini weapons were often poisoned, though this one had done its work simply by slicing cleanly through the boy's chest from spine to breastbone.

Corwyth's voice sounded very close, *too* close, though Kellin could not see him. "A waste of life," the Ihlini said. "You threw it away, Kellin."

"No!"

"You had only to come to me."

"No!"

"And so now you are alone in the dark with an Ihlini." Corwyth's laughter was quiet. "Surely a nightmare all Cheysuli dread."

Urchin was dead. Muttering a prayer to the gods—and an apology to Urchin for the pain he could not feel—Kellin stripped hastily out of his jerkin, tucked it over the exposed spikes, then yanked the wafer from Urchin's chest.

He twisted his head. *Where is—?*

Just behind. "Kellin. Surrender. I promise you no harm."

Kellin lurched upward and spun. "I promise *you* harm!"

He heard Corwyth cry out as the glinting weapon, loosed, spun toward the Ihlini. Kellin did not tarry to see if the Tooth had bitten deeply enough to kill. He fled into darkness again.

Kellin ran until he could run no more, then dropped into a steady jogging trot. Though his breath fogged the air, the first terror had faded, replaced by a simple conviction that if he did not halt, not even to catch that breath, he could remain ahead of Corwyth.

He assumed the Ihlini lived. To believe otherwise was to court the kind of carelessness that might prove fatal. If he had learned one thing from his beloved Ian, it was never to assume one was safe when one could not know.

Deadfall snapped beneath booted feet, then died out gradually as Kellin learned to seek out the thicker shadows of softer, muffled ground. In six strides he learned stealth, reverting to simple instincts and the training of his race.

If I had a lir— But he did not, and wishing for one would gain him nothing save a tense uncertainty of his ability to survive.

At last even his trot collapsed into disarray. Kellin staggered, favoring his right side. Exhaustion robbed him of strength, of endurance; apprehension robbed him of grace. He stumbled once, twice, again. The final tumble sent him headfirst into a tangle of tall bracken, which spilled him into shadow. Kellin lay there, winded, sucking cold air scented heavily with mud, and resin, and fear.

Go on, his conscience told him. But the body did not respond. *Remember what happened to Rogan. Remember what happened to Urchin.*

Kellin squeezed shut his eyes. He had, until the moment of Urchin's death, believed himself inviolable. Ian had died, aye, because the Lion had bitten him, and the fortune-teller had died by the same violent means, but never had Kellin believed death could happen to *him*.

Rogan and Urchin, dead.

I could die, too.

Could the Ihlini's sorcery lead Corwyth directly to Kellin?

Run—

He stumbled to his feet yet again, hunching forward as a cramp bit into his side. He banished the pain, banished the memories of the deaths he had witnessed, and went on again.

—*am a Cheysuli warrior ... the forest is my home—and every creature in it*—

He meant to go home, of course. All the way to

Mujhara herself, and into Homana-Mujhar. There he would tell them all. There he would explain. There he would describe in bloody detail what Corwyth had accomplished.

The sound was a heavy cough. Not human. Clearly animal. A heavy, deep-throated cough.

Kellin froze. He sucked in a breath and held it, listening for the sound.

A cough. And then a growl.

—am Cheysuli—

So he was. But he was also a boy.

The growl rose in pitch, then altered into a roar.

He knew the sounds of the forest. This was not one of them. This was a sound Kellin recognized because it filled his dreams.

He did not cry out, but only because he could not. *Lion?*

"No," Kellin blurted. He denied it vigorously, as he had denied nothing before in his life. Urchin had come, and the Lion had been driven away. The daytime was safe. And only rarely did the Lion trouble his dreams now, since Urchin had come.

But Urchin was dead. And night replaced the day.

"*No!*" Kellin cried. *There can be no Lion. Everyone says.*

But it was dark, so dark. It was too easy to believe in such things as Lions when there was no light.

He fastened himself onto a single thought. "I am not a child anymore. I defeated the Steppesman and knocked down his knife. Lions do not exist."

But the Lion roared again. Kellin's defiance was swamped.

He ran without thought for silence or subterfuge. Outflung hands crushed aside foliage, but some of it sprang back and cut into the flesh of his naked torso, jerkinless in flight. It snagged hair, at eyes, at mouth; it dug deeply into his neck even as he ducked.

Lion!

He saw nothing but shadow and moonlight. *If I stop—*

From behind came the roar of a hungry, hunting lion, crashing through broken brush on the trail of Cheysuli prey.

Huge and tawny and golden, like the throne in Homana-Mujhar.

How can they say there isn't a Lion?

Blood ran into Kellin's mouth, then spilled over open lips; he had somehow bitten his tongue. He spat, swiped aside a snagging limb, then caught his breath painfully on a choked blurt of shock as the footing beneath crumbled.

Wait— He teetered. Then fell. The ground gave way and tumbled him into a narrow ravine.

Down and down and down, crashing through bracken and creepers, banging arms and legs into saplings, smacking skull against rocks and roots. And then at last the bottom, all of a sudden, *too* sudden, and he sprawled awkwardly onto his back, fetching up against a stump. Kellin heard whooping and gulping, and realized the noise was his own.

Lion?

He lurched upward, then scrambled to his feet. He ached from head to foot, as if all his bones were bruised.

Lion?

And the lion, abruptly, was *there*.

Kellin ran. He heard the panting grunts, smelled the meat-laden breath. And then the jaws snapped closed around his left ankle.

"No!"

The pain shot from ankle to skull. Jaws dug

through leather boot into flesh, threatening the bone.

Kellin clawed at the iron teeth of the iron, bodiless beast that had caught boy instead of bear. Fingers scrabbled at the trap, trying to locate and trigger the mechanism that would spring the jaws open.

No lion— It was relief, but also terror; the beast could not be far behind.

Kellin had heard of bear traps. The Cheysuli disdained such tools, preferring to fight a beast on its own level rather than resorting to mechanical means. But some of the Homanans used the heavy iron traps to catch bear and other prey.

Now it's caught ME— Pain radiated from the ankle until it encompassed Kellin's entire body. He twitched and writhed against it, biting into his bloodied lip, then scrabbled for the chain that bound trap to tree. It was securely locked. Designed to withstand the running charge of a full-grown bear, it would surely defeat a boy.

Frenziedly, Kellin yanked until his palms shredded and bled. "Let go—*let go*—LET GO—"

The deep-chested cough sounded again. Through deadfall the lion came, slinking out of shadow, tearing its way through vines and bracken.

Kellin leapt to his feet and ran, and was jerked down almost at once. Iron teeth bit through boot and compressed fragile flesh, scraping now on bone.

—*no—no*—
—no—*no*—NO—"

The lion, still coughing, broke out of shadow into moonlight. Kellin jerked at the chain again, but palms slipped in sticky blood. The weight of the trap was nothing as he tried to stand again, to meet his death like a man.

But then the lion roared. The boy who meant to

die a man was reduced, by sheer terror, into nothing but a child screaming frenziedly for his father.

But his father would not come, because he never had.

Eight

Horseback. And yet he did not ride as a man but as a child, a small child, rump settled across the withers, legs dangling slackly upon one shoulder while the rest of him was cradled securely against a man's chest.

Kellin roused into terror. "Lion—" He was perfectly stiff, trying to flail his way to escape. Terror overwhelmed him. "Lion— LION—"

Arms tightened, stilling him. "There is no lion here."

"But—" He shut his mouth on the protest, the adamant denial of what the voice told him. Then another panic engulfed. *"Ihlini—"*

The man laughed softly, as if meaning no insult. "Not I, my lad. I've not the breeding for it."

Kellin subsided, though his strained breathing was audible. His eyes stretched painfully wide, but saw nothing in the darkness save the underside of a man's jaw and the oblique silhouette of a head. "Who—?" It faded at once. Pain reasserted itself. "My *leg*."

"I'm sorry for it, lad . . . but you'll have to wait for the healing."

It took effort to speak, to forced a single word through the rictus of his mouth. "—whole—?"

"Broken, I fear. But we'll be mending it for you."

Kellin ground his teeth. "—*hurts*—" And then

wished he had said nothing, nothing at all; a Cheysuli did not speak of pain.

"Aye, one would think so." The grip shifted a little, sliding down Kellin's spine to accommodate the weight that was no longer quite so slack. " 'Twas a trap for a bear, not a boy. You're fortunate it left the foot attached."

Kellin stiffened again, craning, as he tried to see for himself.

The other laughed softly. "Aye, lad, 'tis there. I promise you that. Now, settle yourself; you've a fever coming on. You'll do better to rest."

"Who—?" he began again.

The rider chuckled as Kellin tried to sit up. He turned his face downward. "There, now—better? I'm one of you after all."

"One of—me?" And then Kellin understood. Relief washed through him, then ebbed as quickly as it stole his strength away.

Indeed, one of him. The stranger was his grandsire, if stripped of forty years. His accent was Aileen's own. There was only one Cheysuli warrior in all the world who sounded like the Mujhar's Erinnish queen.

"Blais," Kellin murmured. Weakness and fever crept closer to awareness, nibbling at its edges.

The warrior grinned, displaying fine white teeth in a dark Cheysuli face. "Be still, little cousin. We've yet a ways to ride. You'll do better to pass it in sleep."

In sleep, or something like. Kellin slumped against his kinsman as consciousness departed.

He roused as Blais handed him down from the horse into someone else's care. Pain renewed itself, so strongly that Kellin whimpered before he could suppress it. And then he was more ashamed than ever because Blais himself was Cheysuli and knew a warrior did not voice his discomfort.

Sweating, Kellin bit again into a split lip and tasted fresh blood. It was all he could do not to moan aloud.

"My pavilion," Blais said briefly. "Send someone to Homana-Mujhar with word, and call others here for the healing."

The other warrior carried Kellin inside as Blais dismounted and carefully settled him onto a pallet of thick furs. Kellin opened his eyes and saw the shadowed interior of a Cheysuli pavilion. Then the stranger was gone, and Blais knelt down on one knee beside him. A callused palm touched Kellin's forehead.

"*Shansu*," Blais murmured. "I know it hurts, little cousin, no need to fight it so. I'll think none the less of you."

But Kellin would not give in, though he sweated and squirmed with pain. "Can't *you* heal me?"

Blais smiled. His face was kind in a stern sort of way. He was very like them all, though Erinn and Homana ran in his veins as well as Cheysuli blood. Physically the dilution did not show; Blais' features and coloring were purely Cheysuli, even if the accent was not. "Not without help, my lad. I was ill myself last year with the summer fever— well enough now, you'll see, but weak in the earth magic yet. I'd rather not risk the future of Homana to a halfling's meager gifts."

Halfling. Kellin shifted. *What am I, then?* "You have a *lir*. Tanni. I remember from when you visited Homana-Mujhar two years ago."

"Aye, but she came to me late. Don't be forgetting, lad—I was Erinn-raised. The magic there is different. I'm different because of it."

Fever-clad weakness proved pervasive. Kellin squinted at his cousin through a wave of fading vision. "I'm different, too, like you ... will I get my *lir* late?"

" 'Tis between you and the gods." Blais' callused palm was gentle as he smoothed back dampened hair. "Hush, now, lad. Don't waste yourself on talking."

Kellin squirmed. "The Lion—"

" 'Twas a bear-trap, lad."

Kellin shut his eyes because it made him dizzy to keep them open. "An Ihlini Lion ..." he asserted weakly, "and it was after me."

"Lad."

"—*was*—" Kellin insisted. "The Ihlini killed Urchin. And *Rogan*."

"Kellin."

"They were my friends, and he *killed* them."

"Kellin!" Blais caught Kellin's head between two strong hands, cupping the dome of skull easily. "No more of this. The healing comes first, *then* we'll be talking of deaths. D'ye hear?"

"But—"

"Be still, my little prince. Homana has need of you whole."

"But—"

And then the others were there, crowding into the pavilion, and the wave of exhaustion that engulfed Kellin was as much induced by the earth magic as by his fever.

Voices intruded. The murmurs were quiet, but they nonetheless broke apart Kellin's tattered dreams and roused him to wakefulness.

"—harsh for any man to lose his closest companions," Blais was saying from outside as he pulled aside the doorflap. "For a lad, that much the harder."

Light penetrated the interior, turning the inside of Kellin's eyelids red. The answering voice was well-known and beloved. "Kellin has always seemed older than his years," Brennan said as he entered the pavilion. "Sometimes I forget he is naught but a boy, and I try to make him into a man."

" 'Tis the risk any man takes with an heir, especially a prince." Blais let the doorflap drop, dimming daylight again into a wan, saffron tint.

Brennan's voice was hollow. "He is more than that to me. I lost Aidan—" He checked. "So, now there is Kellin. In Aidan's place. In all things, in Aidan's place. He was made to be Prince of Homana before he was even a boy, still but an infant wetting his napkins."

Kellin cracked his lids slightly, only enough so he could see the two men through a fuzzy fringe of lashes. He did not want them to know he was awake. He had learned very young that adults overheard divulged more information than when asked straight out.

Blais' laugh was soft as he settled himself near the pallet. "You had no choice but to invest him when you did. Aidan had renounced the title already, and *I* had come from Erinn. D'ye think I am deaf? I heard all the whispers, *su'fali* ... had you delayed Kellin's investiture, my presence here in Homana might have given new heart to the *a'saii*. Your claim on the Lion would have been threatened again."

"I might have packed you off to Erinn," Brennan suggested mildly.

"Might have *tried*, my lord Mujhar." Blais' tone was amused as he gestured for his guest to seat himself. "When has a warrior been *made* to do anything he preferred not to do?"

Brennan sighed as he knelt down beside his grandson. "Even Kellin. Even a ten-year-old boy."

The humor was banished. "He spoke of a lion, and an Ihlini."

The line of Brennan's mouth tautened. "The lion is something Kellin made up years ago. It is an excuse for things he cannot explain. He is fanciful; he conjures a beast from the lions in banners and signets, and the throne itself. And because he has been unfortunate to witness Ihini handiwork, he interprets all the violence as the doings of this lion."

"What handiwork?"

"The death of a fortune-teller. He was a foreigner and unknown to us, but his death stank of sorcery."

"Lochiel," Blais said grimly.

"He knows very well Kellin offers the greatest threat to the Ihlini."

"Like his father before him."

"But Aidan no longer matters. He sired the next link, and that link now is the one Lochiel must shatter." Brennan's fingertips gently touched Kellin's brow. "It all comes to Kellin. Centuries of planning all comes down to him."

Blais' tone was dry, for all it was serious. "Then we had best see he survives."

"I have done everything I could. The boy has been kept so closely it is no wonder he makes up stories about lions. Had my *jehan* kept me so tied to Homana-Mujhar, I would have gone mad. As it is, I am not in the least surprised he found a way to escape his imprisonment. But Urchin and Rogan are also missing; I can only surmise they, too, were lured away. No Ihlini could get in, and Kellin is too well-guarded within the palace itself. He would go nowhere without the Homanan boy, and Rogan would never permit Kellin to leave if he heard any whisper of it. So I believe we must look at a clever trap set with the kind of bait that would lure all of them out."

Blais' tone was grim. "An imaginary lion?"

Kellin could no longer hold himself back; his eyes popped open. "There *was* a Lion!"

"Cheysuli ears," Brennan said, brows arching, "hear more than they should."

"There was," Kellin insisted. "It chased me into the bear-trap . . . after Urchin and Rogan died."

Brennan shut his eyes. "More deaths."

Blais shifted. He sat cross-legged, one thigh weighted down by the head of a ruddy wolf. His expression was oddly blank as he stroked the wide skull and scratched the base of the ears.

Brennan's momentary lapse was banished. He was calm, unperturbed. "Tell us what happened, Kellin. We must know everything."

Kellin delayed, testing his ankle. "It doesn't hurt any more."

"Earth magic," Blais said. "You've a scar, but the bones are whole."

"A scar?" Kellin peeled back the deerskin coverlet and saw the bared ankle. Indeed, there was a jagged ring of purplish "tooth" marks ringing his ankle. He wiggled his foot again. There was no pain.

" 'Twill fade," Blais told him. "I've more scars than I can count, but hardly any of them show."

Kellin did not care about the scar; if anything, it proved there *was* a Lion. He looked now at his grandsire, putting aside the Lion to speak of another grief. "It was Rogan," he said unsteadily. "*Rogan* betrayed me to the Ihlini."

The Mujhar did not so much as twitch an eyelid. The mildness of his tone was deceptive, but Kellin knew it well: Brennan wanted very badly to know the precise truth, without embellishments or suppositions. "You are certain it was he?"

"Aye." Kellin suppressed with effort the emotions to which he longed to surrender. He would be all Cheysuli in this. "He said he would take me to my *jehan*. That you knew we were to go, just the three of us, but that we meant to go to Clankeep. He said he would send true word to you where we were, but only after we were on our way to Hondarth."

Brennan's face grayed. "Such a simple plan, and certain to work. I was a fool. Lochiel has ways of suborning even those I most value."

"Not money," Kellin said. "So he could have his wife back. Only—" He checked himself, recalling all too clearly the tiny dancing woman and Rogan's horrible ending. "Corwyth killed him first. With sorcery. And then *Urchin*." Pain formed a knot in chest and throat. "Urchin's dead, too."

After a moment the Mujhar touched Kellin's head briefly. Gently, he said, "You must tell me everything you remember about how this was done, and the Ihlini himself. *Everything*, Kellin, so we may prepare for another attack."

"Another—?" Kellin stared hard at the Mujhar, turning over the words. Realization made him breathless. "They want to *catch* me. Corwyth said so. He said he was taking me to Lochiel, in Valgaard."

Brennan's expression was grim, but he did not avoid candor. "You are important to the Ihlini, Kellin, because of who you are, and the blood in your veins. You know about that."

He did. Very well. *Too* well; it was all anyone spoke of. "They won't stop, then." It seemed obvious.

"No."

Kellin nodded, understanding more with each moment. "That's why you set the dogs to guarding me."

"Dogs? Ah." Brennan smiled faintly. "We dared not allow you to go anywhere alone. Not in Mujhara, not even to Clankeep." His jaw tightened.

"Do you recall how you sickened after your Naming Day feast?"

Kellin nodded, recalling with vivid clarity how ill he had been after eating his meal. He had not wanted fish for a sixth-month, after.

"Lochiel had no recourse to sorcery in order to harm you, not so long as you remained in Homana-Mujhar, or at Clankeep, but coin buys people. He bribed a cook to poison the meal. We were forced to take serious steps to safeguard Homana's prince, and his freedom suffered for it." Brennan's words were stated with careful precision. "Rogan understood. Rogan knew why. He comprehended fully how you were to be protected."

That is why they were all so upset when I ran away from the fortune-teller. Guilt flickered. "It was after I heard you speaking with granddame. About how my *jehan* would not have me see him." Kellin swallowed heavily. "Rogan came and said he would take me to my *jehan*."

Brennan's expression was bleak as he exchanged a glance with Blais. "I have learned from this, too, though I believed myself wise in such matters." He sighed heavily. "Nearly every man has his price. Most will deny it, claiming themselves incorruptible, but there is always something that will lure them into betrayal. If they disbelieve it, it is because they have not been offered that which they most desire."

Rogan was offered his wife. Kellin wanted to protest it. It hurt him deeply that Rogan had betrayed him, but he understood his grandfather's words. Hadn't *he* been bought by the promise of his father?

"I would never submit to an Ihlini," he muttered. "Never."

"And that is why you are here." Brennan smiled

faintly, tension easing from his features. "Tell us everything."

Kellin did. By the time he was done he felt tears in his eyes, and hated himself for them.

Blais shook his head. "There is no shame in honest grief."

Brennan's tone was gentle. "Rogan was everything to you for two years, and Urchin was your best friend. We think no less of you because you loved them."

Kellin let that go, thinking now of something else. "You said something about me. To Blais, earlier. That I offer the greatest threat to the Ihlini." He looked first at Blais, then at the Mujhar. "What harm can *I* do them?"

"You can bring down their House," Brennan said quietly, "merely by siring a son."

It was incomprehensible. "Me?"

The Mujhar laughed. "You are young yet to think of such things as sons, Kellin, but the day will come when you are a man. Lochiel knows this. With each passing year you become more dangerous."

"Because of my blood." Kellin looked at the scar ringing his ankle, recalling the warm wetness running down between his toes. "*That* blood."

Brennan took Kellin's wrist into his hand and raised it, spreading the fingers with the pressure of his thumb. "All the blood in here," he said. "In this hand, in this arm, in this body. And the seed in your loins, provided it quickens within the body of a particular woman. Lochiel cannot risk allowing you to sire that son."

"The prophecy," Kellin murmured, staring at his hand. He tried to look beneath the flesh to bone and muscle, and the blood that was so special.

"The Firstborn reborn," Blais said. "The bane of the Ihlini. The end of Asar-Suti."

Kellin looked at his grandfather. "They died because of me. Rogan. Urchin. The fortune-teller. Didn't they?"

Brennan closed the small hand inside his own adult one. "It is the heaviest burden a man can know. Men who are kings—and boys who are princes—carry more of them than most."

His chest was full of pain. "Will more die, grandsire? Just because of me?"

Brennan did not lie. He did not look away. "Almost certainly."

Nine

Kellin felt important and adult: Brennan had said he might have a small cup of honey brew, the powerful Cheysuli liquor. He knew it was his grandfather's way of making him feel safe and loved after his encounter with tragedy, so he sipped slowly, savoring the liquor *and* the intent, not wanting the moment to end because he felt for the first time as if they believed him grown, or nearly so. Nearly was better than not; he grinned into the clay cup.

The Mujhar was not present. When Brennan returned to the pavilion, he, Kellin, and Blais would depart for Homana-Mujhar, but for the moment Kellin was required to stay with his cousin. Brennan met with the clan-leader to discuss the kinds of things kings and clan-leaders discuss; Kellin had heard some of it before and found it tedious. He was much more interested in his kinsman, who was fascinating as a complex mixture of familiar and exotic.

An Erinnish Cheysuli with Homanan in his blood, Blais did not *look* anything but Cheysuli, yet his accent and attitude were different. The latter was most striking to Kellin. Blais seemed less concerned with excessive personal dignity than with being content within his spirit; if that spirit were more buoyant than most, he gave it free rein regardless.

At this moment Blais was working on a bow, replacing the worn leather handgrip with new. His head was bent over his work and a lock of thick black hair obscured part of his face. *Lir*-gold gleamed. Next to him sprawled sleeping Tanni, toes twitching in wolf dreams.

"It could be you," Kellin blurted. "Couldn't it?"

Blais did not look up from his handiwork. "What could, lad?"

"You," Kellin repeated. "The man in the prophecy. The man whose blood can do the things everyone wants it to do."

Now Blais raised his head. "My blood?"

"Aye. You are Cheysuli, Erinnish, and Homanan. You are halfway there."

"Ah, but you are *all* the way there, my lad. I've no Solindish or Atvian blood bubbling in my veins." Blais' face creased in a smile. "You've no fear of me usurping your place."

"But you're older. You are a warrior." Kellin looked at Tanni. "You have a *lir*."

"And so will you, in but a handful of years." Strong fingers moved skillfully as Blais rewrapped the leather.

"But I heard you," Kellin said quietly, grappling with new ideas. "You talked to grandsire about the *a'saii*."

The hands stilled abruptly. This time Blais' gaze was sharp. "I said something of it, aye. You see, lad—I have more cause to concern myself with *a'saii* than any warrior alive."

"They were traitors," Kellin declared. "Rogan told me—" He cut it off abruptly. "Grandsire said they wanted to overthrow the proper succession and replace it with another."

"So they did." Blais' tone was noncommittal. "They were Cheysuli who feared the completion of the prophecy would end their way of life."

"Will it?"

Blais shrugged. "Things will change, aye . . . but perhaps not so much as the *a'saii* fear."

"Do you?" Kellin needed to know. "Do you fear it, Blais?"

An odd expression crossed Blais' smooth, dark face. For only a moment, black brows pulled together. Then he smiled crookedly. "I fear losing what I have only just found," he admitted evenly. "I was born here, Kellin. Keep-born, but reared in Erinn a very long way away. Customs are different in Erinn. I was a part of them, but also longed for others. My *jehana* taught me what she could of the language and customs of Cheysuli, but she was half Erinnish herself, and now wed to an Erinnishman. It was Keely who taught me more, who showed me what earth magic was, and what it could bring me." His smile was warmly reminiscent. "She suggested I come here, to find out who I was."

Kellin was fascinated. "Did you?"

"Oh, aye. Enough to know I belong here." Blais grinned, caressing Tanni's head. "I may not *sound* all Cheysuli, but in spirit I am."

"Why," Kellin began, "do you have more cause to concern yourself with *a'saii* than any warrior alive?"

Blais' brows arched. "You've a good ear to recall that so perfectly."

Kellin shrugged, dismissing it. "The *a'saii* are disbanded. Grandsire said so."

"Formally, aye. But convictions are hard to kill. There are those who still keep themselves apart from other clans."

"But *you* stay here."

"Clankeep is my home. I serve the prophecy as much as any warrior. As much as you will, once you are grown."

Kellin nodded absently. "But why do you have cause?"

Blais sighed, hands tightening on the bow. "Because it was my grandsire who began the *a'saii*, Kellin. Ceinn wanted to replace Niall's son—your grandsire, Brennan—with his own son, Teirnan. There was justification, Ceinn claimed, because Teirnan was the son of the Mujhar's sister."

"Isolde," Kellin put in; he recalled the names from lessons.

"Aye. Isolde. Niall's *rujholla*."

"And Ian's."

Blais grinned. "And Ian's."

"But why *you*?"

Blais' grin faded. "Teirnan was my father. When I came here from Erinn, those who were *a'saii* thought I should be named Prince of Homana when your father renounced his title."

Kellin was astonished. "In my place?"

Blais nodded.

"In my place." It was incomprehensible to Kellin, who could not imagine anyone else in his own place. He had been Prince of Homana all his life. "But—*I* was named."

"Aye. As the Mujhar desired."

Something occurred. "What about you?" Kellin asked. "Did *you* want the title?"

Blais laughed aloud. "I was reared by a man who is the Lord of Erinn's bastard brother. I spent many years at Kilore—I know enough of royalty and the responsibilities of rank to want no part of it." He leaned forward slightly, placing the tip of his forefinger on Kellin's brow. "*You*, my young lad, will be the one to hold the Lion."

"Oh, no," Kellin blurted. "I have to kill it, first."

Blais stilled. "Kill it?"

Kellin was matter-of-fact. "Before it kills all of *us*."

*   *   *

When Kellin—with grandfather, cousin, and numerous liveried and armored guardsmen—entered the inner bailey of Homana-Mujhar, he discovered it clogged to bursting with strange horses and servants. Horse-boys ran this way and that, grasping at baggage-train horses even as they gathered in the mounts of dismounting riders; servants shouted at one another regarding the unloading; while the bailey garrison, clad in Mujharan scarlet, did its best to sort things out.

The Mujhar himself, trapped in the center of the bailey as his horse restively rang shod hoofs off cobbles, finally ran out of patience. "By the blood of the Lion—" Brennan began, and then broke off abruptly as a tall man came out of the palace doorway to stand at the top of the steps.

"Have I made a mess of all your Mujharish majesty?" the man called over the din. "Well, doubtless you are in dire need of humbling anyway."

"Hart!" Brennan cried. "By the gods—*Hart*!"

Kellin watched in surprise as his grandsire hastily threw himself down from his mount and joined the throng, pushing through toward the steps. Brennan mounted them three at a time, then enfolded the other man in a huge, hard hug.

"*Su'fali*," Kellin murmured, then grinned at Blais. "*Su'fali* to both of us. Hart, come from Solinde!"

"So I see." Blais squinted over the crowd. "They are two blooms from the same bush."

"But Hart has blue eyes. And only one hand; an enemy had the other one cut off." Kellin followed Brennan's lead, climbing down with less skill than his longer-legged grandfather, and then he, too, was swallowed up by the crowd. Kellin could see nothing, neither grandfather, great-uncle, nor steps. He considered ducking under the bellies of all the horses, but reconsidered when he thought about the kicks he risked. Like Brennan before him, if with less success, Kellin shoved his way through the milling throng of baggage train and household attendants. Solindish, all of them; he recognized the accent.

His path was more difficult, but at last Kellin reached the steps and climbed to the top. His grandsire and great-uncle had left off hugging, but the warm glints in their eyes—one pair blue, the other yellow—were identical.

So is everything else, except for Hart's missing hand. Kellin looked at the leather-cuffed stump, wondering what it was like to be restricted to a single hand. And Hart had lost more than a hand; the old Cheysuli custom of kin-wrecking still held. He was, because of his maiming, no longer considered in the clans to be a warrior despite his blood and his *lir*, the great hawk known as Rael.

Kellin glanced up. Spiraling in a lazy circle over the palace rooftops was the massive raptor, black edging on each feather delineating wings against the blue of the sky. *I may have a hawk when I am a warrior—*

"Kellin!" Brennan's hand closed over a shoulder. "Kellin, here is your kinsman. You have never seen him, I know, but to know who Hart is a man need only look at me."

"But you *are* different," Kellin said after a brief inspection. "You seem older, grandsire."

It brought a shout of delighted laughter from Hart, who struck his twin-born *rujholli* a sharp blow with his only hand. "There. You see? I have said it myself—"

"Nonsense." Brennan arched a single brow. "You surely count more gray in your hair than I."

"No," Kellin said doubtfully, which moved Hart to laughter again.

"Well, we *are* very like," the Mujhar's twin said. "If there are differences, it is because the Lion is a far more difficult taskmaster than my own Solinde."

"Has Solinde thrown you out?" Kellin asked. "Is that why you have come?"

Hart grinned. "And lose the best lord she ever had? No, I am not banished, nor am I toppled as Bellam was toppled by Carillon. The Solindish love me, now—or, if not love, they tolerate me well enough." He tapped the cuffed stump on top of Kellin's head. "Erinnish eyes, Kellin. Where is the Cheysuli in you?"

"*You* have Homanan eyes," Kellin retorted. "And now your hair is gray; *mine* is all over black."

"Sharp eyes, and a sharper wit," Brennan said dryly. "The Erinnish side, I think."

Hart nodded, smiling, as he assessed his young kinsman. "You are small for twelve, but your growth may come late. Corin's did."

"I am *ten*," Kellin corrected. "Tall enough for ten; grandsire says so."

"Ten." Hart shot a glance at Brennan. "I miscounted, then."

"Aging, are you?" Brennan's eyes were alight. "Forgetting things already?"

Hart demurred at once. "I merely lost track, no more. But I *did* think him older."

"Does it matter?" Brennan asked, laughing. "I am hardly infirm, *rujho*. The Lion will yet be mine a while. Kellin should be well-grown before he inherits."

"I was not thinking of thrones, *rujho*, but of weddings."

"Weddings! Kellin's? By the gods, Hart—"

"Wait you." Hart put up his hand to silence his brother. "Before you begin shouting at me, as you have always done—" he grinned, eyes alight, "—it is for you to say, of course. And now that I see he is so young, perhaps it is too soon."

"Too soon for what?" Kellin asked. "A wedding? Whose? Mine?"

Hart laughed. "So full of questions, *harani*."

"Mine?" Kellin repeated.

Hart sighed, scratching idly at his beardless chin. "I have a daughter—"

Brennan interrupted in mock asperity. "You have four of them. Which one do you mean?"

Hart's shrug was lopsided. "Dulcie is thirteen, which is closer to Kellin than the twins. And—" He shrugged again, letting go what he had begun. "There is reason for this, *rujho* . . . we will speak of it later."

"Too young," Brennan said.

Hart's eyes were speculative. "Too young to marry, perhaps, but not for a betrothal."

"This can wait," Brennan said. "Let us be *ruj-holli* again before we must be rulers."

Hart sighed heavily. "That may be difficult. I have all of them with me."

"Who?"

"They wanted to come," Hart continued. "All but Blythe. She carries her first child after all this time, so we thought it best she remain behind. It will be my first grandchild, after all."

Diverted, Brennan stared at him. "Is she wed? When? I thought Blythe intended never to marry."

"She did not, after Tevis—" Hart paused to correct himself, gritting the name through his teeth. "—after *Lochiel*." He forced himself to relax, blue eyes bright in remembered anger. "But she met a Solindishman of respectable family with whom she fell in love after much too long alone; she *is* past thirty." Hart grinned. "And she would be quite put out if she heard me say that. But she and her lordling married eight months ago, and now there will be a child."

"But the rest ..." Brennan glanced around. "They are here?"

"All of them."

"Ilsa?"

"All of them. They insisted. My girls are—" he paused delicately, "—somewhat firm in their convictions."

Brennan eyed him. "You never were one for self-discipline, Hart. Why should I expect you to be capable of ruling your daughters when you never could rule yourself?"

"I understand discipline quite well, *leijhana tu'sai*," Hart retorted. "But there are times when my girls make such things difficult."

Brennan studied Hart a moment. "You have not changed at all, have you?"

Hart grinned unrepentantly. "No."

"Good." Brennan clapped him on the back. "Now, come inside."

It was abrupt, if unintended, but dismissal nonetheless; they turned as one and strode into the palace without a word or a glance to the boy they knew as the Prince of Homana.

"Wait!" But they were gone, and a hand was on Kellin's shoulder, pulling him back.

"Begrudge them nothing, lad." It was Blais, smiling faintly as he moved to stand beside Kellin.

"But what about me?" Kellin was aggrieved. "Grandsire dismissed the Lion, and now they dismiss *me*."

"They were twin-born, my lad, linked by far more than a simple brother-bond. And they've not seen one another, I am told, for nearly twenty years."

"Twenty years!" Kellin gaped. "I could have been born twice over!"

Blais nodded. "When you are a king, 'tis not so easy to find the time—or the freedom—to go where you will. Hart and Brennan are halves of a whole, parted by title and realm for much too long a time." He briefly touched Kellin's shoulder. "Let them be whole again, lad. They'll be having time for you later."

Kellin scowled. "And weddings, too?"

"Weddings! What has this to do with weddings?" But as Blais stared after his vanished uncles, his expression changed. "Aye, it could be that. 'Tis a topic of much import in royal Houses." He grinned. "Thank the gods *I* am not in line for a throne, or surely they'd be disposing of me, too!"

"And me?" Kellin demanded. "Am I to be married off with no say in the matter?"

Blais did not appear unduly concerned. " 'Tis likely," he confirmed. "You're to be Mujhar of Homana, one day. I'll not doubt there've been letters about your future bride since you were formally invested."

"*Cheysula*," Kellin said darkly, proving to his cousin he knew the Old Tongue, too, "and I'll choose my own."

"Will you, now?" Blais ran a hand through thick black hair, mouth quirking in wry amusement. " 'Tis what Keely claimed of herself, when she chafed at her betrothal—but in the end she wed the man they promised her to."

"Sean." Kellin nodded. "I know all about that." He was not interested in his great-aunt, whom he had never met. He cast a speculative glance up at his kinsman. "Then you are not promised?"

Blais laughed. "Nor likely to be. I'm content to share my time with this woman, or that one, without benefit of betrothals."

Kellin understood. "*Meijhas*," he said. "How many, Blais?"

"Many." Blais grinned. "Would I be admitting *how* many? A warrior does not dishonor his *meij-has* by discussing them casually."

"Many," Kellin murmured. He grinned back at his cousin. "Then I'll have many, too."

Blais sighed and clapped his hand upon a slender shoulder. "No doubt you will. No prince I ever knew lacked for company. Now—shall we go in? I'm for meeting these Solindish kin of ours."

Ten

In short order Blais and Kellin met all of the
Solindish kin en masse in Aileen's sunny solar.
The chamber seemed small of a sudden. Kellin
duly took note of all his assorted kinfolk: Ilsa, the
Lady of Solinde, with her profusion of white-
blonde hair and gloriously expressive gray eyes;
the middle daughters Cluna and Jennet, twins like
Hart and Brennan, who reflected their mother's
coloring and the beginnings of her beauty augmented by Cheysuli heritage; and Dulcie, the
youngest—the girl whom Hart had said might become Kellin's *cheysula*.

To the latter daughter Kellin paid the most attention. His knowledge of weddings and marriages
was slight, but he took it more personally now
that his name had been linked with hers.

He was, however, briefly distracted. Blais, whom
he had decided was everything a warrior should
be—and his rescuer, to boot—was all of a sudden
different. It was a subtle difference Kellin could
not name; he knew only that Blais' attention to
his young cousin was oddly diverted, as if something else far more fascinating had caught his attention. Kellin understood none of it—Cluna and
Jennet seemed silly girls to him, and not worth
more time than was necessary to be polite—but
Blais seemed most disposed to speak with both of
them for a very long time.

Soon enough Blais offered to escort both Cluna and Jennet on a tour of Homana-Mujhar; and the adults suggested that what *they* had to say to one another was better said without Dulcie's and Kellin's presence. Kellin was instructed to do as Blais did: show his cousin every corner of the palace.

Outside in the corridor, Kellin glared mutinously at the closed door. *No one has time for me. The Lion nearly ate me, but no one thinks about THAT—*

Beside him, Dulcie laughed. "They set their traps for him."

Kellin scowled. "What do you mean?" He thought uncomfortably of the bear-trap, conjured by her words.

"Traps," she said succinctly. "They are frivolous women, both of them, only concerned with what is required to catch a handsome man." She grimaced wryly. "I saw it; didn't you?"

Kellin had not. "Of course I did," he said forthrightly, denying his ignorance.

Dulcie eyed him. "He *is* a handsome man, as Cheysuli go; I see now we are all alike, save for some differences in color." She grinned. "Your eyes are green; mine at least are yellow, like a proper Cheysuli's should be."

And proper she was, black-haired and yellow-eyed with skin the same coppery hue as Blais' and every other Cheysuli Kellin had seen. Dulcie was young—*twelve?*—but clearly was Cheysuli in all respects.

Kellin felt a twinge of self-consciousness; just now, faced with Dulcie—and having met Blais—he wanted very much to be as Cheysuli as possible. "I will be Mujhar." He thought it a good offense.

Dulcie nodded. "One of the reasons they want us to marry." She twined a strand of black hair into fingers and began twisting it. "Do you want to?"

Kellin stared at her. How could she be so matter-of-fact about it? Importantly, he said, "That is something I will have to consider."

Dulcie burst out laughing. "*You* consider? They will no more abide by what you wish—*or* me—than a stud horse minds his rider when a mare in season is near."

Kellin had not thought of it that way. "But if I am to be Mujhar, they must listen to me."

Dulcie shook her head. Her brows were straight, serious bars across a sculpted brow. She wore black hair in dozens of braids tied into a single plait and beaded at the bottom. "They will listen to no one, only to the prophecy." Dulcie grimaced. "I have had it stuffed into my ears often enough. It is all about blood, Kellin, and the need to mix it correctly. Don't you see?"

Kellin did not, though once again he claimed he did. "I am the one who is to sire the Firstborn," he declared. "Everyone says so."

Dulcie grinned. "Not without a woman!"

Color stained Kellin's face. "Is that supposed to be you?"

She shrugged, twisting hair again. "What else do you suppose they talk about behind that door but inches in front of your face? They will have us betrothed by supper."

Kellin glared at her. "Why to you? Why not to Cluna, or Jennet?"

"They are too old for you," Dulcie said matter-of-factly, "and likely by now they have both set their caps for Blais. I think neither of them wants a boy for a husband."

It stung. "I am nearly eleven."

"And I nearly thirteen." Clearly, Dulcie was undismayed by his youth. "It has to do with the blood, as I said. There is only one bloodline left to get, Kellin—the one bloodline no Cheysuli desires to acknowledge. But how else do they expect to get the Firstborn? It wants Ihlini blood."

He was startled, recalling Corwyth, and Lochiel's designs. "Ihlini!"

"*Think* about it," Dulcie said impatiently. "They need it from somewhere, from someone who favors the prophecy."

"But not an *Ihlini*—"

"Kellin." Her tone was exasperated. "That is why my father is proposing you and I wed. To get the Ihlini blood."

"But—" It was preposterous. "You do not *have*—"

"Aye," Dulcie answered, "I do. We all of us do: Blythe, Cluna, Jennet, and me. Because of our mother."

"But she is *Solindish*."

Dulcie's tone was freighted with condescension. "Solinde was the birthplace of Ihlini, Kellin. Remember the stories of how they broke away from the Firstborn and left Homana?"

He did. He had not thought of those stories in years. "Then—" Kellin frowned. He did not like the implication. "Then the Ihlini are not so different from the *a'saii*."

Dulcie smiled. "Now you begin to understand."

He eyed her assessively. "Can you conjure *godfire*?"

"Of course not. The Ihlini blood in us goes back more than two hundred years. No arts remain in our House." Dulcie shrugged. "Electra learned a few tricks, but nothing more. Tynstar did not share the Seker's blood with her."

He frowned. "Then why should it matter now?"

"Because no Cheysuli warrior would ever lie down with an Ihlini woman," Dulcie replied. "At least—not a *willing* one. So they will marry *us* off

and hope for the best ... if for no other reason
than to keep the Ihlini from making their own
through you."

"Through me?"

Dulcie sighed. "Are you stupid? If the Ihlini
caught you and made you lie with an Ihlini
woman, there could be a child. It would be *the*
child." She laughed at his expression. "The Ihlini
would use you, Kellin, like a prize Cheysuli stud."

Within hours he was full to bursting on kinfolk—and most of them female, at that, full of gossip and laughter—and so to escape, Kellin went to
his own chamber and climbed up into his huge
bed. He made mountains and hillocks of his coverlet, then planned his own campaigns as Carillon
and Donal must have planned them years before,
when Homana was at war.

"With Solinde," he muttered. He was not at the
moment disposed to like Solinde, since she had
managed to produce a twelve-year-old girl who
believed he was stupid.

The knock at the door was soft, but persistent.
Kellin, startled from his game, called out crossly
for the person to enter.

Aileen came in, not a servant at all. Her hair,
rust threaded with silver, was bound in braids
around her head with pins that glittered in sunlight. Her green gown was simple but elegant. She
wore around her throat a fortune in gold: the
mountain cat torque that marked her Brennan's
cheysula.

Is that what Dulcie expects from me? Kellin
jerked flat his coverlet and slid out of the bed to
stand politely. "Aye, granddame?"

"Sit." Aileen waved him back onto the bed, then
sat down on the edge herself. "Kellin—"

Whenever he spoke with Aileen he unconsciously

echoed the lilt of her accent. He blurted it out all at once before she could finish. " 'Tis done, isn't it? You've betrothed us."

Aileen arched reddish brows. "The idea doesn't please you, then?"

"No." He fidgeted, self-conscious; he liked his granddame very much and did not want to upset her, but he felt he had to tell the truth. "I want to choose for myself."

The faintest of creases deepened at the corner of Aileen's eyes. "Aye, of course you do. So did I. So did Brennan. But—"

"But I can't, can I?" he challenged forthrightly. " 'Tis like Dulcie said: you'll do whatever you want."

The Queen of Homana sighed. " 'Tis true those of royalty have little freedom in matters of marriage."

" 'Tisn't fair," Kellin asserted. "You tell me I will have power when I am grown, but then I am *told* whom I must marry. That is no power."

"No," she agreed quietly. "I had none, nor Corin, whom I wanted to marry in place of Brennan."

"In place of—grandsire?" It was a completely new thought. "You wanted to marry my *su'fali?*"

"Aye."

He blinked. "But you were already betrothed to grandsire."

"Aye, so I was. It did not lessen the wanting, Kellin; it was Corin I loved." Her green eyes were kind. "I know this may shock you, but I thought it fair to tell you. You are young, but not so young the truth should be kept from you, even those truths of men and woman."

"But you married grandsire."

"Aye. It was agreed upon before I was born: Niall's oldest son would marry Liam's daughter." She shrugged, mouth twisted awry. "And so I was *born* betrothed; it was only later, when Corin came to Erinn, that I realized how binding—and how wrong—the agreement was. I fell in love with Corin and he with me, but he was the stronger person. He said the betrothal must stand, and sailed away to Atvia."

"He married Glyn." He had never seen her—he had seen only Hart of his scattered kin—but he knew of the mute woman Corin had wed.

"Years later, aye. But then *I* was wed, and a mother, and my future was utterly settled."

Kellin digested all of it. "You are telling me that I should marry Dulcie."

Aileen smiled. "No."

It stilled him a moment. "No?"

"I told them to give you time, both of you time; to let you grow to adulthood. You've been kept close most of your life, Kellin, and we owe you some measure of freedom." An odd expression crossed her face. "The kind of freedom I had once, before coming to Homana."

Relief overflowed. "*Leijhana tu'sai*, granddame!"

Aileen laughed. "One day marriage will not be such a chore, my lad. That I promise."

"Was it a chore for you?"

The question stopped her. Aileen's eyes filled with memories he could not know, and were not shared with him. "For a very long time, it was," she answered finally. "But not any longer."

"Why?"

"Because when I allowed myself to stop resenting my marriage; when I stopped resenting the Cheysuli *tahlmorra* that dictated I sleep with Brennan instead of with Corin, I fell in love with your grandsire." Her smile was poignant. "And so now I have a new regret: that I wasted so much time in *not* loving him."

Kellin could only stare at his grandmother.

There were no words for what he felt; he knew only that he was young, too young after all, to begin to understand the complexities of adulthood.

Something new came into his head. "Did my *jehana* love my *jehan?*"

Aileen's mouth softened. "Very much, Kellin. 'Twas a match few people experience."

He nodded dutifully, uncomprehending. "But she died when I was born." He looked searchingly at Aileen. "Is that why he hates me? Is that why he gave me up and went away—because I killed his *cheysula?*"

Aileen's face drained. "Oh, Kellin, *no!* Oh, gods, is that what you've been thinking all these years?" She murmured something more in Erinnish, then caught him into her arms and pulled him close. "I'll swear on anything you like that your birth did not kill her, nor did it drive your father away. He gave you up because it was his *tahlmorra* to do so."

"But you believe he was wrong."

She withdrew a little to look into his face. "Have you a touch of the *kivarna*, lad? Have you been hiding the truth from us?"

"No," he blurted, intrigued. "What is it?"

"D'ye know what people feel?" She touched her breast. "D'ye know what is in their hearts?"

Perplexed, he frowned. "No. I just saw it in your face."

Aileen relaxed, laughing a little. "Aye, well—'tis a gift and a curse, my lad. Aidan had it in full measure, and Shona—'twould come as no surprise if it manifested in you."

Kellin was bewildered. " 'Twas in your face, granddame—and your voice." *And what I heard you say to grandsire once before.* But that he would not admit.

Aileen hugged him again briefly, then surrend-

ered him to the bed as she rose and shook out her
skirts. "I think he was wrong," she said firmly. "I
always have. But I'm a woman, Kellin—and though
I'll not swear a man loves his child less, he's not
borne that babe in his body. Aidan did as he believed he had to, to please the gods and his *tahlmorra*. And one day, *I promise*, you will ask him
to his face how he could do such a thing."

He heard the underlying hostility in her tone.
"But not yet."

Aileen's lips compressed. "Not yet."

After a moment Kellin nodded. It was a familiar
refrain. "Well," he said easily, "once I have killed
the Lion, he will *have* to let me see him."

"Oh, Kellin—"

"I will," he declared. "I *will* kill it. And then I
shall go to the Crystal Isle and show *jehan* the
head."

Aileen's mouth, he saw, was filled with all manner of protest. But she made none of them. With
tears in her eyes, the Erinnish Queen of Homana
left her grandson quite alone.

Eleven

Blais' door was ajar. Candlelight crept from the room into the corridor, slotted between door and jamb; Kellin peeked in carefully, not wanting to discover that Blais was not alone at all, but accompanied by Cluna, or Jennet, or Cluna *and* Jennet. They had taken up entirely too much of Blais' time, Kellin felt. It was his turn for his cousin's attention.

He paused there in the slot. He saw no female cousins. Only Blais himself, sprawled across the great tester bed with his *lir*, lovely Tanni, who lay upon her back with legs spread and underparts exposed in elaborate pleasure as Blais stroked belly fur. In that moment she was dog, not wolf; Kellin felt a pang of hope that perhaps he, too, would gain a wolf.

Then again, there was lovely black Sleeta, his grandsire's mountain cat, and Hart's magnificent Rael. There were so many wonderful *lir* in the world; surely the gods would see to it he gained the perfect one.

Blais' arm moved in slow repetition as he stroked Tanni. He lay on his belly, torso propped up on one elbow. Thick black hair fell forward over his shoulders. He wore no jerkin, only leggings; gold shone dully in candlelight against the bronzing of his flesh.

Someday I will have such gold. Kellin wet his lips. "Blais?"

Blais glanced up. Tanni flopped over on her side and bent her head around to inspect Kellin. "Aye?" Blais beckoned, smiling. "Come in, come in—we have no secrets, Tanni and I—and if I wanted privacy I would have shut the door."

Kellin slipped through the slot between door and jamb. Linked behind his back, both hands clutched an object. "I have a question."

His cousin's black brows arched. "Aye?"

He sucked in a deep breath. "Are you going back to Solinde with them?"

"Solinde!" Blais sat upright, shaking hair away from his face. "Why would I go to Solinde?"

"Because of—them." Abashed, Kellin stared at the floor.

"Who?" Blais began, and then he cut off the question. "Why do you ask, Kellin?"

Miserably, Kellin looked up to meet Blais' steady gaze. "I saw you," he whispered. "Earlier today, on the sentry-walk."

"Ah." Blais nodded.

"You were kissing Jennet."

"Cluna."

It stopped Kellin's attempt at explanation. "Cluna? But, I thought—"

Blais laughed. "You were thinking 'twas Jennet I wanted? Well, aye, and so it was—yesterday. Today 'twas Cluna." He shifted into a cross-legged position, one hand tugging gently at Tanni's ear. "You see, Cluna wanted to sample what her *rujholla* had tasted the day before. They compete in everything." He shrugged, grinning. "I accommodated them both."

Kellin was bewildered. "Then which one will you marry?"

"Marry!" Then Blais laughed. "Gods, Kellin—

neither. Were you thinking I would? No. I'll not go
to Solinde, and I'm doubting either of them could
bear to live at Clankeep. There is too much of Solinde in them." He smiled more warmly at his
cousin. "Were you thinking I meant to desert
you?"

Without warning tears welled up. Kellin was astonished and ashamed, but there was a thing he
had to say. "I have no one left," he explained unsteadily. "Only you. Urchin and Rogan—" He bit
into his lip. "There is grandsire and granddame,
but it isn't the same. 'Tisn't like true friends; they
have to like me. But you . . . well—" he swallowed
heavily, spilling it all at once. "I will be Mujhar
one day. I would have need of a liege man."

Blais' face was still. Only his eyes were alive in
the dark mask: fierce and bright and yellow.

Kellin felt all of his muscles knot up. *He'll refuse
me—he will say no.* He wanted it so badly, and yet
he knew it was unlikely. They were years and
worlds apart, and very different in nature.

Blais' tone was muted. "I had not expected
this."

Panic nearly overwhelmed. "Have I offended
you?"

"Offended! That the Prince of Homana desires
me to be his liege man?" Blais shook his head.
"No, there is no offense in this—only honor. And
I never believed myself worthy of such honor."

"But you are!" Kellin cried. "You saved me
from the bear-trap, and the Lion. Your worth is
proved. And—and there is no one else I would
have."

Blais stared hard at Tanni, as if he feared to
give away too much if he looked at Kellin. "There
has been no liege man in Homana-Mujhar since
Ian died."

"He would approve," Kellin said. "He would say you are worthy."

Blais smiled faintly. "Then how could I refuse?" Levity faded again. He was suddenly very solemn. "I will serve you gladly, my lord."

Kellin sighed. From behind his back he took the knife and showed it to Blais. It was gold and steel, with a rampant lion twisted about the hilt. Its eye was a single ruby. Softly, he said, "There is a ceremony."

Blais rose from the bed, knelt upon the floor, and drew his own Cheysuli long-knife. Without hesitation he placed the blade against the inside of his left wrist and cut into the flesh. "I swear," he said quietly, "by this blood; by my name and honor and *lir*, that I will serve as liege man to Kellin of Homana as long as he will have me." Blood ran from the knife cut and dripped crimson on the stone floor. "Will you have me, my lord?"

Wonder welled in Kellin's breast. "I will." And then, quoting the words he had learned long ago: "*Y'ja'hai. Tu'jhalla dei. Tahlmorra lujhala mei wiccan, cheysu.*"

"*Ja'hai-na,*" Blais responded. Then he offered his bloodied knife to his lord and took the other in return.

Kellin looked down upon the Cheysuli weapon with its wolf-head hilt. He felt the tears well up, but he did not care. *I am not alone any more.*

He awoke sweating near dawn, disoriented and fearful. He felt oppressed, squashed flat by dread. — *Lion*—

Kellin wanted to whimper. How could it come to pass? Blais was in the palace. Blais was his liege man. The Lion could not withstand a sworn Cheysuli liege man.

The flesh rose on his bones. "Lion," he murmured. And then, searching for strength, *"Tahl-morra lujhala mei wiccan, cheysu."*

But the sense of dread increased.

Kellin wanted Blais. Together they might vanquish the beast forever. But to summon Blais meant he had to get out of bed.

Kellin shuddered, biting into his bottom lip. He smelled the tang of fear on his flesh and hated himself for it. His scarred ankle ached, though he knew it completely healed.

"Cheysuli," he choked, squeezing his eyes tightly shut. "A *warrior*, someday." Warriors were brave. Warriors did what required doing.

From beneath his pillow he took the Cheysuli long-knife bestowed by his liege man. Stiffly, slowly, Kellin slid down from his bed. He wore only a sleeping tunic that reached to mid-thigh; bare toes dug into the stone floor as if he might take root. *You have a liege man. He will fend off the Lion.* He clutched the knife in both hands, then crept out of his room into the corridor beyond.

False dawn, he thought; even the servants still slept. An ideal time for a lion to stalk the halls.

Kellin chewed his lips painfully, then unclenched his teeth. With the knife as his ward, he moved slowly and deliberately toward the door that was Blais', so far down the corridor as to be a league away.

Kellin pushed open the door. Candlelight from the corridor cressets spilled inside, illuminating the chamber. Kellin saw tousled black hair, the gleam of a *lir*-band, and the glint of Tanni's eyes from the foot of the bed where she lay.

"Blais," he said. "Blais—the Lion is come."

Blais sat up at once, one hand reaching for the royal knife at his bedside. His eyes, pupils expanded in darkness, showed a ring of purest yellow around the edges. "Kellin?"

"The Lion," Kellin repeated. "Will you come? We have to kill it."

Blais ran a hand through his hair. He yawned. "The lion?" And then he came fully awake. "Kellin—" But he cut it off. His expression was masked. "Where is it?"

Kellin gestured with his knife. "Out there. Walking the corridors."

Blais grunted and slid out of bed. He was nude save for *lir*-gold, but paused long enough to slip on leggings. Barefoot, he patted Tanni and murmured a word in the Old Tongue. Then he smiled at Kellin. "A wolf is no match for a lion."

Kellin felt markedly better as Blais followed him out into the corridor. "A sword might be better," he said, "but I am not old enough yet. Grandsire said."

"Have you not begun swordplay?"

"Aye, a little—but the arms-master says it will be a long time before I have any skill. I am too small."

Blais nodded. "A Homanan skill. I am no good at it, myself, though the gods know Sean tried to teach me often enough." He shrugged. "I have no aptitude."

They went on. Torchlight glinted off the earring in Blais' hair. He looked fully awake and alert, Kellin thought in satisfaction. *This time the Lion will lose.*

When they neared the Great Hall, Kellin pressed himself against the wall. A shudder claimed his body from head to toe, stilling only as Blais closed a hand over one shoulder.

"I am your liege man," Blais told him. "I am with you, my lord."

Kellin grinned his relief. " 'Tis inside," he said. "I can feel it." To Blais, it was not difficult to explain; a liege man would know, would understand. "He has come to swallow Homana."

The tone was excessively neutral. "How do you know this?"

"The fortune-teller said so."

Blais seemed briefly dubious, but let it go. He smiled. "Then we shall have to see to it the lion swallows nothing but my knife blade."

Joy and wonder bubbled up in Kellin. *This is what it is to have a liege man!*

Blais pushed open one of the heavy silver doors, sliding effortlessly inside. Kellin slipped through behind him. "Here?" Blais whispered.

"Somewhere . . ." Kellin moved forward slowly, wishing he might have the courage to use the knife he clutched.

Blais stepped out into the center of the long hall and strode the length of the firepit. Coals glowed from its depths beneath an ashen cloak.

The alcove curtain near the massive throne billowed in the darkness. A single coal fell out of the pit and crumbled into ash. *"There!"* Kellin gasped.

Blais reacted instantly, running silently toward the alcove. He caught the curtain and tore it aside, knife glinting.

"Is it there?" Kellin cried. "Blais?"

Blais went rigid, then reeled back from the alcove. Kellin heard the slap of bare torso against the wall. The knife fell from a slack hand. "Tanni!" Blais cried. *"Tanni—"*

Kellin ran. By the time he reached Blais, his kinsman was slumped against wall and floor, body trembling convulsively. Yellow eyes were wide and crazed, turned inside out. Sweat filmed his face.

"Blais!"

Blais shuddered. Then he reached out and caught

Kellin's thin arms, closing his taloned fingers into flesh. "Tanni—Tanni—*lir*—"

"Blais!"

"—gods—oh, gods . . . no—" Blais' face was the color of the ash in the firepit. "Tanni—" He let go of Kellin all at once and lurched to his feet.

"Blais—"

But Blais did not respond. He stumbled toward the end of the hall, seeking doors; his grace was utterly banished, leaving him reeling like a drunken man, or a sick one. He smashed into one of the doors and shoved it open.

Kellin gathered up the fallen knife and ran after his liege man. Fear of the Lion was quite vanquished; what he feared now was that something terrible had befallen Blais. *Don't let him go, too!*

Blais ran even as Kellin caught up, but his body betrayed him. Only his outstretched hands, rebounding off walls, kept him upright. Ropes of muscles stood up in relief against naked flesh.

"Blais!"

And then they were in Blais' chamber, and there was blood everywhere, on the floor and across the bed; a lurid arc against the curtains. Blais tore them aside, then fell down onto the bed. *"Tanni—"*

People crowded in the door. Kellin heard the questions, the startled exclamations, but he answered none of them. He could only stare at the warrior who had been his cousin, his liege man, his friend; who now was a *lirless* Cheysuli.

"Blais—" This time it was a wail because he knew.

Brennan was behind him. "Kellin . . . Kellin, come away."

"No."

Hart was with him, face shiny it was stretched so tautly across the bones of his cheeks. "Come away, Kellin. There is nothing you can do."

"No!" Kellin threw down the knives, then ripped himself out of Brennan's reaching hands. "Blais— Blais—you *cannot*. No! I need you. I *need* you! You are my liege man!" He fastened both hands around one of Blais' rigid arms and tugged, trying to pull his kinsman away from the gutted wolf. "Blais!"

Blais turned a ravaged face on them all. "Take him away . . . take him from here."

"No!" Kellin gulped back the fear. *"Tu'jalla dei—"*

Brennan caught Kellin's arms. "Come away."

"He can't go!" Kellin screamed. "I refuse him leave. I am the Prince of Homana and I *refuse* him leave to go!"

They were all of them in the chamber: Aileen, Ilsa, his Solindish cousins. Dulcie's yellow eyes were wide.

"Tu'jalla dei!" Kellin shrieked. "He has to stay if I say so. He swore. *Tell* him, grandsire! *Tu'jalla dei."*

Brennan's face was stark. "Such things are for gods to do, not men, not even princes and kings. This is the price, Kellin. Blais accepted it when he accepted his *lir*. So did I. So did we all. And so will you."

"I will not! I *will* not!"

Aileen's voice shook. "Kellin—"

"No! No! No!" He writhed in Brennan's grip. "He swore by blood and honor and his *lir*—" Kellin broke it off on a strangled gasp. Indeed, by his *lir*, and now that *lir* was dead. "Blais," Kellin choked. "Don't leave me."

Blais stared blindly. Blood smeared his chest. "I never knew," he said dazedly. "I never knew what pain there was in it."

Brennan looked old beyond his years. "No warrior can. Not before it happens."

Blais held up his bloodied hands. "I am—
empty—" He shoved a forearm across his brow and
left a bloodslick behind, shining in his hair.

"Tu'jalla dei," Kellin said brokenly.

But Blais seemed not to hear. He stripped off
his *lir*-bands and the earring and put them on the
blood-soaked bed. Then he gathered up Tanni's
body into the cradle of naked arms and turned
toward the door.

As one, they all moved aside. Blais went out of
the chamber as wolf blood splashed on stone.

"Blais!" Kellin screamed.

Brennan lifted him from the ground, containing
him easily. "Let him go. He is a walking dead
man; let him go with dignity."

"But I *need* him."

"He needs his ending more." Brennan held him
close. "I wish I could spare you this. But you, too,
are Cheysuli, and the price shall be yours as well."

Kellin stopped struggling. He hung slackly in
his grandfather's arms until Brennan set him
down. "No," he said then, looking up into the face
that looked so old in its grief. "No, there will be
no price. I will have no *lir*."

Hart's voice was kind. "You cannot gainsay
what the gods bestow."

"I will." Kellin's voice took on a hard bitterness.
"I refuse to have one."

"Kellin." Now Aileen, moving forward.

He cut her off at once with an outflung hand. "I
refuse it. Do you hear?" He looked at his kinfolk
one by one. "They all leave. *All* of them. First my
jehan. Then Rogan. Then Urchin ... and now
Blais." His voice sounded alien even to Kellin.
"They all go from me."

Brennan touched his shoulder. "This grief will
pass, one day."

Kellin knocked the hand away. "No! From now

on I walk alone. With no friends, no liege man, no *lir*." He looked at Brennan fiercely. "And I *will not care*."

Aileen was horrified. "*Kel*lin!"

He felt a roaring in his head; felt it rush up from his belly and engulf his chest, threatening his throat. If he opened his mouth, he would vomit.

He knew its name: rage. And a hatred so virulent he thought he might choke on it.

"No more," he said quietly, making it an oath. "The gods cannot take from me what I do not have."

Interval

Naked, the woman lay next to him in the darkness. She had not slept when he was done, for he had, as always, disturbed her with his intensity, and she could not tumble out of passion into sleep the way he could.

She lay very quiet next to him, not allowing her flesh to touch his. If she disturbed him, he would waken in ill humor, and she had learned to avoid his black moods by submitting everything to him: will, body, spirit. She had learned the trick long ago, when she had first become a whore.

She let his warmth warm her, driving away the chill of the winter night. Her dwelling was tiny, not so much more than a hovel, and she could not afford the endless supply of peat and wood that others bought or bargained for to get them through the Homanan winter. She hoarded what she had, although when *he* came she piled it all on the hearth. Even if it meant going without for days after.

He shifted, and she held her breath. One broad hand moved across her belly, then cradled her left breast. The fingers were slack and passionless. He had spent that passion earlier; though he was easily roused, she did not do it now.

She sighed shallowly, not daring to move his hand. He had bought her body, let him fondle it as he chose. It made no difference to her. At least he was a prince.

She had other lovers, of course, but none so fine as he. They were hard men, tough men, with little refinement and less imagination. He, at least, was clean, with a good man smell, lacking the stench of others who had no time for baths, nor the money to buy wood to heat water. It was no trouble to him to bathe whenever he wished; she was grateful for it. She was grateful for *him.*

That he had chosen her was a miracle in itself. She was young still, only seventeen, and her body had not yet coarsened with use, so she presented a better appearance than some of the other women. And she had high, firm breasts above a slim waist, with good hips below. She would lose it all, of course, with the first full-term pregnancy, but so far she had been able to rid herself of the seeds before any took root.

But what of *his* seed?

She laughed noiselessly, startled by the thought. Would she bear a prince's bastard? And if she did, would he provide for her? Perhaps she could leave this life behind and find a good, solid man who would forget about her past. Or would *he* take the child, claiming it his?

It was possible. It had happened in the past, she had heard; the bastards had been sent to Clan-keep, to the shapechangers, to grow up with barren women. He would not risk leaving a halfling with a Homanan woman, lest someone attempt to use it for personal gain.

He called her *meijha* and *meijhana,* words she did not know. She had asked him if he had a wife, and he had laughed, correcting her: *"Cheysula,"* he had said, and then *"No, I have no cheysula. They expect me to wed my Solindish cousin, but I will not do it."*

She turned her head slightly to look at his face. In sleep he was so different, so young, so free of the tight-wound tension. It was a good face in sleep, more handsome than any she had welcomed in her bed, and she longed to touch it. But to do so would waken him, and he would change, and she would see the customary hardness of his mouth and eyes, and the anger in his soul.

She sighed. She did not love him. She was not permitted to love him; he had told her that plainly their first bedding three months before. But she did care. For all his black moods he was kind enough to her, even if it was an unschooled, rough kindness, as if he had forgotten how.

He had spoken harshly to her more often than she would choose, but he had only struck her once; and then he had turned away abruptly with a strange, sickened look in his eyes, and he had given her gold in place of silver. It had been worth the bruise, for she bought herself a new gown she wore the next time he came, and he had smiled at her for it.

Her smile came unbidden; a woman's, slow and smug. *In my bed lies the Prince of Homana.*

He moved. He stretched, flexing effortlessly, and then he sat up. She saw the play of muscles beneath the flesh of his smooth back, the hint of supple spine, the tangle of black hair across the nape of his neck. She lay very still, wondering if she had spoken her thoughts aloud.

For a moment his profile was very clear in the dim light, outlined by the coals in the tiny hearth across the room. She saw the elegant brow and straight nose. He was yet groggy with sleep and soft from it; when the sleep fled, his bones would look older and harder, with black brows that drew down all too often and spoiled the youth of his face.

He slanted her a glance. "Did you dream of me?"

She smiled. "How could I not?"

It was his customary question and her customary answer, but this time neither appeared to please him. He scowled and got out of the narrow bed, then reached to pull on black breeches and boots. She admired as always the suppleness of his muscles, the lithe movements of his body. It was the Cheysuli in him, she knew, though he did not seem other than Homanan. She had seen a warrior up close once and still shivered when she recalled the strangeness of his eyes. Beast-eyes, some folk called them, and she agreed with them.

His were not bestial. They could be disconcertingly direct and nearly always challenging, but they were green, and a man's eyes. For that she was grateful.

He lifted the jug from the crooked table and poured wine, not bothering to don the shirt and fur-lined doublet on the floor beside the bed. She hunched herself up on one elbow. "Are you going?"

"I have had from you what I came for." He did not turn to look at her. "Unless you have discovered yet another position."

She, who believed she could no longer blush, burned with embarrassment. "No, my lord." She had displeased him; he would go, and this time he might not come back.

He swallowed down the wine and set the mug down with a thump. "This vintage is foul. Have you no better?"

"No, my lord."

Her flat tone roused something in him. He turned, and the thin gold torque around his throat glinted. "You reprove *me*?"

"No!" She sat up hastily, jerking the bedclothes

over her breasts in an instinctive bid for a modesty she had surrendered years before. "Never!"

He scowled at her blackly. His mouth had taken on its familiar hard line. And then he smiled all unexpectedly, and she marveled again at the beauty of a man who could be cruel and kind at once. "I have frightened you again." He poured more wine and drank it, seemingly unaffected by its foul taste. "Do you fear I will turn into beast-shape here before you?" He laughed as she caught her breath, showing white teeth in a mocking grin. "Have no fear, *meijhana* ... there is no *lir*-shape for this Cheysuli. I have renounced it. What you see before you is what I am." He still smiled, but she saw the anger in his eyes. "My arms are bare, and my ear. There is no shapechanger in this room."

She held her silence. He had shown her such moods before.

He swore beneath his breath in a language she did not know. He would not come to her bed again this night, to set her flesh afire with a longing she had believed well passed for her until *he* had come with no word of explanation for a prince's presence in a Midden whore's hovel.

A sudden thought intruded. *He might not come back ever.*

The fear made her voice a question she had sworn never to ask. "Will you leave me?"

His eyes narrowed. "Do you care?"

"Oh aye, my lord—very much!" She believed it would please him; it was nonetheless the truth.

A muscle jumped in his jaw. "Do I please you? Do you care for me?"

She breathed it softly. "More than any, my lord."

"Because I am a prince?"

She smiled, believing she had found the proper

answer. "Oh no, my lord. Because you are you. I care for *you*."

He turned from her. Stunned, she watched as he put on his shirt and doublet, then swept up and pinned on the heavy green cloak. It was lined with rich dark fur, and worth more than the house she lived in. She saw the gold cloak-brooch glitter in firelight, ruby gemstone burning. The brooch was worth more than the entire block.

And then he strode across the room to her and caught her throat in his hands, bending over her. "No," he said. "You do not care for *me*. Say you do not."

She grasped at his hands. She wanted very badly to say the proper words. "But I do! Your coin is welcome—I am a whore, for all that, and claim myself no better—but it is *you* I care for!"

He swore raggedly and released her so abruptly she fell back against the wall. He unpinned the brooch and dropped it into her lap. "You will not see me again."

"My lord!" A hand beseeched. "Why? What have I done?"

"You said you cared." His eyes were black in poor light. "And that I will not have."

"Kellin!" She dared to use his name, but he turned away in a swirl of green wool and was gone. The door swung shut behind him.

The brooch that would buy her freedom was cold comfort in the night as she cried herself to sleep.

PART II

One

Kellin stepped out of the slope-roofed hovel into the slushy alley and stopped. He stared blankly at the darkened dwelling opposite and expelled a smoking breath. He inhaled deeply, almost convulsively, and the cold air filled his lungs with the anticipated burning. The alley stank of peat, filth, ordure. Even winter could not overcome the stench of depression and poverty.

He heard movement inside the hovel, through the cracks of ill-made walls: a woman crying.

Too harsh with her. Kellin gritted his teeth. Self-contempt boiled up to replace the thought. *What does she expect? I warned her. I told her not to care. There is nothing in me for anyone to care about, least of all a father . . . I will not risk losing another who claims to care for me.*

The sobs were soft but audible because he made himself hear them. He used them to flagellate; he deserved the punishment.

She was well-paid. That is what she cries for.

But he wondered if there were more, if the woman *did* care—

Kellin gritted his teeth, fighting off the part of his nature that argued for fairness, for a renunciation of the oath he had sworn ten years before. *She is a whore, nothing more. They all of them are whores. Where better to spill the seed for which I am so valued?*

Kellin swore, hissing invective between set teeth. His mood was foul. He detested the duality that ravaged his spirit. He had no use for softness, for compassion; he wanted nothing at all to do with the kind of relationship he saw binding his grandsire and his granddame. That kind of honor and respect simply begged for an ending, and therefore begged for pain.

And what was there for him in a relationship such as that shared by the Mujhar and his queen? Had they not made it clear, all of them, that it was not *Kellin* whom they cared about, but the seed he would provide?

Bitterness engulfed. *Let the whores have it. It will serve them better; expelling it serves ME.*

But the conscience he had believed eradicated was not entirely vanquished. Despite his wishes, he *did* regret his harshness with the woman; did regret he could not see her again, for she had been good to him. There had been a quiet dignity about her despite her life, and a simple acceptance that the gods had seen fit to give her this fate.

Self-contempt made it easy to transfer resentment to the woman. *She would make a good Cheysuli. Better than I do; I, after all, am at war with the gods.*

It was time to leave, lest he give in to the temptation to go back inside the hovel and offer comfort. He could not afford that. It was too easy to succumb, too easy to give in to the weakness that would lead in time to pain. Far better to keep pain at bay by permitting it no toehold in the ordering of his spirit.

Kellin glanced over and saw the familiar guardsmen waiting in the shadows between two ramshackle dwellings. Four shapes. Four watchdogs, set upon his scent by the Mujhar. Even now, even in adulthood, no matter where Kellin went or what he chose to do, they accompanied him. Discreetly, usually, for he was after all the Prince of Homana, but their loyalty was the Mujhar's.

As a boy, he had accepted it as perfectly natural and never thought to question the policy and protection. As a man, however, it chafed his spirit because such supervision, in his eyes, relegated his own abilities, his own opinions, to insignificance. Initially his protests were polite, but the Mujhar's intransigence soon triggered an angrier opposition. Yet the Mujhar remained obdurate. His heir could not—*would* not, by his order—be permitted to walk unaccompanied in Mujhara. Ever.

Kellin had tried losing his dogs, but they tracked him down. He tried tricking them, but they had proved too smart. He tried ordering them, but they were the Mujhar's men. And at last, terribly angry, he tried to fight them. To a man, despite his insults, they refused to honor him so.

He was accustomed to them now. He had trained them to stay out of his tavern brawls. It had taken time; they did not care to see their prince risk himself, but they had learned it was his only escape, and so they left him to it.

Kellin shivered, wrapping the heavy cloak more tightly around his shoulders. It was cold and very clear. The cloud cover had blown away, which meant the nights would be bitter cold until the next snowstorm came. Already he felt the chill in his bones; mouthing a curse, he moved on.

He did not know his destination. He had thought to spend the night with the woman, but that was over now. She had committed the unpardonable; the only punishment he knew was to deny her the comfort of his body, so that he, too, was denied the contentment he so desperately desired despite his vow.

He splashed through crusted puddles. It did not

matter to him how it damaged his boots. He had many more at home. This sort of revenge offered little comfort, but it was something. Let the servants gossip as they would. It gave him some small pleasure to know he was entirely unpredictable in mood as well as actions.

Better to keep them off guard. Better to make them wonder.

As he wondered himself; it was a twisted form of punishment Kellin meted out to bind himself to his vow. If he relaxed his vigilance, he might be tempted to renounce his oath. He would not permit himself that, lest the gods win at last and turn him into a Cheysuli who thought only of his *tahlmorra*, instead of such things as a son badly in need of a father.

Behind him, the watchdogs also splashed. Kellin wondered what they thought of their honorable duty: to spend the night out of doors while their prince poured his royal seed into a whore's body. *They will get no Firstborn of her, or of any other whore.*

Ahead in wan moonlight, a placard dangled before a door. A tavern. *Good. I am of a mind to start a game not entirely like any other.*

Kellin shouldered open the cracked door and went in, knowing the dogs would follow along in a moment. He paused just inside, accustoming his eyes to greasy candlelight, and found himself in a dingy common room. The tables were empty save one, where five men gathered to toss dice and rune-sticks.

For a moment only, Kellin considered joining them. But instead he went to another table and hooked over a stool, motioning with a jerk of his head to the man in the stained cloth apron.

The watchdogs came in, marked where he was, and went to another table. He saw the tavern-

keeper waver, for they wore tunics of the Mujharan Guard and doubtless meant more coin than
a lone stranger.

Smiling faintly, Kellin drew his knife and stuck
the point into wood, so that the heavy hilt stood
upright. The rampant lion curled around the hilt,
single ruby eye glinting in greasy light.

As expected, the tavern-keeper arrived almost at
once. "My lord?"

"*Usca*," Kellin ordered. "A jug of it."

The man nodded, but his gaze flicked to the
guardsmen. "And for them?"

Kellin favored him with a humorless smile.
"They drink what they like. Ask *them*."

The man was clearly puzzled. "My lord, they
wear the Mujhar's crest. And you have it here, on
your knife. Doesn't that mean—"

Kellin overrode him curtly. "It means we have
something in common, but it does not mean we
sleep together." He yanked the broochless cloak
from his shoulders and slapped it across the table.
He waited. The man bowed and hastened away.

When the *usca* was brought, Kellin poured the
crude cup full. He downed it all rapidly, waiting
for the fire. It came, burning his belly and clear
down into his toes. All at once there was life in
his body, filling up flesh and blood, and the pain
that accompanied it.

He had fought it so very long. Because of his
oath, because of his need, he had shut himself off
to emotions, severing his spirit from the Kellin he
had been, because he could not bear the pain. He
had seen the bewildered hurt in his grandmother's
eyes and learned to ignore it, as he learned to
withstand even the scorn in his grandfather's
voice; eventually, in fact, he learned to cultivate
that scorn, because it was a goad that drove him

to maintain his vow even when, in moments of despair and self-hatred, he desired to unswear it.

One day intent became habit, despite the occasional defiance of a conscience battered for ten years into compliance. He was what he *was;* what he had made himself to be. No one could hurt him now.

Kellin drank *usca.* He wanted to fight very badly. When the fire filled head and belly, he rose and prepared to make his way to the table full of Homanans who laughed and wagered and joked.

A man stepped into his path, blocking his way. "Well met, my lord. Shall we share a cup of wine?"

Kellin's tongue was thick, but the words succinct enough. "I am drinking *usca.*"

"Ah, of course; forgive me." The stranger smiled faintly. A lifted hand and a slight gesture beckoned *usca* from the tavern-keeper.

Kellin stared hard at the stranger, struggling to make out the face. The room shifted and ran together so that the colors all seemed one. *Too much usca for conversation.*

When the new jug came, the stranger poured two cups full and offered one to Kellin. "Shall we sit, my lord?"

Kellin did not sit. He set his hand around the hilt of his knife, still standing upright in the table, and snapped it from the wood.

The stranger inclined his head. "I am unarmed, my lord, and offer no threat to you."

Kellin stared into the face. It was bland, beguiling; all mask and no substance. *Perhaps* he *will give me my fight.* He wanted the fight badly; needed it desperately, to assuage the guilt he felt despite his desire not to. *Physical pain is easier to bear than emotional pain.*

For years he had sought it, finding it in taverns

among men who held back nothing. It was a release from self-captivity more wholly satisfying than any other he knew.

This man, perhaps? Or another. Kellin gestured and sat down, laying the knife atop the table as he took the brimming cup.

"A fortune-game?" the other man suggested.

It suited. Kellin nodded and the man took from beneath his cloak a wooden casket, all carved about its satiny sides with strange runic devices.

Kellin frowned. *Wait—*

But the man turned the casket over and spilled out sticks and cubes. The sticks were blank and black. The cubes turned lurid purple and began a dervish-dance.

"Aye," the man said softly, "you *do* remember me."

Kellin was abruptly sober. He marked the familiar blue eyes, the russet hair, the maddeningly serene expression. *How could I have forgotten?*

"Aye," Corwyth said. "Would you care to play out the game?"

Kellin looked for his watchdogs and saw them spilled slackly across their table. Their attitudes bespoke drunkenness to a man who knew no better; Kellin knew better.

He looked then at the other men who wagered near his own table, and saw they seemed not to know anyone else was in the room.

Breath ran shallowly. Kellin tensed on his stool and quietly took up the knife. "You have come for me."

Corwyth watched the bright cubes spin, seemingly undismayed by the presence of a weapon. "Oh," he said lightly, "presently. I am in no hurry." He gestured briefly, and the knife fell out of Kellin's hand. "There is no need for that here."

Kellin swore and grabbed at it, only to find the

metal searingly hot. *"Ku'reshtin—"* He dropped
the knife at once, desiring to blow on burned fingers but holding himself in check. He would not
give the Ihlini any measure of satisfaction.

Corwyth's eyes narrowed assessively. "No more
the boy," he observed, "but a man well-grown,
and dangerous. Someone who must be dealt with."

Kellin did not much care for the implication.
"You tried before to 'deal' with me and failed."

"Aye. I misjudged you. A failing I shall not be
moved to repeat."

The rune-sticks joined the cubes in an obscene
coupling upon the table. Neither man watched.
They looked at each other instead.

A vicious joy welled up in Kellin's soul. Here
was the fight he had wanted. "I will not accom-
pany you."

"One day," Corwyth said. "Be certain of it, Kellin." He gestured, and the cubes and rune-sticks
fell into a pattern: one arrow pointed at Kellin,
the other directly north. "You see? Even the game
agrees."

As he had done so many years before, Kellin
made a fist and banged it down upon the table.
The arrows broke up and fell in disarray to the
floor. Sticks and cubes scattered.

Corwyth showed good teeth. "This is a game,"
he said, "mere prelude to what will follow. If you
think you have the power to prevent it, you are
indeed a fool." Slender fingers were unmoving on
scarred wood. "I do not threaten, Kellin; I come
to warn instead. Lochiel is too powerful. You cannot hope to refuse him."

"I can. I do." Kellin displayed equally good
teeth, but his grin was more feral. "He has tried
before and failed, just as you did. I begin to think
Lochiel is not so powerful as he would have us
believe."

Corwyth's tone was mild. "He need only put out his hand, and you will be in it. He need only close that hand and crush the life from you."

Kellin laughed. "Then tell him to do it."

Corwyth's gaze was steady. "Before, you were a boy. They kept you close, and safe. But you are no longer a boy, and such chains as you have known will bind more than body, but the spirit as well. Do you not fight those chains? Do you not come often into the Midden, fighting a battle within your soul as well as the war with the constraints of your station?"

Kellin's laughter died. Corwyth knew too much. He was overly conversant with what was in Kellin's mind. "I do what I desire to do. That has nothing to do with Lochiel."

"Ah, but it has *everything* to do with Lochiel. You have a choice, my lord: keep yourself to Homana-Mujhar and away from sorcery, yet know there will always be the threat of a traitorous Homanan." His smile was slight as he purposely evoked the memory of Rogan. "Or come out as you will, as you *desire* to, and know that each step you take is watched by Lochiel."

Kellin controlled the anger. Such a display was what Corwyth wanted to provoke; he would not satisfy him. "Then I challenge Lochiel to try me here and now."

Corwyth shook his head. "A game requires time, my lord, or the satisfaction is tainted ... much like a man who spends himself too quickly between a woman's thighs. There are the rules to be learned first, before the game commences." The smile was banished. Corwyth leaned forward. "This night, you shall go free. This night you may go home to Homana-Mujhar—or to whatever whore you are keeping—and may sleep without fear for your soul. But you are to know this: you are not free. Your soul is not unclaimed. Lochiel waits in Valgaard. When he touches you, when he deigns to gather you up, be certain you shall know it."

The Ihlini sat back, but his gaze did not waver from Kellin's. He smiled again, if faintly, and took something else from beneath his cloak. He set it flat on the table between them.

Sorcerer's Tooth.

The years fell away. Kellin was a frightened boy again lost in Homanan forests, with a tutor slain and a best friend dying, and the Lion on his trail.

"Keep it," Corwyth said, "as a token of my promise."

Kellin leapt to his feet, groping for the knife, but a sheet of purple flame drove him away from the table. When the smoke of it shredded away, the Ihlini was gone.

Two

Coughing, Kellin went at once to his watchdogs and found them dead. There were no wounds, no marks, no blood to prove what had befallen them, the four men were simply *dead*. They slumped across the table with blank eyes bulging and their flesh a pallid white.

He looked then for the Homanans, expecting some manner of comment, and discovered they no longer existed. The tavernkeeper had vanished as well. Kellin was quite alone in the common room save for the bodies Corwyth had left behind.

Kellin stood perfectly still. Silence was loud, so loud it filled his head and slid down to stuff his belly, until he wanted to choke on it, to spew it forth and deny everything; to somehow put back to rights the horror that had occurred.

The way I wanted Rogan to be alive again— Kellin shut his teeth. *Rogan was a traitor.*

His grip tightened on the knife. Its heat had dissipated. No longer tainted by Corwyth's wishes, it was merely a knife again, if a royal one. The lion hilt mocked him.

He looked around again. All was as before: four dead watchdogs sprawled across the table in a stinking common room of a Midden tavern Kellin was no longer certain truly existed.

Did Corwyth conjure the Homanans? Is this tav-

ern no more than illusion? If so, he was trapped in it.

Kellin shivered, then swore at the response he interpreted as weakness. He went hastily back to his table, caught up his cloak and threw it around his shoulders. With the knife still clutched in one hand, hilt slick with sweat, he went out into the darkness where the air smelled like air, redolent of winter, but without the stink of Corwyth's sorcery.

The walk to Homana-Mujhar was the longest of Kellin's life. His back was spectacularly naked of watchdogs; he had hated them before but had never wished them dead.

He avoided puddles now. His mouth was filled with the sour aftertaste of *usca.* Drunkenness had passed, as had hostility and the desire to fight. What he wanted most now was to reach Homana-Mujhar and deliver unpleasant news to Brennan, so the burden of the knowledge was no longer his alone.

There were few cobblestones in the Midden. Boots sank into muck, denying easy egress from winding, narrow alleys shut in by top-heavy dwellings. Between his shoulder blades Kellin felt a tingling; the hairs on the nape of his neck rose. He was *lirless* by choice, which left him vulnerable. A bonded warrior would know if an Ihlini was near. He had only his instincts to trust, and they told him it would be a simple thing for Corwyth to take him now, with a Tooth flung into his back.

But the Tooth was back in the tavern. Nothing could have induced him to touch it, let alone to keep it.

Kellin shivered despite the fur-lined cloak. His lips were excessively dry no matter how often he licked them. Corwyth had promised him his freedom tonight; that he might spend the time as he wished. Lochiel was patient.

Muck oozed up, capturing a boot. Kellin paused to free himself, then froze into stillness. A new noise had begun in place of his audible breathing and heartbeat.

The sound was one he knew: a raspy, throaty grunting; the chesty cough of a huge lion.

Gods— He turned convulsively, shoulders slamming against the wall. He heard the scrape of his cloak against brick. Moonlight sparked on the ruby as he lifted the knife.

For one insane moment Kellin saw his shadow on the wall across the narrow alley: the image of a small boy desperate to flee. And then the illusion was banished, replaced with the truth, and he saw himself clearly. No longer the boy. Nightmares were long behind him.

This is how Lochiel intends to take me. This is some trick—

Or perhaps not. After what had happened in the tavern, Kellin was not so certain.

Still, he would not prove such easy prey, to be terrorized by childhood nightmares.

He raised the knife higher. He saw the length of supple fingers, the sinewy back of his hand, the muscle sheathing wrist. He was a man now, and a very different kind of prey.

"Come, then," he said. "If that is you, Corwyth, be certain I am ready. Lochiel will find me no easier to defeat despite opportunity. I am, after all, Cheysuli."

The Lion paused. Noise ceased.

"Come," Kellin goaded. "Did you think to find me so frightened I soiled my leggings? Did you believe it would be *easy*?" He forced a laugh, relying on bravado that was genuine only in part. "Why not banish the Lion's aspect and face me as a man? Or do you fear me after all?"

Grunting and panting faded. The night was silent again.

Kellin laughed as tension fled, leaving him atremble despite his bravado. "So, you prefer to test a boy instead of a man. Well, now you know the truth of it. To take me now, you will have to try harder."

He waited. He thought perhaps Corwyth would resort to ordinary means to attack. But the night was silent, and empty; threat was dispersed.

Kellin drew in a deep breath. *Surely they told stories of my fears when I was a child. It would be a simple matter to shape a lion out of magic now merely to remind me of childhood fears.*

It was a simple explanation, and perhaps a valid one. But a nagging thought remained.

What of Tanni? She was truly gutted.

But men had been bought before: a cook, and Rogan. What if the beast who had slain Blais' *lir* was nothing but a man meant to *make* it look like a beast?

Kellin gripped the knife more tightly. *Corwyth is right. I am no safer now than I was as a child. But I will not order my life around fear; it would be a victory for Lochiel. I will be what I am. If the Ihlini is to take me, he will find it difficult.*

When Kellin reached Homana-Mujhar, he went at once to the watch commander and gave him the news. "Have them brought home," he said. "But also tell those sent to fetch them to touch nothing else. There was an Ihlini abroad tonight."

The captain, a hardened veteran, did not scoff. But Kellin saw the lowered lids, the shuttered thoughts, and knew very well his words were not wholly accepted. Men might be dead, but no Ihlini had come into Mujhara for years. More likely it was *his* fault, from trouble he had started.

It infuriated him. Kellin grabbed a handful of crimson tunic. "Do you doubt *me*?"

The captain did not hesitate. "Who speaks of doubt, my lord? I will of course do your bidding when the Mujhar confirms it."

"The Mujhar—" Kellin cut it off, gritting teeth against the anger he wanted to spew into the man's face. "Aye, tell the Mujhar; it will save me the trouble." He let go of the crumpled tunic and turned on his heel, striding across to a side entrance so as not to disturb the palace with his late return. *Let the captain tell his beloved Mujhar. I will spend my time on other things.*

He climbed the stairs two at a time, shedding cloak with a shrug of shoulders. He hooked it over an arm, heedless of the dragging hem. When he entered his chamber, he flung the cloak across a stool and hastily stripped out of soiled clothing. Naked, he paced to one of the unshuttered casements and scowled blackly into darkness.

He felt stifled. He felt young *and* old, exquisitely indifferent to life, and yet so filled with it he could not ignore its clamor. Something surged through his veins, charging his body with a vigor so intense he thought he was on fire. His hands trembled as if palsied; Kellin suppressed it with a curse.

A surfeit of energy. It set his bones ablaze. He was burning, *burning*.

"Too bright—" Kellin dug fingers into the sill until at last the burning faded. Emptiness replaced it; he was desolate now, with a spirit wholly diminished. Weakness replaced the hideous strength that had knotted all his muscles.

It is only reaction to what occurred earlier. No more than that.

But Kellin was not certain. Panting, he pressed his head into the wall, letting the stone pit flesh.

Fingertips were sore, scraped raw by his grip upon the sill. Everything in him shook.

"Tired." It was much more than that. Kellin staggered to his bed and climbed between the curtains, blessing the servant who had left the warming pan.

But he could not stay there. A restlessness consumed his body and mind and made him accede to its wishes: that he forsake his bed for a physical release that had nothing to do with sex and everything to do with his spirit.

Breeches, no boots. Bare-chested, gripping the knife, Kellin left his chambers and went into the shadowed corridors. He felt as if *he* were a knife, honed sharp and clean and true, balanced in the hand as his own knife was balanced, but the hand which held *him* was none that he knew.

The gods? Kellin wanted to laugh. The old Cheysuli saying about a man's fate resting in the hands of the gods was imagery, no more, and yet he felt as if he fit. As if the hand merely waited.

This is madness. He went to the Great Hall. It had been a long time since he had entered it; it was his grandsire's place. Until Kellin could make it his, he was content to wait: a lean and hungry wolf intently watching its promised meal.

Guilt flickered; was suppressed. *I was bred for it. All the blood that flows in me cries out to rule Homana . . . I was not made of patient clay, and the firing is done.*

He halted before the dais, before the throne, and looked upon the Lion. An old beast, he thought, guarding its pride with aging eyes and older heart, its body tough and stringy, its mouth nearly empty of teeth.

Time runs out for the Lion. Time ran out for them all.

Kellin laughed softly. Slowly he mounted the

steps to the throne and sat himself upon it, moving back into the shadows until his spine touched wood. He placed his arms on the armrests, curled his fingers over the paws and felt the extended claws.

"This is Homana," he said. "*This* is Homana—and one day it will be mine."

His fear of the throne was gone. As a child it had frightened him, but he was no longer a child.

Kellin stared out into the hall. "The lion must swallow the lands. The lion must swallow us all."

He roused at the scrape of a boot upon stone floor. "Not a comfortable bed," the Mujhar remarked.

Kellin jerked upright, blinking blearily, stiff and sore and intensely uncomfortable. He had spent what little remained of the night in the bosom of the Lion. The knife was still in his fist. He was warrior enough for that.

Brennan's expression was masked. "Was there any point to it?"

Kellin challenged him immediately. "I do nothing without a point."

His grandfather's mouth twisted scornfully. "What you do is your concern, as you have made it. I gave up years ago asking myself what could be in your mind, to explain your behavior." He gestured sharply. "Get up from there, Kellin. You do not suit it yet."

The insult was deliberate, and he felt it strike true. He wanted to shout back, but knew it would gain him nothing but additional scorn. Of late he and his grandfather had played a game with the stakes residing in dominance. Brennan was the old wolf, Kellin the new; one day the old would die.

Kellin tapped the blade against wooden claws. "Perhaps better suited than you believe."

"Get up from there," Brennan repeated, "or I shall pull you up myself."

Kellin considered it. At a few years beyond sixty the Mujhar was an aging man, but he was not infirm. His hair was completely silver with white frost around his face, but the fierce eyes were steady, the limbs did not tremble, and the arms with their weight of *lir*-gold did not shrivel and sag. *He is taller and heavier than I, and he might be able to do it.*

Kellin rose with practiced elegance. He made an elaborate bow to his grandfather and turned to walk away, but Brennan reached out and caught one arm.

"How much longer?" he rasped. "This comedy we play? Or is it a tragedy?"

Kellin knew the answer. "Tragedy, my lord. What else could these walls house?"

Brennan's mouth flattened into a thin, compressed line of displeasure. "What these walls *will* house, I cannot say. But what they have housed in the past I can and do say: greater men than you, though they were merely servants."

Kellin wrenched his arm away. "You offer insult, my lord."

"I offer whatever I choose. By the gods, Kellin—will you never grow up?"

Kellin spread his hands in mock display. "Am I not a man?"

"No." Brennan's tone was cold. "You are but a boy grown larger in size than in sense."

"Insult yet again." Kellin was unoffended; it was all part of the game though the Mujhar did not view it as such.

"What is your excuse?" Brennan demanded. "That you lost people close to you? Well, do you think I have not? Do you think none of us has suffered as you do?"

Stung, Kellin glared. "What I suffer is my own concern!"

"*And* mine." Brennan faced him down squarely. "You lack a *jehan*. You know why. You lost a tutor to sorcery, a friend to treachery, and a liege man to Cheysuli custom. You know how. And yet you choose to wallow in grief and make all of Mujhara suffer."

"Mujhara has nothing to do with this!"

"It does." Brennan's tone did not waver. "How many fights have you sought out—or caused, or joined—because of childish vindictiveness? How many men have you fought—and injured—because they were easy prey for your anger? How many bastards have you sired, duly packed off to Clankeep where you need not concern yourself with them?" More quietly, he said, "And how many guardsmen have died because of you?"

"*None* because of me!"

"Oh? Then what of the four men who died last night?"

"But that was not *my* fault."

"Whose was it, then? I thought you led them there on one of your Midden tours."

Anger boiled up. "Only because *you* put them on my trail like hounds upon a fox!" Kellin glared. "Call them off, grandsire. Then no more will die."

Brennan's expression was implacable. "Did you do it?"

"Did *I*—?" Kellin was aghast. "You believe I would *kill* them?"

"Aye," Brennan answered evenly. "I believe you might."

"How?" Kellin swallowed the painful lump in his throat. "I am your own grandson. And you accuse me of murder?"

"You have labored assiduously to make me believe you are capable of anything."

"But ..." Kellin laughed once, expelling air rather than amusement. "I never thought you would *hate* me so."

"Do you think a man must hate another to believe him capable of things another would not do?" Brennan shook his head. "I do not hate you. I know you better than you think, and why you have twisted yourself into this travesty of the Kellin you once were. I cannot understand it, but I am cognizant of *why*."

"Are you?" The anger was banished now, replaced with bitter helplessness. "You are not me."

"Thank the gods, no." Brennan lifted his shoulders briefly, as if shedding unwanted weight. "You are not as hard as you believe. I see it in you, Kellin. You still care what people think. It all matters to you, but you will not permit yourself to admit it. You fight with yourself; do you think I am blind? I need no *kivarna* to see that two men live in your soul."

"You cannot begin to know—"

"I *can*. I see what drives you, I see what shapes you. I only wish you would not give into it. It does *you* more harm than anyone else."

Kellin lashed out. "I do not care what anyone else thinks, only *you*—" He checked abruptly; he had divulged too much.

Brennan closed his eyes a moment. "Then why this charade? If you truly do care what I think—"

"I do. I know what I have done; it was done intentionally. I do not intend to alter it." Kellin's smile was humorless. "This way, I cannot be hurt."

Lines were graven deeply into Brennan's dark face. "You hurt yourself, this way."

"I can live with myself."

"Can you? Can you cohabit with both men? Or

must you destroy one to allow the other more freedom?"

Kellin spat his answer between his teeth. "This is what I wanted. This is what *I* decided. This is what I am."

Brennan made a dismissive gesture. "Another time, then, for this; there is something more important. Tell me what occurred last night."

Kellin sighed and stared down at the knife still clenched in his hand. "It was Corwyth, the Ihlini who killed Rogan and Urchin. He came to the tavern and told me Lochiel still wants me, and will take me whenever he likes. Whenever he wishes, I was told, the Ihlini will put out his hand and I will fall into it."

Brennan nodded. "An old Ihlini trick. He terrorizes victims long before he confronts them."

"I have vanquished the lion," Kellin said, "but he will look for something else. Corwyth has convinced me Lochiel will be as patient as necessary."

"Kellin—"

"They were dead when I reached them." Kellin looked at the knife, recalling the bulging eyes and pallid faces. "There was nothing I could do."

"Then you must stay here," Brennan said. "Homana-Mujhar will shield you."

Kellin barked a laugh. "I would go mad inside a ten-day!"

"There may be no choice."

"*Mad*, grandsire! I am halfway there already." He flipped the knife in his hand, then again, until it spun so the hilt and blade became alternating blurs. In mid-flip he caught it. "I will not stay here."

Brennan's anger showed for the first time since his arrival. "Is this some manner of expiation for your guilt? A twisted version of *i'toshaa-ni*?"

"I feel no guilt," Kellin told him. "*That* is for

my *jehan* to do . . . but I think it quite beyond him.''

Brennan groaned in sheer frustration. ''How many times have I told you? I have said again and again—''

Kellin cut him off. ''You have said, and I have heard. But it means nothing. Not until he says it directly to me.''

Brennan shook his head. ''I will not send word to him again. That is finished.''

Kellin nodded. ''Because the last time he refused to extend hospitality to your messenger and packed him off home again. So, slighted, you surrender. I think my *jehan* must be mad as well, to speak so to the Mujhar of Homana.''

''Aidan does not speak for himself, Kellin. He speaks for the gods.''

''Facile words, grandsire. But listen first to yourself—and then recall that he is your *son*. I know very well who should have the ordering of the other.''

Brennan lost his temper. Kellin listened in startled surprise; he had never thought to hear such language from his grandfather.

''Go, then.'' At last the royal fury was spent. ''Go into the taverns and drink yourself into a stupor. Go to your light women and sire all the bastards you wish so you may leave them as your *jehan* left you, wondering what manner of man you are to desert a child.'' A pale indented ring circled Brennan's mouth. ''Risk your life and the lives of honorable men so you may enter the game with Lochiel. I no longer care. You are Homana's heir for now, but if I must I can find another.''

Kellin laughed at him. ''Who can you find? From where? There are no more sons, grandsire; your *cheysula* gave you but one. And no more grandsons, either; Aidan's loins are empty. He is in all ways but half a man."

"Kellin—"

He raised his head. "There is no heir to be found other than the one you invested twenty years ago."

Brennan reached out and caught the flipping knife easily. "You are a fool," he said clearly. "Perhaps Homana would be better off without you."

Kellin looked at the hand that held his knife. He had not expected the weapon to be caught. Brennan was at least as quick as he; a forcible reminder that the Mujhar of Homana was more than merely a man, but a Cheysuli as well.

He met his grandfather's eyes. "May I have it back?"

"No."

He did not avoid the packleader's eyes. To do so was to submit. "I have need of a knife."

"You have another. Use it."

Kellin clenched his teeth. "That one belonged to Blais. I have sworn never to touch it."

"Then unswear it," the Mujhar said. "*Tu'halla dei*, Kellin. Such things as that come easily to a man who cares for nothing."

It was more than he had anticipated. It twisted within his belly. "It shall be as this, then?"

Brennan did not move. "As you have made it."

After a long moment, Kellin averted his stare. The young wolf, he acknowledged ruefully, could not yet pull down the old.

Three

In his chambers, Kellin sat on the edge of his bed and stared at the small darkwood chest for a very long time. It rested inoffensively on a bench against the wall, where he had placed it many years before. He had looked at it often, stared at it, hated it, knowing what it contained, but once locked it had never been opened again.

He drew in a deep breath, wishing he need not consider doing what was so difficult, because he had made it so. He realized that in truth he need *not* consider it; it was more than possible for him to get another knife despite his grandfather's suggestion. He could buy one in Mujhara, or find one in the palace, or even go to Clankeep and have one of the warriors make him one; everyone knew Cheysuli long-knives were superior to all others, and only one Cheysuli-made was worth the coin. But the challenge had been put forth. The old wolf mocked the young. The young wolf found it intolerable.

His palms were damp. In disgust Kellin wiped them against his breeches-clad thighs. *He tests you with this. Prove to him you are stronger than he thinks.*

Muttering an oath, Kellin slid off his bed and strode without hesitation directly across to the chest. The lid and the key atop it was layered with dust; he had ordered no one to touch the chest.

Dust fell away as he picked up the key, smearing fingertips. He blew the iron clean, squinting against motes, hesitated a moment longer, then swore and unlocked the chest. Kellin flung back the lid so sharply it thumped against the wall.

His lips were dry. He wet them. A flutter of anticipation filled his belly. *I would do better to leave this here, as I vowed. I want no part of this. Blais is dead ten years, but it feels like ten hours.* Kellin's jaw clenched so hard his teeth ached. Then he thrust a hand inside and drew out the contents: a single Cheysuli long-knife.

The grief had not lessened with the passage of years, and the act of retrieving the knife intensified it tenfold. Kellin felt the tightening of his belly, the constriction of his throat, the anguish of his spirit. The wound, despite the decade, was still too fresh.

Kellin held the knife lightly, so that it lay crosswise across his palm. Candlelight glinted off steel because the hand beneath it trembled; he could not help himself. He recalled in precise detail the instant of realization, the comprehension that Blais was doomed because his *lir* was dead. In that moment he had come to understand the true cost of the magic that lived in a Cheysuli's blood. And knew how much he feared it.

The gods give warriors lir not to bless them, but to curse them; to make them vulnerable, so they can never be men but minions instead, set to serve spiteful gods. They give warriors lir simply to take them away.

Kellin stared hard at the knife, daring himself to break down. Beautifully balanced, the steel blade was etched with Cheysuli runes denoting Blais' name and Houses: Homana first, and Erinn. The grip itself was unadorned so as not to interfere with the hand, but the pommel made up for the plainness. An elaborate snarling wolf's head was set with emeralds for eyes.

Kellin's throat closed. To swallow was painful. "A waste," he said tightly. "The gods would have done better to take me in his place."

But they had not, despite his pleas, and he had cursed them for it often. Now he simply ignored them; there was no place in Kellin's life for gods so vindictive and capricious as to first steal his father, then permit his liege man to die.

Anger goaded his bruised spirit. Kellin slammed shut the chest and turned to his belt with its now-empty sheath. He slid the knife home with a decisive motion so that only the wolf's head showed, snarling a warning to the world. *Apropos*, Kellin thought. *Let them all be forewarned.*

He dressed rapidly, replacing soiled breeches with new; a plain wool shirt and velvet doublet, both brown; and Homanan-style boots. Over it all he fastened the belt, brushing the knife hilt with the palm of his hand to make certain of its presence. *Time I tested Corwyth's promise.*

The Mujhar had assigned new watchdogs. Kellin wondered briefly if they knew or were curious about what had become of the last four, but he did not trouble himself to ask. He merely told them curtly to keep their distance, making no effort to befriend them or endear himself to them; he did not want them as friends, and did not particularly care what they thought of him.

This time Kellin rode; so did they. They followed closely, but not so closely as to tread upon his mount's hooves. Testing them—and himself— he led them deep into the Midden to its very heart, where the weight of filth and poverty was palpable. *No one will know me here.* And so they would not; Kellin wore nothing to give away his identify save his ruby signet ring, but if the stone were turned inward against his palm no one would see it. He preferred anonymity. Let those of the Midden believe he was a rich Mujharan lordling gone slumming for a lark; he knew better. He wanted a game, and a fight. As he had told the Mujhar, he did nothing without a point.

The tavern he selected lay at the dead end of a narrow, dark street little better than the manure trench behind the hall garderobe in Homana-Mujhar. It was a slump-shouldered hovel with haphazard slantwise roof; the low door, badly cracked, hung crooked in counterpoint to the roof. The building resembled nothing so much as a drunkard gone sloppy on too much liquor.

Kellin smiled tightly. *This will do.* He dropped off his horse and waited impatiently for his watchdogs to join him on the ground. "Three of you shall remain here," he said briefly. "One I will take with me, because I must in compromise; it seems I have no choice." He thrust the reins to one of the guardsmen. "Wait here, in the shadows. Do what you are honor-bound to do; I make no claim on your loyalty. You answer the Mujhar's bidding, but answer also a little of mine: leave me to myself this night." He gestured toward one of them. The man was young, tall, blocky-shouldered, with pale blond hair and blue eyes. "You will come in with me, but see you it is done without excess attention. And strip off that tunic."

The young guardsman was startled. "My lord?"

"Strip it off. I want no royal dogs at my heels tonight." Kellin appraised him closely. "What is your name?"

"Teague, my lord."

Kellin gestured. "Now."

Slowly Teague stripped out of his crimson tunic with its black rampant lion. He handed it reluctantly to another guardsman, then looked back at Kellin. "Anything else, my lord?"

"Rid yourself of your sword. Do not protest—you have a knife still." He allowed derision to shape the tone. "Surely more than enough weaponry for a member of the Mujharan Guard."

Cheeks burning, Teague slowly divested himself of the swordbelt and handed it over to the man who held his tunic.

Kellin assessed him again, chewing the inside of his cheek. Finally he sighed. "Even a horse with winter hair still shows its blood." He bent and scooped up a handful of mud, then smeared it purposefully across Teague's mail shirt to dull the polished links and to foul the pristine breeches. He ignored the young man's rigidity and pinched mouth. When he was done, Kellin washed his hands in slushy snow, then nodded at the discomfited guardsman. "They will not know you at once."

Distaste was not entirely suppressed though Teague made the effort. "They will not know me at *all*, my lord."

Kellin grinned. "Better. Now, my orders." He waited until his expectant silence gained Teague's complete attention. "Once we are through that door I am not to be called 'my lord,' nor do I desire your interference in anything I undertake."

Teague's jaw was tight. "We are charged with your life, my lord. Would you have me turn my back on a knife meant for yours?"

Kellin laughed. "Any knife meant for *my* back would have to be fast indeed. I doubt I will come to harm—though the gods know I would welcome the challenge." He gestured at the remaining three guardsmen. "Take the horses and move into the shadows."

"My lord?" Teague clearly had not forsaken the honorific. "It is not for me to reprove you—"

"No. It is not."

"—but I think you should know this is not the best of all places to spend your time drinking or dicing."

"Indeed," Kellin agreed gravely. "That is precisely the point. Now—you are to go in and find your own table. I require two things of you only: to sit apart from me, and to be silent."

Teague cast a scowl at his companions waiting in the shadows, then grudgingly nodded. "Aye."

Kellin jerked a thumb at the door, and the muck-smeared guardsman went in muttering under his breath. Kellin waited until enough time had passed to nullify the appearance of companionship, then went in himself.

The stench of the hovel tavern struck him first. Soiled rushes littered the packed earthen floor in crumbled bits and pieces Kellin was certain harbored all manner of vermin. Only a handful of greasy, sputtering tallow candles illuminated the room, exuding an acrid, rancid aroma and wan, ocherous light easily dominated by shadows. An hour in such a place would render his clothing irredeemable, but Kellin had every intention of remaining longer than that. He anticipated a full night.

Teague sat at a small flimsy table in the corner nearest the door. A crude clay jug stood at his elbow and an equally lumpy cup rested in his hands, but he paid attention to neither.

Their eyes met, slid away. Kellin was faintly surprised that Teague would enter so convincingly into subterfuge. There was no hint of recognition in the guardsman's face and nothing about his posture that divulged his true purpose. Mud clung to his mail shirt; a little had spattered across a cheekbone, altering the angle. His hair now also was mussed, as if he had scrubbed a hand through it hastily. Teague's expression was closed, almost sullen, which suited Kellin's orders and the surroundings.

Kellin was deliberate in his perusal of the room and its occupants, knowing the men measured him as carefully. He allowed them time to mark his clothing, bearing, and size, as well as the heavy knife at his belt. He wanted no one to undervalue him, so that when the fight came it would be on equal terms. He admired the elegant simplicity of organized viciousness.

The tavern was crowded, but mostly because its size was negligible. Most of the men spoke in quiet tones lacking aggression or challenge, as if each knew the other's worth and standing within the context of the tavern, and did not overstep. There would be rivals, Kellin knew, because it was the nature of men, but with the arrival of a stranger old rivalries would be replaced with unity. He and Teague, apart or as one, would be suspect, and therefore targets.

He grinned, and let them see it. He let them see everything as he strode to the lone empty table and sat down upon a stool, shouting to the wine-girl to bring him a jug of *usca*.

She came almost at once to judge the cut of his cloth and the color of his coin. Kellin dropped a silver piece onto the table and let it ring, flicking it in her direction with a single practiced finger. Only the gold of his ring showed; the ruby with its etched rampant lion rested against his palm.

"*Usca*," he repeated, "and beef."

She was a greasy, unkempt girl with soiled clothing and filthy nails. She offered him a lone grimy dimple and a smile with two teeth missing. "Mutton and pork, my lord."

"Mutton," he said easily, "and do not stint it."

She wore a stained, threadbare apron over soiled gray skirts, and the sagging bodice gaped to display her breasts. She bent over to give him full benefit of her bounty. He saw more than she intended: flesh aplenty, aye, and wide, darkened nipples pinching erect under his perusal, but also a rash of insect bites. Dark brown hair swung down in its single braid. A louse ran across her scalp.

"My lord," the woman said, "we have more than just mutton and pork."

She was certain of her charms. In this place, he knew, no man would care about her filth, only the fit of his manhood between her diseased thighs. "Later," he said coolly. "Do not press me."

The brief flash of dismay was overtaken at once by enmity. She opened her mouth as if to respond, then shut it tight again. He saw her reassess his clothing, the coin, then forcibly alter hostility into a sullen acceptance. "Aye, my lord. Mutton and *usca*."

Kellin watched her walk away. Her hips swung invitation as if by habit; the rigidity of her shoulders divulged her injured feelings. He laughed softly to himself; he had frequent congress with Midden whores, but not with one such as she. He did not think much of acquiring lice as boon companions in exchange for a dip in her well-plumbed womanhood.

As he waited for *usca* and mutton, Kellin again assessed the room. His entrance, as expected, had caused comment, but that had died. Men gambled again, paying him no mind except for the occasional sidelong glance. Impatiently he pressed the tip of a fingernail into the edge of the silver piece and flipped the coin on the table. Again and again he did it, so that the coin rang softly, and the wan light from greasy candles glinted dully on the sheen of clean silver.

The woman returned with a boiled leather flask, no cup; and a platter of mutton. She thumped down the platter as he tested the smell of the flask. "Well?"

Kellin caught the tang of harsh liquor through the bitterness of boiled leather. He nodded, then flipped the coin in her direction. She caught it deftly, eyed his intent to discern if his mood toward her had changed; plainly it had not, but she bobbed a quick curtsy in deference to the silver. The overpayment was vast, but she accepted it readily enough with no offer of coppers in change. He had expected none.

"Do ye game?" she asked, jerking her head toward a neighboring table.

And so the dance commenced; Kellin felt the knot of anticipation tie itself into his belly. "I game."

"Do ye wager well?"

Kellin drew the Cheysuli long-knife and sliced into the meat. "As well as the next man."

Emerald wolf's-eyes glinted. She marked them, and stared. "Would ye dice with a stranger?"

Kellin bit into the chunk of meat. It was tough, stringy, foul; he ate it anyway, because it was part of the test. "If his coin is good enough, no man is a stranger."

Indecisive, she chewed crookedly at her lip. Then blurted her warning out. "You lords don't come here. The game is sometimes rough."

"Tame ones bore me." He cut more mutton. Emeralds winked.

Her own eyes shone with avarice. "Luce will throw with you. Will ye have him?"

Kellin downed a hearty swallow of *usca*, then tipped the flask again. Deliberately, he said, "I came here for neither the drink nor the meat. Do not waste my time on idle chatter."

She inhaled a hissing breath. Her spine was stiff as she swung away, but he noted it did not prevent her from walking to the closest table. She bent and murmured to one of the table's occupants, then went immediately into the kitchen behind a tattered curtain.

Kellin waited. He ate his way through most of the mutton, then shoved aside the platter with a grimace of distaste. The rest of the *usca* eventually burned away the mutton's aftertaste.

A second flask was slapped down upon the table even as Kellin set aside the first. The hand that held it was not the woman's. It was wide-palmed and seamed with scars. Thick dark hair sprouted from the back. "Purse," the man said. "I dice against rich men, not poor."

Kellin glanced up eventually. "Then we are well suited."

The man did not smile or otherwise indicate emotion. He merely untied a pouch from his belt, loosened the puckered mouth, and poured a stream of gemstones into his hand. With a disdainful gesture he scattered the treasure across scarred wood. His authority was palpable as he stood beside the table, making no motion to guard his wealth. No one in the tavern would dare test him by attempting to steal a gemstone.

Real, every one. Rubies, sapphires, emeralds, and a diamond or two for good measure. All were at least the size of a man's thumbnail; some were larger yet.

Kellin looked at Luce again. The man was huge. The imagery flashed into Kellin's mind: *A bull.* And so Luce seemed, with his thick neck, and a wide-planed, saturnine face hidden in bushy brown beard. His eyes were dark, nearly black. His

crooked teeth were yellow, and he lacked his left
thumb.

A *thief*. But caught only once, or the Mujhar's
justice would have required more than a thumb.

On thick wrists Luce wore heavy leather bracers
studded with grime-rimmed metal. His belt was
identical, fastened with a massive buckle of heavy
greenish bronze. His clothing was plain homespun
wool, dark and unexceptional, but in a concession
to personal vanity—and as a mark of his status—
he wore a chunky bluish pearl in his right earlobe.
In the Midden the adornment marked him a
wealthy man.

A *good* thief, then. And undoubtedly dangerous.

Kellin smiled. He understood why the girl had
gone to Luce rather than to another. She intended
to teach the arrogant lordling a very painful lesson
in payment for his rudeness.

He untied his belt-purse, loosened the mouth,
then dumped the contents out onto the table. Gold
spilled across stained wood, mingling with the
glitter of Luce's stones. With it spilled also silver,
a handful of coppers, and a single bloody ruby
Kellin carried for good luck.

The pile of coins and lone ruby marked Kellin
a rich man also, but it did not begin to match the
worth of Luce's treasure. He knew that at once
and thought rapidly ahead to alternatives. Only
one suggested itself. Only one was worth the risk.

The bearded Homanan grunted and began to
scoop the gemstones back into his pouch. "A poor
man, then."

"No." Kellin's tone was deliberate, cutting
through the faint clatter of stone against stone.
"Look again." With an elegant gesture he pushed
the long-knife into the pile.

He heard the sibilance of indrawn breaths.
Luce's presence at Kellin's table had attracted an

audience. The huge man was among friends in the Midden; Kellin had none. Even Teague, ostensibly there to guard him, slouched at the back of the crowd and appeared only marginally interested in Luce and the lordling who was not, after all, so rich a man as that—except he had now raised the stakes higher than anyone might expect.

The fingers on Luce's right hand twitched once. His eyes, dark and opaque, showed no expression. "I'll touch it."

"You know what it is," Kellin said. "But aye, you may touch it—for a moment."

The insult was deliberate. As expected, it caused a subtle shifting among the audience. Luce's mouth tightened fractionally in the hedgerow of his beard, then loosened. He picked up the knife and smoothed fingers over the massive pommel, closed on the grip itself, then eventually tested the clean steel as an expert does: he plucked a hair from his beard and pulled it gently across the edge. Satisfied, he twisted his mouth. Then it loosened, slackened, and the tip of his tongue showed as he turned the knife in poor light. Emerald eyes glinted.

Luce wet thick lips. "Real."

Kellin's hands were slack on the table top. Compared to Luce's bulky palms and spatulate fingers, Kellin's were almost girlish in their slender elegance. "I carry no false weapons."

Near-black eyes flicked an assessive glance at Kellin. "Cheysuli long-knife."

"Aye."

Flesh folded upon itself at the corners of Luce's eyes. "You'd risk this."

Kellin shrugged in elaborate negligence. "When I dice, there is no risk."

Thus the challenge was made. Luce's brows met, then parted. "This is worth more than I have."

"Of course it is." Kellin smiled faintly. "A Cheysuli knife cannot be bought, stolen, or copied . . . only earned." Idly he rolled his ruby back and forth on the splintered wood. "Be certain, Homanan—if you win that knife from me, you will have earned it. But if it concerns you now that you cannot match my wager, there is something else you may add."

Luce's eyes narrowed. "What?"

"If you lose," Kellin said, "your other thumb."

The tavern thrummed with low-toned growls of outrage and murmurs of surprise. In its tone Kellin heard the implicit threat, the promise of violence; he had challenged one of their own. But the audacity, once absorbed, was worth a grudging admiration. It was a wager to measure the courage of any man, and Luce had more pride than most to risk. They believed in him, Kellin knew, and that alone would move a reluctant man to accept a wager he would not otherwise consider.

Luce set the knife down very deliberately next to Kellin's hand. It was a subtle display of fairness that was, Kellin believed, uncommon to the Midden, and therefore all the more suspect, but was also a salute to Kellin's ploy. The handsome young lordling was no friend to them, but no longer precisely an enemy. He understood the tenor of their world.

Luce smiled. "A wager worth the making, but over too quickly. Let's save us the knife—and the thumb—for last."

Kellin suppressed a smile. "Agreed."

"One more," Luce cautioned, as Kellin moved to sweep the coins into his pouch, "if you lose the knife, an answer to a question."

Easy enough. "If I can give it."

Luce's gaze did not waver. "You'll tell me how you came by such a knife."

That was unexpected. Kellin was accustomed to those in better taverns recognizing him and therefore knowing he was Cheysuli. But Luce clearly knew nothing at all about him, least of all his race, which suited him perfectly. "It is important to you?"

Luce bent and spat. "I have no love of the shape-changers," he said flatly. "If you got a knife from one of them, it can be done again. I want to find the way. Then I would be on equal ground."

It was puzzling. "Equal ground? With the Cheysuli?"

Luce hitched massive shoulders. "They're sorcerers. Their weapons are bound with spells. If I had a knife, I'd share in the power. If I had two, I could rule it."

Kellin smiled. "Ambitious, for a thief."

Luce's eyes narrowed. "A thief, aye—for now. But these men'll tell you what my ambition earns them." One meaty hand swung out to encompass the room. "Without me they earn scraps. *With* me, they earn feasts." His stare was malignant. "The Midden is mine, lordling, and I'll be keeping it so. It'd be easier done with Cheysuli sorcery."

Kellin displayed his teeth in an undiluted grin, then gestured with a sweep of one eloquent hand. "Sit you down, my lord of the Midden, and we shall see precisely what power there is to be won."

Four

By the time Kellin had won some of Luce's jewels and Luce a portion of Kellin's gold, even Teague had joined the crowd surrounding the table. No one paid him the slightest attention, including the prince he was commanded to protect.

Sweat stippled Kellin's upper lip. Except for the cracked door and holes broken in daub-and-wattle walls, the small room was mostly airless. Now that so many had moved in close to watch, ringing the table, he could not draw a single breath without inhaling also the stench of the tavern and the overriding stink of wool- and grime-swathed men who had not bathed since summer.

Kellin impatiently wiped the dampness from his face with the edge of his hand, knowing his nervousness came as much from belated acknowledgment of Luce's dicing skills as the closeness of the room. He had always been good himself, but Luce was better.

The luck has turned. Kellin tossed back a swallow of *usca* from his third flask, trying to diffuse the nagging sense of trepidation. *It favors Luce, not me—and we are nearly through my coin.*

Left were two silver pieces and a handful of coppers, pitiful remainders of Kellin's once-plump purse. Though he had briefly owned a few of Luce's jewels, the giant had easily won them back and more, including the lone ruby.

194

That is where my luck went. Kellin eyed the bloody glint in Luce's pile. *He has it now.*

Luce slapped one meaty hand down across the table, scattering the dice and the last few coins of the current wager. Dark eyes glittered. "Enough," he said. "Put up the rest of it, *all* of it—it's time for the final wager."

To buy time, Kellin assessed him. The big man had consumed cup after cup of *usca*, but nothing of it showed in eyes or manner. There was no indication Luce was any less sober than when the wine-girl first approached him, only a fixed desire to begin the final pattern of the dance.

Kellin inhaled slowly and deeply, trying to clear his head. An unexpected desperation made him nervous and irritable, doubling the effects of his overindulgence in *usca*. His belly was unsettled as well as his spirit. He could not bear the knowledge he might well lose Blais' knife. He had only risked the weapon because he had been certain of keeping it.

Luce smiled for the first time. Behind him, Kellin heard the murmuring of the Homanans. Their anticipation was clearer, as was their absolute faith in Luce's ability. Kellin found it particularly annoying.

He shoved all that remained of his wealth into the center of the table, mingling it with jewels, coins, and dice, then challenged Luce in silence.

The big man laughed. "All, is it?" He flicked onto the pile a glittering diamond. "Worth more than yours," he said off-handedly, "but I'll have it back anyway." Then, with abject contempt, he jabbed a hand toward Kellin. "Your throw. Boy."

The insult stung, as it was intended, but not so much after all. To Luce, he *was* a boy, for the man was much older—but something else was far more imperative than answering a gibe at his youth and inexperience.

If I could win this throw, I could yet string out the game a while and avoid offering the knife. Teeth set tightly, Kellin scooped up the six ivory dice. Carved markings denoted their value. He threw, and counted the values before the dice stopped rolling.

Leijhana tu'sai— Relief crowded out the desperation in Kellin's belly. Sweat dried on his face. He maintained a neutral expression only with great effort, and only because he knew it would annoy Luce. "*Your* throw," he said negligently, relaxing on his stool. Inwardly jubilant, he waited. The crowd around the table stirred; only one value could beat the total on Kellin's dice, and it was not easily accomplished.

Luce grunted and grabbed the dice. His mouth moved silently as he whispered something and shook the cubes in his hand.

A body shifted behind Kellin, breaking his concentration. A voice said irritably: "Don't push!"

Kellin ignored it, watching Luce entreat the dice to fall his way, but within a moment the body pressed close again, brushing his shoulder. Kellin leaned forward in an attempt to escape the crowding. *If they take no care, they will upset the table—*

And they did so just as Luce threw. A body fell into Kellin, who was in turn shoved against the table. Coins, jewels, and dice spilled, showering the rush-littered floor.

Even as Kellin, swearing, rose to avoid overturned *usca*, he recognized the miscreant. The expression in Teague's eyes was one of calculation and satisfaction, not regret or anger, though he voiced a sharp protest against the man who had caused him to fall.

For only a moment Kellin's curiosity roused.

Then he turned back to Luce, who cursed savagely and dropped to his knees, scrabbling for dice. Others were on the floor also, gathering coin and gemstones.

How many will make their way into purses and pockets? And then Kellin reflected that probably none would; Luce's hold over the men was too strong. A copper here and there might disappear, but nothing of significance.

Luce came up from the floor, broad face dark in anger. A malignancy glittered in near-black eyes. "The dice," he grated. "I have them all, but one."

Teague held it aloft. "I have it." His smile was odd as he tossed the cube in his left hand; the right lingered very near his knife.

Luce thrust out a hand. "Give it here."

"I think not." Teague had discarded his truculence and sloppy posture. He looked directly at Kellin. "The die is weighted improperly. You have been cheated."

"A *lie!*" Luce thundered.

Teague tossed the cube to Kellin. "What say you?"

Frowning, Kellin rolled the smooth ivory in his fingers. It felt normal enough. The ploy could well be Teague's way of rescuing him from a difficult situation.

He flashed a glance at the guardsman and saw nothing but a cool, poised patience. Nothing at all indicated Teague might be lying.

Kellin considered. A second test of the cube divulged a faint roughness at one rounded corner, but that could come from years of tavern use rather than purposeful weighting.

"A lie," Luce declared. "Give it here."

Kellin stared back. "You deny the charge."

"I do!"

"Then you will have no objection if we test it." Kellin kicked aside bits and pieces of soiled rushes. He grimaced in distaste as he knelt down on the packed earthen floor. It was a vulnerable position, with Luce towering over him, but he assumed it with as much nonchalance as he could muster. He dared not hesitate now, not before the ring of hostile faces.

"A lie," Luce repeated.

Kellin draped one forearm across a doubled knee. He gripped the die loosely in his right hand. "If it is a fair roll, you shall have the knife." He saw it in Teague's hand, emerald eyes glittering. "Otherwise, your remaining thumb is forfeit."

Luce breathed audibly. "Throw it, then."

Kellin opened his fingers and dropped the cube. It bounced, rattled, then stilled.

"You see?" Luce declared.

Kellin smiled. "Patience is not your virtue." He retrieved the die. "If the identical value shows four more times, I think there will be no question—"

Luce bellowed an order.

Kellin uncoiled from the floor and caught the knife easily as Teague slapped it into his hand. The blade rested against Luce's massive belly, forestalling any attack by others. "I offer you two things," Kellin said clearly. "First, your life; I have no desire to gut you here. It would only add to the stench." He showed the big man his teeth. "The other is the answer to your question. You see, I got this knife—" he pressed the tip more firmly against Luce's belly above the bronze buckle, "—in a sacred ritual. Few Homanans know about it; only one has witnessed it. His name was Carillon." Jubilation welled up in Kellin's spirit. He had risked himself, and won. "It is the custom to exchange knives when a Cheysuli liege man swears blood-oath to serve the Prince of Homana."

Luce's disbelief and fury began as a belly-deep growl and rose to a full-throated roar. *"Prince—"*

Kellin cut it off with a firmer pressure against the heavy belly. "Cheysuli as well, Homanan. *Tahlmorra lujhala mei wiccan, cheysu.*" He laughed, delighted to see the comprehension in Luce's face. "Now, perhaps we should discuss your thumb."

"Gut me, then!" Luce roared, and brought his knee up sharply.

The knife did not by much beat the knee to its target, but Kellin's thrust was almost immediately rendered ineffective. He *intended* to sheath the steel in Luce's belly, but the man's upthrust knee, driving home with speed and accuracy, deprived Kellin of everything except a burst of incredible pain, and the knowledge—even as he collapsed— that he had made a deadly mistake.

—never hesitate— But he had. Now he lay writhing on the filthy floor of a dirtier tavern, wondering if he would survive long enough to find out if he could bed a woman again.

He had cut Luce, perhaps deeply, but not deeply enough to kill; he heard the man shouting orders to his confederates. Hands closed on Kellin even as he groaned and tried to swallow the *usca* that threatened to exit his body. Bile burned in the back of his throat.

Teague. Somewhere. But they were two against too many.

For a fleeting moment Kellin wished he had not been so adamant about posting the remaining watchdogs outside, but there was no time for recriminations. He had lost his knife on the floor and had only his wits and skills with which to save his life.

Hands dragged him upright. Kellin wanted very badly to lie down again, but he dared not if he were to preserve his life. So he tapped the pain, used the pain as a goad, and channeled it into a weapon.

He tore loose of the hands holding him, jabbing with elbows and stomping with booted feet. One man he butted so firmly beneath the chin that teeth crunched. Something sharp sliced across his outflung hands, grated across knuckles; a second knife jabbed him in the back. But its tip fouled on the heavy winter doublet as he spun away.

Kellin lashed out with a boot and smashed a knee, then jammed an elbow into the man's face as he doubled over. Blood spurted as the nose broke, spraying Kellin as well as the Homanan.

Teague. Near, he knew; he could hear the guardsman swearing by the name of the Mujhar. Kellin hoped Teague was armed with more than oaths. *If I could find the door—*

A table was shoved into his path. Kellin braced, then swung up onto it, kicked out again, caught one man's jaw flush. The head snapped back on its neck. The man fell limply even as another replaced him.

Someone slashed at his leg. Kellin leapt high into the air and avoided the knife, but as he came down again the flimsy table collapsed. In a spray of shattered wood and curses, Kellin went down with it.

Something blunt dug into his spine as he rolled. *Wood, not blade—*

"Mine!" Luce roared. "He's mine to kill!"

"Teague!" Kellin shouted.

"My lord—" But the answering shout was cut off.

Kellin thrust himself upward. Arms closed around his chest, trapping his own arms in a deadly hug. His spine was pressed against the massive belt buckle; his head beneath Luce's chin. The Homanan's strength was immense.

A sharp, firm squeeze instantly expelled what little breath was left in Kellin's lungs. The human vice around his chest denied him another. Speckles crept into the corners of his eyes, then spread to threaten his vision.

Kellin writhed in Luce's grasp. He kicked but struck air, and the big man laughed. "Boy," Luce said, "your gods can't hear you now."

He had not petitioned the gods. Now he did, just in case, even as he snapped his head backward in a futile attempt to smash Luce's face. He struck nothing but muscled neck. Luce's grip tightened.

Frenziedly, Kellin fought. His breath was gone, and his strength, but desperation drove him. He would not give up. A Cheysuli warrior never gave up.

Luce, laughing, shook him. A rib protested. "Little prince," he baited, "where is your liege man now?"

Blais would not permit this— Kellin arched his body in a final attempt at escape, then went limp. Blood dripped from the corner of his mouth. He hung slackly in thick arms.

Luce squeezed him a final time, threw him down. "I'll have that knife now."

Kellin's breath came back in a rush. He heard himself gasping and whooping as his lungs filled slowly, then understood what Luce intended to do. "No knife—*mine*—" And it was there, kicked beneath shattered wood; Kellin clawed for it, touched it, closed trembling fingers upon it even as Luce saw his intent. But before the big man could react, Kellin's hand closed over the hilt.

He came up from the floor in one awkward lunge, still gasping for breath, still doubled up from the pain of his bruised ribs. But to hesitate or protect himself guaranteed death; Kellin slashed out repeatedly, carving himself a clearing. He saw the glint of a swordblade—*no, two*—and realized the watchdogs were present at last. Teague had reached the door, or else they had heard the commotion.

Luce?

The man was there, armed as well. The knife he held was not so elaborate as Kellin's but its blade was equally deadly. Near-black eyes were fastened on Kellin's face. "I'll have that long-knife yet."

Blood trickled into Kellin's right eye as he sucked at air. He scrubbed a forearm across his brow, shook back damp hair, then grinned at the big man. Without the breath to answer, Kellin beckoned Luce on with the waggle of one hand.

By now most of the fighting had been stopped, or stopped of its own accord. It had come down to Kellin and Luce. The silence in the tavern was heavy with expectation.

Luce still watched him, judging his condition. Kellin knew it well enough: he was half-sick on *usca* and the blow from Luce's knee, as well as bruised about the ribs. He was stippled by half a dozen nicks and slices, and a cut across his brow bled sluggishly, threatening his vision.

Kellin forced a ragged laugh. "Are you truly the king of the Midden? Do you think yourself fit to rule? Then *show* me, little man. Prove to a Cheysuli you are fit to hold his knife."

Luce came on, as expected. Kellin stood his ground, watching the man's posture and the subtle movements of his body; when Luce's momentum was fully engaged, his intent divulged, Kellin slipped aside and thrust out a boot. Luce stumbled, cursed, then fell against a table. His hands thrust out to brace himself.

With a single definitive blow of Blais' knife, Kellin chopped down and severed the thief's remaining thumb. "There," he said, "the debt now is paid."

Luce screamed. He clutched his bleeding hand against his chest. "Shapechanger sorcery!"

Kellin shook his head, still trying to regain his breath. "Just a knife in the hand of a man. But enough for you, it seems."

The conquest of Luce ended the fight entirely. Kellin saw bloodied faces and gaping mouths, torn clothing and gore-splattered hair. The crimson tunics of the watchdogs glowed like pristine beacons in the smoky shadows of the tavern.

He ached. His profaned manhood throbbed. He wanted no more than to lie down in the slushy snow and cool the heat of pain, to drive away the sickness, to regain in the bite of winter the self-control he had forfeited to a despised desperation.

Kellin wanted no one, thief or guardsman, to see how much he hurt. Without a word, without an order, he turned and walked through the crowd and pushed open the cracked door, taking himself from the tavern into the cold clarity of the alley. The stench was no better there, but the familiar glitter of stars was an infinite improvement over the opaque malignancy of Luce's enraged stare.

Kellin looked at the horses and very nearly flinched. He could not bear the idea of riding.

"My lord?" It was Teague, exiting the tavern. He was bloodied and bruised and very taut around the mouth. "We should get you to Homana-Mujhar."

The response was automatic. "If I choose to go."

Teague neither flinched nor colored. His tone was pitched to neutrality. "Are you done for the evening, my lord?"

Kellin gifted him with a scowl as the other guardsmen filed out of the tavern. "Is there something else you wished to do?"

Teague shrugged. "I thought perhaps you might desire to find another game." He paused. "My lord."

As he collected breath and wits, Kellin considered any number of retorts. Most of them were couched in anger or derision. But after what Teague had done, he thought the guardsman deserved better.

He blew out a frosted breath, then drew another into a sore chest. He wanted to lie down, or bend over, or lean against the wall, but he would do none of those things or risk divulging discomfort. Instead, he asked a question. "*Was* the die improperly weighted?"

Teague grinned. "As to that, I could not swear. But when Luce spread his hand down across the pile and challenged you to the final throw, I saw one die replaced with another. It seemed logical to assume it was weighted to favor Luce."

Kellin grunted agreement. "But it was not replaced before."

"No, my lord."

"You are certain?"

"My lord—" With effort, Teague suppressed a smile and did not look at his companions. "I am moved to say your luck was bad tonight."

"And, no doubt, my tavern selection." Kellin sighed and pressed a hand against sore ribs. "I am going home. You may come, or go, as you wish. It is nothing to me."

Teague considered it. "I think I will come, my lord." The faintest glint brightened his eyes. "I would like to hear what the Mujhar has to say when you arrive on his front step."

It was momentarily diverting. "To me, or to you?"

"To you, my lord. I have done my duty."

Kellin scowled. "It is not the Mujhar who concerns me."

"Who, then?"

It was an impertinence, but Kellin was too tired and sore to remind Teague of that. "The queen," he muttered. "She is Erinnish, remember? And possessed of a facile tongue." He sighed. "My ears will be burning tonight, as she can no longer redden my rump."

Teague surrendered his dignity to a shout of laughter. Then he recalled whom it was he served— the royal temper, Kellin knew, was notorious— and quietly gathered up the reins of his own mount and Kellin's. "I will walk with you, my lord."

The assumption stung. "And if I mean to ride?"

"Then I will ride also." Teague lowered his eyes and stared inoffensively at the ground. "But I daresay *my* journey will be more comfortable than yours."

Kelin's face burned. "I daresay."

The Prince of Homana walked all the way home as his faithful watchdogs followed.

Five

The Queen of Homana pressed a wine-soaked cloth against the wound in her grandson's scalp. "Sit still, Kellin! 'Tis a deep cut."

He could not help himself; he lapsed into an Erinnish lilt in echo of her own. "You'll be making it deeper, with this! D'ye mean to go into my brain?"

" 'Twould keep you from further idiocy, now, wouldn't it?" The pressure was firm as she worked to stanch the dribbling blood.

"That I doubt," Brennan said. "Kellin courts idiocy."

" 'Twould seem so," Aileen agreed equably. Then, when Kellin meant to protest, "Sit *still*."

Between them, they will slice me into little pieces. Kellin sat bolt upright in a stool in his chambers, bare to the waist. He was not in the slightest disposed to remain still as she pressed liquor into his scalp, because he could not. It stung fiercely. The right side of his chest was beginning to purple from Luce's affectionate hug, but Kellin was not certain Aileen's ministrations—or her words—would be gentler.

"You could bind his ribs," she suggested crisply to Brennan, "instead of standing there glowering like an old wolf."

"No," Kellin answered, knowing the Mujhar's

hands would be far less gentle than hers. "You do it, granddame."

"Then stop twitching."

"It *hurts.*"

Aileen sighed as she peeled back the cloth and inspected the oozing cut beneath. "For a Cheysuli warrior, my braw boyo, you're not so very good at hiding your pain."

"The *Erinnish* in me," he muttered pointedly. "Besides, how many Cheysuli warriors must suffer a woman to pour liquid fire into their skulls?"

Aileen pressed closed the cut. "How many *require* it?"

Kellin hissed. He slanted a sidelong glance at his grandfather. "I am not the first to rebel against the constraints of his rank."

The gibe did not disturb the Mujhar in the least. He stood quietly before his battered grandson with gold-weighted arms folded, observing his queen's ministrations. "Nor will you be the last," Brennan remarked. "But as that comment was aimed specifically at me, let me answer you in like fashion: dying before you inherit somewhat diminishes the opportunity to break free of my authority." He arched a brow. "Does it not?"

Kellin gritted his teeth. "I'm not looking to die, grandsire—"

"You give every indication of it."

"—merely looking for entertainment, something to fill my days, something to quench my taste—"

"—for rebellion." Brennan smiled a little. "Nothing you tell me now cannot be countered, Kellin. For that matter, you may as well save your breath, which is likely at this moment difficult to draw through bruised ribs—" the Mujhar cast him an ironic glance, "—because I know very well what you will say. I even know what *I* will say; it was said to me and to my *rujholli* several decades ago."

Kellin scowled. "I am not you, or Hart, or Corin—"

"—or even Keely," Aileen finished, "and I've heard this before, myself." Her green eyes were bright. "Now both of you be silent while I wrap up your ribs."

Kellin subsided into glum silence, punctuated only by an occasional hissed inhalation. He did not look again at his grandsire, but stared fixedly beyond him so he would not provoke a comment in the midst of intense discomfort.

He had told them little of the altercation in the tavern, saying merely that a game had gone bad and the fight was the result. No deaths, he pointed out; the Mujhar, oddly, asked about fire, to which Kellin answered in puzzlement that there was no fire, only a little blood. It had satisfied Brennan in some indefinable way; he had said little after that save for a few caustic comments.

Kellin sat very still as Aileen worked, shutting his teeth against the pain—he would *not* permit her to believe he was less able than anyone else to hold his tongue—and said nothing. But he was aware of an odd sensation that had little to do with pain.

"—still," she murmured, as a brief tremor claimed his body.

Kellin frowned as she snugged the linen around his ribs. *What is*—? And then again the tremor, and Aileen's muttered comment, and his own unintended reaction: every inch of flesh burned so intensely he sweated with it.

Brennan frowned. "Perhaps I should call a surgeon."

"No!" Kellin blurted.

"If there is that much pain—"

"—isn't *pain*," Kellin gritted. "Except—for that—" He sucked in a hissing breath as Aileen pulled linen taut against sore flesh. "Call no one. Grandsire."

He held himself still with effort. It *wasn't* pain, but something else entirely, something he could not ignore, that burned through flesh into bone with a will of its own, teasing at self-control. Fingers and toes tingled. It spread to groin and belly, then crept upward to his heart.

"Kellin?" Aileen's hands stilled. "*Kel*lin—"

He heard her only dimly, as if water filled his ears. His entire being was focused on a single sensation. It was very like the slow build toward the physical release of man into woman, he thought, but with a distinct difference he could not voice. He could not find the words. He knew only there was a vast and abiding *thing* demanding his attention, demanding his body and soul.

"Ihlini?" he murmured. "Lochiel?"

He need only put out his hand, Corwyth had said, and Kellin would be in it.

His ribs were strapped and tied. He could not breathe.

—could not *breathe*—

"Kellin!" Aileen's hands closed on his naked shoulders. "Can you hear me?"

He could. Clearly. The stuffy distance was gone. The burning subsided, as did the tremors. He felt it all go, leaching him of strength. He sat weak and trembling upon the stool, sweat running down his face. Damp hair stuck to his brow.

Gods— But he cut it off. He would not beg aid or explanation from those he could not honor.

Kellin clenched his teeth within an aching jaw. For a moment the room wavered around him, running together until all the colors were gone. Everything was a fleshy gray, lacking depth or substance.

"Kellin?" The Mujhar.

He could make no answer. He blinked, tried to focus, and vision eventually steadied. His hearing now was acute, so incredibly acute he heard the soughing of the folds of Aileen's skirts as she turned to Brennan. He could smell her, smell *himself:* the bitter tang of his own fear, the acrid bite of rebelling flesh.

"Brighter—" he blurted, and then the desolation swept in, and emptiness, and a despair so powerful he wanted to cry out. He was a shell, not a man; a hollow, empty shell. Shadow, not warrior, a man lacking in heart or substance, and therefore worthless among his clan.

In defiance of pain, Kellin lurched up from the stool. He shuddered. Tremors began again. He felt the protest of his ribs, but they did not matter. He took a step forward, then caught himself. For a moment he lingered, trapped upon the cusp, then somehow found the chamberpot so he could spew his excesses into pottery instead of onto the floor.

Even as Aileen murmured sympathy, Brennan cut her off. "He deserves it. The gods know Hart and Corin did, *and* Keely, when they followed such foolish whims."

"And what of *your* whims?" she retorted. "You did not drink overmuch, but you found Rhiannon instead."

Kellin stood over over the chamberpot, one arm cradling his chest. It hurt to bend over, hurt to expel all the *usca,* hurt worse to draw a breath.

He straightened slowly, irritated by his grandparents' inconsequential conversation, but mostly humilated by the dictates of his body. He felt no better for purging his belly. Sickness yet lurked within, waiting for the moment he least expected its return.

Brennan's tone was uncharacteristically curt,

but also defensive as he answered his *cheysula.*
"Rhiannon has nothing to do with *this.*"

"She was your downfall as much as gambling
was Hart's and *I* was Corin's!" Aileen snapped.
"Don't be forgetting it, Brennan. We all of us do
things better left undone. Why should Kellin be
different?"

He shivered once more, and then his body
stilled. In quiescence was relief, carefully Kellin
sought and found a cloth to wipe his mouth. It
hurt too much to move; he leaned against the
wall. Brickwork was cool against overheated flesh.

Distracted by his movement, Aileen turned from
her husband. "Are you well?"

"How can he be well?" Brennan asked. "He has
drunk himself insensible and now suffers for it, as
well as for a fight that nearly stove in his chest."
His mouth hooked down in derision. "But he is
young, for all of that; he will begin again tomorrow."

"No," Kellin managed. "Not tomorrow." The
room wavered again. He caught at brickwork to
keep from falling.

"Kellin." The derision was banished from Brennan's tone. "Sit down."

The floor moved beneath Kellin's feet. Or was
he moving?"

"He's ill!" Aileen cried. "Brennan—*catch*—"

But the command came too late. Kellin was
aware of a brief detached moment of disorientation, then found himself sprawled across the floor
with his head in the Mujhar's arms.

He was cold, so *cold*—and a wail of utter despair
rose from the depths of his spirit. "—empty—" he
mouthed. "—*lost*—"

Brennan sat him upright and held him steady,
examining his eyes. "Look at me."

Kellin looked. Then vision slid out of focus and

the wail came back again. A sob tore loose in his chest. "Grandsire—"

"Be still. Look at me." Brennan cradled Kellin's head in his hands, holding it very still.

"Are you wanting a surgeon?" Aileen asked crisply.

"No."

"Earth magic, then."

"No."

"Then—"

"*Shansu*," Brennan told her. "This is something else, *meijhana*. Something far beyond the discontent caused by too much *usca*."

It was indeed. If not for the Mujhar's hands holding him in place, Kellin believed he might fall through the floor and beyond. "—too hard—" he whispered. "Too—"

"—empty," Brennan finished, "and cold, and alone, torn apart from the world and everything in it."

"—*lost*—"

"And angry and terribly frightened, and very small and worthless."

Kellin managed to nod. The anguish and desolation threatened to overwhelm him. "How can— how can you know?"

Brennan's severity softened. "Because I have felt it also. Every Cheysuli does when it is time to bond with his *lir*."

"*Lir!*"

"Did you really believe you would never have one?" Brennan's smile was faint. "Did you believe you would not need one?"

"I renounced it!" Kellin cried. "When Blais left—I *swore*—"

"Some oaths are as nothing."

"I renounced a *lir*, and the gods." It was incomprehensible that now, after so long without one, he might require a *lir;* or that he should have to battle the interference of gods he did not honor.

"Clearly the gods did not renounce *you,*" Brennan said dryly. "Now the time is come."

Kellin summoned all his strength; it was a pathetic amount. "I refuse."

The Mujhar smiled. "You are welcome to try."

Aileen was shocked. "You are overharsh!"

"No. There is nothing he can do. It is his time, Aileen. He will drive himself mad if he continues this foolishness. He must go. He is Cheysuli."

"And—Erinnish ... and Homanan—and all the other lines—" Kellin shivered. " 'Tis all I count for, is it not? My seed. My blood. Not Kellin at *all!*" His spirit felt as cold and hard as the floor. Desperately, he said, "I renounce my *lir.*"

"Renounce as you will," Brennan said, "but for now, get up on the stool."

Kellin gritted his teeth. "You are the Mujhar, blessed by the gods. I charge you to take it away."

"What—the pain? You earned it. The emptiness? I cannot. It can only be filled with a *lir.*"

"Take it away!" Kellin shouted. "I cannot live like this!"

Brennan rose. His eyes, so intensely yellow, did not waver. "You have the right of *that,*" he agreed. "You cannot live like this."

"Grandsire—"

"Get up, Kellin. There is nothing to be done."

He got up. He ached. He swore, even before Aileen. He was profoundly empty, bereft of all save futility and a terrifying *apartness.* "I renounced it," he said, "just as I renounced the gods. They have no power over me."

Brennan turned to Aileen. "I will have *usca* sent up. Best he dulls his pain with that which caused it; in the morning he will be better—" he slanted a glance at his grandson, "—or he will be worse."

She was clearly displeased. "Brennan."

The Mujhar of Homana extended a hand to his queen. "There is *nothing* to be done, Aileen. Whether or not he likes it, Kellin is Cheysuli. The price is always high, but no warrior refuses to pay it."

"I do," Kellin declared. "*I* refuse. I will not accept a *lir*."

Brennan nodded sagely. "Then perhaps you should spend the next few hours explaining that to the gods."

Six

"*Leijhana tu'sai,*" Kellin murmured as his grand-parents shut the door behind them. He was sick to death of Brennan's dire predictions and Aileen's contentiousness; could they not simply let him alone? *They try to shape me to fit their own idea of how a prince should be.*

Or perhaps they attempted to shape him into something other than his father who had re-nounced his rank and title as Kellin renounced his *lir.*

He drew in a hissing breath and let it out again, trying to banish pain as he banished the previous thought. Kellin had no desire to consider how his behavior might affect his grandparents, or that the cause of his own rebellion was incentive for the very expectations he detested. Such maunderings profited no one, save perhaps the occasional flicker of guilt searching for brighter light. He had no time for such thoughts; his ribs ached, and his manhood as yet reminded him of its abuse. Best he simply took to his bed; perhaps he would fall asleep, and by morning be much improved in health and spirit.

But restlessness forbade it even as he approached the bed. He was dispirited, disgruntled, highly un-settled. Even his bones itched. His body would not be still, but clamored at him for *something—*

"What?" Kellin gritted. "What is it I'm to do?"

He could not be *still*. Frustrated, Kellin began to pace, hoping to burn out the buzz in blood and bones. But he managed to stop only when he reached the polished plate hanging cockeyed on the wall.

He stared gloomily at his reflection: a tall man, fair of skin—*for a Cheysuli*, he thought, *though dark enough for a Homanan!*—with green eyes dilated dark and new bruises on his face.

Aileen's applications of wine had stiffened his hair. Kellin impatiently scrubbed a hand through it, taking care to avoid the crusting cut. The raven curls of youth were gone, banished by adulthood, but his hair still maintained a springy vigor. He scratched idly at his chest, disliking the tautness of the wrappings. The linen bandages stood out in stark relief against the nakedness of his torso.

Kellin stared at his reflection, then grinned as he recalled the cause of sore ribs. "And what of the thumbless thief?"

But the brief jolt of pleasure and vindication dissipated instantly. Luce was not important. Luce did not matter. Nothing at *all* mattered except the despair that welled up so keenly to squash his spirit flat.

Kellin turned from the plate abruptly. Better he not look; better he not *see*—

Emptiness overwhelmed, and the savage desire to tear down all the walls, brick by brick, so he could be free of them.

He burned with it. Cursing weakly, Kellin lurched to the narrow casement. Beyond lay Homana of the endless skies and meadows, the freedom of the air. He was confined by walls, oppressed by brickwork; every nerve in his body screamed its demand for freedom.

"Get out—" he blurted.

He needed desperately to get out, get free, get *loose*—

"Shadow," he murmured. "Half-man, hollow-man—" And then he squeezed shut his eyes as he dug fingers into stone. "I will *not* . . . will not be what they expect me to be—"

Cold stone bit into his brow, hurting his bruised face; he had pressed himself against the wall beside the window. Flame washed his flesh and set afire every nick, scratch, and cut. Rising bruises ached as blood throbbed in them, threatening to break through the fragile warding of his skin.

He paced because he could not help himself; he could not be still. A singing was in his blood, echoing clamorously. He paced and paced and paced, trying to suppress the singing, the overriding urge to squeeze himself through the narrow casement and fling himself into the air.

"—fall—" he muttered. "Fall and break all my bones—"

Hands fisted repeatedly: a cat flexing its claws, testing the power in his body, the urge to slash into flesh.

He sweated. Panted. Swore at capricious gods. He wanted to open the door, to tear it from its hinges, to shatter the wood completely and throw aside iron studs.

Kellin sat down on the stool and hugged bare arms against wrapped chest, ignoring the pain. He rocked and rocked and rocked: a child in need of succor; a spirit in need of release.

Tears ran down his face. "Too many—" he said. "Too *many* . . . I will not risk losing a *lir*—" Only to lose himself to an arcane Cheysuli ritual that robbed the world of another warrior despite his perfect health.

Lirless warriors went mad, he had been taught, as all Cheysuli were taught. Mad with the pain and the grief, the desperate emptiness.

"—mad *now*—" he panted. "Is this different?"

Perhaps not. Perhaps what he did now was invite the very madness he did not desire to risk in bonding with a *lir*.

Brickwork oppressed him. The walls and roof crushed his spirit.

"Out—" he blurted. But to go out was to surrender.

He rocked and rocked and rocked until he could rock no more; until he could not countenance sitting on the stool another moment and rose to pace again, to move from wall to wall, to stand briefly at the casement so as to test his will, to dare the desperate need that drove him to pace again, until he reached the door.

Unlocked. Merely latched. He need only *lift* the latch—

"No." A tremor wracked Kellin's body. He suppressed it. He turned away, jubilant in his victory, in the belief he had overcome it—and then felt his will crumble beneath the simplicity of sheer physical need.

It took but a moment: boots, doublet, russet wool cloak, long-knife. Emeralds winked in candlelight.

Kellin stared at the knife. Vision blurred: tears. Tears for the warrior who had once sworn by the blade, by his blood, by the *lir* whose death had killed him.

He thought of the words Blair had offered him a decade before.

It hurt. It *squeezed*, until no room was left for his heart; no room remained for his spirit.

"*Y'ja'hai*," Kellin breathed, then unlatched and jerked open the door.

He did not awaken the horse-boy sleeping in straw. He simply took a bridle, a horse—without benefit of blankets or saddle—and swung up bareback.

Pain thundered in Kellin's chest. He sat rigidly

straight, daring himself to give in as sweat trickled down his temples. Scrapes stung from the taste of salt, but he ignored them. A smaller pain, intrusive but less pronounced, reminded him of his offended netherparts, but that pain, too, he relegated to nothing in the face of his compulsion.

Winter hair afforded him a better purchase bareback than the summer season, when mounts were slick-haired and the subsequent ride occasionally precarious. It was precarious now, but not because of horsehair; a rider was required to adapt to his mount's movements by adjustments in body both large and small, maintaining flexibility above all else, but the skill was stripped from Kellin. With ribs bruised and tightly strapped, he was forced to sit bolt upright without bending his spine, or risk significant pain.

He knew the way so well: a side-gate in the shadows, tucked away in the wall; he had used it before. He used it now, leaving behind the outer bailey, then Mujhara herself as he rode straight through the city to the meadowlands beyond. The narrow track was hard footing in the cold, glinting with frost rime in the pallor of the moon.

No more walls— Kellin gritted his teeth. *No more stone and brick, no more streets and buildings—*

Indeed, no more. He had traded city for country, replacing cobbles with dirt and turf, and captivity for freedom.

But the emptiness remained.

If I give myself over to the lir-bond, I will be no different from any warrior whose promise to cheysula and children to care for them always is threatened by that very bond.

It seemed an odd logic to Kellin. How could one promise supersede the other, yet still maintain its worth? How could any warrior swear himself so profoundly to *lir* and family knowing very well one of the oaths might be as nothing?

For that matter, how could *cheysula* or child believe anything the warrior promised when it was made very clear in the sight of gods and clan that a *lir* came first always?

Kellin shook his head. *A selfish oath demanded from selfish gods—*

The horse stumbled. Jarred, sore ribs protested; fresh sweat broke on Kellin's brow and ran down his face. Cold air against dampness made him shiver convulsively, which set up fresh complaint.

He cast a glance at the star-freighted sky. *Revenge for my slight? That I dare to question such overweening dedication to you?*

The horse did not stumble again. If the gods heard, they chose not to answer.

Kellin, for his part, laughed—until the despair and emptiness shattered into pieces the dark humor of his doubts, reminding him once again that he was, if nothing else, subject to such whims as the gods saw fit to send him.

Merely because I am Cheysuli— He gripped the horse with both knees, clutching at reins. He recalled all too well what his grandsire had said regarding madness. He recalled even more clearly the wild grief in Blais' eyes as the warrior acknowledged a far greater thing than that he must give up his life; Tanni's death and the severing of the *lir*-bond had been, in that moment, the only thing upon which Blais could focus himself, though it promised his death as well.

Irony blossomed. *Certainly he focused nothing upon me, who had from him a blood-oath of service.*

One sworn to the gods, at that.

Kellin and his mount exchanged meadowlands for the outermost fringes of the forest. His passage stirred the woods into renewed life, startling

birds from branches and field warren from bur-
rows. Here the moon shone more fitfully, frag-
mented by branches. Kellin heard the sound of his
horse and his own breath expelled in pale smoke.
He pulled the russet cloak more closely around his
shoulders.

The horse stopped. It stood completely still, ears
erect. Its nostrils expanded hugely, fluttered, then
whuffed closed as he expelled a noisy snort of
alarm.

"Shansu—" Even as Kellin gathered rein to forestall him, the horse quivered from head to toe.

From the shadows just ahead came the heavy,
throaty coughing of a lion.

"Wait—" But even as Kellin clamped his legs,
the horse lunged sideways and bolted.

Seven

In the first awkward lunge, Kellin felt the slide of horsehair against breeches and the odd, unbalanced weightlessness of a runaway. With it came a twofold panic: first, the chance of injury; the second because of the lion.

He had ridden runaways before. He had fallen off of or been thrown from runaways before. It was a straightforward hazard of horsemanship regardless how skilled the rider, regardless how docile the horse. A horseman learned to halt a runaway mount with various techniques when footing afforded it; here, footing was treacherous, and vision nonexistent. This particular runaway—at night, in the dark, with customary reflexes obliterated by pain and disorientation—was far more dangerous than most.

Kellin's balance was off. He could not sit properly. He was forced to ride mostly upright, perching precariously, breaking the fluid melding of horse and rider. Vibrations of the flight, instead of dissipating in his body, reverberated painfully as the horse broke through tangled undergrowth and leapt fallen logs.

Branches snagged hair, slapped face, cut into Kellin's mouth. A clawing vine hooked the bridge of his nose and tore flesh. He felt something dig at one eye and jerked his head aside, cursing helplessly. *One misstep—*

He tried to let reflexes assume control, rather than trusting to himself. But reflexes were banished. His spine was jarred as the horse essayed a depression in the ground, which in turn jarred his ribs. Kellin sucked in a noisy breath and tried to ease his seat, to let the response of muscles to his mount's motion dictate the posture of his body, but failed to do so.

The horse stumbled, then dodged and lurched sideways as it shied from an unseen terror. Kellin blurted discomfort, biting into his cheek; he thought of snubbing the horse's nose back to his left knee in the classic technique, but the trees were too close, the foliage too dense. He had no leeway, no leverage.

The horse hesitated, then leapt again, clearing an unseen impediment. It seemed then to realize it bore an unwanted rider. Kellin felt the body shifting beneath his buttocks, away from clamping legs; then it bunched and twisted, elevating buttocks, and flung its rider forward.

Awkwardly Kellin slid toward the horse's head, dangling briefly athwart one big shoulder. Hands caught frenziedly at mane as he tried to drag himself upright, clutching at reins, digging in with left heel, but the horse ducked out from under him.

Kellin was very calm as he hung momentarily in the air. He was aware of weighty darkness, encroaching vines and branches, the utter physical incomprehensibility that he was unconnected to his mount—and the unhappy acknowledgment that when he landed momentarily it would hurt very much.

He tucked up as best he could, cursing strapped ribs. One shoulder struck the ground first. He rolled through the motion, smashing hip against broken branches shrouded in tangled fern, then flopped down onto his back as the protest of his ribs robbed him of control. He landed flat and very hard, human prey for the hidden treacheries of unseen ground.

For a moment there was no pain. It terrified him. He recalled all too clearly the old Homanan soldier who had taken a tumble from his horse in the bailey of the castle. The fall had not been bad; but as fellow soldiers—and Kellin with them—gathered to 'trade jests, it became clear that though old Tammis lived, his neck was broken. He would not walk again.

The panic engendered by that image served as catalyst for the bruised strength in legs and arms. Kellin managed one huge jerking contortion against broken boughs and fern. It renewed all the pain, but he welcomed it. Pain was proof he could yet move.

I will *walk again.* But just now, he was not certain he wanted to. Now that he *could* move he did not, but lay slack and very still against a painful cradle. He forced himself not to gasp but to draw shallow breaths through the wreckage of his chest.

When he at last had wind again, Kellin gasped out a lengthy string of the vilest oaths he knew in Homanan, Old Tongue, and Erinnish. It used up the breath he had labored so carefully to recover, but he felt it worth it. Dead men did not swear.

The horse was gone. Kellin did not at that moment care; he could not bear the thought of trying to mount. He wished the animal good riddance, suppressing the flicker of dismayed apprehension—a long and painful walk all the way to Mujhara—then set about making certain he was whole. Everything *seemed* to be, but he supposed he could not tell for certain until he got up from the ground.

Sound startled him into stillness. But a stride

or two away came the coughing grunt of beast, and the stink of its breath.

It filled Kellin's nostrils and set him to flight. It might be bear, mountain cat— He flailed, then stilled himself.

Lion?

It bore Corwyth's hallmark.

With effort Kellin pulled his elbows in to his sides and levered his torso upright, lifting a battered chest until he no longer lay squashed and helpless. "Begone," he said aloud, using the scorn of royalty. "You have no power over me."

The odor faded at once, replaced with the damp cold smells of winter. A man laughed softly from the shadows shielding the beast. "The lion may not," he said, "but be certain that *I* do."

Kellin's breath hissed between set teeth as Corwyth exited the shadows for the star-lighted hollow in which the prince lay. The Ihini wore dark leathers and a gray wool cloak. Pinned by a heavy knot of silver at one shoulder, the cloak glowed purple in the livid shadows of its folds.

Knowledge diminished pain; made it no longer important. "Corwyth the Lion. But the guise is now ineffective; I have learned what you are."

Corwyth affected a negligent shrug. "I am whatever it serves me—and my master—to be. For you, it was a lion." The Ihlini walked quietly toward Kellin, crackling no branches, snagging no vegetation. His hands were gloved in black. "Indeed, we heard of the small prince's fear of lions. It permitted us certain liberties, even though we were powerless within the palace itself. Fear alone can prove effective, as it did in your case. You believed. That belief has shaped you, Kellin; it has made you what you are in heart and spirit, and placed you here within my grasp."

Kellin longed to repudiate it, but he could not

speak. What Corwyth said was true. His own weakness had provided the Ihlini with a weapon.

The gloved hands spread, displaying tiny white flames that transformed themselves to pillars. They danced against Corwyth's palms. "Ian's death in particular was most advantageous. Your certainty that the Lion had killed him was unfounded—it was but a child's imagination gone awry, interpreting a passing comment into something of substance—but that substance, given life, nearly consumed you." The flames within his palms bathed Corwyth's smiling face with lurid illumination. His eyes were black pockets in a white-limned mask. "That, too, served, though it was none of ours. A fortuitous death, was Ian's. We could not have hoped for better."

Kellin stirred in protest, then suppressed a grunt of pain. He wanted very badly to rise and face the Ihlini as he would face a man, but pain ate at his bones. "Lochiel," he said.

Corwyth nodded. "The hand at last is outstretched. It beckons, Kellin. You are cordially invited to join your kinsman in the halls of Valgaard."

"Kinsman!"

Corwyth laughed. "You recoil as if wounded, my lord! But what else are you? Shall I recount your heritage?"

Kellin's silence was loud.

The Ihlini continued regardless. "Lochiel was Strahan's son. Strahan was Tynstar's son, who got him on Electra of Solinde. She was, at the time, married to Carillon and was therefore Queen of Homana; but her tastes lay with her true lord rather than the Mujhar who professed to be." White teeth shone briefly. "Strahan was her son. He was brother—*rujholli*?—to Aislinn, who bore Niall, who sired Brennan—and a multitude of others—who in turn sired Aidan. Your very own *jehan."* Corwyth nodded. "The line is direct, Kellin. You and Lochiel are indeed kinsmen, no matter what you might prefer."

Something slow and warm trickled into Kellin's eyes. He was bleeding—the cut Aileen had stanched? Or another, newer one?

Corwyth laughed. "Poor prince. So battered, so bruised . . . and so entirely helpless."

Kellin pressed himself up from the ground in a single painful lunge, jerking from its sheath the lethal Cheysuli long-knife. It fit his grasp so well, as if intended for him. *Blais could not have known—* He flipped it instantly in his hand and threw, arcing it cleanly across the darkness toward the Ihlini sorcerer. *My own brand of Tooth!*

But Corwyth put up a gloved hand now free of flames. The knife stopped in midair. Emerald eyes turned black.

"No!" Kellin's blurted denial was less of fear than of the knowledge of profanation. *Not Blais' long-knife!*

Corwyth plucked the weapon from the air. He studied it a moment, then tucked it away into his belt. His eyes were bright. "I have coveted one of these for a century. I thank you for your gift." The young-looking Ihlini smiled. "Without you, I might never have acquired one; Cheysuli warriors are, after all, well-protected by their *lir.*" Corwyth paused to consider. "But you lack a *lir* and therefore lack the protection. *Leijhana tu'sai,* my lord."

Kellin wavered. His fragile strength, born of panic and fury, was spent. Nothing was left to him, not even anger, nor fear. An outthrust hand earned him nothing but empty air, certainly little balance. Fingers closed, then the hand fell limply as Kellin bit into his lip to forestall collapse. He would not, *would not*, show such weakness to the Ihlini.

"Give in to it," Corwyth suggested gently. "I am not here to be cruel, Kellin . . . you paint us so, I know, and it is a personal grief; but there is no sense in maintaining such rigid and painful control merely out of pride."

The darkness thickened. Sorcery? Or exhaustion compounded by pain? "I am Cheysuli. I do not in any way, in words or deed or posture, even by implication, suggest that I am inferior to an Ihlini."

Corwyth laughed. "Inferior, no. Never. We are *equal*, my lord, in every sense of the word. Sired by the gods, we are now little more than petty children quarreling over a toy." His hand closed over the wolf-headed knife tucked into his belt. "Once, we might have been brothers. *Rujheldi*, as *we* say—is it not close to *rujholli*?" Corwyth did not smile. "Uncomfortably close, I see, judging by your expression. But it is too late now for anything more than enmity. The Cheysuli are too near fulfillment. The time is now to stop the prophecy before it can be completed. Before *you*, my Cheysuli *rujheldi*, can be permitted to sire a child upon an Ihlini woman."

Kellin wanted very much to spit. He did not because he thought it was time he showed self-restraint. He, who had so little. With careful disdain, he asked, "Do you believe I would so soil my manhood as to permit it entry into the womb of the netherworld?"

Corwyth laughed. It was a genuine sound kiting into darkness. It stirred birds from a nearby tree and reawakened Kellin's apprehension. "A man is a fool to trust to taste and preference in a matter so important. I recite to you your own history, Kellin: Rhiannon, Lillith's daughter, sired by Ian himself—"

"Ian was tricked. He was bespelled. He was *lirless*, and therefore helpless."

"—and Brennan, your grandsire, who lay with Rhiannon and sired the halfling Ihlini woman at whose breast you suckled."

Kellin's belly clenched. "My grandsire was seduced."

"But *you* are above such things?" Corwyth shook his head. "A single birth, Kellin . . . a single seed of yours sowed in fertile Ihlini soil, and the thing is done." His eyes were black and pitiless in the frosted darkness. "We are not all of us sworn to Asar-Suti. There are those Ihlini who would, to throw us down, try very hard to insure the child was conceived. The prophecy is not dependent upon *whose* blood mingles with yours, merely that it be Ihlini."

Kellin summoned the last of waning strength. In addition to battered chest, a hip and shoulder ached. Welts and scratches stung. Bravado was difficult. "So, will you kill me here?"

Corwyth smiled. "You are meant for Lochiel's disposition."

Kellin dredged up scorn. "If you mean to take me to Valgaard, you will do it against my will. That much you cannot take from me, *lirless* or no."

"That may be true," Corwyth conceded, "but there are other methods. And all of them equally efficient."

He gestured. From the shadows walked two cloaked men and a saddled horse. Kellin looked at them, looked at the mount, and knew what they meant to do.

"A long ride," Corwyth said, "and as painful as I can make it." He glanced to the horse, then looked back at Kellin. "How long do you think you can last?"

Eight

Kellin awoke with his mouth full of blood. He gagged, spat it out, felt more flow in sluggishly from the cut on the inside of his cheek. Pressure pounded in his head. It roused him fully, so that he could at last acknowledge the seriousness of his situation.

Corwyth's companions had flung him belly-down across the saddle, little more than a battered carcass shaped in the form of a man. Ankles were tied to the right stirrup, wrists to the left. The position was exceedingly uncomfortable; the binding around his ribs had loosened with abuse and provided no support.

He recalled his defiant challenge: Cheysuli to Ihlini. He recalled losing that challenge, though little of anything afterward; the pain had robbed him of consciousness. Now consciousness was back. He wished it were otherwise.

Kellin gagged and coughed again, suppressing the grunt of pain that exited his throat and was trapped with deliberate effort behind locked teeth. Regardless of the discomfort, despite the incipient rebellion of his discontented belly, he would not disgrace himself by losing that belly's contents in front of an Ihlini.

A thought intruded: *Had I listened to my grandsire*— But Kellin cut it off. Self-recrimination merely added to misery.

The horse moved on steadily with its Cheysuli burden. Every stride of the animal renewed Kellin's discomfort. He wanted very much to sit upright, to climb down from the horse, to lie down quietly and let his headache subside. But he could do none of those things.

A crackling of underbrush forwarned him of company as a horse fell in beside him. Kellin's limited head-down view provided nothing more of the world than stirrup leather and horsehair.

Then Corwyth spoke, divulging identity. "Awake at last, my lord? You have slept most of the night."

Slept? I have been in more comfortable beds. Kellin lifted his head. His skull felt heavy, too heavy; it took effort to hold it up. The light now was better; he could see the Ihlini plainly. Dawn waited impatiently just outside the doorflap.

Corwyth smiled. There was no derision in his tone, no contempt in his expression. "One would hardly recognize you. A bath would undoubtedly benefit. Would you care to visit a river?"

The thought of being dumped into an ice-cold river bunched the flesh of Kellin's bones. He suppressed a shiver with effort and made no answer.

The Ihlini's smile widened. "No, that would hardly do. You might sicken from it, and die . . . and then my lord would be very wroth with me." Blue eyes glinted. "I pity you, Kellin. I have seen Lochiel's anger before, and the consequences of it."

Kellin's mouth hurt. "Lochiel has tried to throw down my House before." It was mostly a croak; he firmed his voice so as not to sound so diminished. "Why do you believe he will succeed this time?"

"He has you," Corwyth said simply.

"You have me," Kellin corrected. "And I would

not count a Cheysuli helpless while his heart still beats."

Russet brows arched. "Shall I stop it, then? To be certain of my safety? To convince you, perhaps, that you are indeed helpless despite your Cheysuli bravado?"

Kellin opened his mouth to retort but found no words would come. Corwyth's gloved hand was extended, fingers slack. They curled slowly inward.

There was no pain. Just a vague breathlessness that increased as the fingers closed, and a constriction in his chest that banished the ache of his ribs because this was much worse. Bruised ribs, even cracked ones, offered little danger when a man's heart was threatened.

Kellin stirred in protest, but his bonds held firm. The horse walked on, led by Corwyth's minions. The Ihlini's fingers closed.

He felt each of them: four fingers and a thumb, distinct and individual. Each was inside his chest. They touched him intimately, caressing the very muscle that kept him alive.

It was, he thought, rape, if of a very different nature.

Kellin desired very much to protest, to cry out, to shout, to swear, to scream imprecations. But his mouth would not function. Hands and feet were numb. He thought the pressure in his head might cause his eyes and ears to burst.

He could not *breathe*.

Corwyth's hand squeezed.

Kellin thrashed once, expelling breath and blood in a final futile effort to escape the hand in his chest.

"Your lips are blue," Corwyth said. "It is not a flattering color."

Nothing more was left. *Piece of meat—*

It was, Kellin felt, a supremely inelegant way to die.

Then the hand stilled his heart, and he *was* dead.

Kellin roused as Corwyth grabbed a handful of hair and jerked his head up. "Do you see?" the Ihlini asked. "Do you understand now?"

He understood only that he had been dead, or very close to it. He sucked in a choking breath, trying to fill flaccid lungs. The effort was awkward, spasmodic, so that he recognized only the muted breathy roaring of a frightened man trying desperately to breathe.

I am frightened— And equally desperate; he felt intensely helpless, and angry because of it. Lochiel's ambassador had humiliated him in the most elemental of ways: by stripping a Cheysuli of freedom, strength, and pride.

"Say it again," Corwyth suggested. "Say again Lochiel cannot throw down your House."

Kellin said nothing. He could not manage it.

The hand was cruel in his hair. Neck tendons protested. "You have seen nothing. *Nothing*, Kellin. I am proud, but practical; I admit my lesser place without hesitation or compunction. The power I command is paltry compared to his."

Paltry enough to kill him with little more than a gesture.

Corwyth released his hair. Kellin's neck was too weak to support his skull. It flopped down again, pressing face against winter horsehair. He breathed in its scent, grateful that he could.

"Think on it," Corwyth said. "Consider your circumstances, and recall that your life depends entirely upon the sufferance of Lochiel."

Kellin rather thought his life depended entirely on his ability to breathe, regardless of Lochiel's intentions. As he lay flopped across the saddle, he concentrated merely on in- and exhalations. Lochiel could wait.

When they cut him from the horse and dragged him down, Kellin wondered seriously if death might be less painful. He bit into his tongue to keep from disgracing himself further by verbal protestation, but the sudden sheen of perspiration gave his weakness away. Corwyth saw it, weighed it, then nodded to himself.

"Against the tree," the Ihlini ordered his companions.

The two hauled Kellin bodily to the indicated tree and left him at its foot to contemplate exposed roots as he fought to maintain consciousness. Sweat ran freely, dampening his hair. He lay mostly on one side. His wrists, though now cut free of the stirrup, were still tied together. He no longer was packed by horseback like so much fresh-killed meat, but the circumstances seemed no better.

Kellin blew grit from his lips. The taste in his mouth was foul, but he had been offered no water.

The sun was full up. They had been riding for hours without a single stop. In addition to the residual aches of the Midden battle and the discomfort of the ride, Kellin's bladder protested. It was a small but signal irritant that compounded his misery.

Kellin eased himself into a sitting position against the tree trunk. He sagged minutely, testing the fit of his ribs inside their loosened wrappings and bruised flesh, then let wood provide false strength; his own was negligible.

I am young, strong, and fit . . . this is a minor inconvenience. Meanwhile, he hurt.

Corwyth strode from his own mount to Kellin,

who could not suppress a recoil as the Ihlini touched the binding around his wrists. "There, my lord: freedom." The wrappings fell away. Corwyth smiled. "Test us as you like."

Kellin wanted to spit into the arrogant face. Corwyth knew *he* knew there was no reason to test. No man, Cheysuli or not, would risk his heart a second time to Ihlini magic.

"Are you hungry? Thirsty?" Corwyth gestured, and one of his companions answered with a wrapped packet and leather flask delivered to Kellin at once. "Bread, and wine. Eat. Drink." Corwyth paused. "And if you refuse, be certain I shall make you."

Immediately Kellin conjured a vision of his own hands made by sorcery to stuff his mouth full of bread until he choked on it. His heart had been stopped once; better to eat and drink as bidden than risk further atrocity.

With hands made stiff and clumsy by the weight of too much blood, he unwrapped the parcel. It was a lumpy, tough-crusted loaf of Homanan journey-bread. He set it aside carefully, ignoring Corwyth's interest, and unstoppered the flask. Without hesitation—he would give nothing to the Ihlini, not even distrust—he put the flask to his cut lips and poured wine down his throat.

It stung the inside of his mouth. Kellin drank steadily, then restoppered the flask. "A poor vintage," he commented. "Powerful you may be, but you have no knowledge of wine."

Corwyth grinned. "Bait me, my lord, and you do so at your peril."

Kellin stared steadily back. "Unless you heal me, Lochiel may well wonder what you have done to render his valuable kinsman so bruised."

Corwyth rose. "Lochiel knows you better than that. Everyone in Homana—*and* Valgaard—has heard of the Midden exploits undertaken by the Prince of Homana.''

Midden exploits. He detested the words. He detested even more Lochiel's knowledge of them. To forestall his own comment, he put bread into his mouth.

"Eat quickly," Corwyth said. "We ride again almost immediately."

Kellin glared at him. "Then why stop at all?"

"Why, to keep you and anyone else from claiming me inhumane!" With a glint in blue eyes, the young-seeming Ihlini turned away to his mount, then paused and turned back. "Would you like me to help you rise so you may relieve yourself?"

Kellin's face caught fire. Every foul word he knew crowded into his mouth, which prevented him from managing to expell even one.

"Come now," Corwyth said, "it is an entirely natural thing. And, as you are injured—"

"No," Kellin declared.

Blue eyes glinted again. "Hold onto the tree, my lord. It might help you to stand up."

Kellin desired nothing more than to ignore the suggestion entirely. But to do so was foolish in the face of his need. Pride stung, but so did his bladder.

"I will turn my back," Corwyth offered. "Your condition presupposes an inability to escape."

The comment naturally triggered an urge to prove Corwyth wrong, but Kellin knew better than to try. If the Ihlini could play with his heart, Kellin had no desire to risk a threat to anything else.

"Hurry," Corwth suggested. He turned away in an elaborate swirl of heavy cloak.

"Ku'reshtin," Kellin muttered.

Silence answered him.

*   *   *

Corwyth's companions escorted Kellin to his horse when it was time to ride on. Corwyth met him there. "You may ride upright, if you like. Surely it will prove more comfortable than being tied onto a saddle."

Kellin gritted teeth. "What will it cost me?"

"Nothing at all, I think—save perhaps respect for my magic." Corwyth caught Kellin's wrists before he could protest. The Ihlini gripped tightly, crossed one wrist over the other, and pressed until the bones ached in protest. "Flesh into flesh, Kellin. Nothing so common as rope, nor so heavy as iron, but equally binding." He took his hands away, and Kellin saw the flesh of his wrists had been seamlessly fused together.

Gods— Immediately he tried to wrench his wrists apart but could no more do that than rip an arm from his body. His wrists had *grown* together at the bidding of the Ihlini.

He could not help himself: he gaped. Like a child betrayed, he stared at his wrists in disbelief so utterly overwhelming he could think of nothing else.

My own flesh— It sent a shudder of repulsion through his body. *My heart, now this . . . what will Lochiel do?*

"A simple thing," Corwyth said easily. Then he signaled to his companions. "Help him to mount his horse. I doubt he will resist." Corwyth moved away, then hesitated as if in sudden thought, and swung back. "If he does, I shall seal his eyelids together."

They rode north, toward the Bluetooth River, where they would cross into the Northern Wastes and then climb over the Molon Pass down into Solinde, the birthplace of the Ihlini, and on to Valgaard itself. Kellin had heard tales of the Ihlini fortress and knew it housed the Gate of Asar-Suti. It was, Brennan had said, the Ihlini version of the Womb of the Earth deep in the foundations of Homana-Mujhar.

Kellin rode upright with precise, careful posture, trying to keep his torso very still. His legs conformed to the shape of saddle and horse, but his hands did not control the horse. The reins had been split so that each of Corwyth's companions—*minions?*—led the prisoner's mount. Corwyth rode ahead.

They kept to the forest tracks, avoiding main roads that would bring them into contact with those who might know the Prince of Homana. Kellin doubted anyone would recognize him. His face was welted and bruised, his lower lip split and swollen. He stank of dried sweat mixed with a film of grit and soil, and leaves littered his hair. Little about him now recommended his rank.

Snow crackled in deep shadows, breaking up beneath shod hooves. As afternoon altered to evening, the temperature dropped. Kellin shrugged more deeply into his cloak as his breath fogged the air.

When at last they halted, it was nearly full dark. Kellin was so sore and weary he thought he might topple off the horse if he so much as turned his head. *Let them see none of it.* Slowly he kicked free of stirrups, slung a leg across the saddle, and slid from his mount before the Ihlini could signal him down; a small rebellion, but successful.

He made no attempt to escape because to try was sheerest folly. Better to bide his time until his strength returned, then wait for the best moment. Just now all he could do was stand.

Kellin leaned against the horse a moment to steady himself, flesh cold beneath a film of newborn perspiration. He shivered. Disorientation broke up

the edge of consciousness. Weariness, perhaps—
*Or—? He stilled. *Sorcery? Corwyth's attempt to
tease me?*

One of the minions put his hand on Kellin's
shoulder; he shrugged it off at once. The rebuke
came easily in view of who received it. "No one is
permitted to touch the Prince of Homana without
his leave."

Corwyth, dropping off his own mount, laughed
in high good humor. "Feeling better, are we?"

Kellin felt soiled by the minion's touch. An urge
to bare his teeth in a feral snarl was suppressed
with effort. He swung from the black-eyed man,
displaying a taut line of shoulder.

Corwyth pointed. "There."

Kellin lingered a moment beside his horse. His
head felt oddly packed and tight, so that the Ihlini's order seemed muted. A second shiver wracked
his body, jostling aching bones. *Not just cold—
more—*

"Sit him down," Corwyth said, but before the
minion could force the issue, Kellin sat down by
himself. "Better." Corwyth tended his own mount
as his companions tended Kellin's.

Kellin itched. It had nothing to do with bruises
and scrapes, because the itching wasn't in his skin
but in his blood. Flesh-bound hands flexed, curling
fingers into palms, then snapping out straight
again.

He could not eat, though they gave him bread,
nor could he drink, because his throat refused to
swallow. Once again he leaned against a tree, but
this time he needed its support even more than
before. He felt as if all his bones were soft,
stripped of rigidity. His spirit was as flaccid.

He shifted against wood, grimaced in discomfort, then shifted again. He could not be still.

Just like in Homana-Mujhar. He fixed his eyes on

Corwyth, who sat quietly by a small fire. "Was it you who drove me from the palace?"

"Drove you?"

"With sorcery. Was it you?"

Corwyth shrugged. "That required neither magic nor skill. I know your habits. You gamble, you drink, you whore. All it required was the proper time."

Kellin shifted again, hiding flesh-bound wrists beneath a fold of his cloak because to look on them was too unsettling. "You set the trap. I put myself into it."

The Ihlini smiled. "A happy accident. It did save time."

"Accident? Or my *tahlmorra*?"

That provoked a response. "You believe the gods might have planned this? This?" Corwyth's surprise was unfeigned. "Would the Cheysuli gods risk the final link in the prophecy so willingly?"

Kellin scowled. "Who can say what the gods would do? I despise them . . . they have done me little good."

Corwyth laughed and fed a stick to the flames. "Then perhaps this *is* their doing, if you and the gods are on such bad terms."

Kellin shivered again. "If Lochiel knows so much about me, surely he knows I have already sired children. Why kill me now? Before, certainly—to prevent the precious seed from being sown—but now it is too late. The seed is well sowed."

"Three children," Corwyth agreed. "But all bastards, and none with the proper blood. Halfling brats gotten on Homanan whores." He shrugged elegantly. "Lochiel only fears the Firstborn child."

Kellin stilled. Was it a weapon? "Lochiel is afraid?"

Corwyth's expression was solemn. "Only a fool

would deny he fears this outcome. I fear it. Lochiel fears it. Even the Seker fears fulfillment." Flames illuminated his face. It was starkly white in harsh light, black in hollowed contours. "Have you never thought what fulfillment will bring?"

Kellin laughed. "A beginning for the Cheysuli. An ending for the Ihlini."

Flames consumed wood. A pine knot cracked, shedding sparks. Corwyth now was solemn. "In your ignorance, you are certain."

"Of course I am certain. It has been promised us for centuries."

"By the very gods you despise." Corwyth did not smile, nor couch his words in contempt. "If that is true, how then can you honor their prophecy?"

Kellin licked a numb lip. His body rang with tension, as if he were a harp string wound much too taut on its pegs. "I am Cheysuli."

"*That* is your answer?" Corwyth shook his head. "Perhaps you are more Cheysuli than you believe, even *lirless* as you are. Only fools such as your people dedicate themselves to the fulfillment of a mandate that will destroy everything they know."

Kellin's mouth twisted. "I have heard that old tale before. When the Ihlini cannot win through murder or sorcery, they turn to words. You mean to undermine our customs."

"Of *course* I do!" Corwyth snapped. "And if you had any wit to see it, you would understand why. Indeed, the prophecy will destroy Ihlini such as myself . . . but it will also destroy the Cheysuli." He extended an empty hand. "The prophecy of the Firstborn will close its fist around the heart of the Cheysuli, just as I did yours, and stop it." He shut his hand. "Just like this."

It was immediate. "No." Kellin twitched, then rolled his head against bark. "You play with words, Ihlini."

"This is not play. This is truth. You see me as I am: a man, not an Ihlini, but simply a *man* who fears the ending of his race in the ascendancy of another."

"Mine," Kellin agreed.

"No." Corwyth placed another stick on the fire. His gloved hand shook. "The ascendancy is that of the Firstborn." In firelight his eyes were hidden by deep pockets of shadow. "Your child. Your son. When he accepts the Lion, the new order replaces the old."

"*Your* order."

Corwyth smiled faintly. "Tell me," he said, "is your prophecy complete? No—I do not speak of the words all of you mouth." His tone was ironic. " 'One day a man of all blood shall unite, in peace, four warring realms and two magical races.' What I speak of is the prophecy *itself* in its entirety. It was passed down century after century, was it not?"

"The *shar tahls* make certain of that."

"But do they know the whole of it? Do they have record of it?"

"Written down?" Kellin frowned. "Such things can be lost if not entrusted to *shar tahls* in an oral tradition."

Corwyth nodded. "Such things *were* lost, Kellin. I know very well what the *shar tahls* teach are mere fragments . . . pieces of yarn woven together into a single skein. Because that is all they know. In the schism that split the Firstborn into Cheysuli and Ihlini, very little was left of the dogma on which your future hangs." He shook his head. "You know nothing of what may come, yet you serve it blindly. *We* are not such fools."

Kellin said nothing.

The Ihlini pulled his dark cloak more closely around his shoulders. "This profits nothing. I will

leave it to my lord to prove what I say is true."
Corwyth glanced at his companions. "I will leave
it to Lochiel, and to Asar-Suti."

Kellin shivered. *Lochiel will kill me. Not for myself. For the child. For the seed in my loins.*

In the scheme of the gods he detested, it seemed
he counted for very little.

Nine

Kellin watched the three Ihlini prepare to sleep. Though his wrists remained sealed, he was certain something more would be done to insure he could not escape. Perhaps Corwyth *would* seal his eyelids, or stop his heart again.

But Corwyth did not even look at his captive. The sorcerer quietly went about his business, pacing out distances. Each time he halted, he sketched something in the air. The rune glowed briefly purple, then died away.

Wards, Kellin knew. To keep him in, and others out.

He watched them lie down in their cloaks. Three dark-shrouded men, sorcerers all, who served a powerful god no sane man could possibly honor.

Unless there is something to what Corwyth says. But Kellin shut off the thought. Corwyth's declarations of a separate Ihlini prophecy—or of the Cheysuli one entire—was nothing but arrant nonsense designed to shake Kellin's confidence.

But one telling question had been posed. *How do I justify serving the prophecy for gods I cannot honor?*

Kellin shivered. He did not attempt to sleep. He sat against the tree, wrists still bound by flesh, and tried to think himself warm, tried to ease his mind so it did not trouble itself with questionings of Cheysuli customs.

But why not? It was a Cheysuli custom that killed Blais, not an Ihlini.

Heresy.

Is it?

Kellin inhaled carefully, held his breath a moment as he expanded cramped lungs, then blew the air out again in a steady, hissing stream. He stared across the dying fire to the three cloaked shapes beyond. To Corwyth in particular. Kellin knew very well the Ihlini worked merely to undermine his own convictions, which would in turn undermine a spirit that might yet protest its captivity; he was not stupid enough to believe there was no motive in Corwyth's contentions. But his mind was overactive, his thoughts too restless; even when he tried to think of nothing at all, an overabundance of *somethings* filled his head.

It is a long journey to Valgaard. The trick is to lure them into a false sense that I will attempt nothing.

A mountain cat screamed. The nearness of the sound was intensely unnerving. Kellin sat bolt upright and immediately regretted it. He reached for his knife and realized belatedly he had none, nor the freedom of hands to use it.

The scream came again from closer yet, shearing through darkness and foliage. Corwyth and the others, too, were up, shaking cloaks back from shoulders and arms. Corwyth said something in a low voice to the others—Kellin heard Lochiel's name mentioned—then scribed a shape in the air. Runes flared briefly, then went down. Corwyth's men were free to hunt.

Kellin could not remain seated. He climbed awkwardly to his feet and waited beside the tree. The cat's voice lacked the deep-chested timbre of the lion's, but its determination and alien sound echoed the beast that had haunted so much of Kellin's life.

Corwyth spared him a glance, as if to forestall any attempt on Kellin's part to escape. But Kellin was no more inclined to risk meeting the cat than he was to prompt Corwyth to use more sorcery on him.

The Ihlini bent and put new kindling on the fire, then waved a negligent hand; flames came to life. "The noise is somewhat discomfiting," he commented, "but even a mountain cat is not immune to sorcery. I will have a fine pelt to present my master."

It seemed an odd goal to Kellin, in view of his own value and Lochiel's desire for his immediate company. "You would take the time to kill and skin a cat?"

"Lochiel has an affinity for mountain cats. He says they are the loveliest and most dangerous of all the predators. Fleet where a bear is slow; more devious than the wolf; more determined than a boar. And armed far more effectively than any man alive." Corywth smiled. "He keeps them in Valgaard, in cages beneath the ground."

A fourth scream sounded closer yet. Even Corwyth got to his feet.

A shudder wracked Kellin. "What is—" he grittened his teeth against another assault. "—*ku'reshtin*—" he managed. "What threat do I offer?"

Corwyth cast him a glance. "What inanities do you mouth?"

A third shudder shook him. Kellin gasped. His bones were on fire. "What are you—"

Lir, said a voice, *the wards are down. I have done what I could to lead the others astray. Now it is up to you.*

He understood then. "No!" Kellin cried. "I want none of you!"

I am your only escape.

Corwyth laughed. "You may want none of me, but I have you nevertheless."

Kellin was not talking for the Ihlini's benefit. What consumed him now was the knowledge his *lir* was near. If he gave in, it would win. And he would be no freer than any other Cheysuli bound by oaths and service.

He wavered on his feet. *I renounced you. I want no part of you.*

Would you rather go to Valgaard and let Lochiel destroy you? The tone was crisp. *His methods are not subtle.*

His spirit screamed with need. The *lir* was close, so close—he had only to give in, to permit the channel to be opened that would form a permanent link.

He repudiated it. *I will not permit it.*

Then die. Allow the Ihlini to win. Remove from the line of succession the prince known as Kellin, and destroy the prophecy.

He gritted his teeth. *I will not pay your price.*

There is no other escape.

It infuriated him. Kellin brought his flesh-bound hands into the moonlight. *A test, then,* he challenged.

The *lir* sighed. *You believe too easily what the Ihlini tells you to. His art is in illusion. Banish this one as you banished the lion.*

Kellin stared hard at his wrists. The skin altered, flowing away, and his wrists were free of themselves.

Corwyth marked the movement. He turned sharply, saw the truth, and jerked the knife from his belt.

"The wards are down," Kellin said, "and your minions bide elsewhere. Now it is you and I."

You will have to kill him, lir. He will never let you go.

"Go away," Kellin said. "I want nothing to do with you."

Corwyth laughed. "Is this your attempt at escape? To bait me with babbled nonsense?"

You must kill him.

He wanted to shout at the *lir*. *He is armed*, Kellin said acidly. *He is also Ihlini.*

And has recourse to no arts now that I am here.

We have not bonded. I will not permit it.

The tone was implacable. *Then die.*

"Come out!" Kellin shouted. "By the gods, I will fight you both!"

Corwyth's laughter grated. "Have you gone mad? Or do you use this to bait me?"

Distracted by a battle fought on two fronts, Kellin glared. "I need no *lir* for you. I will take you as a man."

"Do try," Corwyth invited. "Or shall I stop your heart again?"

He cannot, the *lir* declared. *While I am here, such power is blunted.*

Then why do I hear you? Near an Ihlini, the link is obscured.

You forget who you are. There is that within you that breaks certain rules.

"My blood?" Kellin jeered. "Aye, always the blood!"

Old Blood is powerful. You have it in abundance. The voice paused. *Have you not read the birthlines lately?*

"Do you want your blood spilled?" Corwyth asked. "I can do that for you ... Lochiel will not punish me for that."

Kill him, the *lir* said. *You are weary and injured. He will defeat you even without sorcery.*

Kellin laughed. *With what? My teeth?*

Those are your weapons, among others. The tone

was dryly amused. *But mostly there is your blood. If a man's form does not serve, take on another.*

Yours? But I do not even know what animal you are!

You have heard me. Now hear me again. The scream of a mountain cat filled the darkness but a handful of paces away.

Corwyth's face blanched. "I am Ihlini!" he cried. "You have no power here!"

Show him, it said. *Let him see what you are.*

Kellin was desperate. "How?"

Forget you are a man. Become a cat instead.

Kellin looked at Corwyth. The knife in the Ihlini's hand had belonged to Blais. Kellin wanted it back.

Corwyth laughed. "You and I, then."

Kellin was angry, so angry he could hardly hold himself still. His bones buzzed with newfound energy and flesh hardened itself over tensing muscle and tendon. He shook with the urge to shred the Ihlini into a pile of cracked bone and bloodied flesh.

A beginning, the *lir* said.

And then he understood—to accomplish what was required he must shed all knowledge of human form, all human instincts. Anger could help that. Anger could assist him.

I want Corwyth dead. I want the knife back.

There is only one way to gain what you desire. I have given you the key. Now you must open the door.

To what future?

To the one you make.

"Come, then," Corwyth said. "I will shatter all your bones, then knit them together again. Lochiel need never know."

Kellin smiled. He forgot about his ribs and all the other nagging pains. He thought about *lir-*

shape instead. He thought about mountain cats, and the instincts that served them.

"You cannot," Corwyth declared. "This is a trick."

Kellin laughed. "Do you forget who I am? You know so much about me and the others of my House—surely you recall that we claim the Old Blood." He paused. "With all of its special gifts."

Corwyth lunged. He was quick, very quick, and exceedingly supple. Kellin dodged the outthrust knife with no little effort or pain, then ducked a second thrust.

Concentrate, the *lir* commanded. *Fingers and toes are claws. Flesh is thickly furred. The body is lean and fit. Jaws are heavy and powerful, filled with tongue and teeth. All you desire is the taste of his flesh in your mouth—his blood spilling from his throat into yours—and the hot sweet scent of his death.*

The knife nearly caught his side. Kellin twisted, grimacing as ribs protested.

Mountain cat, it said. *Far superior to any beast bred by god or demon.*

Kellin rolled as Corwyth struck a third time. He panted audibly, trying to divorce his mind from his body, to let his instincts dictate motion.

Now.

Anger fed his strength. Kellin saw the glint of the knife in Corwyth's hand—*Blais' knife!*—and then, briefly, everything faded. The world was turned inside out, and when it came right again it was a very different place.

His mouth dropped open to curse the Ihlini, but what issued forth was a rising, angry wail. He felt the coiling of haunches to gather himself; the whip of a sinuous tail; the tightness in his empty—*too empty!*—belly. Kellin bunched, and sprang.

The knife glinted again. Kellin reached out in

midair with a hind leg and slashed the weapon from Corwyth's hand. He heard the Ihlini's cry, and then Kellin was on him.

Corwyth went down easily. Lost in the killing frenzy, Kellin did not think about what he did. He simply closed powerful jaws on the fragile throat of a man and tore it away.

There was no sense of jubilation, vindication, or relief. Merely satiation as the cat fed on the prey's body.

Ten

What am I—? Comprehension was immediate. Kellin hurled himself away from the body on the ground. No more the cat but a man, appalled by what had occurred. *Gods—I did THAT?*

Corwyth was messily dead. He lay sprawled on the ground with blood-soaked cloak bunched up around him, gaping throat bared to the moon.

I did.

He was shaking. All over. He was bloodied to the elbows. Blood soaked his doublet. Blood was in his mouth. *Everywhere, blood*—and the taste of Corwyth's flesh.

Kellin thrust himself from the ground to his knees, then bent and hugged sore ribs as his belly purged itself. He wanted very much to purge his mind as well, to forget what he had seen, to forget what he had *done*, but the memory was livid. It excoriated him.

He scrubbed again and again at his face, trying to rid it of blood, but his hands, too, were bloody. Frantically Kellin scooped up double handfuls of dirt and damp leaves and scoured hands, then face, pausing twice to spit.

Lir.

Kellin jumped. He spun on his knees, panting, bracing himself on one stiff arm, and searched avidly for the mountain cat who had driven him beyond self. There was no sound. No cat. He saw nothing but star-weighted darkness and the scalloped outline of dense foliage.

Gone. Breathing steadied. He scraped the back of a hand across his chin. Fingers shook.

Lir. The tone was gentle. *The death was required. Just as the deaths of the minions were required.*

"You killed them?"

They are dead.

He barked a hoarse laugh. "Then you have broken one of the most binding rules of the *lir*-bond. You are not supposed to kill Ihlini."

The tone was peculiar. *We are reflections of one another.*

"What does *that* mean?"

You do that which you are commanded not to do. And now I as well.

It astounded him. "Because of *me* you broke the rule?"

We are very alike.

He contemplated that. He knew himself to be a rebel; could a *lir* be so also? If so, they were indeed well matched.

He cut it off at once. "I want nothing to do with you."

It is done. The men are dead.

Kellin stiffened. He refused to look at Corwyth's body. "There was no warning—you said nothing of what I would feel!"

You felt as a cat feels.

"But I am a *man*."

More, it said. *Cheysuli.*

Kellin spat again, wishing he had the strength of will to scour his mouth as well as his flesh. A quick glance across the tiny campsite offered relief: Ihlini supplies laid out in a neat pile.

"Water." He pressed himself from the ground and walked unsteadily to the supplies. He found a leather flask and unstoppered it, then methodically rinsed his mouth and spat until the taste of blood and flesh was gone. As carefully, he poured the contents of a second flask into one hand and then the other, scraping flesh free of sticky blood with cold, damp leaves.

"*I'toshaa-ni,*" he murmured, and then realized that the ritual merely emphasized the heritage that had led him to this.

Dripping, Kellin rose again. He made himself look. The view was no better: a sprawled, stilled body with only the pallor of vertebrae glistening in the ruin of a throat.

He shuddered. "I renounced you," he declared. "I made it very plain. Now more than ever it is imperative that I do not bond with a *lir.* If *that* is what it means—"

"That" was necessary. "That" was required.

"No." He would not now speak inside his head but say it as a man, so there existed no doubt as to who—and what—he was. "It was butchery, no more."

It was to save your life. The tone was terse, as if the *lir* suppressed a great emotion. *What the Ihlini do, they do to preserve their power. Lochiel would have killed you. Or gelded you.*

"Gelded—"

Do you think he would permit you to breed? You are his ending. The moment your son is born, the world begins anew.

Kellin wiped damp hands across his face, warping it out of shape as if self-inflicted violence would banish acknowledgment. "I want nothing to do with this."

It is too late.

"No. Not if I renounce you, as I have. Not if I refuse to bond with you."

Too late, the *lir* repeated. The tone now was muted.

Suspicion flared. He had been taught to honor all *lir*, but at this moment, conversing with this *lir*, he was afraid to assume it beneficent. "Why?" Alarm replaced suspicion. "What have you done?"

It was necessary.

It filled him with apprehension. "What have you done?"

Lent you a piece of myself.

"You!"

Required, it insisted. *Without that part of me, you would never have accomplished the shapechange.*

A shudder wracked Kellin from head to foot. The flesh on his scalp itched as if all his hairs stood up. "Tell me," he said intently. "Tell me what I have become."

Silence answered him.

"Tell me!" Kellin shouted. "By the gods, you beast, *what have you done to me?*"

The tone was odd. *Why does a man swear by gods he cannot honor?*

The inanity amazed him. "If I could see you—"

Then see me. A shadow moved at the edge of the trees. *See me as I am. Know who Sima is.*

A soft rustle, then nothing more. In the reflection of dying flames, gold eyes gleamed.

Kellin nearly gaped. "You are little more than a *cub*!"

Young, Sima conceded. *But old enough for a lir.*

"But—" Kellin blurted a choked laugh, then cut it off. "I want nothing to do with you. With you, or with any of it. No *lir*, no bonding, no shapechange. I want a full life . . . not a travesty always threatened by an arcane ritual that needlessly wastes a warrior."

Sima blinked. *I would die if you died. The cost is equally shared.*

"I do not *want* to share it! I want not to risk it at all."

A tail twitched. She was black, black as Sleeta, the Mujhar's magnificent *lir*. But she was small, as yet immature, gangly as a half-grown kitten. Incongruity, Kellin thought, in view of her intransigence.

I am empty, Sima said. *I am but a shadow. Do you sentence me to that?*

"Can I? I thought you said it was too late."

Gold eyes winked out, then opened again. *If you wish to renounce me, you may. But then the Ihlini will be victorious, because both of us will die.*

She did not sound young. She sounded ineffably old. "Sima." Kellin wet his lips. "What have you done to me?"

The sleek black head lowered. Tufted ears flattened. The tail whipped a branch to shreds.

"Sima!"

Caused you to change before the balance was learned.

Kellin's mouth felt dry. "And that is a bad thing?"

If balance is lost and not regained, if it is not maintained, a warrior in lir-shape risks his humanity.

His voice sounded rusty. "He would be locked in beast-shape?"

If he lost his balance and spent too long in lir-shape, he could lose knowledge of what he was. Self-knowledge is essential. Forgotten, the man becomes a monster caught between two selfs.

After a long moment, Kellin nodded. "*Leijhana tu'sai,*" he said grimly, "for giving me the chance to become a child's nightmare."

I gave you the chance to survive. Corwyth would not have killed you, but he would have brought you pain. And Lochiel would have done worse.

Kellin did not argue. He would not speak to her. He would give her no opportunity to drag him deeper into the mess she had made of his life.

Because he could not stay in the clearing with the mutilated body, Kellin took Corwyth's horse for his own. He turned the other mounts loose; he had no time for ponying.

Sima did not honor his moratorium on speech. *They would have killed me.*

He knew immediately what she referred to. For the first time, he contemplated what it was to a *lir* to experience guilt. He understood there was no choice in killing the minions; they would have skinned her and taken the pelt to Valgaard for presentation to Lochiel.

Even as they presented me. Grimly Kellin said, "I would wish that on no one, beast or no."

Leijhana tu'sai. Sima twitched her tail.

Kellin slanted her a hard glance as he snugged the girth tight. "You know the Old Tongue?"

Better than you do.

He grunted. "Privy to the gods, are you? More favored than most?"

Of course. All lir are. The cat paused. *You are an angry man.*

"After what you have made of me, do you expect gratitude?"

No. You are angry all the time.

He slipped fingers between girth and belly to check for a horse's favorite trick: intentional bloating to keep the girth loose. "How would you know *what* I am?"

I know.

"Obscurity does not commend you."

Sima thumped her tail. *A difficult bonding, I see.*

"No bonding at all." As the horse released its breath in response to an elbow jab, Kellin snugged the girth tighter. "Go back to wherever it is *lir* come from."

I cannot.

"I will not have you with me."

You cannot NOT have me.

"Oh?" Kellin cast her an arch glance. "Will you stop me with violence?"

Of course not. I am sworn to protect you, not injure you.

"That is something." He looped reins over the bay gelding's neck. "Go back to the gods, cat. I will have none of you."

You have no choice.

"Have I not?" Kellin gritted his teeth and put a boot toe into the left stirrup. Swearing inventively, he swung up into the saddle and settled himself slowly. "—I think I have every choice, cat."

None. Not if you wish to survive.

"There have been *lirless* Cheysuli before."

None who survived.

Kellin gathered in reins. "General Rowan," he said briefly. "Rowan was meticulous in teaching my history. Rowan was one of Carillon's most trusted men. He was a *lirless* Cheysuli."

He did not lose a lir. He never had one. He was kept from the bonding by the Ellasians who did not know what he was.

"I know what I am. I know what you are." He swung the horse southwesterly. "Go back to the gods who sent you. I will have none of them, or you."

Lir—

"No." Kellin spared a final glance at the body beside the fire. In time the beasts would eat it. He would not be one of them; he had done his part already. *"Tu'halla dei,"* he said. "Or whatever the terminology from warrior to renounced *lir.*"

The sleek back cat rose. *I am Sima. I am for you.*

Kellin kicked the horse into a walk. "Find another *lir.*"

There IS none! she cried.

For the first time he heard the fear in her tone. Kellin jerked the horse to a halt. He turned in the saddle to stare angrily at the mountain cat. "I saw what became of Tanni. I know what became of Blais. I am meant to hold the Lion and sire a First-born son—do you think I dare risk it all for you? To know that if you die, the prophecy dies also?"

Without me, you die. Without you, I do. With both of us dead, there is no need for the prophecy.

Kellin laughed. "Surely the gods must see the folly in this! A *lir* is a warrior's weakness, not his strength. I begin to think the *lir*-bond is nothing more than divine jest."

I am for you, she said. *Without you, I am empty.*

It infuriated him. "Tell it to someone who cares!"

But as he rode from the campsite, the mountain cat followed.

Eleven

Kellin was exhausted by the time he reached Clan-keep. He had briefly considered riding directly to Homana-Mujhar—no doubt Brennan and Aileen wondered what had become of him—but decided against it. Clankeep was the answer. His problem had nothing at all to do with the Homanan portion of his blood, but was wholly a Cheysuli concern.

I will tell them what has happened. I will explain what I was forced to become, and the result—surely they cannot countenance a warrior who in lir-shape compromises every bit of his humanity. He stead-fastly ignored the shadow slinking behind him with gold eyes fixed on his back. *They will understand that this kind of bonding cannot be allowed to stand.*

Kellin sighed relief. He felt better already. Once his plight was explained, all would be understood. He had spent portions of his childhood in Clankeep and knew the pureblood Cheysuli could be a stiff-necked, arrogant lot—he had been accused of his share of arrogance by the castle boys in childhood—but they had to acknowledge the difficulty of his position. Kellin knew very well his request would be neither popular nor readily accepted, but once they fully understood what had occurred the Cheysuli would not refuse. He was one of their own, after all.

I will speak to Gavan. Gavan was clan-leader, a man Kellin respected. *He will see this is serious, not merely an inconvenience. He will know what must be done.*

Kellin felt gingerly at the bridge of his nose. It was whole, but badly scratched. His left eyelid was swollen so that a portion of his vision was obstructed. His clothing was crusted with dried blood. *I can smell myself.* It shamed him to show himself to Gavan and the others this way, but how better to explain his circumstances save with the gory proof before them?

He was not hungry though his belly was empty. The idea of food repulsed him. He had eaten the throat of a man; though he was free now of the taste, his memory recalled it. Kellin wanted nothing at all to do with food.

He listened for and heard the faint rustling behind. Sima did not hide her presence, nor make attempt to quiet her movements. She padded on softly, following her *lir.*

Kellin's jaws tautened. *Gavan will see what has happened. He will know what must be done.*

Clankeep, to Kellin, was perfectly ordinary in its appearance. He had been taught differently, of course; the keep had been razed twenty years before on the night of his birth, when Lochiel himself had ridden down from Valgaard with sorcerers at his beck. The Ihlini had meant to destroy Clankeep and kill every living Cheysuli; that they had failed was in no way attributable to their inefficiency, but to the forced premature birth of Aidan's son. Cut from his mother's belly before the proper time, Kellin was at risk. Lochiel had immediately returned to Valgaard. In that retreat, a portion of Clankeep and her Cheysuli were left alive.

Kellin, gazing with gritty, tired eyes on the

painted pavilions clustered throughout the forest like chicks around a hen, saw nothing of the past, only of the present. That the unmortared walls surrounding the pavilions were, beneath cloaks of lichen and ivy, still charred or split by heat did not remind him of that night, because he recalled nothing of it. He had no basis for comparison when he looked on the present Clankeep. To Kellin it was simply another aspect of his heritage, without the depressing weight of personal recollection.

Despite the hour he was welcomed immediately by the warriors manning the gate and was escorted directly to the clan-leader's pavilion. In the dark it stood out because of its color: a pale saffron bedecked with ruddy-hued foxes. Moonlight set it softly aglow.

Kellin dismounted as his escort ducked into Gavan's pavilion; a second warrior took Corwyth's horse and led it away. Kellin was alone save for the cat-shaped shadow nearby. He ignored her utterly.

In only a moment the first warrior returned and beckoned him inside, pulling aside the doorflap. Kellin drew in a deep breath and went in, acutely aware of his deshabille. He paused inside as his eyes adjusted to the muted glow of a firecairn, then inclined his head to the older man who waited. Gavan offered the ritual welcome in the Old Tongue, then indicated a place to sit upon a thick black bear pelt. Honey brew and dried fruit also were offered. Kellin sat down with a murmured word of thanks and accepted cup and platter. Irresolute, he stared at both, then set aside the fruit and drank sparingly of the liquor. Like the Ihlini wine, it burned his cut mouth.

Gavan wore traditional leathers, though tousled graying hair indicated he had risen hastily from bed. In coal-cast shadows his dark Cheysuli face was hollowed and eerily feral, dominated by yellow eyes above oblique, prominent cheekbones. Some of Gavan's face was reflected in Kellin's, though his own was less angular and lacked the sharpness of additional years.

The clan-leader sat quietly on a bear pelt before Kellin, a ruddy dog-fox curled next to one knee. His eyes narrowed minutely as he observed Kellin's state. "Harsh usage."

Kellin nodded as he swallowed, then set aside the cup. "Ihlini," he said briefly. He was flattered by the instant response in Gavan's eyes: sharp, fixed attention, and a contained but palpable tension. Kellin wondered fleetingly if Gavan had been present during the Ihlini attack. Then he dismissed it, thinking of the man instead. *I will have more care from him than from my own jehan.*

"Lochiel?" the clan-leader asked.

Kellin shook his head. "A minion. Corwyth. Powerful in his own right . . . but not the master himself."

Gavan's mouth compressed slightly. "So the war begins anew."

Kellin swallowed heavily. "Lochiel wants me captured and taken to Valgaard. No more does he want me killed outright, but brought to him *alive.*" Though his mouth was clean, he tasted Corwyth's blood again. It was difficult to speak. "In my dying—or whatever he decrees is to be my fate—I am to be Lochiel's entertainment."

Gavan set aside his cup. "You have not gone to the Mujhar."

"Not yet. I came here first." Kellin suppressed a shudder as the image of throatless Corwyth rose in his mind; this man would not understand such weakness. "There is a thing I must discuss. A *frightening* thing—" he did not like admitting such to Gavan, but it was the simple truth, "—and a

thing which must be attended." It was more difficult than expected. Kellin flicked a glance at the
mountain cat who lay so quietly beside him. He
longed to dismiss her, but until all was explained
he did not dare transgress custom. A *lir* was to
be honored; arrant dismissal would immediately
predispose Gavan to hostility. "I killed Corwyth,
as I said—but not through a man's means."

Gavan smiled faintly as he looked at Sima. "It
is my great personal joy that the bonding has at
last occurred. It is well past time. Now you may
be welcomed into the clan as a fully bonded warrior . . . it was of some concern that the tardiness
of the *lir*-bonding might cause difficulty."

Kellin's mouth dried. "Difficulty?"

Gavan gestured negligent dismissal. "But it is
of no moment, now. No one can deny your right
to the Lion."

This was a new topic. "*Did* someone deny it?"

A muscle jumped briefly in Gavan's cheek. "There
was some talk that perhaps the mixture of so many
Houses in your blood had caused improper dilution."

"But the mixture is *needed*." Kellin fought to
control his tone; he realized in a desperation fray-
ing into panic that things would not be sorted out
so easily after all. "The prophecy is very explicit
about a man of *all* blood—"

"Of course." Neatly, Gavan cut him off. "A man
of all blood, aye . . . but a man clearly Cheysuli."
He smiled at Sima. "With so lovely a *lir*, you need
fear no warrior's doubts."

Kellin found it difficult to breathe. To gain time
he looked around the interior of the pavilion: at
the dog-fox next to Gavan; at the glowing firecairn; at the bronze-bound trunk with a handful
of Cheysuli ornaments scattered across its closed
lid; at the compact warbow—once called a hunting bow—leaning against the trunk; at the shad-

ows of painted *lir* on the exterior of the pavilion fabric.

Lastly, at Sima. Gold eyes were unblinking.

Kellin picked up the cup of liquor and drained it. It burned briefly, then mellowed into a warmth that, in an empty belly, set his vision to blurring.

His lips felt stiff. "Carillon had no *lir.*"

Gavan's black brows, as yet untouched by the silver threading his hair, moved more closely together. Clearly, he was baffled by the non sequitur. "Carillon was Homanan."

"But the clans accepted him."

"He was the next link. After Shaine: Carillon. After Carillon: Donal."

"Because Carillon sired only a daughter. A Solindish halfling."

"Aislinn. Who wed Donal and bore Niall." Gavan smiled then, his faint consternation clearing. "Is this because Niall, too, was late receiving his *lir*? Did you fear, as they say he did, that you would never receive one?" He smiled, nodding his head in Sima's direction. "You need fear nothing. Your future is secure."

Kellin drew in a deep breath, ignoring the twinge in his chest. Gavan's words seemed to come from a great distance. "What if—" He broke off, then began again. "What if I had never received a *lir*?"

Gavan shrugged. "There is no profit in discussing what did not occur."

Kellin forced a smiled. "Curiosity. What if I had never received, nor bonded with a *lir*?" He was no good at disingenuity; the smile broke up into pieces and fell away. "I am well beyond the age a warrior receives a *lir*. Surely before now there must have been some discussion in case I never did."

The clan-leader made a dismissive gesture. "Aye, it was briefly discussed; there is no sense in hiding it from you. It is a serious matter. Because you are the only direct descendant with all of the proper bloodlines—"

"Save one."

Gavan inclined his head slightly. "—save one, aye . . . still, it remains that you *are* the only one with all of the necessary lineage required to produce the man we await."

"The Firstborn."

"Cynric." Gavan's eyes were bright. "So your *jehan* has prophesied."

Kellin did not desire to discuss his *jehan*. "Had I not received my *lir*, what would have happened? Would you have questioned my right to inherit?"

"Certainly clan-council would have met to discuss it formally at some point."

"Would *you* have questioned it?" Suddenly, it mattered. It mattered very much. "Would the Cheysuli have rejected my claim to the Lion?"

"The Mujhar is in no danger of giving up *his* claim any time soon." Gavan smiled. "He is a strong man, and in sound health."

"Aye." Kellin's nerves frayed further. It seemed no matter how careful he was, how meticulous his phrasing, he could not get the answer he wanted; yet at the same time he knew what the answer was, and dreaded it. "Gavan—" He felt sweat sting a scrape on one temple as the droplet ran down beneath a lock of hair. "Would the Cheysuli accept a *lirless* Mujhar?"

Gavan did not hesitate. "Now? No. There is no question of it. We are too close to fulfillment . . . a *lirless* Cheysuli would prove a true danger to the prophecy. We cannot afford to support a Mujhar who lacks the most fundamental of all Cheysuli gifts. It would provide the Ihlini an opportunity to destroy us forever."

"Of course." The words were ash. If he opened

his mouth too widely, he would spew it like a dismantled firecairn.

Gavan laughed. Yellow eyes were bright and amused, and wholly inoffensive. "If you are feeling unworthy in the aftermath of bonding, it is a natural thing. The gift—and the power that comes with it—is entirely humbling." He arched black brows. "Even for Mujhars—and men who will *be* Mujhar."

All of Kellin's anticipated arguments in favor of severing the partial bond with Sima evaporated. He would get no understanding from Gavan; likely, he would get nothing even remotely approaching sympathy. He would simply be stricken from the birthlines and summarily removed from the succession.

Leaving no one. "Blais," he said abruptly. "There was a time when some warriors wanted Blais to be named prince in my place."

"That was many years ago."

Kellin felt the dampness of perspiration stipple his upper lip. He wanted to brush it dry, but to do so would call attention to his desperation. "The *a'saii* still exist, do they not? Somewhere in Homana, separate from here . . . they still desire to make their own *tahlmorras* without benefit of the prophecy."

Gavan lifted his cup of honey brew. "There are always heretics."

Kellin watched him drink. *If Blais had survived—* He put it into words. "If Blais had survived, and I had gained no *lir*, would he have been named to the Lion?"

Gavan's eyes were steady. "In lieu of a proper heir, there would have been no other. But such a thing would have delayed completion for another generation, perhaps more. Blais lacked the Solindish and Atvian bloodlines. It would have taken time—more time than we have. . . ." Gavan drank, then set aside his cup. "But what profit in this, Kellin? You are a warrior. You have a *lir*. It falls to you, now, without question. It all falls to you."

Coals crumbled in the firecairn. Illumination wavered, then stilled. It glowed in Gavan's eyes.

"Too heavy," Kellin murmured, swallowing tightly.

Gavan laughed aloud. A hand indicated Sima. "No burden is too heavy if there is a *lir* to help you bear it."

Twelve

Though offered a place in Clankeep, Kellin did not accept it. There was something else he wanted—*needed*—to do; something he should have done years before. He had avoided it with a steadfast intransigence, taking a quiet, vicious pleasure in the wrong done him because it fanned the flames of rebellion. A part of him knew very well that without what he perceived as true cause, his defiance might yet be warped into something other than a natural maturing of personality. He was expected to be different from others because of his heritage and rank; hot temper and hasty words were often overlooked because of who he was. That in itself sometimes forced him to more rebellion because he needed to provoke a response that would mitigate self-contempt.

He knew very well what the mountain cat said was right. He *was* too angry, and had been for years. But he knew its cause; it was hardly his fault. A motherless infant prince willingly deserted by a father had little recourse to other emotions.

Kellin stood outside the pavilion. Like Gavan's, it also bore a fox painted on its sides, though the base color was blue instead of saffron. The pavilion was difficult to see in the darkness; moonlight was obscured by clustered trees and overhanging branches. The Cheysuli had moved Clankeep after the Ihlini attack, for a part of the forest had burned. Only rain a day or two later had prevented more destruction.

Accost him now, just after awakening, so he has no time to marshal defenses or rhetoric. Kellin drew in a deep breath that expanded sore ribs, then called through the closed doorflap that he desired to see the *shar tahl.*

A moment only, and then a hand drew aside the flap so that the man stood unobstructed. He wore leather in place of robes, and *lir*-gold weighted his arms. He was alert; Kellin thought perhaps the man had not been asleep after all.

"Aye?" And then the warrior's expression altered. An ironic arch lifted black brows. "I should have expected this. You would not come all the times I invited you in the daylight ... this suits your character."

It sparked an instant retort. "You know nothing about my character!"

The older man considered it. "That is true," he said at last. "What I know of you—now—has to do with the tales they tell." He widened the doorflap. "By your expression, this is not intended to be a sanguine visit. Well enough—I had gathered by your continued silence you did not accept my offers of aid as anything other than insult."

"Not insult," Kellin said. "Unnecessary."

"Ah." The man was in his late fifties, not so much younger than the Mujhar. Thick hair grayed heavily, but the flesh of his face was still taut, and his eyes were intent. "But now there is necessity."

Kellin did not look at Sima. He simply pointed to her. "I want to be rid of that."

"Rid?" The *shar tahl*'s irony evaporated. "Come in," he said curtly.

Kellin ducked in beside him. Hostility banished the dullness engendered by Gavan's honey brew;

nerves made him twitchy. He stood aside in stiff silence as the *shar tahl* permitted the mountain cat to enter.

He waited edgily. There were many things he wanted to say, and he anticipated multiple pointed responses designed to dissuade him. The *shar tahl* would no more understand his desire than Gavan would have; the difference was, Kellin was better prepared to withstand anything the *shar tahl* might suggest by way of argument. He disliked the man. Dislike lent him the strength of will to defy a man whose service was to the gods, and to the preservation of tradition within the clans.

"Be seated," the *shar tahl* said briefly. Then, to Sima, "You are well come to my pavilion."

The cat lay down. Her tail thumped once. Then she stilled, huge eyes fixed on Kellin.

With a grimace of impatience, Kellin sat down. Neither food nor drink was offered; tacit insult, designed to tell him a thing or two. *Then we are well matched. I have things to say as well.*

"So." The older man's expression was closed, severe in its aloofness. "You want to be rid of your *lir.* Since it is well known you had none, I can only assume this is a very recent bonding."

"Aye, very recent; last night." Pointedly, Kellin added, "When I was a captive of the Ihlini."

The *shar tahl's* expression did not alter; he seemed fixed upon a single topic. "Yet now you wish to sever that bond."

Kellin's hands closed into fists against crossed legs. "Does it mean nothing to you that the Prince of Homana was captured by the Ihlini, and less that he escaped?"

The *shar tahl's* mouth tightened minutely. "We will speak of that later. At this moment the Prince of Homana's desire to sever what the gods have made for him is of greater concern."

"Because it has to do with gods, and you are a *shar tahl*." Kellin did not bother to hide the derision in his tone. "By all means let us discuss that which you believe of more import; after all, what is the welfare of Homana's future Mujhar compared to his desire to renounce a gift of the gods?"

"Yet if you renounce this bond, there is no more need to concern ourselves with the welfare of Homana's future Mujhar, as he would no longer *be* heir." The *shar tahl's* eyes burned brightly. "But you know that. I can see it in your face." He nodded slightly. "So you have been to Gaven already and what you have heard does not please you. Therefore I must assume this meeting is meant merely to air your grievance, though you know very well nothing can come of it. You cannot renounce the *lir*-bond, lest you be stripped of your rank. And *you* would never permit that; it would echo your *jehan's* actions."

Kellin's response was immediate. "I did not come to speak of my *jehan*!"

"But we will." The older man's tone allowed no room for protest. "We should have had this conversation years ago."

"We will not have it now. My *jehan* has nothing to do with this."

"Your *jehan* has much to do with this. His desertion of you has to do with everything in your life."

"Enough."

"I have hardly begun."

"Then I will end it!" Kellin glared at the man. "I am still the Prince of Homana. My rank is higher than yours."

"Is it?" Black brows arched. "I think not. Not in the eyes of the gods ... ah, of course—you do not recognize their sovereignty." The *shar tahl* lifted a quelling hand. "In fact, you detest them because you believe they stole your *jehan* from you."

Much as he longed to, Kellin knew better than to shout. To give in to such a display was to weaken his position. "He was meant to be the heir. Not I. Not *yet;* my time was meant for later. They *did* steal him."

"A warrior follows his *tahlmorra.*"

"Or obstructs the prophecy?" Kellin shook his head. "I think what they say of him is true: he is mad. No madman bases his actions on what is real. He does as he does because his mind is addled."

"Aidan's mind is no more addled than your own," the *shar tahl* retorted. "In fact, some would argue it is more sane than yours."

"Mine!"

The warrior smiled grimly. "Your reputation precedes you."

For only an instant Kellin was silent. Then he laughed aloud, letting the sound fill the pavilion. "Because I drink? Because I wager? Because I lie with whores?" The laughter died, but the grin was undiminished. "These actions appear to be a tradition within my family. Shall I name you the names? Brennan, Hart, Corin—"

"Enough." The irony was banished. "You came because you wish to renounce your *lir.* Allow me to do my office. Bide a moment, my lord." The *shar tahl* rose abruptly and moved to the doorflap. He ducked out, leaving Kellin alone with a silent black mountain cat. After a moment the priest returned and resumed his seat. His smile was humorless. "How may I serve my lord?"

Kellin's impatience faded. Hostility dissipated. If the man *could* aid him, he had best mend his manner. "The bonding was done hastily, to enable me to escape the Ihlini. Even she admits it." He did not glance at Sima. "She speaks of balance, and the danger in lacking it. I have none."

The *shar tahl* now was serious. "You assumed *lir*-shape in anger?"

"In anger, fear, panic ..." Kellin sighed; the vestiges of pride and hostility faded utterly. Quietly, he explained what had happened—and how he had killed a man by tearing out his throat.

The dark flesh by the older man's eyes folded upon itself. His eyes seemed to age. "A harsh bonding. But more than that, an improper one. It is only half done."

"Half?" Kellin looked at the cat. "Do you mean I *could* renounce her?"

"No. Not safely. Your *lirlessness* is ended; half-bonded or no, you will never be what you were. The question now is, what will you permit yourself to *be*?"

Alarm bloomed. "What do you mean?"

"You are angry," the *shar tahl* said. "I perhaps understand it better than most—your *jehan* and I have shared many confidences." The severity of the face now was replaced with a human warmth that nearly unmanned Kellin. "Aidan and I have spent much time together. It was why I desired to speak with you before, to explain his reasoning."

"Let *him* explain it!"

The *shar tahl* sighed. "The proper time is not yet come."

Bitterness engulfed. "There never *will* be a 'proper time'!" Kellin cried. "That is the point!"

"No." The *shar tahl* lifted a hand, then let it drop. "That is not the point. There will come a time, I promise ... when the gods intend that you should meet."

"When *he* intends, you mean ... and he never will." Kellin gathered himself to rise. "This is bootless. It wastes my time."

"Sit down." The tone was a whipcrack. "You have come to me with a serious concern that needs to be addressed. Set aside your hatred and hostility long enough, if you will, to permit me to explain that you are in grave danger."

"I have escaped the Ihlini."

"This has nothing to do with the Ihlini. This has to do with yourself. It is of the balance I speak." The *shar tahl* glanced at Sima. "Has she explained what could happen?"

"That I might be locked in beast-form if I lose my balance?" Kellin's mouth twisted. "Aye. *After* she urged me to take *lir*-shape."

"Then she must have believed it necessary." The *shar tahl* studied Sima with something very akin to sympathy, which seemed an odd thing to Kellin; the *lir* were considered far wiser than their warriors. "The *lir* are proscribed from attacking Ihlini. If she urged you to assume *lir*-shape before the proper time, fully cognizant of the risk, it was because she believed it necessary to preserve your life." The yellow eyes were intent. "The life has been preserved. Now we must insure that the mind within the body is preserved as well."

"Burr—" Kellin cut it off. It was time for truth, not protest. Defiance crumbled in the face of his admission. "I have resented you for years."

"I know." The *shar tahl* reached for a jug and cups, then poured two full. "Drink. What you must know will dry your mouth; wet it first, and then we shall begin."

"Can I learn it by dawn?"

"A thing so vital as this cannot be learned in a night. It requires years." Burr sipped his honey brew. "A young warrior is taught from the day of his birth how to strike the balance in all things. We are a proud race, we Cheysuli, and surpassingly arrogant—" Burr smiled, "—because we are,

after all, the children of the gods ... but we are
not an angry race, nor one much given to war
except when it is required. The Homanans have
called us beasts and predators, but it is because
of what we can do with our bodies, not our desire
for blood. We are a peaceful race. That desire for
peace—in mind as well as lifestyle—is taught from
birth. By the time a young man reaches the age
to receive a *lir*, his knowledge of self-control is
well-rooted. His longing for a *lir* supercedes the
recklessness of youth—no young Cheysuli would
risk the wrath of the gods that might result in
lirlessness."

"Is that true?" Kellin asked. "You are a *shar
tahl*—would the gods deny a boy a *lir* because he
does not suit their idea of a well-behaved
Cheysuli?"

Burr laughed. "You are the most defiant and
reckless of Cheysuli I have ever known. Yet there
is the proof that the gods do as they will." A hand
indicated Sima. "You have your place, Kellin. You
have a *tahlmorra*. Now it is your task to acknowledge the path before you."

"And take it?"

"If it is what the gods intend."

"Gods," Kellin muttered. "They clutter up a life.
They bind a man's spirit so he cannot do as he
will."

"You, I believe, are a perfect example of the fal-
lacy in that logic. You do—and have always
done—precisely as you desire." Burr sipped liquor, then set the cup aside. "You must fully accept your *lir*. To remain half-bonded sentences
both of you to a life to which no man—or *lir*—
should ever be subjected."

"Madness," Kellin said. He worked a trapped
twig from the weave of soiled breeches. "What if
I told you I believed it was arrant nonsense, this

belief that *lirlessness* results in madness? That I believe it is no more than a means for a man's misplaced faith in his gods to control him, or destroy him?"

Burr smiled. "You would not be the first to suggest that. In fact, if you were not the heir to the Lion and therefore assured of your place, I would say your defiance and determination resembles the *a'saii*." He drank, watching Kellin over the rim of his cup. "It is not easy for a man to accept that one moment he is in the fullness of his prime, healthy and strong, while the next he is sentenced to the death-ritual despite his continued health and strength. It is the true test of what we are, Kellin; do you know of any other race which willingly embraces death when there appears to be no reason to die?"

"No. No other race is so ludicrously constrained by the gods." Kellin shook his head, tapping the twig against his knee. "It is a *waste*, Burr! Just as *kin-wrecking* is!"

"That, I agree with," Burr said. "Once, the custom had its place . . . there was a need, Kellin."

"To cast out a man because he was maimed?" Kellin shook his head. "The loss of a hand does not render a man incapable of serving his clan or his kin."

"Once, it might have. If a one-handed warrior failed, because of his infirmity, to protect a single life, he was a detriment. There was a time we dared not permit such a risk, lest our people die out entirely."

Kellin gestured. "Enough. I am speaking now of the death-ritual. I contend it is nothing more than a means of control, a method by which the gods— and *shar tahls*, perhaps?—" he grinned in arch contempt, "—can force others to do their will."

Burr was silent. His eyes were partially hidden

behind lowered lashes. Kellin thought perhaps he might at last have provoked the older man into anger, but when Burr at last met his eyes there was nothing of anger in his expression. "What the gods have required of men is duty, honor, reverence—"

"And self-sacrifice!"

"—and sacrifice," Burr finished. "Aye. I deny none of it. But if we had not offered any of these things, Kellin, you would not be seated here before me contesting the need for such service."

"Words!" Kellin snapped. "You are as bad as the Ihlini. You weave magic with words, to ensorcell me to your will."

"I do nothing but state the truth." Burr's tone was very quiet, lacking all emotion. "If a single man in your birthline had turned his back on his *tahlmorra*, you would not be the warrior destined to inherit the Lion."

"You mean if my *jehan* had turned his back on his *tahlmorra*." Kellin wanted to swear. "This is merely another attempt to persuade me that what my *jehan* did was necessary. You said yourself you are friends . . . I hear bias in his favor."

"It was necessary," Burr said. "Who can say what might have become of you if Aidan had not renounced his title? Paths can be altered, Kellin— and prophecies. If Aidan had remained here, he would be Prince of Homana. You would merely be third in line behind Brennan and Aidan. That extra time could well have delayed completion of the prophecy, and destroyed it utterly."

"You mean, it might have prevented me from lying with whatever woman I am supposed to lie with—*according to the gods*—in order to sire Cynric." Kellin tossed aside the twig. "A convenience, nothing more. No one *knows* this. Just as no one knows for certain a warrior goes mad if his *lir* is killed." He smiled victory. "You see? We have come full circle."

Burr's answering smile was grim. "But I can name you the proofs: Duncan, Cheysuli clan-leader, kept alive by Ihlini sorcery though his *lir* was dead, and used as a weapon to strike at his son, Donal, who was meant to be Mujhar."

Kellin felt cold; he knew this history.

"Teirnan, Blais' *jehan*, who assumed the role of clan-leader to the heretical *a'saii*. A warrior who would have, given the chance, pulled Brennan from the Lion and mounted it himself." Burr's tone was steady. "Tiernan renounced his *lir*. In the end, completely mad, he threw himself into the Womb of the Earth before the eyes of your *jehan* and *jehana* in an attempt to prove himself worthy to hold the Lion. He did not come out."

Kellin knew that also.

Burr said softly, "First we will speak of your *jehan*. Then of the balance."

Kellin wanted it badly. "No," he said roughly. "What I learn of my *jehan* will be learned from him."

Burr looked beyond him to the slack doorflap. He said a single word—a name—and a warrior came in. In his arms he held a small girl asleep against his shoulder; by his side stood a tousle-haired boy of perhaps three years.

"There is another," the *shar tahl* said. "Another son; do you recall? Or have you forgotten entirely that these are your children?"

"Mine—" Kellin blurted.

"Three royal bastards." Burr's tone was unrelenting. "Packed off to Clankeep like so much unwanted baggage, and never once visited by the man who sired them."

Thirteen

Kellin refused to look at the children, or at the warrior with them. Instead he stared at Burr. "Bastards," he declared, biting off the word.

The *shar tahl's* voice was calm. "That they are bastards does not preclude the need for parents."

Kellin's lips were stiff. "Homanan halflings."

"And what are you, my lord, but Homanan, Solindish, Atvian, Erinnish. . . ?" Burr let it trail off. "*I* am pure Cheysuli."

"*A'saii?*" Kellin challenged. "You believe I should be replaced?"

"If you refuse your *lir*, assuredly." Burr was relentless. "Look at your children, Kellin."

He did not want to. He was desperate not to. "Bastards have no place in the line of succession—"

"—and therefore do not matter?" Burr shook his head. "That is the Homanan in you, I fear . . . in the clans bastardy bears no stigma." He paused. "Did Ian know you felt so? He, too, was a bastard."

"Enough!" Kellin hissed. "You try to twist me inside out no matter what I say."

"I shall twist you any way I deem necessary, if the result achieved is as I believe it should be." Burr looked at the boy. "Young, but he promises well. Homanan eyes—they are hazel—but the hair is yours. And the chin—"

"Stop it."

"The girl is too young yet to show much of what she shall be—"

"*Stop* it!"

"—and of course the other boy is but a handful of months." Burr looked at Kellin, all pretenses to neutrality dropped. "Explain it away, if you please. Justify your actions with regard to these children, though you refuse to permit your *jehan* the same favor."

"*He traded me for the gods!*" It was a cry from the heart Kellin regretted at once. "Can you not see—"

"What I see are two children without a *jehan*," Burr said. "Another yet sleeps at the breast of a Cheysuli woman who lost her own baby. I submit to you, my lord: for what did you trade *them*?"

Words boiled up in Kellin's mouth, so many at first he could not find a single one that would, conjoined with another, make any sense at all. Furious, he thrust himself to his feet. At last the words broke free. "I get nothing from you. No truths, no support, no honorable service! Nothing more than drivel mouthed by a man who is truer to the *a'saii* than to his own Mujhar!"

Burr did not rise. "Until you can look on those children and acknowledge your place in their lives, speak no word against Aidan."

Kellin extended a shaking hand. He pointed at Sima. "I want no *lir*."

"You have one."

"I want to be rid of her."

"And open the door to madness."

"I do not believe it."

Burr's eyes glinted. "Then test it, my lord. Challenge the gods. Renounce your *lir* and withstand the madness." He rose and took the small girl from the silent warrior's arms, settling her against his shoulder. Over her head, he said, "It will be a true test, I think. Certainly as true as the one Teirnan undertook at the Womb of the Earth."

Desperate, Kellin declared, "I have no room in my life for the impediment of halfling bastards!"

"That," Burr said, "is between you and the gods."

Kellin shut his teeth. "You are wrong. All of you. I will prove you wrong."

"*Tahlmorra lujhalla mei wiccan, cheysu,*" Burr said. Then, as Kellin turned to flee, "*Cheysuli i'halla shansu.*"

Kellin did not stay the rest of the night in Clankeep but took back his borrowed mount and rode on toward Mujhara. He had moved beyond the point of weariness into the realm of an exhaustion so complex as to render him almost preternaturally alert. Small sounds were magnified into a clamor that filled his head, so that there was no room for thought. It pleased him. Thought renewed anger, reestablished frustration, reminded him yet again that no matter what he said—no matter who he *was*—no Cheysuli warrior would accept him as one of them so long as he lacked a *lir.*

They would sooner have me go mad with *a lir than go mad because I renounce one.*

It made no sense to Kellin. But neither did the mountain cat who shadowed his horse, loping in its wake.

He had tried to send her away. Sima refused to go. Since he had made very clear his intentions to forswear her, the cat had said nothing. The link was suspiciously empty.

As if she no longer exists. And yet here she was; he had only to glance over a shoulder to see her behind him.

Would it not be simpler if he shut off that link

forever? Certainly less hazardous. If Sima died while as yet unbonded, he could escape the death-ritual.

Though Burr says I will not.

Kellin shifted in the saddle, attempting to lessen the discomfort of his chest. The *shar tahl* had challenged him to test the conviction that a *lirless* warrior went mad. And he had accepted. Part of the reason was pride, part a natural defiance; uneasily Kellin wondered what might happen if he lost the challenge. If, after all, the Cheysuli belief was based on truth.

What does it feel like to go mad? He slowed his mount as he approached the city; star- and moon-light, now tainted by Mujhara's illumination, made it difficult to see the road. *What was Teirnan thinking, as he leapt into the Womb?*

What had his father thought, and his mother, as the warrior without a *lir* tested his right to the Lion, and was repudiated?

I would never throw myself into the Womb of the Earth. It was— He brought himself up short. *Madness?*

Kellin swore the vilest oaths he could think of. An arm scrubbed roughly across his face did nothing to rid his head of such thoughts. It smeared grime and crusted blood—he had left Clankeep without even so much as a damp cloth for cleaning his face—and tousled stiffened hair. His clothing was rigid with dried blood and scratched at bruised flesh. Inside the flesh, bones ached.

He did not enter Mujhara by way of the Eastern Gate because they knew him there. Instead he angled the horse right and rode for the Northern Gate. Of all the gates it was the least used; the Eastern led toward Clankeep, the Southern to Hondarth, the Western to Solinde. The Northern opened onto the road that, followed to its end, led to the Bluetooth River; beyond lay the Northern Wastes, and Valgaard.

Kellin shivered. *I would have gone there, had Corwyth persevered.*

Through the Northern Gate lay the poorer sections of Mujhara, including the Midden. Kellin intended to ride directly through, bound for Homana-Mujhar on its low rise in the center of the city. He wanted a bath very badly, and a bed—

His horse—Corwyth's horse—shied suddenly, even as Kellin heard the low-pitched growling. He gathered rein, swearing, as the dog boiled out of the darkness.

Kellin took a deeper seat, anticipating trouble, but the dog streaked by him. Then he knew.

The link that had been so empty blazed suddenly to life, engulfing him utterly. He heard the frantic barking, the growls; then Sima's wailing cry. The link, half-made though it was, reverberated with the mountain cat's frenzied counterattack.

"Wait!" It was a blurt of shock. Stunned by the explosion within the link, Kellin sat immobile. His body rang with pain and outrage; yet none of it was his own. "Hers." She had said they were linked, even if improperly. He felt whatever the cat felt.

Freed of the paralysis, Kellin jerked the horse around, feeling for the long-knife retrieved from Corwyth. He saw a huddle of black in the shadows, and the gleam of pale slick hide as the dog darted in toward Sima. It was joined by another, and then a third; in a moment the noise would bring every dog at a run.

They will kill— The rest was lost. A man-shaped shadow stepped out of a dark doorway and, with a doubled fist, smashed the horse's muzzle.

Kellin lost control instantly, and very nearly his

nose. The horse's head shot skyward, narrowly missing Kellin's bowed head. The animal fell back a step or two, scrabbling in mucky footing, flinging his head in protest.

Before Kellin could attempt to regain control of the reins, hands grabbed his left leg. It was summarily jerked out of the stirrup and twisted violently, so that Kellin was forced to follow the angle or risk having his ankle broken. The position made him vulnerable; a second violent twist and a heave tipped Kellin off backward even as he grabbed for the saddle.

"Ku'reshtin—" He twisted in midair, broke free of the hands, then landed awkwardly on his feet— *leijhana tu'sai!*—and caught his balance haphazardly against the startled horse's quivering rump.

Before he could draw a breath, the man was on him.

Inconsequentially, even as he fought, Kellin believed it ironic. He had no coin. All anyone would get from him was a Cheysuli long-knife; which, he supposed, was reward enough.

His own breathing was loud, but over his noise he heard the yowling of the mountain cat and the clamor of dogs. His concentration was split—for all he wanted no *lir*, he did not desire her to be killed or injured—which made it that much harder to withstand his assault.

Booted feet slipped in muck. The alley was narrow, twisted upon itself, hidden in deep shadow because dwellings blocked out much of the moon. Kellin did not hesitate but grabbed at once for Blais' knife; massive hands grasped his right arm immediately and wrenched his hand away from the hilt. The grip on his arm was odd, but firm enough; then it shifted. Fingers closed tautly on flesh, shutting off strength and blood. Kellin's hand was naught but a lifeless blob of bone, flesh, and muscle on the end of a useless arm.

"Ku'resh—"

The grip shifted. A knee was brought up as Kellin's captive forearm was slammed down. The bones of his wrist snapped easily against the man's thigh.

Pain was immediate. Kellin's outcry echoed the frenzy of the mountain cat as she fought off the dogs. But the attacker was undeterred. Even as Kellin panted a shocked protest colored by angry oaths, the stranger wound his fists into the blood-stiffened doublet. He lifted Kellin from the ground, then slammed him against the nearest wall.

Skull smacked stone. Lungs collapsed, expelling air. A purposeful elbow was dug deeply into Kellin's laboring chest, rummaging imperiously amidst the wreckage of fragile ribs. Bones gave way.

He inhaled raggedly and managed a breathless string of foul words in a mixture of Homanan, Old Tongue, and Erinnish, depending on the words to give him something on which he might focus. The pain was all-consuming, but not nearly so astounding as the violence of the attack itself.

Sima's screaming echoed in the canyon of cheek-by-jowl dwellings. A dog yelped, then another; others belled a call to join the attack.

Lir— It was instinctive. He meant nothing by it. The appeal faded immediately, though not the knowledge of it.

Kellin sagged against the wall, pinned there by a massive body. A shoulder leaned into his chest. His broken wrist remained trapped.

The odd grip tightened, shifting on his forearm. "First the thumb," the attacker grunted.

There was no air, no air at all—but *pain*—

"First the thumb, then the fingers—"

Kellin sucked frantically at air.

"—and lastly, the *hand*—"

He knew the truth then. "Luce!" Kellin gasped. "Gods—"

"None here, little princeling. Only me." A grin split Luce's beard in the pallor of the night. "I'll hold the hand just so—" He did it one-handed, while the other snagged the long-knife from Kellin's belt.

One word, no more, *"Wait—"*

"What? D'ye think to buy me, princeling? No, not Luce—he's enough coin to last him, and ways of getting more." Luce's breath stank. He hooked an elbow up and slammed it into Kellin's jaw. The back of Kellin's skull smashed against stone wall; he felt a tooth break from the blow, and weakly spat out the pieces. Luce laughed. "A love-tap, nothing more . . . and speaking of that, perhaps I should make you mine to use as I will—a royal sheath for my sword—"

Kellin squirmed against the wall. His vision yet swam from the blow, and he tasted blood in his mouth. He did not know if it came from the empty root socket, or was expelled from pierced lungs.

Luce still pinned the broken wrist against the wall. In the other hand gleamed the knife. He set the point between Kellin's spread legs and tapped cloth-warded genitals. "The Midden's a harsh place full of desperate people—but *Luce* would protect you. Luce would make you his—"

"Sima!" Kellin shouted, spraying blood and desperation. In the distance he heard growls and yelps, and the wailing cry of an infuriated cat. *"Sim—"*

But Luce shut it off with a dig of an elbow into broken ribs. "First the thumb," he said.

Kellin understood what a *lir* was for. He had repudiated his own. What, then, was left?

He hurt very badly. The injuries were serious. Even if Luce did nothing else, he would probably die regardless.

Sima had said before she had given him the key. Now it was his task to open the door again.

Kellin used the pain. He used the pain, the fury, the frustration, the fear. He *feasted* on it, and allowed it to fill his spirit until there was nothing left of the man but the elemental drives to kill, and to feed.

As the knife came down to sever the thumb from his hand, the hand was no longer there. In its place was the flexing paw of a mountain cat.

Fourteen

With a shocked cry, Luce let go. The knife glinted briefly, then tumbled into muck. Kellin dropped four-footed to splayed, leathery pads, then twisted sinuously in the body made for fluid movement, like water over stone; like runoff in the ancient cut of a waterfall over sheer cliffs.

He will learn what it means to harm a Cheysuli— But then the thought spilled away into a jumble of crazed images tumbled one against another, all stuck together like layers of leaves adhered one on top of another, until vision fell out of focus and no longer mattered at all. What mattered now was scent and the stink of a frightened man; the sound of the man's sobbing; the taste of promised revenge.

The cat who was Kellin reached out. Easily— *so* easily!—he slapped a negligent paw across the giant's thigh. Claws dug in sharply; blood spurted through rent cloth.

Luce screamed. Thumbless hands clutched at his bleeding thigh, trying to stanch it. Lazily, exultant in his strength, Kellin reached out again and slapped at the other meaty thigh so that it, too, bled. As Luce sobbed and whimpered, he curved a playful paw around one ankle and dug claws into bone. With a snarl that warped his mouth slantways, he jerked the man to the ground. The sound of the skull splitting was swallowed by his snarl.

The noise of the hounds was gone. Tail lashed anticipation, beating against cold air. Kellin moved to stand over his meal so no one else could steal it.

Lir!

Kellin did not listen.

Lir! Do not!

It was easier to frame the feelings, the images, not the words. His mouth was no longer human. His response was built of instinct, not the logic of a man. *You want it.*

No. No, lir. Leave it. A bleeding Sima was free of dogs, though some lay dead, others dying, while another ran off yelping. *Leave it.*

He challenged her. *YOU want it.*

No.

I hunger. Here is food. He paused. *Are you my mate?*

Come away.

He panted. He drooled. Hunger was paramount, but pain ate at his spirit. It was easiest to give in, to let instinct rule a comprehension that was, even more quickly now, flowing away from him. *I hunger. Here is food.*

You are man, not cat.

Man? I wear a cat's shape.

You are man. Cheysuli. Shapechanger. You have borrowed this shape. Give it back. Let the earth magic have it back. When you have learned the proper balance, you can borrow the shape again.

He let his tail lash. *Who am I, then?"*

Kellin. Not cat. Man.

He considered it. *I do not feel like a man. THIS is man, this food here beneath me.* Saliva dripped from his jowls. *You want it for yourself.*

Come away, she said. *You have wounds to be healed. So have I.*

The dogs hurt you?

I have hurts. So do you. Come away, lir. We will have them healed.

Nearby a door was opened. Someone looked out into the street. He heard a gabble of voices. He understood none of the words. Noise, no more; the noise of puny humans.

He lowered his jaws. Blood, sweat, urine, fear, and death commingled in a powerful perfume. He would taste it—

NO. The female was at his side. She leaned a shoulder into his. Her chin rubbed at his head. *If you would feed here, there will be no choice but to kill you.*

Who would kill me? Who would dare?

Men.

Inner knowledge gloated. *They could not accomplish it.*

She leaned harder, rubbing against his neck. *They could. They would. Come away, lir. You are badly hurt.*

Another door opened. A slash of candlelight slanted into the street. In its illumination he saw the dead hounds, the slack hulk of a man. Voices cried out, full of terror.

Away? he asked. *But—the food—*

Leave it, she said. *There is better elsewhere.*

The big cat hurt. His wounds were uncounted, and untended; he required tending. He went with her then because the urge to feed had left him. He felt disoriented and distant, unsure of himself. She led him away from the alley to another not far away and found a hidden corner.

Here, she said, nudging at a shoulder.

She was wounded, he saw. Blood spiked the fur on her spine. He turned to her, tending the bites, licking to wash the blood away. She had been hurt by the hounds, torn and tainted by the audacity of mere beasts who did not know what it was to be gods-blessed.

Leave it, she said. *Remember what you are.*

He paused. *I am—* He checked.

Gold eyes were intent. *What are you?*

I am—as you see me.

No.

I am—I am—

Remember! she snapped. *Recall your knowledge of self.*

He could not. He was what he was.

She leaned against him. He smelled her fear, her blood. She was alien to him, who did not know what she was to him. *Stay here. You are too badly wounded to walk. Wait here for me.*

It frightened him. *Where are you going?*

For help. Stay here.

She left him. He crouched against the wall, tail whipping a counterpoint to the pain in his foreleg, in his ribs, in his jaws. Licking intensified pain. He flattened his ears against his head and pulled back his lips from his teeth in a feral grimace of pain and fear.

She had left him alone, and now he was helpless.

Men came. And torches. The big cat shied back, huddling into a corner as he snarled and growled a warning. He slitted eyes against the flame and saw silhouettes, man-shapes holding sticks with fire blooming from them. He smelled them: they stank of anticipation, apprehension; the giddy tang of an excitement nearly sexual, as if they hoped to mate once the task was done. The odor was strong. It filled up his nostrils and entered his head, causing the reflex response that dropped open his jaws. Raspy in- and exhalations as he scented the men made him sound like a bellows.

Lir. It was the female. Sima. *Lir, do not fear. They have come to help, not harm.*

Fire.

They will come no closer, save one. She slunk out of the blinding light into his slime-coated corner. Blood crusted across her shoulders; she had run, and bled again. *Let the man come.*

He permitted it. He pressed himself against the wall and waited, one swollen paw dangling. Breathing hurt. He hissed and shook his head; a tooth in his jaw was broken.

The man came away from the fire. Kellin could not judge him by any but a cat's standards: his hair was silver like frost in winter sunlight, and his eyes glowed like coals. Metal glinted on naked arms, bared by a shed cloak despite the winter's bite.

"Kellin." The man knelt down on one knee, unmindful of the muck that would soil his leathers. "Kellin."

The cat opened his mouth and panted. Pain caused him to drool.

"Kellin, you must loose the cat-shape. There is no more need."

The cat rumbled a growl; he could not understand.

The man sighed and rose, turned back to the men with flames. He spoke quietly, and they melted away. Light followed them, so that though empty of men the corner still shone with a sickly, frenzied pallor.

The men were gone. In their places was a void, a blurred nothingness that filled the alley. And then a tawny mountain cat stalked out of the fading flame-dazzle with another at his side: a magnificent black female well into her prime. Her grace denounced the gangliness of the young female with Kellin who was, after all, little more than a cub.

Three mountain cats: two black, one tawny gold. In his mind formed the images that in humans would have been speech; to him, now, the images made promises that they would lend him required strength, and the healing he needed so badly.

In their eyes he saw a man. Human, like the others. His hair was not winter-frost, but black as a night sky. His eyes were green coals in place of ruddy or yellow. He did not glint with gold; he wore no gold at all. He was smooth and sleek and strong, with the blood running hot in his veins.

Pain blossomed anew. Broken bones protested.

Three cats pressed close. The tawny male mouthed his neck; Kellin flattened his ears and lowered his head. He hurt too much to display dominance postures to one who was clearly much older and wiser than he.

Come home, the cat said. *Come home with me now.*

Kellin panted heavily. In the muck, his pads were damp with sweat. Weakness overrode caution. He let them guide his mind until he saw what "home" meant: the true-body that was his. Fingers and toes in place of claws. Hair in place of fur, and smooth, taut flesh too easily bruised by harsh treatment.

Come home, the tawny cat said, and in its place was a man with eyes that understood his pain and the turmoil in his soul. "I have been there," he said. "My weakness is my fear of small dark places . . . I will be with you in this. I understand what it is to fear a part of yourself over which you have no control." Then, very softly, "Come home, Kellin. Let the anger go."

He let it go. Exhaustion engulfed, and a blurred disorientation. Spent, he slumped against the half-grown female. She licked at his face and scraped a layer of skin; human skin, not feline.

Kellin recoiled. He pressed himself into the stone wall.

"Kellin." Brennan still knelt. Behind him torches flared. "*Shansu*, Kellin—it is over."

"I—I—" Kellin stopped. He swallowed hard against the sour taste of bile. He could frame no proper words, as if he had lost them in his transformation. "I."

The Mujhar's expression was infinitely gentle. "I know. Come with me." Brennan paused. "Kellin, you are hurt. Come with me."

He panted shallowly. He cradled his wrist against a chest that hurt as much. His legs were coiled under him so he could rise instantly in a single upward thrust.

Brennan's hand was on his shoulder.

Kellin tensed. And then it mattered no longer. He closed his eyes and sagged against the stone. Tears ran unchecked through grime, perspiration, and blood old as well as new. He was not ashamed.

Brennan's hand touched his blood-stiffened hair softly, tenderly, as if to frame words he could not say. And then the hand was gone from Kellin's hair, closing instead on the arm that was whole. "Come up from there, my lord."

His grandsire had offered him no honor in manner or words for a very long time, nor the deep and abiding affection that now lived in his tone.

Kellin looked at him. "I am not . . . not . . ." He was still too close to the cat. He wanted to wail instead of speak. "Am. Not. Deserving . . ." He tried again in desperation, needing to say it; to recover the human words. "—not of such *care*—"

Tears shone in Brennan's eyes. "You are deserving of many things, not the least of which is care. *Shansu*, my young one—we will find a balance for you. Somehow, we will find a proper balance."

Torchlight streamed closer. Kellin looked beyond his grandfather and saw the royal guard. One of the men was Teague.

Their faces had been schooled to show no emotion. But he had seen it. He had seen them, and the fear in their eyes as they had looked upon the cat who had been to all of them before nothing more than a man.

Kellin shuddered. "I was—I was . . ." The wail was very near. He shut his mouth upon it, so as to give them no more reason to look upon him with fear and apprehension.

They were the elite guard of a warrior who became a mountain cat at will. It was not new to them, who had seen it before. But Brennan was nothing if not a dignified man of immense self-control. Kellin was not and had never been a dignified man; self-control was nonexistent. In him, as a human, they saw an angry man desirous of shedding blood.

In him now, as a cat, they saw the beast instead.

They know what I have become. What I will always be to them. It spilled from Kellin's mouth, accompanied by blood. "Grandsire—*help me*—"

Brennan did not shirk it. "We will mend the body first. Then we shall mend the mind."

Fifteen

He was but half conscious, drifting on fading awareness that told him very little save his wounds were healed at last, his broken bones made whole—yet the spirit remained flaccid. He wanted badly to sleep. Earth magic drained a man, regardless of which side he walked.

His eyes were closed, sticky lashes resting against drawn cheeks. Earth magic reknit bones, but did not dissipate bruises or prevent scarring from a wound that would otherwise require stitching. It merely restored enough health and strength to vanquish immediate danger; a warrior remade by the earth magic was nonetheless well cognizant of what had occurred to require it.

Kellin's face bore testimony to the violence done him. The flesh across the bridge of his nose had been torn by a thorn; welts distorted his cheeks; his bottom lip was swollen. He had drunk and rinsed out his mouth, but the tang of blood remained from the cuts in his lip and the inside of his cheek.

A hand remained on Kellin's naked shoulder. Fingertips trembled against smooth, freshly sponged flesh; Aileen had seen to the washing. *"Shansu,"* Brennan murmured hoarsely, lifting the hand. He, too, was drained, for he had undertaken the healing alone. It would have been better had there been another Cheysuli to aid him, but

Brennan had not dared waste the time to send for a warrior. He had done the healing himself, and now suffered for it.

Kellin was dimly aware of Aileen's murmuring. The Mujhar said something unintelligible, then the door thumped closed. Kellin believed himself alone until he heard the sibilance of skirt folds against one another, the faint slide of thin slipper sole on stone where the rug did not reach. He smelled the scent she favored. Her presence was a beacon as she sat down by his bed.

"She is lovely," Aileen said quietly. "This must be very much what Sleeta looked like, before she and Brennan bonded."

He lay slumped on one side with his back to her. A shoulder jutted skyward. Along his spine and the curve of his buttocks lay warmth, incredible warmth; the living bulk of a mountain cat.

Kellin sighed. He wanted to sleep, not speak, but he owed Aileen something. Into the limp hand curled against his chin, he murmured, "I would sooner do without her, lovely or no."

"D'ye blame her, then? For being what you are?"

It jerked him out of lassitude into startled wakefulness. He turned over hastily, thrusting elbows beneath his spine to lever his sheet-draped torso upright. "Do you think *I*—"

"*You,*" Aileen said crisply; she was not and had never been a woman who deferred, nor did she now blunt her words because of his condition. "Are you forgetting, my braw boyo, that I've lived with a Cheysuli longer than you've *been* one?"

It took him aback. He had expected sympathy, gentleness, her quiet, abiding support. What Aileen offered now was something other than that. "It is because of Sima that I—did that."

"Did what? Killed a man? Two?" Aileen did not

smile. "I'm born of the House of Eagles; d'ye think the knowledge of killing's new to me? My House has been to war more times than I can count ... my birthlines are as bloody as yours." She sat very straight upon the stool, russet-hued skirts puddled about slippered feet. "You've killed an Ihlini sorcerer, and a Homanan who meant to kill—or maim—you; as good as dead to the Cheysuli; I know about *kin-wrecking*." Aileen's tone was steady, as were her eyes. "The first killing won't be questioned; he was an *Ihlini*."

His mouth flattened into a grim, contemptuous line. "But the other was Homanan."

"Thief or no," she said, "some will call you a beast."

Memory was merciless. "I *was*."

"So now you're blaming your lovely *lir*."

"She is not my *lir*. Not yet. We are not fully bonded."

"Ah." Aileen's green eyes narrowed. She looked more catlike for it, with a fixed and unsettling stare. "And you're for ending it, are you?"

She read him too easily. Kellin slumped back onto bolsters and bedclothes. She was due honor and courtesy, but he was very tired. Bones were healed, but the body was yet unaware of its improved condition, save the blazing pain was gone. Stiffness persisted; after all that had happened in the space of two days, his resiliency was weakened. Youth could not usurp reality though its teeth be blunted. "I have no choice. *She* made me become—"

"I'm doubting that." Aileen's tone was level, unforgiving; she offered no platitudes designed to ease his soul, but harsher truths instead. "By the gods, I'm doubting *that*! You're the blood of my blood, Kellin, and I'll not hear a word against you from others—but *I* will say what I choose. In this instance, I hide none of it behind kindness and love, but tell it to you plainly: you've only yourself to blame."

His protest was immediate, if incomplete. *"Me?"*

"No Cheysuli warrior alive is without anger, Kellin. He merely controls it better. You control nothing at all, nor make any attempt."

He had no time to think, merely the need to fill the toothed silence yawning between them; to fight back with words from a heart that was filled to bursting with despair and desperation: could *she* not understand? She was his own blood. "I did not *want* to kill them, granddame—at least, aye, perhaps the Ihlini—he threatened *me*, after all!—but not the Homanan, not like *that*—he was a thief, aye, and deserving of roughness, but to kill him like that?" He gestured impatiently, disliking his incoherency; it obscured the strength of intent. "Kill him, aye, because he meant to kill me, or maim me in such a way as to cut me off from my clan, but I never wanted to kill *him*—at least, not as a cat . . . as a man, *aye*—"

"Kellin." She cut him off sharply with voice and gesture; a quick motion of eloquent hand. It was a Cheysuli gesture. "If you would listen to what you just said—or *tried* to say!—you would understand why it is imperative that you fully accept your *lir*."

All his muscles stood up inside flesh in mute repudiation. "My *lir*—or the beast who would *be* my *lir*—has nothing to do with this."

Aileen rose. She was in that moment less his granddame than the Queen of Homana. "You are a fool," she declared. "A spoiled, petulant boy trapped in a man's body, and dangerous because of it. A boy filled to bursting on anger and bitterness can do little harm; a man may do more. A man who is half a beast may do more yet."

"I am *not*—"

"You are what you are," she said flatly. "What are we to think? Aye, a man under attack will do as he must to survive—d'ye think I will *excuse* a man who means to kill my grandson?—but a man such as you, gifted so terribly, can never *be* a man."

Gifted so terribly. He had not looked on it as such. "Grandsire also wears the shape of a cat."

Her mouth was compressed. She permitted herself no latitude in the weight of her displeasure. "No man in all of Homana, not even a Midden thief, need fear that the Mujhar of Homana would ever lose himself to the point he sheds his humanity and *feeds* as a beast."

It shook him. Her face was taut and pale; his own felt worse. He felt it would stretch until the bones of his skull broke through, shredding thinning flesh, thereby displaying the true architecture lying too near the surface.

Human? Or beast? Kellin swallowed heavily. "I want nothing to do with it. *You* are not Cheysuli— surely you can understand how I feel. Does it not frighten you that the man whose bed you share becomes a cat at will?"

"I know the man," she said evenly. "I'm not knowing you at all."

"But—I am *I*!"

"No. You are a bared blade hungry for blood, with no hand on its hilt to steady its course."

"Granddame—"

"He is old," Aileen said, and the cracks of desperation in her self-control began abruptly to show. "He is the Mujhar of Homana, in whose veins the Old Blood flows, and he serves the prophecy. There is no doubt in him; what he does,

he does for the Lion, and for the gods who made
the Cheysuli. What I think does not matter, though
he honors me for it; he does what he must do."
Her hands trembled slightly until she hid them in
skirt folds. "How do you think it felt to be given
a tiny infant and told the future of a realm depended on that infant, because the infant's father
was meant for the gods, not men?"

Kellin did not answer. There were no words in
his mouth.

"How do you think it felt for him to realize the
entire fate of Homana and his own race depended
solely on that infant; that there would be no others
to shore up the claim. If that infant died, the
prophecy died with him. Aidan can sire no more."

Beside him, Sima stirred.

"How do you think it has been for him to watch
what you became? To see you waste yourself on
whores, when there is a cousin in Solinde . . . to
see you risk yourself in the Midden, when there
are safer games nearby . . . to hear you rant about
fatherlessness when *he* has been a father in every
way but seed, and even *then* he is your grandsire!
How do you think it feels?"

He wet dry lips. "Granddame—"

Aileen's face was white and terrible. "How do
you think it feels to know that your grandson—
the only heir to the Lion—lacks the balance that
will maintain his humanity; that if he does not
gain it, the beast in him will prevail?" Aileen
leaned close. "He is my husband," she declared.
"He is my *man*. If you threaten him with this, be
certain you shall suffer."

It shocked him. *"Granddame!"*

She was not finished. "I wasted too many years
not honoring him enough. That time is past. I will
do what I must do to keep him from destroying

himself because a spoiled, defiant grandson refuses to grow up."

"Granddame, you cannot know—"

"*I* know," she said. "I saw his face when he looked at you. I saw his fear."

The Erinnish possessed his tongue. "I'm not knowing what to *do!*"

Aileen stepped close to the bed. Her hand touched Sima's head. "Be what you are. Be a Cheysuli warrior. You're in need of the gods' care more than any man I know."

It filled his mouth before he could prevent it, lashing out to punish. The question was utterly unexpected, yet even as he asked it, Kellin knew he had desired to frame the words for many, many years. "Does it mean nothing to you at all that your son repudiates you?"

Color spilled out of her face.

Kellin was appalled. But the words were said; he could not unsay them. "I only mean—"

"You only mean that he deserted his mother as well as his son, yet she does nothing?" Aileen's eyes were a clear, unearthly green, and empty of tears. "She has not done nothing, Kellin—she has done everything within her power to convince him to come home. But Aidan says—*said*—no, when he answered my letters at first. He answers nothing now; he said I need only ask the gods." Her chin trembled minutely. "He has a powerful faith, my son—so powerful it blinds him to the needs of other people."

"If you went there—"

"He forbids it."

"You are his *jehana!*"

Her fingers folded themselves into her skirts. "I will not go as a supplicant to my own son. I have some measure of pride."

"But it must hurt you!"

Her eyes dimmed behind a glaze of tears. "As it hurts you. As it hurts Brennan. We are all of us scarred by the absence of Aidan."

Cold fury filled Kellin. "And you wonder why I want nothing to do with a *lir*, or with the gods! You have only to look at *him*, and what obsession has made of him. I will not be so bound."

"You will be Mujhar one day. That will bind you even as it does your grandsire."

Kellin shook his head. "That is different. What kind of a Mujhar risks himself by bonding with an animal who might be the death of him? Does he not therefore risk his realm as well—*and* the prophecy?"

Aileen's voice was steady. "What is worth having if you are naught but a beast, and your people desire to kill you?"

Sixteen

One hundred and two steps. Kellin counted them as he climbed down from the Great Hall into the undercroft of Homana-Mujhar, where the Womb of the Earth lay within *lir*-warded walls. As a boy he had gone once with Ian, and once with the Mujhar. He had never gone alone.

Not entirely alone. The cat is with me.

He did not want her there. But she was the reason he went down to the Womb at all.

One hundred and two steps. He stood in a small closet made of stone and depressed the keystone. A wall turned on edge, and the Womb lay before him.

Air was stale, but did not stink of an ending. The passageway walls were damp-slicked and shiny. He carried a torch; it smoked and streamed, shedding fragile light as he put it forward to illuminate the Womb.

Kellin tensed, though he knew what to expect; three visits were not enough to diminish the impact. *Lir* leapt out of walls and ceiling, tearing free of stone. They were incredibly lifelike, as if a sculptor had captured living animals and *encased* them in marble rather than carving them. They stared back at him from hard, challenging eyes: creamy ivory veined with gold.

The Womb gaped. Its rim was nonexistent in distorting light, so that he could not see the rune-worked edge. Only the deeper blackness that marked its mouth.

Kellin wet drying lips and moved past the *lir*-carved door slowly, holding the torch outthrust so he did not mistake the footing and tumble to his death.

But would I die? I am meant to be Mujhar ... those to be Mujhar can survive the rebirth.

He did not have the courage to accept the challenge.

Kellin stepped inside. The Womb's maw expanded as the torch, held in an unsteady hand, illuminated the truth: a perfectly rounded hole that had accepted men before and refused to give them a second birth.

"Carillon," he murmured. "The last Prince of Homana to enter into the Womb and be born in the shape of a king."

He had learned the histories. He knew his birthline. Carillon of Homana, the last Homanan Mujhar.

"After him, Donal. Then Niall. Then—Brennan." Kellin's jaws tightened. *The next should have been my jehan, had he the courage to understand.*

But Aidan had renounced it. Aidan had been a coward.

Should I leap into the Womb to prove my worthiness? Can I atone for my jehan's weakness with my own strength? He stared hard at the marble *lir.* "Is that what they want?"

No answer. The *lir* stared back in silence.

Kellin turned and set the torch into a bracket. Carefully he took three steps to the edge of the Womb, then squatted down beside it. Buttocks brushed booted heels. Sore thighs protested, as did newly knit ribs.

Silence.

Kellin's mouth went dry. In the presence of the

Lion, he had felt many things. But the Womb was not the Lion. It spoke to him of a heritage far older than the Lion's, who was, in the unbiased nature of measurement, naught but a newmade thing. A cub to the Womb's adulthood. The walls were man-made, and the *lir* carved within stone, but before men had meddled to glorify what they perceived as the tangible proof of power, there had been the Womb.

"A gate," Kellin murmured. "How many have gone through it?"

Movement caught his attention. A black shadow paced into the vault, then rounded the Womb. It sat down across from him so that the Womb lay between, black and impenetrable. Gold eyes threw back smoky torchlight, opaque and eerily slanted.

Now, she said. *Your choice.*

He did not speak as a *lir*. "Is it?"

It has always been your choice.

"According to the prophecy, there can be no choice. If a warrior repudiates his *tahlmorra,* his service to the prophecy, he is denied the afterlife."

Her tail twitched once, then folded over arched toes. He had seen housecats sit so; incongruity. She was not and could never be tame. *A man may turn his back on life after death. It is his right to do so. It is the price of living.*

"To choose how he will live after he is dead?" Kellin grinned derisively. "I sense obscurity. I smell the kind of argument that must content my *jehan,* who traffics with the gods. How else could a man be made to repudiate his son?"

He did not. He answered his tahlmorra. Her tail twitched again. *He created* your *tahlmorra in the following of his own.*

Kellin frowned. "I mislike oblique speech. Say what there is to say."

That it is a warrior's choice to be other than the gods might prefer him to be.

"And therefore alter the prophecy?"

Your jehan might say that altering of the prophecy also follows its path.

Kellin swore and sat down upon his rump, letting his heels slide forward. With blatant disregard for proprieties, he dangled both legs into the void. "You are saying that a man who turns his back on the prophecy also *follows* it by that very repudiation. But how? It makes no sense. If I made myself celibate and sired no more children, there would be no Firstborn. How would that serve a prophecy that exists solely to *make* another Firstborn?"

You have already sired children.

He thought about it. So he had. They, too, each of them, claimed the proper blood. *Save for the final House, the final link in the chain.* Kellin drew in a deep breath. "If I went to Solinde and found myself an Ihlini woman with whom I could bear to lie and got a child upon her, the task is finished. The prophecy complete."

Sima's tail twitched. She offered no answer.

"I could do it tomorrow, if I decided to. Leave. Go to Solinde. Find myself a woman, and end this travesty."

Sima displayed her teeth. *No one ever said it would be difficult.*

Kellin exploded. "Then if it is so *easy* to do—" But he let it trail off. "The blood. It comes to that. Ian lay with Lillith and sired Rhiannon. Rhiannon lay with my grandsire and bore—who? A daughter? The one who in turn lay with Lochiel and bore *him* the daughter with whom I shared a cradle?" Kellin hitched his shoulders. "And who, no doubt, would be the unlikeliest woman with whom I should be matched—and therefore is, in the perversity of the gods, the very woman they *intend* for me to lie with. To sire the proper son. Cynric, the Firstborn.'"

Sima held her silence.

The image was vivid before him. "Lochiel will geld me. He will show the woman to me—or, rather, me to her—and then he will *geld* me! So that I know, and she knows, how very close we came—and how superior the Ihlini are despite our Cheysuli gifts."

Sima bent her head and licked delicately at a paw.

"No answer?" Kellin asked. "No commentary? But I believed the *lir* were put here to *aid* their warriors, not obfuscate the truth."

The cat lowered her paw. She stared directly at him across the black expanse of the Womb. Feral gold eyes dominated the darkness. *I am not your lir. Have you not declared it? Have you not renounced me as your jehan renounced you?*

Had he? Had he?

A *lirless* warrior was destined to go mad. A *lirless* Cheysuli was not a warrior at all. A *lirless* Cheysuli could never be Mujhar. Could never hold the Lion. Could never sire the Firstborn because the Cheysuli would look to another.

A solution presented itself. An answer to the questions.

Kellin shuddered once. Sweat ran down his temples and stung the scratches on his face. Breathing was shallow, though the ribs now were healed. A flutter filled his belly, then spilled to genitals.

He swallowed painfully because his throat was dry and tight. He pressed both hands against cold stone on either side of his thighs. Fingertips left damp marks. Within the link, he said, *Let the gods decide.*

Kellin, prince of Homana, thrust himself into the Womb.

No top. No bottom. No sides.

No beginning, nor an ending.

Merely a *being*.

Kellin bit his lips bloody so he would not scream. It would diminish him to scream. Such noise would dishonor the gods.

Gods? What did he know of gods? They were, he had said, little more than constructs invented by men who desired to rule others, to keep lesser men contained so that *they* maintained the power.

Gods. His father worshiped them. *Jehan*, father, sire . . . there were so many words. None of them made sense. Nothing at all made sense to a man who leapt into the Womb.

The only sense in such folly was the *search* for sense, so he might understand what manner of man he was and what he was meant to be in the context of the gods.

Gods. Yet again.

If he renounced them, if he repudiated them, would they permit him to die?

If there *were* no gods, then surely he was dead.

Kellin fell. There was no bottom. He did not scream at all.

What were the Cheysuli but children of the gods? It was what the word meant.

Upon such unflagging faith was a race made strong, so others could not destroy it.

Men who had nothing in which to believe soon believed in Nothing. Nothing destroyed a man. Nothing destroyed a race.

Was Nothing, then, a demon?

Belief replaced Nothing. Belief destroyed the demon.

The Cheysuli were, if nothing else, a dedicated

race. Once a thing made sense within the context of their culture, belief was overriding. Belief was their champion; it overwhelmed Nothing so the demon died of disuse, of DisBelief.

In the Womb, Kellin laughed. What had Sima said as Kellin looked upon flesh-bound wrists? *"You believe too easily in what the Ihlini tells you to. His art is illusion. Banish this one as you banished the Lion."*

Illusion was another's successful attempt to make a man believe in something that did not truly exist. The key to banishing illusion was to *dis*believe.

Corwyth, and other Ihlini, had tried very hard to make the Cheysuli disbelieve in the prophecy.

The Ihlini disbelieved. Teirnan and the *a'saii* had—and did—disbelieve. And if *dis*belief could defeat illusion, and yet the prophecy survived, was it therefore a true thing, a thing with substance?

Or was it simply that the Cheysuli who believed in it believed *so strongly* that the weight of their faith, the contents of their spirits, destroyed the disbelief?

The champion of the gods, called Belief, destroyed the demon whose true-name was DisBelief.

Kellin cried out in the confines of the Womb: *"I do not understand!"*

History rose up. So many lessons learned. The hours and days and weeks and months Rogan had spent with him, laboring to instruct so that Kellin comprehended the heritage of the races he represented.

He could name all his races, all the Houses in his blood. They were each of them necessary.

So was it necessary for him to have a *lir;* to renounce the bond was to renounce his very self and the legacy of the blood.

A *lirless* Cheysuli had hurled himself into the Womb. He had placed his fate within the hands of the gods.

Kellin's shout echoed: *"Tahlmorra lujhalla mei wiccan, cheysu!"*

He had invited them to decide. If a man did *not* believe, would he risk himself so? If DisBelief ruled him, he would therefore commit suicide by issuing such a challenge, for a challenge with no recipient was no challenge at all but the substanceless defiance of an ignorant child.

Suicide was taboo.

Paradox, Kellin thought: Suicide was taboo, yet a *lirless* Cheysuli undertook the death-ritual. His sojourn in the forest was meant to find his death however it chose to take him; it was nothing else *but* suicide, though a man did not stab himself, or drink poison knowingly.

He died because of beasts. He died as prey to predator, as meat for the gods' creatures.

From flesh-colored clay in the hands of the gods, a man became meat.

The Wheel of Life turned so that the clay was fired in the kiln of the gods and set upon the earth to live as the clay willed. Believing or DisBelieving.

Kellin understood.

"Y'ja'hai!" he shouted.

Clay without the blood of a *lir* was nothing but colorless powder. Unmixed. Unmade. Never thrown upon the Wheel.

Kellin understood.

Kellin Believed.

The image of Sima's face flashed before blind eyes.

"I accept," he said. *"Y'ja'hai."* Then, desperately, "Will you accept me?"

The words rang in his head. *Ja'hai-na*, she said.
Y'ja'hai.

The *lir*-link meshed, locked, sealed itself together. Nothing could break it now but the death
of warrior or *lir*.

That knowledge no longer mattered to Kellin.
He was whole. He was Cheysuli.

The Womb of the Earth was fertile. The *Jehana*
gave birth once again after nearly one hundred
years, to suckle the newborn man upon the bosom
of his *tahlmorra*.

The Prince of Homana would one day become
Mujhar.

He roused to torch-smudged darkness and the
gaze of marble *lir*. He lay sprawled on his back
with arms and legs splayed loosely, without purpose or arrangement, as if a large negligent hand
had spilled him from its palm onto the vault floor.

He thought perhaps one had.

"Lir?" He gasped it aloud, because before he had
refused to honor her in the link. "Sima?" And
then, scraping himself up from the floor, he
wrenched his body sideways, to grasp frenziedly
at the cat who sat quietly by the hole into which
he had pushed himself. *Lir?* This time in the link,
so there was no room for doubt. There would
never be doubt again. He would not permit it;
could not *allow* himself—

Sima blinked huge eyes.

He scrabbled to her on awkward knees, needing
to touch her fur; requiring to touch the body that
housed the blazing spirit. *Lir? Lir?*

Sima yawned widely to display fearsome fangs.
Then she shook her head, worked wiry whiskers,
and rose. She padded all of two steps, pressed her
head into his shoulder, then butted him down. She
was ungentle; she wanted him to acknowledge the

power in her body despite its immaturity. She was *lir*, after all; far superior to *cat*.

He could say nothing but her name. He said it many times despite the fur in his mouth as she leaned down upon him; despite the weight on his chest as she lay down across him; despite the warping of his mouth as her tongue reshaped his lips.

Lir—lir—lir. He could not say it enough.

Sima kneaded his shoulders. Smugly, she said, *Better now than never*.

While the tears ran down his face.

Seventeen

Kellin clattered down the stairs to the first floor, intent on his destination. Behind him came Sima, glossy in mid-morning light; gold eyes gleamed. Daily her gangliness faded and was replaced by a burgeoning maturity, as if full bonding had at last loosed the vestiges of cubhood. She would one day, Kellin believed, rival Sleeta for size and beauty.

A month ago you would not have considered it, she told him.

A month ago I was lirless, and therefore lacked a soul. What man without a soul can acknowledge his lir's promise?

Within the link, she laughed. *How we have changed in four weeks!*

He left behind the staircase and strode on toward the entryway. *Some would argue I have not changed at all; that I still frequent taverns—*

But not those in the Midden.

No, but taverns all the same—

And the women in them?

Kellin grinned; its suddenness startled a passing serving-woman, who dropped into an awkward, red-faced curtsy even as he went by. *Is there something you have neglected to tell me? Is there more to a link between warrior and female lir than I have been led to believe?*

That is vulgarity, lir.

Of course it is. You had best get used to it. No one has ever argued for my kindness and decency—have you not heard the stories?

Sima padded beside him, bumping a shoulder into his knee. *I need hear nothing, lir. What you are is in your mind.*

So I gave up privacy when I linked with you.

She yawned. *When a warrior bonds with a lir, he no longer desires privacy.*

It was true. He shared everything with Sima, save the intimacy his vulgarity implied. And while she did not climb into the bed he shared with a woman, she nonetheless was fully aware of what passed within it; she merely curled herself on the floor and slept—or pretended to. Kellin had gotten used to it, though he supposed there was gossip exchanged regarding a certain perverse affinity for a mountain cat as onlooker; and he was not certain he disapproved. Let them wonder about him. He would sooner be of interest than taken for granted, as he believed the Mujhar was.

"Kellin! Kellin?" It was Aileen, silver threads more evident in fading hair. "Have you a moment?"

He paused as she came down the corridor. "Now?" He displayed the warbow he carried, and the suede quiver full of white-fletched arrows. "I was bound for a hunt with my watchdogs." Kellin grinned. "They require activity. Of late I bore them, now I am reformed."

Aileen arched an ironic eyebrow. "You are not 'reformed,' my lad, merely *diverted*. And 'twill only take a moment; a letter has come from Hart. Brennan wants you in the solar."

"Bad news?"

Aileen touched a fingertip to her upper lip. "I'm thinking not," she said neutrally, "depending on point of view."

"On point of—" His suspicions blossomed as he saw the glint in green eyes. "Gods—'tis Dulcie, isn't it? Grandsire's put off Hart long enough, waiting for me to measure up . . . and now that he believes I've done it, he begins a discussion about marriage!"

"There was discussion of it a decade ago," she reminded him. " 'Tis nothing new, and should not surprise you. You are both well-grown."

He put up a silencing hand. "Enough. I will go. Will you send word to the watchdogs I will be delayed?"

" 'Tis sent," Aileen said. "Now, go to Brennan. Whatever complaint you have to make is better made to him."

"Aye. You argued *against* the marriage that decade ago." Kellin sighed. "But now you are for it, undoubtedly; catch the feckless warrior before he becomes less malleable."

"You are not now and never will be malleable," Aileen retorted, "merely occasionally less inclined to defy." She pointed. "Go."

Kellin went.

The solar was less bright now that the sun had moved westward, but displayed no shadows. The Mujhar sat in his usual chair with his legs propped on a stool and a wine cup in his hand. Against his thigh rested a creased, wax-weighted parchment held down by a slack hand.

The door stood ajar. Kellin shouldered it open more fully and crossed the threshold, tapping rattling arrows against one knee. "So, I am to be wed. This year, or next? In Homana, or Solinde?"

Brennan smiled. He showed more age now; the healing of his grandson had left its mark. "Have you no objection?"

"A mouthful, but you will hear none of them."

Kellin tapped arrows again as he halted before his grandsire. "What does Hart say?"

"That there is no sense in putting off what must be done."

"How cognizant of tenderness is my great-uncle of Solinde." Kellin sighed. "I suppose it must, then. To link Houses, and bloodlines . . . and no doubt beget the child who will fulfill the prophecy." Irony spilled away. "Neither of us has a choice, grandsire. Neither Dulcie, nor me. Like you and granddame; like Niall and Gisella; like Donal and Aislinn."

"Nor did Carillon and Solindish Electra, through whose blood comes the proper match." Brennan's mouth twisted. "So many years, so many marriages—all designed to bring us to this point."

"Not to *this* point, surely; to the birth, grandsire. Wedding Dulcie means nothing at all to the gods, only the son born of the union." Kellin gestured with the warbow. "Have it carved in stone, if you will, like the *lir* within the Womb: Kellin of Homana shall wed Dulcie of Solinde, and so beget the Firstborn."

Brennan's fingers creased soiled parchment. "Left to your own devices—"

Kellin took it up. "Left to my own devices, I would doubtless waste my seed on a dozen different whores for the rest of the month, then turn to a dozen more." He shrugged. "Does it matter? I have known since I was ten it would come to this . . . Dulcie knew it, too. It may as well have been settled as we soiled our royal wrappings; there never was a chance we could look another way."

"No," Brennan conceded. "We are so very close, Kellin—"

"Then be done with it. Have her come here, or I will go there. I do not care." He waved bunched arrows. "Write it now, if you will. Let me be about my hunt. My watchdogs wait."

Brennan's mouth compressed though the faint displeasure engendered by flippancy was less pronounced than resignation. "Be about it, then. I will have this sent tomorrow."

Glumly, Kellin nodded. "My last hunt in freedom."

Brennan barked a laugh. "I doubt *Dulcie* will curtail your hunting, Kellin! She is very much Hart's daughter, in spirit as well as tastes."

"Why? Does she wager? Well, then, perhaps we will make a match of it after all." But levity faded in the face of his future now brought so near. Kellin shrugged. "It will do well enough. At least she is half Cheysuli; she will understand about Sima."

"Indeed," Brennan said gravely; a glint in his eye bespoke the irony of the statement because but four weeks before Sima was sheer impediment rather than half of Kellin's soul.

Kellin, who knew it; who saw the look in his grandsire's eye and colored under it, lifted his arrows. "I will help replenish the larder." Erinn slid into his words. " 'Twill take a day or two— don't be expecting me back before then." He grinned. "And aye, I'll be taking my watchdogs; they'll be hunting as well!"

Spring had arrived fitfully, turning snow to slush, slush to mud, then freezing it all together in a brief defiant spasm before resolving itself to its work. Kellin felt an affinity for the season as he rode out with Teague and the others; now more than ever he longed to remember winter, because *then* there had been no cause to concern himself with a wife.

"Cheysula," he muttered.

Teague, next to him on a red roan, lifted inquisitive brows. "What?"

Kellin repeated the word. "Old Tongue," he said, "for 'wife.' "

"*Ah.*" Teague understood at once. "That time at last, is it?"

Kellin knew the incident in the Midden tavern had sealed their friendship, though Teague was careful to keep a distance between them so familiarity did not interfere with service. The others also had relaxed now that their lord was easier in himself; he knew very well the prevailing opinion was that Sima had worked wonders with the prince's temperament. For all he had initially disturbed them the night he was trapped in cat-form, they did not in any way indicate residual fear.

"That time," he agreed glumly. "I hoped it might wait a year or two more—or three, or four—"

"—or five?—"

"—but they'll not wait any longer. I'll be wed before summer, I'll wager."

Teague laughed. "Then you know nothing of women, my lord. She will be wanting an elaborate wedding with all the Houses of the world invited so they can bring her gifts."

Kellin considered it. "She did not appear to be much concerned for such things when I saw her last."

"How old was she?"

"Twelve?" He shrugged. "Or thirteen; I have lost track."

The young watchdog grinned. "Then she'll be *just* the age to demand such elaboration! You will not escape, my lord. But it offers you respite; it will take at least until *next* winter to prepare for such a feast!"

Kellin slanted a glance at Sima across one

shoulder. "I do not know which is worse: wedding immediately with little ceremony—" he turned back to guide his mount, "—or putting it off a year so that so much can be made of it!"

One of the others joined in: a man named Ennis, who was Teague's boon companion. "Better now than tomorrow," he offered. "That way we can be done with our duty that much the sooner."

Kellin looked at him blankly.

Ennis grinned. "Do you think the Princess of Homana will desire our company?"

He had not considered that. Perhaps his marriage *would* offer him respite from the watchdogs, but Kellin was not convinced trading one for the other would prove so good a thing.

They left Mujhara and headed directly north, toward the woods that fringed the road. Because not so many people traveled the North Road, hunting was better. It did not take long for Kellin and his watchdogs to flush game. He hung back slightly, letting the Homanans do much of the work, and waited until they were so caught up in chasing down a hart that they forgot about him entirely.

Satisfied, he glanced down at Sima. *Now we can test it.*

She fixed him with an unwavering stare. *Best to know now what the last four weeks have wrought.*

Kellin dismounted and dropped reins over a limb thrust slantwise from a tree. He left the horse, quiver, and warbow and walked farther into the woods, conscious of the anticipatory flutter in his belly.

Be not so fearful, Sima suggested, following on his heels. *We have time.*

How much? he asked uneasily. *What should happen if, driven to anger in the midst of political tur-*

moil, I forget my human trappings and become nothing more than a beast?

Time, she repeated. *What turmoil is there to be? You are prince, not king. You matter little yet for the turmoil to involve you.*

A humbling reminder. Kellin sighed and beat his way through brush to a small clearing, then closed his hand on the wolf's-head pommel of Blais' knife. "Strength," he murmured, invoking his kinsman's memory. "You had your share of it, and of courage; lend a measure to me."

Sima pressed against one knee, then flowed away to take up position nearby. She sat with tail tucked over toes, ear-tufts flicking minutely. *You have learned much in four weeks.*

Kellin rubbed at too-taut shoulders, trying to ease the tension. *I have learned advice in four weeks. The doing yet remains, and that is what I fear.*

Be what you are, Sima said. *Kellin. That is all you can be, regardless of your shape.*

"More," he said. "I was more, *twice.*"

Sima blinked. *That was before.*

"Before you?" He grinned. "Aye, and therefore did not count; I was *lirless,* and unblessed." Humor spilled away. "Well enough. Let us see what I become when I trade my shape for another."

He squeezed the hilt once more, then let his hand fall away. With careful deliberation Kellin detached himself from the moment and let his awareness drift from the *here and now* to the *there,* with no sense of time, where the magic resided deep in the earth.

Power pulsed. At first it was coy, caressing his awareness so he knew it was there for the taking, then flowing away to tease him yet again with insubstantiality.

It was frustrating. *Sima*—

Yours to do, she told him.

He concentrated. Power flirted, seduced; he wanted it very badly. His body rang with tension that was almost sexual, an intense and abiding need. He let himself go into it until awareness of self became awareness of need, of what would satisfy him, and then Power uncovered itself like a woman shedding draperies and let him touch it.

—different—

It was. Before he had merely thought of the beast, neglecting to recall that he was a man with a man's distinct needs. The beast had overtaken all that was man, until he was helpless and unaware, beaten down from his humanity into animal instinct. This time he knew. His name was Kellin, not cat, and he was a *man*. A fully bonded Cheysuli warrior who had recourse to the magic that lived in the womb of the earth.

He touched it. It set his fingertips atingle.

Kellin, he whispered. *Man, not cat—but lend me the shape, and I will do it honor.*

Senses flared. Images broke up his mind. No longer human images of a human world, but the patterns of a cat.

Am I—?

Not yet, Sima said. *There is more yet to be done.*

More. He did not know more.

He fell. He was in the Womb again, empty of everything save a vague but burning awareness that he was a man who desired, but briefly, to give his human form to the earth so he might, for only a while, walk the world as a cat.

Not so much to ask.

Vision exploded. His eyes were open, but he saw nothing save a disorientation so great it threatened equilibrium. Kellin thrust out a staying hand intended to hold him upright, but it broke through the crust of the earth and sank deep into the river of Homana's Power.

Earth magic. There for the taking.

Kellin took it.

There, Sima said. *Not so difficult after all.*

Smells engulfed, replacing reliance on sight. In cat-form, Kellin exulted.

Let us run, Sima suggested. *Let us run as cats, so you know what it is to honor the gods.*

He did not think much of gods. But in this form, filled with the glory of *lir*-shape, Kellin could not protest.

If it was gods who were responsible, he would honor them.

Eighteen

Kellin ran through the sun-dappled forest with Sima at his shoulder, lovely, magnificent Sima—no other warrior's *lir* was half so beautiful!—and took joy in the pure, almost sensual freedom the cat-shape gave him. He explored it as he ran, marking the differences within his brain, yet the samenesses as well. His awareness of self was unchanged despite the body's alteration; he knew perfectly well he was a man in a *borrowed* form that would, when he chose, be exchanged once again for the proper body. There was no division in his soul other than that his awareness permitted; he did not wish himself one or the other. He simply was what he was: a Cheysuli warrior with magic in his blood, who could, when he desired to, become a mountain cat.

You see? Sima asked.

Kellin exulted. He believed he understood himself at last, and the needs that lived in his soul; he could control himself in this shape as easily as he could in human form. He need only remember, to keep alive the spark of self-knowledge that recalled he was Kellin, and human, so as not to tip the balance from *lir*-shape into beast form.

Not so difficult. His muscled body stretched, fluid in graceful motion, stronger by far than the human shape. *She has taught me much in the past weeks. I understand better. I understand what it is.*

Sima interrupted. *A stag, just ahead. Fit for Homana-Mujhar?*

He saw it; it was. A fine, huge stag with a magnificent rack of antlers.

Kellin slowed, then stilled even as Sima did. The stag stood unmoving, poised in a patch of sunlight. Flanks heaved from exertion; was he prey to someone's hunt?

Kellin did not care. The stag was *theirs*, now, and indeed fit for Homana-Mujhar. He was large and would no doubt prove difficult to take down, but there were two of them. Together they could manage it.

First leap to you, Kellin said.

Sima was pleased. She crouched even as he did, tail barely twitching at the tip. She tensed in a perfect stillness, tufted ears motionless.

Now— She was instantly in motion: a black, sleek blur that sprang effortlessly from the ground and hurled herself through the air.

Sima screamed. For an instant Kellin pinned tufted ears, wondering why she would startle the stag into flight and risk losing the prey, then saw the feathered shaft of an arrow protruding from her flank as she twisted in midair and fell.

She screamed again, and so did he. Her pain was his own, and the shock that consumed her body. She was down, twisting to bite frenziedly at the shaft.

Kellin heard a human voice shouting in fear and horror. A man burst through the bushes on foot. His face was drained; when he saw both cats, his horror was redoubled. "My lord! My lord, I did not mean it! It was the stag—the arrow was loosed before I saw her!"

The *lir*-link was alive with Sima's pain. Kellin shuddered with it, and the hair along his spine stood up straight. The shout of rage that issued from his throat was not that of a man, but of the beast instead.

The arrow in Sima's flesh dug deeply into his own. Pain, shock, and weakness merged into fury, and the comprehension of hideous truth: his *lir* was dying; so, then, was he.

Kellin screamed, and leapt.

The man thrust up a warding arm, but made no effort to draw the knife that might have saved his life. His mouth warped open in horror, but he did not move. It was as if he did not believe that his Cheysuli lord, though bound now by *lir*-shape, would ever truly harm him.

The man went down beneath the cat and gave up his life in an instant. He did not even cry out as the throat was torn from his body.

Other men burst from the trees on horseback and drew up in a ragged, abrupt halt that set horses' mouths to gaping and men to swearing. Kellin dared them to attack. He stood over the prey and dared them to take it.

The keening scream welled in his chest and burst from his throat. Their faces twitched and blanched. None of them moved.

"Teague," one said, though the word made little sense. "Gods—he has killed *Teague*!"

Sima panted behind him. Kellin turned his dripping head and saw her sprawled on her right side, feathered shaft buried deep in her left flank. It bore the Mujhar's colors, and the richer crimson of her blood.

She panted. Her tongue lolled. The gold eyes dimmed.

Lir! Kellin cried.

She was beyond speech. He felt only her fear and pain and the bewildered questioning of what had happened.

Anger burned fiercely. Kellin swung back to the

others and took a single step toward them. Horses snorted uneasily; one jibbed at the bit.

"My lord," a man said; his hands shook on the reins. A companion broke and ran, then a third, then a fourth. The one who had named the prey remained behind. "My lord," he said again, and his young face twisted in a mingling of shock and outrage. "Do you even know whom you have killed?"

Kellin tried to say it: *"The man who nearly killed Sima!"* But none of the words came out. Only a keening growl.

"He was your friend!" the Homanan shouted, tears filling his eyes. "Or now that you are a beast, do you only count *them* as friends?" In his anger, the young man drew his knife and threw it to the ground. "There! You may have it. I want none of it! I forswear my service; I renounce my rank. I want nothing to do with a prince who kills his friends, for assuredly he is not the man I want as my king!" He scrubbed hastily at his face. "The Mujhar is a man I honor, but I owe you nothing. I *give* you nothing; I am quit of royal service as of this moment!"

Kellin could not form the words. With effort he beat back the pain within the link, the knowledge of Sima's condition, and concentrated long enough to banish the shape that prevented communication. Human-form came quickly, too quickly; he stumbled to his knees, bracing himself upright with one hand thrust into deadfall. *"Wait—"* he blurted.

"Wait? Wait?" It was Ennis; Kellin's human eyes recognized him now. "For what? So you may change again, and tear out *my* throat?" Ennis's grief was profound. "He was my friend, my lord. We grew up together, and now you have killed him. Do you expect me to *wait* while you fashion an explanation?"

"Sima—" Kellin panted. He hung there on hands and knees, then scrubbed haphazardly at his bloodied face. "My *lir*—in her pain, I could not stop." Sima's pain still ruled him, though now he was a man. Breathlessly he insisted, "He attacked her! What else was I to do? Permit him to kill her? Then he kills *me*!"

"He wanted the *stag*, my lord! None of us saw the cat." Ennis reined in his restive horse. His anguished face was twisted. "Will you permit me, my lord, to recover the body? I would prefer to give it a proper burial before you decide to eat it!"

Disorientation faded. The link remained strong, as did the pain contained within it, but Kellin was no longer a cat and he felt Sima's pain another way. He understood the difference between her senses and his own.

A man dead? By his doing? Still weak from the abruptness of his shapechange, Kellin turned awkwardly and saw the body sprawled in deadfall; the torn and bloodied throat. He recognized the man, acknowledged the handiwork. In that moment he fully comprehended what he had done. *"NO!"*

"Aye," Ennis retorted. "You have blood on your mouth, my lord; royalty or not, you cannot hide the truth from a man who has seen the Prince of Homana murder an innocent man."

Nearby, Sima panted. Blood matted her flank.

Brief concentration broke up in response to renewed pain. The link was filled with it, stuffing Kellin's head. He could think of nothing else but his *lir*. "Sima—"

"May I take the body?" Ennis persisted. "You may find another dinner."

Teague. It was Teague. He had killed Teague.

Lir? Sima's tone was weak. *Lir, you must heal me. Waste no time.*

"Will you permit me the leave to take my friend back?" Ennis asked.

Now, Sima said. Her tongue lolled from her mouth. *Lir—*

Teague was dead. Sima was dying. No doubt at that moment Ennis would prefer his prince died also, but Kellin could not give in merely to please him. He would not permit the travesty to go forth.

"Take him," he rasped, moving toward the cat, thinking only of the cat so he could avoid the truth. "Take him to my grandsire."

Ennis blurted a laugh that was profound in its anguish. "Be certain I shall! The Mujhar shall be told of this. He needs to know what manner of beast is his heir."

The tone flayed. *"Go!"* Kellin shouted. "It is a matter of balance—I have no control! If *you* would live, take Teague and go!" He knelt down at Sima's side. *What am I to do? How do I heal you?*

You are Cheysuli, she said. *Rely on that which makes you a warrior, and use it to heal me.*

The instructions he found obscure, but her condition alarmed him. It was all he could do not to fling back his head and howl his fear and pain. "Magic," he panted. "Gods—give me the magic."

He *was* Cheysuli. The power came at his call.

When it was done, Kellin came awake with a snap and realized in his trance he tread close to sleep, or to collapse. His bloodied hands were yet pressed against Sima's side, but the arrow was gone. He saw a few bits of feathers lying on the ground with the arrowhead itself, but the shaft was gone, as if burned to ash.

The breath came back into his lungs all unexpectedly, expanding what had collapsed, refilling what was empty. He coughed painfully. The world slid sideways; braced arms failed and spilled him to the ground, so that he landed flat upon his spine. The back of his skull thumped dully against leaf-strewn ground.

Sima stirred next to him. *The healing is complete. You have done well.*

He could not so much as open his eyes. *Had I not, we would both be bound for the afterlife. I was not in so much of a hurry.*

Nor I. She shifted closer yet, pressing the warmth of her body against his right side. *The magic drains a man. There is balance in that, also . . . we have time, lir. No need to move at once.*

He did not much feel like moving ever, let alone at once. Kellin sighed, welcoming the coolness of the deadfall beneath him. His itching face felt crusted. He longed to scratch it, but to do that required him to move a hand. It was too much to attempt.

Lir. Sima again, resting her chin upon his shoulder. *I am sorry for the man.*

"What m—" He broke off. Kellin thrust himself to hands and knees and hurled himself over, to look, to seek, to reassure himself that none of it was true.

Teague's body was gone, but bloodied leaves and hoofprints confirmed the truth Kellin desired to avoid. Teague indeed had died, and Ennis had carried him home.

Kellin touched his crusted face with fingers that shook. *Teague's blood.*

"Gods," he choked aloud, "why do you *permit* this?"

Lir. Sima rose, butted at an arm. *Lir, it is done. It cannot be undone.*

"I killed—" He could not voice it, could not find the words. "I killed *Teague*—"

Reflex, she told him. *A cat, to protect himself, strikes first. You struck to protect me.*

"Teague," Kellin mouthed.

Even the comfort of the *lir*-link was not enough.

He had killed a man who was not an Ihlini, not a thief, not an enemy.

I have killed a friend.

Kellin sank down to the ground and pressed his face against it, unmindful of bloodied leaves.

I have killed a friend.

He recalled Teague's presence in the Midden tavern where Luce held sovereignty, and how the Homanan had aided him. How Teague had, of them all, not looked upon him as a beast the night he had nearly killed Luce because Teague had a better understanding of what lived in his lord's mind.

I swore to have no friends because I lost them all—because they all died . . . and now when I let one come close again after so much time, I kill him MYSELF—

He wound rigid hands into his hair and knotted them there, then permitted himself to shout as a man might shout to declare his grief and torment.

But the sound, to Kellin, was naught but a beast's wail.

Nineteen

It was demonstrably obvious, when Kellin reached Homana-Mujhar, that Ennis and the others had carried word before him. The horse-boy who took his mount did so with eyes averted and led the horse away quickly, not even waiting for his customary coin. Off-duty men gathered before the guardhouse in the bailey fell silent as Kellin walked by them, breaking off conversation to stare from the corners of their eyes. They measured him, he knew; they looked for the proof in his face, in his clothing, in the expression in his eyes.

What do they see?

He had washed the blood from face and hands, and scrubbed at his jerkin. He believed no bloodstains remained, but possibly none were required; he wore guilt in his posture despite his desire not to.

Sima padded beside him. They watched her, too, marking her apparent health. She did not limp or show any indication an arrow had but hours before driven her toward death. It was a natural healing, but to the Homanans, who had little knowledge of such things, it seemed to suggest that Kellin's reaction was one of whim, not of need; as if he had killed Teague because the idea had occurred, and because he could.

Kellin paused inside the palace to inquire as to the Mujhar's whereabouts, and was told to go at once to the Great Hall. Inwardly, Kellin's spirit quailed. *Not in privacy? Or is it that he will discuss it with me as Mujhar, not grandsire, nor even Cheysuli warrior?*

Sima bumped his leg. *I am with you.*

No. Kellin paused. *This is for me to face alone. Go up to my chambers and wait.*

She hesitated, then turned and padded away.

Kellin brushed haphazardly at the perspiration stippling his upper lip, then went on toward the Great Hall. Foreboding weighted his spirit until he twitched with it, desiring to scratch at stinging flesh.

Brennan was on the throne. The Lion's head reared above the Mujhar in a display of wooden glory. Aged eyes stared blindly; Kellin was grateful the Lion could not see what had become of a prince who would one day inherit it.

It was nearing sundown. Light slanting through stained glass formed lattices on the stone floor, so that Kellin walked through sharp-etched pools of pure color. In spring, the firepit was unlighted. Kellin walked its length steadily, though more slowly than was his wont; he would not shirk the confrontation but did not desire to hasten it. What would come, would come; no need to accelerate it.

He reached the dais all too soon. And then he saw Aileen standing at Brennan's right side with one hand on the Lion. *It is serious—* Kellin clamped closed his teeth, feeling again the emptiness in his jaw where Luce had broken a tooth. Healing had sealed it closed, but the tooth was banished forever.

His grandsire looked old. The years had been kind to him for a long time, but now the kindness was banished. The healing four weeks before had left its mark, and the knowledge Ennis had brought. Dark skin no longer was as supple and taut, permitting brackets to form at nose and mouth, and webwork patches beside his eyes. The Mujhar's hands rested lightly over the curving, clawed armrests, but the knuckles were distended.

Kellin halted before the dais. Briefly he inclined his head to Aileen, then offered homage to the Mujhar. He waited in tense silence, wishing Sima stood beside him; knowing it as weakness. It was time he acknowledged it.

Brennan's eyes did not waver. His voice was steady. "When a king has but a single heir, and no hope of any others, he often overlooks such things as the hot blood of youth, and the trouble a boy can rouse. Gold soothes injured pride and mends broken taverns. It will even, occasionally, placate an angry *jehan* whose daughter has been taken with child. But it does not buy back a life. Even a king dares not overlook that."

Kellin wet dry lips. "I do not ask you to overlook it. Merely understand it."

"I have been told by Ennis and the others that they heard Teague cry out; that he knew he had made a mistake."

"My lord, he did."

"And yet you used the power of *lir*-shape to kill him anyway."

It would have been better, Kellin decided, if the Mujhar had shouted at him, because then he could rely upon anger. But Brennan did not; he merely made quiet statements in a grave and habitual dignity that Kellin knew very well he could never emulate.

He inhaled a trembling breath. "My lord, I am moved to remind you of what you already know: that a warrior in *lir*-shape encounters all of the pain his *lir* does. It—affects—him."

"I *do* know it," Brennan agreed. "But a warrior

in *lir*-shape is yet a man, and understands that a Homanan who acknowledges his mistake is not to be murdered."

Behind his back, Kellin balled his hands into fists. It would undermine his appeal if he shouted; and besides, he *was* guilty. "Sima was wounded. She was dying. All I could think about was that he had shot her, that she was badly hurt, and that if *she* died, I died also." The words were hard to force past a tight throat. "He was my friend, my lord. I never meant to kill him."

"You did. In that moment, you did indeed intend to kill him." Brennan's hands closed more tightly over the armrest. "Do you think I cannot see it? I am Cheysuli also."

Grief and anguish commingled to overwhelm. "Then why confront me like this?" Kellin cried. "By the gods, grandsire—"

But Brennan's sharp gesture cut Kellin's protest off. "Enough. There are other things to concern ourselves with than whether I understand what led to the attack."

"What other things?" Kellin demanded. "You yourself have said we cannot buy back Teague's life, but I will do whatever I must to atone for my mistake."

Brennan leaned forward. "Do you hear what you are saying? You speak of Teague's death as a mistake, an unfortunate circumstance you could not avoid."

"It was!"

"Yet when Teague makes a mistake, you respond by killing him." Brennan's face was taut. "Tell me where the difference lies. Why is one mistake excused—because you are a prince?—while one results in murder?"

"I—" Kellin swallowed heavily. "I could not help myself."

"In *lir*-shape."

"Aye." He understood now what Brennan meant him to see. "I felt her pain, her fear—"

"And your own."

"And my own." Kellin's face warped briefly. "I feared for her, grandsire—I had not had her very long, yet I could not imagine what it would be like to lose her. The grief, the anguish—" He looked at Brennan. "I thought I might go mad."

"Had she died, you would have." The Mujhar sank back into the Lion. "It is the price we pay. All your arguments against the death-ritual now mean nothing."

Kellin stared hard at the stone beneath his boots. "Aye."

"Through the link, her pain was yours . . . and you feared she would die. Knowing what it would cost."

"My life," Kellin murmured.

"So you took his, even though you might have turned to Sima at once and begun the healing that would have saved two lives: hers, and Teague's."

His mouth was stiff, awkward. "I could not help myself."

"No," Brennan agreed in abject weariness, "you never have been able to. And that is why you are here before us now: to decide what must be done."

He looked up sharply. "What must be done?" he echoed. "But—what *is* there to do? There are rituals for Teague, and his family to tend, and *i'toshaa-ni* for me—"

"Kellin." Brennan's voice was steady. He glanced briefly at Aileen, whose expression was so taut as to break, then firmed his mouth and looked back at his grandson. "Tell me why the *qu'mahlin* came about."

It was preposterous. Kellin nearly gaped. "Now?"

"Now."

"You desire a history lesson?"

"I desire you to do whatever I require of you."

"Aye." It was blurted before Kellin thought about it. Frowning his perplexity, he began the lesson. "A Homanan princess ran away with a Cheysuli. Lindir, Shaine's daughter—she went away with Hale, Shaine's liege man." In the face of Brennan's expectant patience, Kellin groped for more. "She was meant to wed Ellic of Solinde, to seal an alliance between Homana and Solinde, but she ran away instead with Hale." He paused. "That is what I was taught, grandsire. Is there more you want?"

"Those are the political concerns, Kellin. What the elopement did as regards Homana and Solinde was to destroy any opportunity for peace to flourish; the two realms remained at war. But *that* would not cause the birth of the *qu'mahlin*, which was a strictly Homanan-Cheysuli conflict."

"Shaine's pride was such that he declared them attainted, subject to punishment."

"That is part of it, Kellin. But think a moment . . . consider something more." Brennan's fingers tightened against aged wood. "It is one thing for a king to declare his daughter and his liege man attainted; he has the right to ask for their lives if he chooses to. It is quite another for that king to declare an *entire race* attainted, and set all of Homana against it."

Kellin waited for more. Nothing more was said. "Aye," he agreed at last. "But Shaine was a madman—"

"Even a madman cannot lead his people into civil war if they *do not believe* what he has said. What did he say, Kellin?"

He knew it very well; Rogan had been at some pains to instruct him, and the Cheysuli at Clankeep as well. "He said we were demons and sorcerers and had to be destroyed."

"*Why* were we demons and sorcerers? What was his foremost proof?"

"That we could assume the shape of animals at will—" Kellin broke it off. He stared blindly at his grandsire. "That we could assume beast-shape and kill all the Homanans." He felt ill. "As—I killed Teague."

"As you killed Teague." Brennan sighed deeply. "In the days of Shaine, the Homanans believed themselves in danger. It was far easier to kill all the Cheysuli than risk their sovereignty. And so they tried. Shaine began it, and others carried it out. It took many years, including Ihlini and Solindish domination, before the Cheysuli were admitted again to Homana without fear of extermination."

"Carillon," Kellin murmured. "He ended the *qu'mahlin*."

"And made a Cheysuli Prince of Homana when he sired no sons of his own." A silver forelock had frosted to white. "Before the Lion came into the hands of Homanans, it was a Cheysuli legacy. The kingdom of Homana was a *Cheysuli* realm. But we gave it up rather than have the Homanans fear us, knowing that someday it would fall again to us, and to the Firstborn who would bind four realms and two magical races in a true peace." Brennan drew in a breath. "How can the Homanans permit a man to rule them who cannot control himself when he assumes *lir*-shape? He is, to them, nightmare; a beast without self-control. And I am not so certain, just at this moment, the Homanans are wrong."

It shocked. *"Grandsire—"*

"I know what it is to share pain through the link. I know what it is to be driven half-mad by

fear—you have heard stories, I know, of how I am
in small places—but I do not *kill*."

"Grandsire—"

"What if it happens again?"

"Again!" Kellin stared. "You believe it might?"

"I must. These four weeks you have achieved
much, but obviously self-control in *lir*-shape is not
one of them. I cannot risk it, Kellin."

"Given time, guidance—"

"Aye. But I cannot risk it while you remain in
Homana-Mujhar. It gives the Homanans too broad
a target."

Kellin's belly clenched. "Clankeep, then." Where
he would have to explain to Gavan, and to Burr,
and to men and women who would not understand how a Cheysuli warrior could permit such
atrocity in the name of his *lir*, whom once he had
meant to banish. "Balance," he murmured. "If I
can learn the balance . . ."

"There is another balance, Kellin. One which
has eluded you through all of your life, and which
I have, in my ignorance, permitted to warp that
life. I am as much to blame as you are, in this."

Aileen stirred. "No. Not you. I will not allow
you to blame yourself."

Kellin looked at her. Aileen's green eyes blazed
with conviction as she stared at her husband; he
would get no support from her. He longed for
Sima, but would not call her to him. "Banish-
ment, then."

"The Council has approved."

Kellin winced.

"It is not a permanent thing. You will be permitted home when I am assured you have learned
what you need to know."

"And when the rumors have died down." Kellin
sighed. "I understand, grandsire. But—"

"I know." Brennan's eyes were filled with compassion. "It has happened before. My own *jehan* grew weary of the excesses of his sons, and banished two of them. Hart he sent to Solinde, Corin to Atvia. Neither wanted to go any more than you desire to go. As for me—" he smiled briefly at Aileen, "—I was made to wed before either of us was ready."

Aileen's face was rigid. "I do not regret it now."

"We both did then." Brennan turned back to his grandson. "For a six-month, a year—no longer than is necessary."

Kellin nodded. "When?"

"In the morning. I have made arrangements for the journey, and a boat will be waiting."

"Boat?" Kellin stared. "A boat? Why? What need have I of a boat?" Trepidation flared into panic. "Where are you sending me?"

"To the Crystal Isle. To your *jehan.*"

Panic transmuted itself to outrage. *"No!"*

"It is arranged."

"*Un*arrange it! I will not go!"

"You wanted this for years."

"Not now. Not for *ten* years, grandsire! I have no intention of going to my *jehan.*"

Brennan's gaze was level. "You will go. For all your anger and bitterness, and the multiplicity of your small rebellions, you are still a warrior of the clan. I am Mujhar. If I bid you to do so, you will go."

"What has *he* to do with this? This is something I must deal with on my own! I do not require the aid of a man who cannot keep his son but must give up everything to live on an *island*—"

"—where you will go." Brennan rose. "Aidan has everything to do with this. We could not have predicted it then, and I doubt it occurred to him— he was in thrall to the gods, and thought of nothing else but the *tahlmorra* meant for him—but it is something we must deal with now. You will go to the Crystal Isle and see your *jehan*."

"Why? *Why* do you think this will help me?"

"Because perhaps he can remove the boy's anger and replace it with a man's understanding that what the world—and gods—mete out is what he must deal with in a rational, realistic manner, without recourse to an anger that, in asserting itself, kills men." The muscles flexed in Brennan's jaw. "Because there is nowhere else I can send you and not be afraid."

Kellin stared. Shame banished outrage. "Of me? You are afraid of *me*?"

"I must be. I have seen what happens when the anger consumes the man." His eyes were bleak. "You must go to the source of your pain. To someone who can aid you."

"I want nothing to do with *him*!"

"He shaped you. By his very distance, by his own *tahlmorra*, he shaped you. I think it is time the *jehan*, and not the grandsire, tended the clay that his own loins sired." Brennan pushed a trembling hand across his brow. "I am too old to raise you now. It is Aidan's turn."

"Why," Kellin spat out between clenched teeth, "did you wait so long for this? I begged it all those years!"

"He did not wish it, and I believed you did not need it."

"Does he wish it now?"

"No."

"But now you believe I need it."

"Aye."

It congealed into bitterness. "Would I need it now if I had had it *then*?"

Brennan shut his eyes. "Gods—I cannot say . . . if so, I *am* to blame for what you have become—"

"No!" Aileen cried. "By all the gods of Erinn,

Brennan, I've said it before—I'll not have you blaming yourself for this! What must I do to convince you? He is what he is. Let him take it to his father. Aidan is more fit to deal with aberration than either of us!"

"Why?" Kellin asked. "Because he is 'aberration,' and now I am also?"

Aileen looked at him. "You are my grandson," she said. "I love you for that—I will *always* love you for that—but I cannot comprehend a man who lacks the self-control to prevent him from killing other men." Her hands balled into fists. "I am Erinnish, not Cheysuli—I cannot understand the soul of a Cheysuli. That it is wild, I know, and untamed, and unlike that of any other, I know. But it is an honorable soul also, well-bound by the gods, and duty . . . yours is unbound. Yours is as unlike Brennan's—or Corin's—than any I have known. It is most like Aidan's in its waywardness, but with a blackness of spirit that makes you dangerous. Aidan was never that." Aileen glanced at Brennan briefly, then back to her grandson. "Go to your father. 'Tis what you need—and, I'm thinking, Aidan also."

Kellin's jaws hurt. "You said—'no longer than is necessary.' How am I to know?"

Brennan reached for and took into his own one of Aileen's hands. "Until Aidan sends you back."

He looked at Aileen in desperation. "Was it your idea?"

She offered oblique answer though her face was wasted. "In Erinn," she said quietly, "a man accepts his punishment. And the will of his lord."

Kellin stood there a long time. Then, summoning what little pride remained, he bowed and took his leave.

Interval

He had, since coming to the Crystal Isle, seen to it that much of its wildness was tamed, at least so much that a man might walk freely along a track without fearing to lose an eye to an importunate branch. And yet not so much wildness was vanquished that a man, a Cheysuli, might feel his spirit threatened by *too* much change.

It was incongruity: to make the wildness useful without diluting its strength. And to offer change within a culture whose very strength was wildness.

He wore leathers, as always, snug against flesh that did not as yet begin to wither with age, and *lir*-gold on bare arms that did not surrender muscle. He was fit, if but a few years beyond his prime; a young man of twenty would call him old—perhaps, more kindly, old*er*—but to another man he represented all that was remarkable about a Cheysuli.

He paused at the border between woodlands and beach. Sunlight glinted off water, scouring white sands paler yet, so that he was forced to lift his hand against the blinding glare.

Blobs swam before his eyes, robbed of distinctness by the brilliance of the sun. They coalesced along the horizon, where the sea lapped in. He saw the blobs take shape, forming legs, tails, heads. He whistled. The blobs paused, then came flying, transmuting sundazzled formlessness into spray-dampened bodies recognizable as canine.

Tongues lolled. Tails whipped. They lashed their own bodies in a frenzy to reach him, to display a devotion so complete as to render words obsolete.

They were his now. The big male had died nearly twenty years before—of grief, he believed—but the others had survived despite the death of the woman who had caused them to be born. Most of those were dead, now, also—giant dogs died sooner—but they had bred as well, so that the island never lacked for companionship of a sort no Cheysuli had known before; they did not keep pets.

Nor were *these* pets; they were, by their existence, in the beating of great hearts, living memorials to Shona.

To him, they were sanity.

He paused as they joined him. The exuberance of their greeting endangered those parts most revered by a man; grinning, he turned a hip each time a tail threatened, then grabbed two or three until the dogs, all astonished, spun to whip tails free. Then it began again, until he told them with false sternness that the game was over; that they were to be still.

He sat down there in the sand, warding off inquisitive noses, until the dogs, too, settled with grunts and great rumbling sighs. Wise eyes watched him, waiting for the sign that he meant to rise and find a stick to toss for their pleasure; but he did not, and after a time they slept, or lay quietly: an ocean of storm-hued wolfhounds sprawled upon the beach of an island, in its begetting, very alien to their souls. They were Erinnish, though none of these had been there.

They were all he had of her. The son she had borne in the midst of her dying, in the flames of a burning keep, was not and never had been his to tend. Another man might have grieved, then done what he could to raise up the living soul whose heart was partly hers, but he was denied that comfort. All he had of her, in the days and the darkness, were memories and dogs.

He honored the gods with his service. He did not question its needs, or the path he had taken; it was his *tahlmorra*. A great security resided in the knowledge that what he did served a greater purpose; that sacrifices made in the name of that greater purpose, no matter how difficult, would in the end bear out his seeming madness. Let them attach scorn to his name now, but one day, long after his bones had rotted, they would call him something else.

"But my spark is nothing compared to the flame of his." Aidan smiled. "My name is a spark, and Kellin's a bonfire—but *Cynric's* will blaze with all the terrible splendor of a wildfire as it devours the land around it."

He knew they would curse him. Men were often blind when it came to needed change. When they acknowledged what had happened—and what still would come—they would claim him an emmissary of a demon not to their liking, when all he did was serve the gods who had decided to mend what had broken.

"Revolution," he said; the dogs twitched ears. "If they knew what was to come, they would none of them agree; they would all become *a'saii*."

But he would not permit it. That was his purpose, to guide his people closer to a true understanding that out of devouring flames would rise a new world.

It would be difficult. But the gods would see to it he had a means to persevere. If it required a weapon, a weapon would be given.

Aidan was content. He knew his path very well. All he had to do was wait for the weapon, then set it on *its* path.

PART III

One

The chapel was built of standing stones set into a tight circle. Most of them still leaned a little, like teeth settling badly in a diseased jaw, but some-one had taken the time—probably years—to see that many of the stones had been pushed back into proper alignment. The circle was whole again, with a carved lintel stone set over the darkened entrance, and a heel stone put up in front. Kellin went slowly to it, drawn by its singular splendor.

The side facing him was unnaturally flat, chipped and rubbed smooth. Across the dark gray face ran runic symbols he had seen but once be-fore, in his Ceremony of Honors. He recognized most of them, but he was not perhaps as conver-sant in the Old Tongue as he should be. *I have lived too long among Homanans.*

Kellin was transfixed by the shapes carved into the stone. The runes were incised deeply; he thought the carvings no more than fifteen or twenty years old. The heel stone was older yet, but not so ancient as the circle itself. *An infant stand-ing within the shade of his fathers.*

Standing, the heel stone reached Kellin's chest. As he knelt, the runes became clearer. He put a finger upon their shapes to trace them out. "One day . . . blood . . . magic."

"One day a man of all blood shall unite, in peace,

four warring realms and two magical races," said
the voice. "And if those few words you mouthed
are all you know of the Old Tongue, it is well you
come to me for instruction."

Kellin did not move. His fingers remained extended to touch the runes. Only the tips trembled.
*Not what I expected a jehan to say to his son as
he sees him for the first time.* It served to fuel his
anger.

Aidan stood in the chapel doorway. The sunlight
was full on his face, glinting off the gold freighting
arms and ear. It struck Kellin as incongruity;
oddly, he had expected a simple man, not a warrior. But Aidan was that, and more; best Kellin
remember it.

He wanted very badly to say all manner of
things, but he desired more to find just the right
challenge. Let Aidan lead him, then; he would
await the proper moment.

"Get up from there," Aidan said. "I am not the
sort of man to require homage."

He does not know me. It shook him; he had expected Aidan to know. It altered his intent. "You
gave that up," Kellin said, forgoing patience.
"Homage."

Aidan smiled. "That, as well as other unnecessary things." He hesitated. "Well, will you rise?
Or have you come with broken legs to have them
made whole again?"

Kellin wanted to laugh but suppressed the
sound. He was not certain he could control it.
"No," he said only.

"Good. I am not a god; I do not perform
miracles."

Delicate contempt. "Surely you can heal. You
are Cheysuli."

"Oh, aye—I have recourse to the earth magic.

But you are too healthy to require it." Aidan gestured. "Rise."

Kellin rose. He found no words in his mouth, only an awkward, wary patience inhabiting his spirit.

Aidan's ruddy brows arched. "Taller than I believed . . . are you certain the clan desires to lose you?"

It was perplexing. "Why should you believe the clan might lose me?"

"Have you not come for the teaching?" It was Aidan's turn to frown. "The clans send to me those men—and women—who wish to learn what it is a *shar tahl* must do. I serve the gods by interpreting and teaching divine intentions . . ." He shrugged. "*I* make no differentiation between a man who is physically more suited to war than to study, but the clans often do. I am persuaded they would labor most assiduously to talk you out of coming here." The glint in his eyes was fleeting. "Surely the women would."

It was disarming, but Kellin would not permit it to vanquish his irritation. He used the reminder that his appearance was considered by most, especially women, as pleasing to look for himself in Aidan. He saw little. Aidan's hair was a rich, deep auburn, almost black in dim light, save for the vivid white wing over his left ear. His eyes were what a Cheysuli would describe as ordinary, though their uncompromising yellowness Homanans yet found unsettling. His flesh was not so dark as a clan-bred warrior, but then neither was Kellin's.

There we match; in the color of our flesh. But not, I am moved to say, in the color of our hearts.

Aidan's tone was polite. "Have you come to learn?"

It nearly moved him to a wild, keening laughter;

what he wanted to learn had nothing to do with gods. In subtle derision, he said, "If you can teach me."

Aidan smiled. "I will do what I can, certainly. It is up to the gods to make you a *shar tahl*."

"Is that—?" Kellin blurted a sharp sound of disbelief. "Is that what you think I want?"

"What else? It is what I do here: prepare those who desire to serve the gods more closely than others do."

Kellin moved around the heel stone. He marked that the sun had been in Aidan's eyes; that what his father saw of him was little but silhouette, or the pale shadow of three dimensions.

He sees a warrior, somewhat taller than expected, but nonetheless kneeling in communion with the gods. Well, I will have to see to it he knows me for what I am, not what he presupposes. He moved to the front of the stone, permitting Aidan to see him clearly. *Now what do you say?*

Aidan's skin turned a peculiar grayish-white. His flesh was a chalk cliff in the sun, showing the damage done by rain and damp and age. Even the lips, carved of granite, were pale as alabaster.

"Echoes—" Aidan blurted, "—but Shona. The *kivarna*—" He was trembling visibly.

Kellin had not believed he much resembled his dead mother; they said she was fair, and her eyes brown. But obviously there was something; Aidan had seen it too quickly. *Or perhaps only feels it because of his kivarna.*

Contempt welled up. He wanted badly to hurt the man. "She did bear me," he said. "There should be something of her in me."

Aidan's face was peeled to the bone so the shape of his skull was visible. The eyes, so calm before, had acquired a brittle intensity that mocked his former self-possession. His mouth was unmoving, as if something had sealed it closed.

Is this what I wanted, all those years? Or do I want more yet?

Aidan drew in a breath, then released it slowly. He smiled a sad, weary smile. The chalk cliff of his face had lost another layer to the onslaught of exposure; in this case, to knowledge. "I knew you would hate me. But it was a risk I had to take."

Kellin wanted to shout. "Was it?" he managed tightly. "And was it worth it?" He paused, then framed the single word upon years of bitterness. *"Jehan."*

In Aidan's eyes was reflected as many years of conviction. "Come inside," he said. "What I have to say is best said there."

He did not want to—he felt to do as asked would weaken his position—but Kellin followed. The chapel was not large inside, nor did it boast substantial illumination; a tight latticework roof closed out the sun. Kellin allowed his eyes to adjust, then glanced briefly around the interior. A rune-carved alter stood in the center. Set against the tilted walls were stone benches. Torch brackets pegged into seams in the stonework were empty.

"Where is your *lir*?" Aidan asked.

"She led me here, then disappeared."

"Ah." Aidan nodded. "Teel disappeared this morning as well, so that all I had were the dogs; it was a conspiracy, then, that we should meet without benefit of *lir*."

Kellin did not care overmuch about what the *lir* conspired to do. He was wholly fixed on the acknowledgment that the man who stood before him had planted the seed which had grown in Shona's belly, only to be torn free on a night filled with flames. *He loved her, they say. Could he not have loved her son as well?*

Aidan sat down on one of the benches. Kellin, pointedly, remained standing. Bitterly he said, "Surely with your *kivarna*—aye, I know about it— you must have known I was coming."

Color had returned to Aidan's face. It was no longer stretched so taut, no longer empty of a tranquillity that annoyed one who lacked it. "I do not question your right to bitterness and hatred, but this is not the place for it."

Kellin barked a harsh laugh. "Is that why you brought me in here? To tame my tongue and render me less than a man?" He wanted to jeer. "You forget, *jehan*—I have none of your reverence, nor your humility. If I choose to honor the gods, I do it in my own fashion. And, I might add, with less elaboration." He cast a scornful glance over the chapel. "I did not know a man would exchange the flesh of his own son for the confines of *stone*."

Aidan waited him out. "I would not expect you to offer reverence *or* humility. You are not the man for it."

It was veiled insult, if Kellin chose to take it so. Another might acknowledge it as simple statement of fact. "Do you believe me too weak to be as you are? No, *jehan:* too strong. I am not a coward. I do not turn my face from its proper place to hide upon an island with a mouth full of prophecies."

"Indeed, you are not weak. Nor are you a coward." Aidan shrugged. "Nor am I, but I give you the freedom to believe as you will—just now, there is more. What you are is a confused, angry young man who only now confronts his heritage—and knows his ultimate fate lies in other hands." He overrode the beginnings of Kellin's protest. "You mentioned my *kivarna* first—shall we let the gift guide me in the examination of your soul?" He smiled without intending offense, reminding quietly that what he could do was what few others could. "You will do as I did when the time has come: acknowledge and fully accept what the gods have designed for you in the ordering of your life."

"If you know it, then tell me!" Kellin cried. "You claim communion with the gods. *Tell* me now and save me time wasted in discovering it for myself!"

"And deny you the chance to grow into the man the gods intend you to be?" Aidan smiled. "A warrior cannot circumvent a *tahlmorra* so easily ... he is charged to become what he is meant to become in the husbandry of his soul. Were I to *tell* you what becomes of you, I might well alter what is meant to happen."

"Obscurity," Kellin charged. "That is what you teach here: how to speak in riddles so no man can understand."

"A man *learns*," Aidan countered, "and then he understands."

Kellin laughed. "Tell me," he challenged. "If indeed you can. Prophesy for me. For your only son."

Aidan did not move upon the bench. His hands lay in his lap. "Do you forget who I am?"

"Who *you* are? How could I? You are the man I have sought all my life—even when I denied it—and now that I have found you I am at last able to tell you precisely what I think of you and your foolish claims!"

"I am the mouthpiece of the gods."

Kellin laughed at him.

And then his laughter died, for Aidan began to speak. "The Lion shall lie with the witch. Out of darkness shall come light; out of death: life; out of the old: the new."

"Words," Kellin began, meaning to defame the

man who said them, to leech them of their power, but his challenge died away.

"The Lion shall lie with the witch, and the witch-child born of it shall join with the Lion to swallow the House of Homana and all of her children."

"Jehan!"

Yellow eyes had turned black. Aidan stared fixedly at Kellin, one hand raised to indicate his son. "The Lion," he said, "shall devour the House of Homana."

"Stop—"

His voice rose. "Do you think to escape the Lion? Do you think to escape your fate?" Lips peeled back. "Small, foolish boy—you are *nothing* to the gods. It is the Lion's cub they desire, not the Lion himself . . . you are the means to an end. *The Lion shall lie down with the witch.*"

Kellin was instantly taken out of himself, swept back ten years. To the time of Summerfair, when he had put on his second-best tunic to go among the crowds and see what he would see, to taste *suhogla* again and challenge a Steppes warior. To enter the tent filled with a sickly, sweetish odor; to see again the old man who sat upon his cushion and told who he was, and what would be his fate.

"Lion—" Kellin whispered, staring at his father. "There is a lion—after all—"

Aidan smiled an odd, inhumane smile. "Kellin," he said plainly, "you *are* the Lion."

Two

"I am sorry." Aidan's tone was quiet, lacking its former power. "But I warned you. It is never a simple thing—and rarely pleasant—to learn your *tahlmorra.*"

Kellin clung to the heel stone for support. He did not precisely recall how he had reached it. He remembered, if dimly, stumbling out of the shadow-clad chapel into clean sunlight—and then he had fallen to his knees, keeping himself upright only by virtue of clinging to the heel stone as a child to its mother's neck.

He continued to clutch it. He twisted his head to ask over a shoulder. "Do you know what you said?"

Aidan, squinting against sunlight, sighed and nodded. "Most of it. I can never recall clearly what I say when I prophesy, but the intent remains in my mind." His eyes were steady, if darkened by the acknowledgment of what had occurred. "Despite what you led me to believe with regard to your ignorance of your *tahlmorra,* it is not the first time you have heard such words."

"I was ten." Kellin stood up and relinquished his grip on the stone, aware of a cold clamminess in his palms. "But I did not *know*—"

"No," Aidan agreed, "a child could not. Nor many men. You were not ready. Even now you are not."

Resentment congealed. "So you did it to prove something."

Mildly, Aidan said, "You did ask. In plain and impolite words."

Another time he would have fought back. Just now something else struck him as more important. "You said—" He looked warily at the chapel, as if it were responsible for putting the thoughts inside his head. "You said *I* am the Lion."

"You are."

"But *how*? I am a man. Not even in *lir*-shape am I a lion!"

Aidan nodded. "Where words will not serve, symbols often do." He traced the runes inscribed in the heel stone. "These are symbols. And so is the Lion."

"The Lion is a throne."

"That, too, is a symbol." Aidan smiled. "You are a man in all the ways in which a man is measured; fear nothing there. But you are also the next link in the prophecy of the Firstborn. It may somewhat devalue my dedication to say this so baldly, but prophecies are sometimes little more than colorful pictures, like the *lir* we paint on pavilions."

It gave Kellin something, a tiny bit of strength with which to reassert his challenge. "Then there is no truth to it."

"Of course there is truth to it. Does the painted animal shape mean there is no living *lir*?" Aidan shook his head. "A prophecy does not lie. At times circumstances change, and the fate itself is changed; they gave us free will, the gods. The ultimate result may be altered, but what served as catalyst was never a falsehood. It is not graven in stone." He tapped fingertips against the heel stone. "This will remain here forever—for as long as the world has—to speak of the prophecy and all it entails. Eighteen words." His smile was not

condescending, but unadorned serenity; he was
certain of his place within the prophecy. "Eighteen simple words that have ruled our lives since
before we were even conceived."

Kellin looked at the runes. " 'One day—' " But
he broke off reflexive quoting. There was another
matter he considered more important. "How can
I be the Lion?"

"You *are.* No more than that. You are the Lion
. . . just as I was the broken link."

Kellin wanted to deny it all, to accuse the *shar
tahl* who was also his father that purposeful obscurity offered no one an answer. But what came out
of his mouth was a simple truth: "I do not
understand."

"That is one of my purposes here: to explain
things more fully."

Bitterness reasserted itself. "To other men
whose lives have been twisted by their
tahlmorras?"

"Come with me."

It provoked. "Where? To that palace? I have
seen it. You do not live there."

"To my pavilion." The smile, now lacking the
unearthly quality of prophecy, was freely offered
again with nothing more in its shaping than hospitality. "I am Cheysuli, Kellin. Never forget that."

Aidan's pavilion clustered with others in a
smaller version of Clankeep. It was pale green
with ravens adorning its sides; on the ridgepole
sat the model.

Sima, sprawled on a rug before the doorflap,
blinked sleepily in the sun. *You found him.*

Kellin scowled. *As you meant me to. That is why
you left me.*

She was unrepentant. *Teel and I thought it best.
I do not appreciate such secrecy in my own lir.*

Nor does your jehan. She twitched her tail. *Even now he chastises Teel.*

He deserves it. So do you. He did not stoop to pat the cat but went on by her and into the pavilion as his father pulled back the flap.

Aidan seated himself on a brown bear pelt and gestured for Kellin to make himself comfortable. "We built the Keep here because I saw no sense in inhabiting a palace. We are Cheysuli. We are here to rebuild what we can of the old religion, while imbuing it with new." He smiled. "I am somewhat controversial with regard to my beliefs; some elders name me a fool."

Kellin said nothing. He had come for none of this.

"This is a place of history and magic," Aidan continued, "and we treat it as such. Palaces have no place here."

He disputed at once. "I thought the Cheysuli built it. There are runes in the pillars. Old Tongue runes, like those on the heel stone." It was proof; it was enough; it trapped his traitorous father.

"Runes can be carved later, as those on the heel stone were."

Kellin exhaled patience. He was wrung dry of it. "So, it is a Homanan palace after all. Should that matter? The Homanans are our people, too."

Aidan smiled. "If that was a test, then assuredly you have passed it."

In succinct Homanan, Kellin swore. "I did not come for this!"

"No." Aidan rested his hands on his knees. "Ask what you will, Kellin."

Kellin did not hesitate. The question had been formed nearly twenty years before. He had mouthed it every night, practicing in his bed, secure in his draperies as a child in its mother's womb. Now he could ask it in the open, in the light, of the man who knew the answer. "Why did you give me up?"

Aidan did not hesitate. "It was an infinitely Cheysuli reason, and one you will undoubtedly contest, though you should know better; you, too, are Cheysuli."

Kellin inhaled angrily on a hissing breath. "*Tahlmorra.* That is your answer."

"The gods required me to renounce my title, rank, and inheritance. I was the *broken* link. The chain could only be mended—and therefore made much stronger—if I gave precedence to the next link. Its name was Kellin." Aidan's eyes did not waver. His tone did not break. His demeanor was relaxed. All of his self-possession was very much in opposition to the words he spoke. "It was the hardest thing I have ever done."

Through his teeth, Kellin said, "Yet you did it easily enough."

The first crack in Aidan's facade appeared. "Not without regret. Not without pain. When I set you into my *jehana's* arms—" Aidan broke it off, as if afraid to give up too much of himself after all. His tone was husky. "You were Shona's child. You were all I had of her. But I was, in that moment, a child of the gods—"

"It is a simple thing to blame gods."

Aidan's lips parted. "It was done for Homana."

"Homana! Homana, no doubt, would have been better off with a contented prince instead of one who lacked a *jehan.* Do you know what my life has been?"

"Now, aye—the *kivarna* has told me."

"And what does it mean? Nothing? That I spent my childhood believing myself unworthy, and my adulthood cognizant that *I* mean nothing at all, save I can sire a son?" Kellin's fists trembled against his thighs. "Use your famous *kivarna* and see what you did by renouncing a son in favor of the gods."

"Kellin." The chalk cliff sloughed another layer; soon it would be bare, and the true man uncovered. "I never intended for you to suffer so. I knew it would be hard, but it had to be done . . . and you are not, above all things, a malleable man. You choose your own path—have *always* chosen your path—no matter the odds."

"I was a *child*—"

"So was I!" Aidan cried. "I had *dreams*, Kellin— nightmares. To me, the Lion was a vastly frightening thing." With effort, he let it go. He smiled sadly, no longer hiding his truths. "Do you know what it is like for a *jehan* to at last acknowledge that the thing which frightens him most is his own son?"

Kellin was nearly incoherent with outrage. "Is this your excuse for giving me up? That you are *afraid*—"

"It was necessary. There was a purpose in it for me—and one, I believe, for you."

Kellin jeered. "Facile words, *jehan*."

"True words, Kellin."

"Why would you be afraid of me? I am your *son*."

"You are the Lion. You are meant to lie down with the witch. You are meant to sire the First-born." Aidan's eyes did not waver. "It is one thing to serve the gods, Kellin, knowing what you work toward—it is entirely another to realize that what you do *matters* in the ordering of the world." His smile was without humor. "Men who honor no gods, who fail to serve the gods, cannot understand the enormity of the truth: that the seed of a single man's loins can alter forever the shape of a world."

Kellin was furious. "You will not blame *me* for

this! You will not for one moment lay this at *my* doorflap! Do you think I am a fool? Do you think me so ignorant as to be led by facile words? By the gods, *jehan*—by *any fool's gods*—I will not be turned aside by your faith, by your admirable devotion, by the mouthings of a madman when I want to know the answer to a single, simple question!"

"And I have told you why!" Kellin had at last shattered Aidan's composure. It loosed the final layer of cliff and laid bare the underside of the man, not the *shar tahl;* the once-born Prince of Homana who had bequeathed it all to his infant son. "My *tahlmorra.* You should understand a little of that, now that you know what yours is."

"*Jehan*—"

"Would you have me hold you by the hand and lead you through it? Are you so blind—or so selfish—that you cannot permit yourself to see another man's pain?"

Kellin expelled a curse framed upon the Old Tongue. "What manner of pain could lead a man to renounce his son?"

"The pain in knowing that if he did not, an entire race might be destroyed."

"*Jehan*—"

"The throne was never meant for me. *Here* is where I was bound. The link—*my* link—was shattered in Valgaard; do you understand what I mean? I was broken, Kellin . . . *I* was . . . my link— a symbol—was destroyed. Yours was left whole. *Whole*, Kellin—to be joined with the rest of the chain when Brennan is dead, and a new king ascends. Do you see? I was in the way. I was *unnecessary*. The gods required a prophet, not another rump upon the throne . . . someone to proclaim the coming of the Firstborn. Someone to prepare the way."

"Jehan—"

"You are the Lion. You are meant to devour the House of Homana."

Kellin's face spasmed. "You say first I am the Lion, and then I am a link in a chain ..." He shook his head in emphatic denial. "I understand none of it!"

Aidan's voice was hoarse. "We are all but links. Mine was shattered. Its destruction sundered the chain. Even now it lies in Valgaard, in Lochiel's keeping."

"A *real* chain?"

"A real chain."

"Broken."

"I broke it. I broke *me* to strengthen you."

Kellin bared his teeth. "What good does it do, then, if Lochiel holds it?"

"Someone must get it back."

"From *Lochiel*?"

"Someone must take the two halves and make them one again."

Kellin understood. He sprang to his feet. "By the gods—not *I*! I will not be used in a personal revenge that concerns only you."

Aidan's eyes were infinitely yellow. "Lochiel killed your *jehana*."

Kellin recognized the battle and struck back at once, using all his weapons. "I never knew her. What does it matter?"

"He cut you from her body as he burned down all of Clankeep."

It hurt desperately. He had blamed himself so long for his mother's death. "No—"

"He wanted the seed," Aidan said. "He wanted to raise you as his own, to turn you against your House ... to defang the Lion utterly before it reached maturity."

Kellin fastened on a thing, a small, cruel thing,

because he needed to, to salvage his anger, to shore up his bitterness. They were things he knew. "Where were *you*," he asked viciously, "while Lochiel the Ihlini cut open my mother's belly?"

Aidan's eyes mirrored Kellin's desperation. "Where do you think I got this?" A trembling hand touched the white wing in his hair. "A sword. It broke open my skull and spilled out all the wits, all the words, all the things that make a man . . . and turned me into someone no one, not even I, can truly understand." His face was wasted. "Do you think, in all your hatred, when you lie awake at night cursing the man who left you, that any man, any father, would *ask* the gods to give him such a fate?"

Kellin was shaking. He could not stop himself. "I want—I want . . ." He wet dry lips. "I want to be free of the beast."

"Then kill it," Aidan said.

"How?"

"Go to Valgaard. Rejoin two halves of a whole."

"And that will make *me* whole?" Kellin's wild laugh tore his throat. "Expiation for *your* weakness does nothing to destroy my own!"

"Go to Valgaard."

Kellin bared his teeth. "You have not seen what I have become!"

"Nor has Lochiel." Aidan rose and opened the doorflap. "Perhaps the beast in you is a weapon for us all."

"*I killed a friend!*" Kellin cried. "Do you say it was necessary, that the gods required *this* to fashion a weapon?"

The chalk cliff shapechanged itself to granite. "The gods required me to give up my son. Now that son provides a way for us to destroy an Ihlini who would, given the chance, bring down all of us. He would smash the Lion to bits, then feed it chip by chip into the Gate of Asar-Suti." Aidan's tone was unflinching. His eyes condemned the weakness that would permit a man to refuse. "Make the sacrifice worth it. Make the death of your friend count for something—as Shona's death did."

Kellin's throat hurt. "This is not what I came for."

"It is," Aidan said. "Have I not said I am the mouthpiece of the gods?"

Kellin gestured helplessness. "All I ever wanted—all I *ever* wanted—was some word, some indication you cared, that you knew I *existed* . . . but you gave me nothing. Nothing at all."

Silence lay heavy between them. Then the faintest of sounds, so subtle that in another time, in another moment, no one would have marked it. It was the soft sibilance of a man's hand crumpling fabric.

Tears stood in Aidan's eyes as he clung to the doorflap. "What I gave you—what I gave you was what I believed you had to have." His mouth worked briefly. "Do you think I did not know what it would cost you?"

"But you never *came.*"

Aidan's laugh was a travesty. "Had I come, I would have taken you back. Had I sent word, I would have told you to come. For the sake of your son, Kellin, I had to give up my own."

"For *my* son!"

"Cynric," Aidan whispered, and the blackness in his eyes ate away the yellow. "The sword and the bow and the knife—"

"No!" Kellin shouted. "What of me? What of me? *I* am your son, not he! What about me?"

Aidan's eyes were empty of all save prophecy. "You are the Lion, and you shall lie down with the witch."

"*Jehan*—" he said brokenly. "Is this what they have done, your beloved gods? Made you over into this?"

"The Lion shall devour the lands."

For the first time in his life, Kellin put his hands on his father.

For the second time in Aidan's life, he put arms around his son. "Do not be ashamed," he said. "There is no shame in tears."

Muffled, Kellin said, "I am—a warrior."

"So am I," Aidan agreed. "But the gods gave us tears nonetheless."

Three

They stood upon the dock, facing toward the city of Hondarth sprawled indistinct on the distant shore: the former Prince of Homana, who might have been Mujhar, and the present prince, his son, who one day *would* be.

The sea-salt breeze blew into their faces, ruffling hair, tickling eyelashes, softly caressing mouths. Behind him, silent wolfhounds gathered at the border between wooden dock and paler sand, waiting for their master. Perched in a nearby tree sat the raven called Teel, while the lovely mountain cat, blue-black in the light of the sun, waited mutely beside her warrior.

Kellin slanted a pensive, sidelong glance at his father. They did not, he had decided, much resemble one another. The son of Shona and Aidan appeared to be a mixture of everyone in his ancestry—which was, he felt, a stew of hybrid spices—save that the cat at his side and the gold on his flesh marked him as something more distinct than merely human.

He does not look so old as I thought yesterday. Kellin stripped a wayward lock of hair from an eye, blinking away the sting. *Yet if one looks at the eyes, he seems older than anyone else.* "So—you expect me to go." He snapped his fingers. "Just like that."

Aidan's smile was faint, with a hint of irony in it.

"It would be folly indeed to expect *quite* so much acquiescence ... surely you still have questions."

"A multitude. This one, to begin: how can you say I am the Lion who is meant to lie down with the witch? What witch? Who is it? How can it be done?" Kellin gestured incomprehension. "Even now my grandsire discusses a marriage between me and Dulcie—and I sincerely doubt *Dulcie* is this witch."

Aidan's smile was unabated, as was the irony. "Marriages, no matter how well planned, do not always occur."

It provoked Kellin to retort sharply. "As one nearly did not occur between Aileen of Erinn and the Prince of Homana?"

Aidan laughed, unoffended. "Old history. They are well content, now; and that marriage *did* occur."

"What of mine?"

"Oh, I believe you will indeed be married." Aidan nodded. "One day."

It seemed important to know. "To this witch?"

Aidan's tone was deliberate, akin to Rogan's when the tutor labored to instruct an easily distracted student. "What *precisely* have I said, when I prophesy?"

"That the Lion will lie with the witch." Kellin sighed. "I have heard it more than once."

"Lying down with a 'witch' does not necessarily mean you will marry her."

"Ah." Black brows sprang upward. "Then you advocate infidelity."

Aidan showed his teeth in a challenging grin that Kellin saw, in surprise, was very like his own. "I advocate merely that you do what must be done. *How* it is done is up to you."

"To sleep with an Ihlini ..." Kellin hitched his shoulders because the flesh between them prickled; the idea was unattractive. "That is what she is, this witch, is she not? An Ihlini?"

"It has been done before."

"Oh, aye—grandsire did. Ian did. I know the stories."

"Do you?" Aidan's brows slanted upward in subtle query. The wing of white hair, against deep russet, was blinding in the sunlight. "Do you also know that *I* slept with one?"

"You!" It was entirely unexpected from a man who was *shar tahl*. "They say you bedded no one after my *jehana* died."

"I did not. I cannot. Surely they told you the cost of *kivarna*, when the partner dies. It is much like a *lirless* warrior, save the body does not die. Only the portion of it that might, given opportunity, given the wherewithal, sire another child."

"But—I am the only one."

"And will ever be." Aidan looked at him. "In Atvia, before I married Shona, I bedded an Ihlini woman. And the second time, I knew it."

"Willingly?"

"With Lillith?" Aidan sighed. "To excuse myself, to justify my action, I might prefer to say that even that first time she ensorcelled me . . . but it would be a lie. What I did, I did because I desired it; because I could not, in my maleness, deny myself the gratification found in a woman's body, despite whom she might be."

"Lillith . . ." Kellin tasted the name and found it oddly seductive. "It was she who lay with Ian and bore him a child."

"Rhiannon, who later lay with my *jehan* and bore *him* a child. Melusine is her name."

"You know it?"

"She is the woman who sleeps with Lochiel. She bore *him* a child . . . while she herself, Melusine, was born of Cheysuli blood as well as Ihlini—yet chooses to serve Asar-Suti.''

It seemed surpassing odd. "How do you know all this?''

"Lochiel sees to it I know. Lochiel and I—" Aidan's taut, angled smile was strangely shaped, "—have long been adversaries on more battlefields than the obvious ones. He sends me messages.''

"*Lochiel?*" Kellin found it incomprehensible. "Why?''

"To make certain I know." Wind ruffled the white wing against Aidan's temple. "Her name is Melusine, and she bore him a daughter. It was that daughter with whom you shared a cradle.''

Kellin grunted. "I know something of that.''

"Do you?" Aidan's gaze was steady. "Shall I tell you the whole of it, then, so you may have another thing for which to hate me?''

"What? More?" It might have stung once; it might have been a weapon Kellin took pride in wielding, but no longer. Much remained between them, but some of the pain was assuaged. "Then tell me, and I will decide if I should rekindle my hatred.''

Aidan looked directly at him. "I *bargained* for you. It was little more, to him, than a simple trade. I was to *choose*—" He rubbed briefly at his forehead as if it ached, then glanced away toward distant Hondarth. "There were two babies, as you know: you, and Lochiel's daughter. I had no way of telling which was which. You were both of you swaddled, and asleep; it is somewhat difficult to tell one infant from another, in such circumstances.''

"Aye. How did you?''

"I did not.''

"But—you chose *me*.''

"I left Valgaard with a child in my arms. I did not know which one it was." Aidan sighed. "Not until I unwrapped you and saw you were male. Then I knew, and *only* then, that my choice had been correct.''

"But—if you had chosen the *girl* . . ." Kellin let it go. The repercussions he saw were too complex to consider.

"If I had, you would have been reared as Lochiel's son."

And the girl as a princess within the bosom of Homana-Mujhar, where she might have worked against us. The flesh rose on Kellin's bones. He rubbed at his arms viciously, disliking the weakness that made his fear so plain. "So." It seemed enough.

"So." Aidan nodded. "You know the whole of it."

Kellin stared fixedly across the lapping water. He could not look at his father. He had spent too long hating from a distance to give way easily, to admit to circumstances that might persuade a man to act in such a way as to ignore his son. "You risked a great deal."

"It was my only choice. It was Homana's only chance."

Kellin frowned fiercely. "You said—the Lion will devour the House. Is that not the same fate Lochiel aspires to give us?"

"There is a difference between swallowing the lands, and *destroying* them. Words, Kellin—symbols. Intent is divulged with words. Think of the prophecy."

"Eighteen words, again?"

" '—*shall unite, in peace*—' " Aidan said. "Well?"

Kellin sighed, nodding. "Then to unite the lands, I must swallow them. Swallowing, one might argue, is a form of uniting."

Aidan smiled. "Vivid imagery. It helps a man to

remember." He looked at the waiting boat. "We all make choices. You shall make yours."

Kellin saw his father form the eloquent Cheysuli gesture he had detested so long. He matched it easily with his own hand. *"Tahlmorra."*

Aidan's answering smile was serene. "You have run from it long enough."

"So, now you send me *to* it. To Lochiel and Valgaard—and to the witch?"

"That," Aidan said, "is for the gods to know."

Kellin sighed disgust. "I have not had much congress with gods. They are, I am convinced, capricious, petty beings."

"They may indeed be so, as well as other things perhaps not so reprehensible." Aidan was unoffended. "The example for all manner of behavior lies before you; we all of us are their children."

"Even the Ihlini?"

"Stubborn, resentful children, too spoiled in their power. It is time they recalled who gave it to them."

Kellin chewed his lip. *"Why* am I to bring you this chain? What are you to do with it?"

"Tame the Lion."

"Tame me!" He paused. "Tame *me?"*

"Who shall, in his turn, swallow the·Houses—*unite* them, Kellin!—and bring peace to warring realms."

He clamped his teeth together. "All because of a chain. Which you broke. And left, like a fool, in *Valgaard!"*

"Aye," Aidan admitted. "But then I have never suggested I am anything else."

" 'Mouthpiece of the gods,' " Kellin muttered. "You claim yourself *that.*"

"And so I am. But the gods made all men, and there *are* foolish ones." He smiled. "Bring me back the chain, and the beast shall be tamed."

"A quest," Kellin gritted.

"The gods do appear to enjoy them. It passes the time."

Kellin shook his head. There was much he wanted to say, but too little time in which to say it. He had been given his release; time he took it, and went.

"*Shansu*," Aidan said. "*Cheysuli i'halla shansu.*"

Kellin's tone was ironic. "If there is any such thing in Valgaard." He paused. "You said you would not go to Homana-Mujhar because you feared you would bring me back."

"Aye."

"I am here now. That risk is gone." He hesitated. "Will you go home now?"

The wind teased auburn hair. "This is my home."

"Then—to visit. To be hosted by the Mujhar and his queen." It was hard to force the words past the lump in his throat. "She wants nothing more, *jehan*. Nor does he. Can you give them that now?"

Aidan's soft laugh was hoarse. "You believe me so much a monster as that . . ." He sighed. "There is still much to be done here."

"But—"

"But one day I will return to Homana-Mujhar."

Kellin smiled faintly. "Is that prophecy?"

"No. That is a *jehan* who is also a son, and who would like to see his parents."

Kellin sighed. There yet remained one more thing.

He looked away to the distant shore, then turned back and stared hard at Aidan as Sima leapt into the boat. "Fathers desert their children." He used Homanan purposely; he did not in this moment intend to discuss his own sire, but those of other children.

The wind stripped auburn hair back from Aidan's face. It bared, beneath the skin, the architecture of bone that was ineffably Cheysuli, if housed in paler flesh. "Aye."

"Other fathers ... Homanan, Ellasian, Solindish—they must do it all over the world—" *I did it myself. I banished three to Clankeep.* "—Is there ever a reason?"

"Many reasons."

It was not the proper answer. Kellin reshaped the question. "Is there ever *justification*?"

"Only that which resides in a man's soul," Aidan answered. "To the child, bereft of a father, bereft of the *kivarna* that might explain the feelings that caused the father to leave, there is nothing save an emptiness and a longing that lasts forever."

"Even if—" Kellin hesitated. "Even after the father is dead?"

"Then it is worse. A deserted child dreams of things being put to rights, of all the missing pieces being found and rejoined. A deserted child whose dreams die with the father's death knows only a quiet desperation, a permanent incompleteness; that the dream, even born in hatred, pain, and bitterness, can now never come true."

Kellin swallowed with difficulty. Unevenly he said, "A hard truth, *jehan*."

"And the only one there is."

Four

Kellin bought a horse in Hondarth, rode it across the city, then traded it for another at a second livery. The second mount, a plain brown gelding disinclined to shake his entire body with violent dedication every four steps, proved considerably more comfortable. The ride commenced likewise.

It crossed his mind once, as he and Sima neared the turning to Mujhara, that he could go home. What would the Mujhar do, send him away again? But the order had been for him to remain with his father until Aidan saw fit to send him home; Kellin could, he thought, argue that it was done.

Except he knew better. It most decidedly was *not* done, it being the ludicrous quest to fetch out of Valgaard two halves of a chain his father had broken, then foolishly left behind.

He might have kept it for himself and saved me the trouble.

Sima flanked his horse. *Aye. Then we would be where we were three weeks ago: banished to the island.* She paused. *Where there are dogs.*

Kellin laughed aloud. "Fastidious, are we? Disinclined to consort with *dogs*?" He grinned at his horse's ears; he knew the cat sensed his amusement within the link. "They are good dogs, Sima, regardless of your tastes. They do not bark like terriers, snatching at ankles if you move . . . nor do they bell like hounds on the morning you most desire to sleep."

No, she admitted. *But I am quieter even than those Erinnish beasts.*

"Usually," he said. "Your purring, beside my ear, is enough to shatter my skull."

You told me once it helps you to go to sleep.

"If I *cannot* sleep, aye; there is something soothing about it. But when you sprawl down next to me and take up with rumbling when I am *already* asleep . . ." He let her fill in the rest. *You are not a housecat, lir. You are considerably larger in many aspects, most markedly in your noise—and in the kneading of your claws.*

Sima forbore to answer.

It grew cold as they drew closer to the Bluetooth River. Kellin was grateful he had thought to buy a heavier cloak in Hondarth; he wished now it was fur-lined. But it was nearly summer, and people in the lowlands did not think of such things when the sun shone so brightly.

He shivered. *If I were home in Homana-Mujhar, or within a woman's arms—* Kellin sighed. *That is my favorite warmth.*

I thought I was.

He grinned. *There are certain kinds of warmth not even a lir may provide.*

Then I must assume you would prefer a roadhouse woman and her bed to the cold ground tonight.

He straightened in the saddle. *Is there one?*

One? Or both?

Either. A woman without the roadhouse would prove warm enough, as would a roadhouse without a woman. But a woman in *a roadhouse would be the best of all.*

Then you may rest well tonight. There is one around the curve of the road.

So there was. Content, Kellin rode up to the stable and dropped off his horse with a sigh of relief. There was no boy to do the work for him, so he led the horse inside the daub-and-wattle building, stripped his mount of tack, then rubbed him down and put him into an empty stall with hay and a measure of grain. He left saddle and bridle beneath drying blankets, then went out into the twilight to look for Sima.

She waited beneath a tree, melding into dusk. Kellin dropped to one knee and butted his brow against hers. *Tomorrow we go on.*

She butted back. *Do we?*

You saw the cairn at the turning. It is but three leagues to the ferry. We will cross first thing . . . by sundown tomorrow, we will be in Solinde.

Sima twisted her head and slid it along his jaw, so that a tooth scraped briefly. *And by sundown the day after that, Valgaard?*

His belly tightened. *I would sooner avoid it—but aye, so we will.*

Sima butted his cheek, tickling his left eye with the tuft of an ear. He buried his face in the silk of her fur, then climbed back to his feet. *Keep yourself to the trees.*

Keep yourself to one wine.

Kellin grinned. *But not to one woman? So much faith in me, lir!*

No, Sima answered. *There* is *only one woman.*

Kellin did not care. One would be sufficient.

The common room was small but well-lighted, and the rushes were clean. *Prosperous place . . .* Kellin glanced around. As well it should be, so close to the ferry crossing and the North Road out of Ellas, frequently traveled by merchants. He made arrangements for a room, moved to a table nearer the kegs than the front door, and looked for the girl.

It did not take long to find her, nor for her to find him. Even as he hooked out the stool from beneath the small table, she was at his side. Deft hands unpinned his cloak, then stripped it from his shoulders.

The girl froze. Black eyes were avid as she saw the gold on his arms; a glance quickly flicked at his left ear assured her that her assessment was correct.

She smiled, black eyes shining bronze in the light as *lir*-gold glinted. She was young and pretty in a wild, black-eyed way, bold in manners and glances. Content with the weight of his wealth, she eyed the fit of his leggings.

She was quite striking, though in time her looks would coarsen. For now, she would do. *Better than most.* Kellin smiled back. It was an agreement they reached easily without speaking a word; when he tossed the silver coin down on the table to pay for his food and drink, she caught it before it bounced. *Indeed, she will do—much better than expected.*

"Pleasure, my lord?"

He grinned briefly. It was a two-part question, as she well knew when she asked it. "For now, *usca*. If you have it."

"We hae it." White teeth flashed as the coin disappeared into a pocket in her voluminous woolen skirt. She wore a faded crimson blouse and a yellow tabard-smock over it, but both were slashed low to show off small, high breasts. She had pinned her thick black hair at the back of her neck in a bundled mass, but locks had come loose and straggled down her back. Finer strands curled against the pallor of her slender neck.

Kellin found the disarray, and the neck, infinitely appealing. "And what else?" he asked.

She showed her teeth again. "Lamb."

"Lamb will do." He let her see his assessment of her; she would mark it flattery, in the glint of green eyes. "What do they call you?"

"*They* call me whate'er they like," she said frankly. "So may you. But my name be Kirsty."

"Kirsty." He liked it. "Mine is Kellin."

She measured him avidly. "You're a shape-changer, are ye no', wi' all that gold . . . ?" She nodded before he had a chance to answer. "I ne'er seen a shapechanger w'out the yellow eyes."

He found her northern speech as appealing as her slender neck with its weight of hair. He gave her the benefit of a slow, inviting smile he had found years before to be most effective. "Do I frighten you?"

Arched black brows shot up. "You?" Kirsty laughed. "I've been all my life a wine-girl . . . 'tisn't much a man *hae* to frighten me!" She paused consideringly. "Do ye *mean* to, then?"

Her hand rested against the table. He put out his own and gently touched the flesh that lacked the smooth silken feel of the court women he had known before turning to the Midden; he found her hand familiar in its toughened competence, and therefore all the more attractive. "No," he said softly. "I would never mean to hurt *you*."

Kirsty promised much with eyes that bespoke experience without prevarication. "I'll bring your lamb, then, and the *usca* . . . but I'm working, now. I canna gie ye my company till later."

He turned his hand against hers so she could see the bloody glow of the ring on his forefinger. It was unlikely a north country girl would recognize the crest, but she would know its value well enough.

Black brows rose again. "You'd nae gie me *that* for a night, nor a *week* of nights!"

"Not this, perhaps—" he could not; it signified his rank, "—but certainly this." He touched the torque at his neck.

Her eyed widened. " 'Tis too *much*! For a wine-girl? Hae ye no more coin?"

"I 'hae' coin." He mimicked her accent. "But you hae a pretty neck."

She assessed the torque again. "A man's, no' a woman's . . . t'would lie low—here—" She touched her collar bone, then drew her fingers more slowly to the cleft of her high breasts and smiled to see his eyes.

He understood the game. "Do you not want it, then?"

For her, the game was ended. Dreams filled her eyes as the breath rushed out of her mouth. "Wi' *that* I could go to Mujhara! Am I a fool? Nae, I'd take it. But what d'ye want for it?"

"Your company. Now."

"Bu' . . ." She glanced around. "Tam'd turn me out, did I no' tend the others."

"I will pay Tam, too."

A smooth brow knitted. "Hae it been so long, then, that ye're *that* hungry?"

"Hungry," he answered, "for all the things that satisfy a man." He clasped her fingers briefly, then released her hand. "Food and drink first. Come when you can."

Her eyes were on the torque. "Promises made are no' kept, sometimes. D'ye think I'm a fool, then?"

For answer Kellin rose and stripped the torque from his neck. He hooked it around her own, then settled its weight low, on delicate collar bones. Its patina glowed richly against the pallor of her skin.

Her fingertips touched it. "Oh . . ."

Kellin grinned. "But you will earn it, my lass, with *me*."

Kirsty laughed aloud, then bent close to him. "Nae, I think not—'tis a *gift*! I'd hae done you for naught at all."

"For naught!"

"Aye!" Her laugh was throaty. "I've no' seen a man like you in all o' my days!"

Chagrined, he clapped a hand to her rump and found it firm and round. "Lamb and *usca*, then, before I die of hunger."

"Won't be hunger *you* die of!" She swung and was gone before he could retort.

Kellin ate lamb, drank *usca*, and laid a few wagers on the fall of the dice in a friendly game at another table. He was marked as Cheysuli, but no one appeared to resent it. Eyes followed the glint of gold when he moved in the lamplight, but the greed was friendly and lacking in covetous intent.

Kirsty appeared at last and ran deft fingers down his arm. Then she touched the buckle of his belt and tugged. "I'm done," she said. "Are you?"

"That depends," he gathered up his modest winnings, "on which game you refer to. With this one, aye; most certainly I am done. The other is not yet begun—" he grinned, "—and like to last all night."

She laughed softly. "Then coom prove it to me."

He rose and hooked a finger through the torque. He lifted it; then, using it, he pulled her closer, very close, so his breath warmed her face. "What more proof of my intent is necessary?"

Her hand was skilled as she slid it between his legs. "There's proof—and there's *proof*."

Kellin laughed quietly. "*Shansu, meijhana*—or would you prefer an audience?"

"Those words," she said, brows lifting. "What are those *words*?"

He said it into her ear. "I will explain them elsewhere."

Kirsty laughed and hooked an arm around his waist as his settled across her shoulders. "This way, my beastie—"

"No." He halted her instantly, humor dissipating. "Do not refer to me so."

" 'Twas just . . ." Her defense died. She nodded.

Kellin pulled her close, sorry he had broken the mood. "You know better where my room is."

Kirsty took him there.

He awakened hours later, aware of *usca* sourness in his mouth and a certain stiffness in his shoulders. Kirsty had proven her mettle, and had certainly drained him of his.

The room was dark. It took Kellin a moment to adjust his eyes. The stub of a candle had long since melted down, so that the only illumination was from the seam of moonlight between ill-fitted shutters. It lent just enough light to see the pallor of Kirsty's shoulder, jutting roofward. Raven hair and blankets obscured the rest of her.

I like black hair—and such white, white skin. She was curled against him like a cat, rump set against his left hip. *Would she purr, like Sima?*

But his mind drifted in search of an answer to an unknown question. He wondered what had wakened him. Usually he slept the night through, unless he dreamed of the Lion; but it had been weeks since the last nightmare, and he believed Kirsty had effectively banished the beast for the night. He lay in perfect silence, listening to her breathing.

Lir, Sima said, *has the girl stolen your senses along with other things? I have called for you three times.*

Ah. Kellin sighed and rubbed at his eyes. *What is it?*

If you wish to ride to Valgaard, you had better leave your bed.

Why? Do you want to leave now? It was ludicrous. *I said we would go in the morning.*

Your horse is leaving. Sima sounded smug.

My horse— He understood at once.

Kellin sat up, swearing, and tossed the covers aside. Kirsty mumbled a protest and dragged the blankets back. His clothing lay in a tangled heap on the floor, and no doubt the leather was cold. Kellin swore again and reached for leggings.

Kirsty turned as he buckled his belt. "Where d'ye go?"

"To rescue my horse." He meant to take his cloak, but Kirsty had pulled it up around her shoulders.

She stared at him. "How d'ye know it *wants* rescuing?"

"My *lir* told me." He bent to pull on his boots.

"Yer *beast*?"

"Not a beast. She is a mountain cat." He grinned briefly, tossing her the bone. "Her fur is as black and lovely as your hair."

Kirsty hunched up beneath blankets and cloak, unsure of the compliment. "Will ye coom back?"

Kellin pulled open the door. "Would a man be so foolish as to desert *you* in the midst of a cold night?"

Kirsty laughed. "Then I'll gie ye sommat to remember me by." She flung back cloak and coverlet, displaying cold-tautened breasts, and it was only with great effort that Kellin departed the room.

Upon exiting the roadhouse, Kellin was sorry he had left the cloak behind. The night was clear and cold, belying the season. Bare arms protested with pimpled flesh; he rubbed them vigorously, sliding fingertips across cooling *lir*-gold, and strode on toward the stable intending to settle the business at once, then hasten back to bed.

The building was a black, square-angled blob in the moonlight, blocky and slump-roofed. He approached quietly, accustomed to making no sound in the litheness of his movements, and touched the knife hilt briefly.

Sima's tone was clear. *They are taking the saddle, too.*

Kellin swore beneath his breath. Just as he reached the stable two men appeared, and a horse. *His* horse. The gelding was bridled and saddled, as if they intended to ride immediately.

He recognized them from the common room. *Greedier than I thought*— Kellin moved out of shadow into moonlight. "I doubt you could pay my price. You lost in the game tonight."

They froze. One man clung to the horse, while his companion stiffened beside him. Then the first put up his chin. "Go back to Kirsty," he said, "and we'll let ye be. 'Twill be a gey cold night, the other."

The dialect was thick. Kellin deciphered it, then added his own comment. " 'Twill be a gey cold night, withal—for *one* of us. . . ." He slipped into the lilt he had learned from his grandmother. Erinnish was similar. "But I'll be keeping yon horse for myself as well as the bonny lass."

Both men showed their knives. Kellin showed his. The display resulted in a muttered conversation between the two Homanans, as Kellin waited.

Eventually his patience waned. "We each of us has a knife. In that, we are well-matched. But are you forgetting I am Cheysuli? If a knife will not do to persuade you who is better, *lir*-shape will."

It sufficed. The man holding the reins released the gelding at once as the other stepped away. The horse wandered back toward the warm stable.

Kellin sighed. "Go on your way. *That* way." He gestured. "You'll be bedding down elsewhere, my boyos."

The men goggled at him. "We have a room!"

"Not any more."

"Ye canna *do* this!"

" 'Tis done." He grinned at them. "You tried to steal my horse, but that's done for the night. Now I've stolen your bed." He gestured. "On your way."

They muttered something to one another, then turned toward the road.

Kellin raised his voice. *"Cheysuli i'halla shansu!"*

They did not, either of them, offer an answer he understood.

"No, I thought not." Kellin went after the horse, caught and gathered dragging reins, then led the gelding into the stable. "Disturbed your sleep, did they?" He reached for the knotted girth. "Then we are a proper pair—though I dare say I miss the woman more than—" He turned. The noise was slight, but his hearing better than most.

It was too late. Weight descended upon him. Kellin went down with only a blurted protest.

Five

It was the cold that finally woke him. The earthen floor was packed hard as stone, and was twice as cold. The scattered straw offered no protection. Kellin's flesh, as he roused, rose up on his bones all at once and he shivered violently in a sustained, convulsive shudder that jarred loose the fog from his head.

"Gods—" His teeth clicked together and stayed there, clamped against the chattering he would not acknowledge.

Awake again?

He started to hitch himself up on one elbow, thought better of it almost at once, and stayed where he was. He rolled his head to one side and felt at the back of his skull, marking the lump. Something crusted in his fingers: dried blood, he guessed; at least it wasn't still flowing.

"*Lir?* Where are—uh." He scowled as he found her seated very close to his side. Aggrievedly, he said, "You might have at least lay down *next* to me! Some warmth is better than none!"

The last time we spoke of warmth, you claimed a woman's better than mine.

"That was in *bed*. Am I in bed now? No! I am lying sprawled on an icy stable floor with not even a *saddle* blanket for my—" He broke it off in astonishment. "—nor any *clothing*, either! My leathers—"

Sima slitted gold eyes against a stream of invective. When he at last ran out of oaths he stopped, caught his breath, and shut his eyes against the pain in his battered head.

He felt *empty*, somehow—and then Kellin clutched a naked earlobe. "My *lir*-gold!" He sat upright, unmindful of his headache. "Gods—they took my *gold*!"

Sima twitched her tail. *Gold is gold. Blessed or no, its value to a man remains the same.*

"But—it took me so long to get it—"

You were in no hurry, she reminded him primly. *You denied it—and me—for a very long time.*

Kellin gingerly rubbed the back of his tender skull, then felt the stiffness of abused neck tendons and attempted to massage the pain away. "Gloating does not become you."

Everything becomes a lir.

"And Blais' knife, too." Acknowledgment of a further atrocity sent a shudder through his body. "Oh, gods—oh, *gods* . . . my ring. My signet ring. Gods, *lir*—that ring signifies my rank and title!" He clutched the naked finger. "It has adorned the hand of every Prince of Homana since, since—" He gave it up. *"Lir—"* And then a burst of ironic laughter crowded out his panic. "Fitting, is it not? For ten years I rebel against the constraints of my rank—and now thieves steal its symbol from me! Surely the gods had a hand in this."

Or a foolish warrior.

Levity vanished. "You are not in the least surprised."

I warned you. She licked a paw.

"Does it mean nothing to you that what they have done is heretical? To rob a Cheysuli warrior of his *lir*-gold, and the Prince of Homana of his signet—"

—is brave, if nothing else; I admire them for their

gall. Sima blinked, then slitted eyes. *You can fetch it back.*

"In a saddle blanket? They have taken everything else!"

Surely the girl can bring you clothing.

"The girl likely was part of this." Realization stabbed him. "What coin I have left is in my room—" he reconsidered it, "—or *was.*"

Then you will have to tend it yourself.

Kellin swore again. Then, with excessive care, he got off the cold ground at last, found the nearest saddle blanket, and wrapped it around his loins. He was just tucking in the end when the stable door creaked open.

Kirsty stood silhouetted in moonlight, swathed in his cloak. He saw the tabard and woolen skirt, and leather shoes. Unbound hair, tangled from the evening's sport, hung below her hips.

Sima blinked again. *A conclusion perhaps best not jumped to.*

"Thieves," Kellin declared in answer to Kirsty's expression. "Did you know nothing of it?"

She put up her chin. "If I knew aught, I'd be other than here, ye muddle-headed whelp! D'ye think me so foolish as to *coom* to ye if I knew?"

"A clever woman would, merely to mislead me." He was curt in his headache and humiliation. "Have you clothing I can put on?"

Kirsty tossed back her untamed mane. "Ye'd look gey foolish in *my* clothing, ye ken."

Kellin sighed. "Aye, so I would. Have you *men's* I might put on?"

"Tam'll hae some. T'will cost, and nae doot'll be no' to your liking, but better than ye wear now." Her grin was abruptly sly. "Not that *I'm* minding, ye ken."

"I ken," he said dryly. "And I will pay Tam.

Though the gods know that torque alone would buy me a trunkful."

She clutched at it. " 'Tis mine! Ye *said* so!"

" 'Tis yours. I said so. Keep it, Kirsty—run and fetch the clothing." Silently he said, *If I can trust you to come back.*

Kirsty swung on her heels and hastened away while Kellin sat down on a haphazard pile of grain sacks and tried to ignore the cold and the thumping in his head.

She was back after all in but a handful of moments, and had the right of it; the clothing was not at all to his liking. But he put on the grimy smock and woolen baggy trews without complaint, then stuffed straw into the toes of Tam's oversized, decaying boots so they at least remained on his feet. The soles were worn through, the poor heels all run down, but even tattered leather was better than bare feet.

His earlobe hurt. The thieves had paid scant attention to the wire and how it hooked; they had wrenched it out of the hole with little regard to his flesh. But the lobe, if sore, was whole; he recalled very clearly that his grandsire lacked all of his.

Kirsty touched his arms. "No' the same wi' nae gold."

Anger got the best of him. "Is that what you wanted all along?"

She drew back, warding the torque against his eyes. "Nae! And I only meant ye dinna look the same wi'oot it, not that I *wanted* it! Now ye look like a Homanan, and a poor one at that!"

He laughed with little amusement. "So I do; one might mistake me altogether as a common low-born roadhouse-keeper." He regretted the words at once; what had she done to deserve them? "I am sorry—I am poor company. My thanks for the clothing. Now—which way did they go?"

"They?"

"The thieves. You know them, do you not?"

Kirsty said nothing.

"I saw them earlier, in the common room. They knew you, Kirsty, and you knew them." He paused. "I do not intend to kill them, merely fetch back my things. What they took is—sacred." He left it at that.

Kirsty chewed on a lock of hair. "North," she said finally, "across the river."

It was very near dawn. Already the sky behind her began to lighten. "Into Solinde."

She shrugged. "They're Solindish. They coom onc't a four-week."

"To steal."

"To work."

"One and the same, perhaps?" Kellin sighed. "Which way across the river?"

"Westward." She jerked her head. "They might ha' hurt ye worse."

"I said I will not kill them." He glanced at the stalls. "I have need of a horse."

Sima questioned that. *What of lir-shape?*

Within the link, he refused. *Too dangerous. No balance, yet—and now no time to learn it.* Kellin shivered. *For now, I will ride a horse.*

Kirsty stared. "*Now* ye want a horse? Ye hae no such coin in your purse, ye ken. I looked—*here* 'tis—*I* dinna want it!" She slapped it into his hand. "I only meant, how will ye buy the horse?"

"On promises," he said.

"Promises o' what? You've naught left; you've said so."

He turned from her and moved to the nearest stall. "This one will do. Where is the bridle?—ah."

He took it down from its peg, slipped the posts that fenced in the horse, and slipped inside.

"You'll no' turn *thief*," she said. "That be Tam's horse."

"Not yours."

"Nae. I own nothing but what I wear—and this." She clutched the torque. Her black eyes were very bright, but it was not from good humor; Kellin thought perhaps tears. "Unless you mean to take it back."

"No, I will do no such thing. Here, have back the coin—it will pay for the clothing. But I also need a horse. If you would have Tam repaid for *that*, there is a thing you can do." He bridled the piebald horse, then led it from the stall. He would not take saddle also; he took too much already. "If you would pay back Tam—and put coin in your pockets, as well—you need only go to Mujhara, and then to Homana-Mujhar."

"Homana-Mujhar!" She gaped. "To the palace?"

"They'll give you coin for the torque." He swung up bareback onto the piebald back and winced; the spine was well delineated. "That way it will stay with like pieces instead of winding up with a money-lender ... tell them I used it to pay a debt."

"Tell *who*?" She tossed back her head. "The Mujhar himself?"

He grinned. "They do know me there."

She was instantly suspicious. "I'm to tell them Kellin sent me to trade this for coin? Och, aye— they'll toss me oot i' the street!"

"Not immediately. After a meal, perhaps." He glanced at Sima. *Coming?*

She stood up from the shadows and shook her coat free of straw, then slid out of darkness into the dawn of a new day. Kirsty let out a startled shriek and leapt back three paces.

"My *lir*," he said briefly. "Do you see what I mean about her fur and your hair? Both such a lovely, glossy black."

The girl clutched at the shining torque. "In the eyes," she mumbled, staring at him. "E'en wi'*oot* the gold!"

"I thank you," Kellin said. "It is a compliment."

As he rode away from the stable, Kirsty called a final farewell. "Homana-Mujhar, indeed! I'll be keeping this for *myself*!"

Kellin sighed as he settled himself carefully athwart the treacherous spine. "Worth a trunkful of clothing and an entire *herd* of horses."

But less than your missing lir-gold, your ring— and your kinsman's knife.

Kellin offered no answer. Sima, as always, was right.

By the time they reached the ferry, Kellin's discomfort in his nether regions matched the thumping in his head. He was altogether miserable, wishing for his horse back, and all his gold back, and the knife, and most particularly the saddle that would have made things, even on *this* horse, much easier to bear.

He thought his head might burst. A closer inspection with fingers had not divulged anything he did not already know—the swelling was soft and tender, the cut dried. He wondered what they had struck him with—the roadhouse, perhaps?

He began a complaint to Sima. *They might have been*— Halfway through the comment he cut off the communication through the link. It made his head hurt worse. He waved a gesture at the cat that dismissed conversation; she flicked tufted ears and held her silence accordingly, but he thought she looked amused.

The ferry was docked this side of the river. Relieved, Kellin halted the piebald and slid off carefully, so as not to jar his head. A man was slumped against a cluster of posts roped together, the stub of a pipe clenched in his teeth. His eyes were closed, but he was not asleep.

Kellin led the horse up. "Did you give passage to two men early this morning? Just before dawn?"

One eye opened. Graying brown hair straggled around his face beneath a threadbare cap. " 'Twould be hard for a body to *walk* across, would ye no' say?"

Kellin suppressed a retort. "Then you did."

"Dinna see bodies in the river, do ye?—though they be carried awa' by now." The other eye opened. "She's angry in the spring."

Kellin looked beyond the man he took to be the ferry-master to the river beyond. It *was* spring, and the river did seem angry; the thaw had thickened the Bluetooth so that it ran nearly out of its banks, with a high, fast current that would suck a man down all too easily.

"They robbed me," Kellin said. "I am angry, also."

The ferry-master squinted. "Doesna look like ye had so much to steal."

"Now, no. Before, I did. This is the best I could do," he paused. "Did you give two Solindishmen passage across the river?"

"If I said aye, would ye be after passage, too?"

"The woman said it was where they were bound."

"Kirsty?" The man brightened. He was, Kellin judged, nearly as old as the Mujhar. "Did she send ye, then?"

"She sent me."

He raked Kellin with a glance from brown eyes set deeply in shadowed sockets. "Then ye must ha' pleased her. She's no needing to be sending a

robbed man after those who coom to see her onc't
a four-week."

Kellin hung onto his patience with effort. The
thudding in his head made it increasingly difficult.
"We pleased each other well enough. Did the men
cross here?"

"Dinna walk, did they?" He heaved himself
from the planking and jabbed the pipe in Sima's
direction. "She tame, yon cat?"

Kellin opened his mouth to vigorously deny that
a *lir* could be tamed; he shut it once he recalled
what Kirsty had said: that he could, in Tam's
clothing, pass as a Homanan. This close to Solinde, this close to Valgaard, it might be better to
keep his mouth shut with regard to *lir*. "Aye," he
said. "Tame enough."

"Then you'd best go no farther north," the ferry-
master warned. "There's a man o'er the Pass who
pays gold and jewels for cats like her."

He was indignant. "*Who* does?"

The ferry-master made a sign against evil. "A
man," he said only. "He'd hae *her* faster than the
river would eat a man." His truculence now was
vanished. "Aye, they crossed. Will ye?"

"I will. At once."

The man unwound the coil of rope tying up the
ferry. "Hae ye coin for it?"

"I have—" No. He did not. "—this horse."

"*That* horse! That one? What would I be doing
wi' Tam's old nag?"

"Mine was stolen," Kellin said tightly through
his teeth. "I bought this one to track the thieves,
so I might get back my *own* mount—which is, I
might add, considerably better than 'Tam's old
nag.'"

"Aye, it would be, ye ken? Not many *worse* than
Tam's old nag." He jerked his head toward the
ferry. "Coom aboard, then, you and yon cat . . . if

Kirsty sent ye after them, there's a reason for't. I'll no' take the nag." He grinned briefly. "Kirsty'll make it right."

Knowing how she spent her nights, Kellin judged she would. Nonetheless, he was grateful.

Almost as soon as he was aboard, Kellin was sorry. The Bluetooth fought the ferry every inch of the way, spuming over the sides of the flat, thick platform until the boards ran white with foam. The old piebald spread his legs and dropped his head even as Kellin grabbed hold of a rope; Sima dug claws into aged wood and lashed her tail angrily in counterpoint to the heaves the ferry-master put to the ropes.

By the time they reached the other side, Kellin's tattered clothing was soaked. Sima bared her teeth and shook droplets free of her coat. As soon as the ferry thumped the bank she sprang for land; Kellin led the piebald off and thanks the gods for putting firm land beneath his feet.

"Aye," the ferry-master said, "she's a gey wicked bitch in the spring. Summer's better." He jerked his head westward. "That way, they went. They won't be expecting ye, so they willna be in a hurry. Ye'll hae them by sundoon."

Kellin nodded thanks. "Is this because of Kirsty?"

"Och, she's a right'un, that lass . . . but ye've a pinched look in the eyes that says they hit ye a mite too hard." He grinned around the pipe. "And ye speak too well for a man born to wear Tam's clothes." He jerked his head again. "Gi' on wi' ye, then. Ye'll be back by tomorrow, and ye can *pay* for your ride."

Kellin smiled. *"Cheysuli i'halla—"* He broke it off instantly, cursing the headache that mangled his wits so.

The ferry-master's eyebrows shot up beneath the

lock of greasy hair. "Ah. Well, then. Not tame after all, is she?" He coughed. "Yon cat."

"No." Kellin swung up onto the piebald and wished immediately his pride had permitted him to find a log and mount, like a woman. "There are times I wish she were."

The brown eyes were sharp. "Then 'tisn't the horse you're wanting, or the coin ... more like cat-shaped gold, is't?"

"More like," Kellin said. He kicked the horse into motion.

"Aye, well ... I've no' known them to be so foolish before." He briefly showed a gap-toothed grin that gave way to the pipestem. "Be wary of Solinde. Up here so close to Valgaard—well ..." He let it go. "They'd be wanting more than yon cat."

This time he did not hesitate. *"Leijhana tu'sai. Cheysuli i'halla shansu."*

Six

The westward road was not so well-traveled as the one cutting down from the Bluetooth into the center of Homana. It was narrow and twisty, winding its way through silted huddles of downed trees and acres of water-smoothed boulders carried this way and that by a temperamental river gone over its banks to suck back again, leaving detritus in its wake. Tam's old nag was not a particularly coordinated horse, and Kellin spent much of his time trying to keep his head very still upon his neck as the horse stumbled its way along.

"By sundown," Kellin muttered in reference to the ferry-master's prediction as the piebald tripped again. "By then, I may well be lacking a head entirely. It will have fallen off and rolled to a halt amidst that pile of boulders, *there*, and when the crows have picked it clean no one will know the difference between it and that rock, *there*."

Sima chanced the *lir*-link. *I will go on ahead. Let me find them—I will come back and fetch you.*

It pulsed within his skull. Kellin hissed in pain and shut his eyes against it, then waved her on. "Go. I am little threat to them if I find them in this state. They will laugh, and be on about their business with no fear of me."

The cat whipped her tail, then left at a springy lope.

The horse stumbled on. After a while Kellin balanced himself, shut his eyes, and gave himself over to a state very akin to sleep, in hopes that when he awoke the pain would be dispersed.

He roused to a quiet voice pitched over a rush of water. "I had expected to eat alone, but your horse has other ideas." A pause. "I am glad of the company; will you share my meal?"

Kellin opened his eyes. He slumped atop the piebald, which had in turn wandered off the road to a cluster of tumbled boulders very near the river's edge. He smelled smoke and fish. It made his belly rumble.

The stranger laughed. "I will take that as acceptance."

"Where am I?" Kellin glanced around. The road was not so far; he could see it winding westward.

"Here," the man said, amused. "At my campsite, such as it is; but I have had good fortune in my fishing, and there is enough for us both." His hazel eyes were friendly. The piebald snorted against the hand that held his bridle; the stranger grinned and pushed the muzzle away. "You have been hard used; I have wine for the ache."

He was a young, fine-featured man, perhaps Kellin's age or a year or two older. His hair was dark, nearly black, and fell smoothly to his shoulders. His clothing was spun of good wool of uniform yarn. Kellin marked him a well-to-do man: linen tunic died blue, with black embroidery at the collar; black-dyed breeches; good boots, and a brilliant crimson cloak thrown on loosely over shoulders.

Kellin considered refusing. There were the thieves to think about. But his head did ache, his belly did rumble—and Sima was on their trail. He need only wait for her, and by the time she returned, his condition would be improved.

"My thanks," he said. Then recalled what he looked like. "But I have nothing—"

The stranger waved a hand. "Your company is enough. I am not so far from my destination; I can be generous." He smiled again. "You might do better to walk, then to go another step atop *this* horse."

"Aye." Kellin smiled crookedly and slid off, gritting his teeth against the pounding in his head. It was worse, not better; but the road was hard and the horse clumsy. He was lucky his head remained on his neck.

"My name is Devin," the stranger said as Kellin pulled the reins over the piebald's neck. "The wine I have is Solindish white; will it do?"

Kellin followed. "Any wine will do. I am not fit to judge its taste." A glance from Devin told Kellin he had perhaps misphrased his answer; he had meant because of his head, but Devin's quick assessment indicated the stranger believed he meant his station. *He thinks me a poor man; well, for the moment, I am.* He led the piebald to the water-wracked, uprooted tree at the riverbank and tied him to a branch next to Devin's mount, a fine glossy bay very like Kellin's stolen horse.

A fire was built between a tumble of clustered boulders and the water's edge, hosting two speckled fish speared and hung belly-up along two stripped branches resting in crotched braces. The lap of the river was but paces away, so the sound was loud. Devin squatted near the fire, digging through packs. "Here." He tossed the wineskin. "I have another; drink as you will. I will tend the fish."

Kellin caught the skin as he turned from the piebald and swallowed, glad of the liquor's bite. If he drank enough, it would dull the pounding in his head, but that would be poor manners. He

owed Devin sober companionship, not the rudeness of a man undone by misfortune.

Devin made conversation as he inspected the
sizzling fish. "I misjudged the distance," he said,
"or I would have stayed the night in the last roadhouse I passed. The ground is a hard bed when
one is used to better." He lifted one of the speared
fish. "Here. Trout. I daresay it will complement
the wine."

Kellin accepted the proffered fish-laden stick
with thanks and sat down against the closest boul-
der. He thought Devin was indeed accustomed to
better; a sapphire gleamed on one hand, while a
band of twisted gold glinted on the other.

Devin took the other fish for himself and sat
back against his packs, blowing to cool the meat.
"Have you a wife?" he asked.

Kellin shook his head. His mouth was full of
fish.

"Ah. Well, neither do I—for but a four-week
more!" He grinned. "I am bound for my wedding.
Wish me good fortune, my friend, and that the girl
is comely . . . I have no wish to share my bed with
a plain woman!"

Kellin swallowed. "You have never seen her?"

"No. A dynastic thing, this marriage. To bind
the bloodlines closer." Devin chewed thoughtfully.
"A man like you weds for love, or lust—or because
the woman has conceived, and her father insists!—
but a man like me, well . . ." He sighed. "No
choice for either of us. The match was suggested
by her father, and mine accepted eagerly; one cannot help but to rise in service to a powerful lord."

Kellin's smile was crooked. "No."

"I envy you. You need not wed at all, if that is
your desire—well, I should not complain; my lot
is better than yours." Devin's attitude was friendly

enough, but all too obviously he believed Kellin lowborn. "What is your trade?"

Kellin wanted to laugh. If he told Devin the truth— He grinned, thinking of the thieves. "What other trade is there but to aspire to higher in life— and the coin to make it possible?"

Devin's eyes narrowed consideringly as he washed down trout with wine. "You are a passing fair mimic."

"A mimic?"

"Ayè. Put on finer clothing, wash the grime from your face, you could pass for a highborn man." He stoppered the wineskin. "You might make a mummer."

Kellin laughed, thinking of his grandparents. "There are those who have accused me of that very thing. I did but playact the role, they said— then admonished me to learn my part better." He jerked his head westward. "When you came down the road, did you pass two men with a bay very like your own?"

Devin shrugged. "I passed many people. I do not recall the horse." His eyes brightened over the fish. "Why?"

"The horse they have is mine. It was stolen from me . . ." He ran a hand through tousled hair. "You see, I am not precisely the man I appear to be." Kellin plucked at Tam's grimy tunic. "They took more than my horse."

"And left you with that piebald horse and another's clothing?" Devin shouted a laugh. "Aye, it makes sense—you have not the manner of a lowborn man, either."

Kellin thought of the Midden and his visits. "Some might argue with that."

"Well, at least they left you your life. Did they knock you on the head?" He grinned as Kellin grimaced an answer. "I thought so. The dullness in

your eyes ... aye, well, drink more wine." He finished his fish. "If I were not expected, I would
help you catch the thieves. I have certain gifts that
would improve the sport."

"Gifts?"

Devin grinned. "Arts." He reached for the wineskin, then turned as movement on the road caught
his eyes. Almost at once he froze. "Be still!" He
put out a hand. "Do not move—gods, but what a
beauty ... and a fitting gift for the girl's father.
He covets them. I shall have to see if I can take
her."

Kellin turned, asking, "Covets what—?" And
broke off immediately. Suspicion blossomed.

He dropped the fish, set down the wineskin quietly, and wished he had his knife. He stared hard
at the friendly stranger.

"She is *lovely*!" Devin breathed.

Kellin did not answer. He reached out very carefully and closed his hand around the hilt of Devin's knife.

Devin twisted at once, slapping down at Kellin's
grasping hand. "What are you—*wait*—" He rolled
and scrambled up, poised for attack. The light in
his eyes was gone, replaced by a cold, piercing
stillness. Quietly, he said "Only a fool steals from
an Ihlini."

The cold knot solidified in Kellin's belly. He
knelt on one knee with the other booted foot
planted, grasping a stolen knife. "And only a fool
thinks he can capture a *lir*."

Realization kindled in Devin's eyes, then damped
to coals. He shook his head. "You have no power
before me."

"Nor you before me."

Devin raised his hands. "I have these."

"And I have your knife."

Devin's eyes narrowed. His young face was

stretched taut across prominent cheekbones. His lips were bloodless. He studied Kellin carefully, then murmured something beneath his breath. "They say—" He shut his mouth, then began again. "They say we are very alike. Ihlini and Cheysuli. That we are bloodkin." He remained half crouched, prepared to receive an onrush. "Do you believe it?"

"Does it matter?"

"It does. If there is truth to it. If we are to kill one another."

"Are we?"

Devin shrugged. "To serve Asar-Suti, I will kill whomever I must—" In one smooth motion he ripped his cloak from his shoulders and swirled it at Kellin, snapping weighted corners.

The blaze of crimson came at his face, aimed for his eyes. Kellin ducked the cloak easily enough, but it served merely as distraction; Devin scooped up and hurled a river rock that nearly struck Kellin's head.

Ku'resh— As Kellin dodged it, the Ihlini hurled himself forward.

They went down together hard, smashing into rocks spewed up by the Bluetooth River. Devin's fingers dug into Kellin's throat. He squirmed beneath the Ihlini, thrashing legs to gain leverage, and managed to thrust a knee upward that imperiled Devin's balance. The Ihlini tensed, shifted, and Kellin bucked him off. The knife was lost somehow, but he scrambled to his feet even as Devin came up clawing.

It was an obscene dance, an intercourse of grasping hands reaching to crush a throat. Kellin was aware of Sima's nearness by the sound of her growls and snarls, but the link was completely empty. In its place was an odd disorientation, a buzzing interference that told him all too clearly what he should have known before; what he *would* have known before had his wits not been so muddled.

They were too near the river. Sand shifted. Rocks rolled. Kellin's feet slid inside oversized, straw-stuffed boots. *No foothold*— He slipped even as Devin changed grasp, and Kellin stumbled. He brought the heel of his right hand up against the underside of Devin's jaw, meaning to snap the neck, but the Ihlini twisted his head sharply aside.

This, then— Kelin hooked a foot and caught Devin's ankle. He dropped the Ihlini, then turned and lunged for the knife but a pace away.

Devin's feet scissored out. Kellin, caught, fell hard, trying to twist, but Devin's hands were on him. *—knife—*

The Ihlini had it. Kellin saw the brief glint, saw the tip meet Tam's grimy fabric, then plunge through.

Gods—Sima— He squirmed, sucking in his belly.

Devin gasped a triumphant laugh. Steel dug through flesh and slid between ribs. The Ihlini's mouth was a rictus of victory and exertion. "*Who wins this one?*"

Kellin jerked himself off the blade, willing himself not to think of the pain, the damage, the risk. He saw the blood smearing steel, saw the crimson droplets staining damp sand, but refused to acknowledge it.

He twisted his torso and brought up a booted foot. One thrashing thrust jarred against Devin's thigh, then glanced off. It was enough. Kellin levered himself up, grasping hair and tunic, and threw Devin over. He let his weight fall and pinned the Ihlini, then grabbed handfuls of dark hair and began to smash the skull against the sand.

The wound was bad. If he did not kill Devin

soon, he would soon bleed to death. What a sweet irony if they killed one another.

Devin bucked. An upthrust knee missed Kellin's groin but not his belly. Pain blossomed anew, and bleeding. His tunic was sodden with it.

"—wait—" Devin gritted. "—only need to *wait*—" But he did not. He bucked again, broke Kellin's grasp, and scrambled away from him. "Now—"

Kellin staggered upright, sealing the wound closed with his left arm pressed hard against his ribs. He fell back two steps, stumbled over a rock, tried to steady his footing. Strength was fading fast.

Devin laughed. His face was scratched and reddened in patches; it would bruise badly if he lived long enough. "Cheysuli blood—" he gasped, "—is red as Ihlini—red as my *own* . . . are we kinsmen, then?" He smeared an arm across his face. "I have only to wait—you will do me the favor of dying even if I never touch you again."

"My *lir*—will touch—*you*—" It was all Kellin could manage as he labored to keep his breath.

"Your *lir*? I think not. The *lir* are proscribed against harming Ihlini. Have you ever wondered why?" Devin's breath was returning.

Kellin backed up. He heard the rush of the river, the promise of its song. What he needed was time to recover himself, but time he did not have. Devin had time.

He could not hold the blood in. It crept through his fingers, then dripped to the sand. A rock was red with it, turning slowly black. Behind Kellin the river roared louder.

"Enough," Devin said, bending to grab the knife. "I am expected in Valgaard. This foolish dance delays me."

Kellin bent and scooped up a round stone. He let fly, then scooped another and threw again.

Devin ducked, but did not let go of the knife. He knew better; why loose the only weapon and chance the enemy's retrieval?"

The Ihlini advanced. "One more throw, and your heart will burst. Do you think I cannot tell?"

Kellin retreated, clutching bloodied wool against his chest. The world around him blurred. *Not like this—not what I could ask for in the manner of my death—*

Sima screamed. Devin lunged.

Kellin twisted from the knife as the blade was thrust toward him. He caught the outstretched arm in both hands and wrenched, snapping it over, trying with grim determination to break the limb entirely.

Devin shouted. The knife fell free, then the Ihlini stumbled forward and threw his weight against Kellin.

A curious warmth flowed throughout his chest. Kellin saw the Ihlini's mouth moving, but heard no words. He sagged, thrust out a braced foot to hold himself up, and clung to Devin.

The bank behind them broke. Both flailing bodies tumbled into the river.

Kellin loosed his grasp on Devin as the waters closed over his head. He thrust himself upward, thrashing; ill-fitting boots filled with water and dragged him down again.

Sima—

He clawed, sealing his mouth shut, trying to make his way upward where he could breathe again. The boots were pulled off his feet.

Sima—

The river rolled. He broke the surface briefly and sucked air. Then the beast caught him again, threw him over, hurled him downward. He tumbled helplessly, clawing at current, holding his breath in lungs that refused to serve him.

He was briefly embraced within the treacherous arms of a buried tree, deep in the water. Then the tunic tore loose and he was free of it, of snag and tunic; he thrashed again but could no longer tell which was surface and which was bottom.

He breathed water. He was hurled against a rocky protuberance, then scraped off again and tumbled, limbs flailing uselessly. His right leg caught, wedged into a cleft between the rocks. Kellin twisted in the current, was tumbled helplessly, and felt the dull snap.

No pain. His leg was numb. *Both* legs were numb. His entire body was nothing but a blob of useless flesh, too vulnerable, too fragile, to withstand the beast in full spate.

The river dragged him free, then threw him heedlessly against another promontory. He surfaced briefly, coughed a garbled plea for air, for aid, then the river reclaimed him.

This time she was cruel. She hurled him into her depths and kept him there, like a cork caught in a millrace, and when she threw him out again, into the lesser current, she did not notice if the broken body breathed or not.

Interval

The master of Valgaard was found deep in the undercroft of the fortress, feeding his cats. They did not cluster at his feet as housecats do, courting morsels, demanding affection, because they were not pets, but mountain cats, tawny, russet, and black, who prowled the confines of their cages baring great teeth, snarling as he dangled promised offal before them, and red, bloodied meat.

He was a handsome man, and knew it; it pleased him to know it, though breeding almost assured it. And young, less than thirty, clearly in his prime—though that was won from the Seker and was not a natural thing. He kept his dark, springy hair closely cropped against a well-shaped head balanced on an elegant neck, and adorned supple fingers with a clutch of rings. They glinted bloody and bronze in the torchlight.

A man arrived. He stood in the archway and did not step into the chamber. His voice was pitched very quietly, so as not to disturb the cats; more importantly, so as not to disturb the master. "My lord."

Lochiel did not look away from his cats; he enjoyed their ferocity. "Have you news of Devin?"

The man folded his hands before him, eyes fixed on the floor so as not to offer offense. "We are not certain, my lord. We believe so."

Lochiel turned. His eyes were a clear ale-brown

set beneath winged brows that on another man might suggest femininity; on him, they did not. No one alive would suggest he was less than a man. The structure of his face was of peculiar clarity, as if the gods had labored long to make him perfect. "Why are you uncertain?"

"We found a horse, and packs containing certain articles belonging to Devin—included among them was the ring your daughter sent him—but Devin was not with the horse. There were signs of violence, my lord—bloodied sand, and a fallen knife . . . but no body. At least, not there." The servant did not look up from the floor. "We found a man downriver not far from the horse, thrown up in the bank like driftwood."

"Dead?"

"He was not when we found him. He might be now. He is sore hurt."

Lochiel threw meat to the cats, one by one, and smiled to see unsheathed claws trying to fish meat bestowed from one cage into another. "Where is my daughter?"

"With him, my lord. She was hawking out of the defile, in the canyon—she saw us bring him up."

Lochiel sighed. "Not the most impressive way to meet your bridegroom." He glanced at bloodied hands and wished them clean; they were. "It will be an annoyance if Devin dies. I researched his pedigree most carefully."

"Aye, my lord."

Lochiel observed the cats. His day was now disturbed. "They will have to wait. I will have them eat no meat save it comes from my hands."

"Aye, my lord. My lord?"

Lochiel arched an inquisitive brow.

"We saw a cat, my lord. As we came over the

Pass. A sleek, black female, young but promising well. She hid herself almost at once."

"Had she a mate?"

"None we saw. We were thinking of the man, and came straight on to the fortress."

"Very well. I will send you out tomorrow to learn the truth of her." He glanced at the black male who eyed him hungrily. "Perhaps if you are good, I shall give you a mate." He frowned pensively. "It would be a pity if my daughter lost hers. I need children of them." He touched one of his rings. *If Cynric is born—* His mouth compressed, robbing the line of its purity.

If Cynric were born after all, there was only one sure way, one certain course to defeat him; but such insurance was costly and required a sacrifice. Yet *he* he had failed in all his attempts. Asar-Suti did not countenance failure.

The Ihlini studied his rings, considering, knowing the answer already. If Kellin lived to sire the child, that sure way, that exacting, definitive course would have to be taken.

Lochiel sighed. *If we are to block the Firstborn, I shall have to make a child for the Seker to inhabit.*

PART IV

One

"You should not be here," my mother declared.

I heard the rustle of her skirts as they dragged across the threshold. She wears them long and full, using up bolts of costly cloth that might better be distributed among several women instead of only one. But that was my mother; she lived solely for her position as Lochiel's wife, as if it might mislead a stranger into forgetting what she herself detested: that the taint of Cheysuli blood also ran in her veins.

"Undoubtedly," I agreed. "But I am here now; proprieties no longer matter." I glanced at her then, and saw the skirts were the deep, rich red of the thickest Homanan wine. She glittered with jet. *All black and red, and white.* . . . Even to carmined lips against the pallor of her flesh. She bleaches it deathly white, to hide the Cheysuli taint.

"Who is he?" She moved closer.

"A man," I answered evenly, with off-handed negligence. Then, to prick her: "He may well be Devin."

She cast me a sharp, well-honed glance designed to discover the truth; I hid it behind the mask. I had learned it of my father, who said *he* had learned it to turn the witch from the door.

It was his jest to say so. We are all of us witches.

"Devin or no, you had best take yourself elsewhere," she said. "There are servants who can tend him, and I am better suited to intimacy than you."

Aye, so she would be; she encouraged it constantly.

I shrugged. "I have already seen him. I met them in the canyon when they brought him up; they wrapped him in a blanket, but that was taken off when they put him in the bed." I paused. "I know what a man looks like."

Carmined lips compressed into a thin, retentive seam. She looked at the man lying so still in the bed. He was well-covered now, but I had seen the naked flesh. It was blue from the water, and slick with bleeding scrapes reopened by the ride. They had brought him to Valgaard trussed like a new-killed stag. The marks still dented wrists and ankles.

"Will he live?" she asked.

I shrugged. "If my father desires him to."

Her glance was sharp. "If he *is* Devin, be certain your father will indeed desire it."

I shrugged again. Everyone in Valgaard knew I was meant to wed Devin of High Crags no matter what *I* wanted; men, particularly fathers, are not often disposed to ask women what they prefer.

My father was less disposed to ask anything at all of anyone; Lochiel need never do so. What was not given, he took. *Or* made.

Well, so did I. Given the chance.

I looked at the man in the bed. *Devin? Are you Devin?*

My mother made a noise. She bent, studied his scraped and swollen face, then shook her head slightly. "He is damaged."

"Somewhat," I agreed dryly. "Whoever he is, he survived the Bluetooth. Worth respect, for that . . .

would you expect a man who goes in handsome to come out better for it?"

He was, at present, decidedly *un*handsome; the river robs a body of the blood that lends flesh color, the heart that maintains life, and the spirit to drive the heart. He was a slab of flesh made into the form of a man, with two arms, a head, and two legs, though one of the legs was broken. I had seen the end of the bone pressing hard against bruised flesh below the knee, turning it white and shiny, but it had not broken through.

"His ear is torn," she said, "and his lip badly split."

"Aye," I agreed. There was much more than that. The entire left side of his face was mottled black with bruising, and bled colorless fluid from abrasions. "Turn back the covers, lady mother. There is worse yet to see."

She did; I expected it. But she looked first at something that was not, so far as we knew, injured by the river. He was a man, and whole.

I shut my teeth very tightly. There is in my mother a quality of *need*, as if she requires a man to note her beauty, to remark upon it, and to profess his ardent interest. She is indeed beautiful, but no man in Valgaard is foolish enough to give her more than covert glances. She is Lochiel's wife.

It had never been so bad as the past two years. I knew its cause now, though realization was slow, and comprehension more sluggish yet. No daughter desires to see her mother made jealous by her daughter's ascension to adulthood. But she was. It had been a hard truth, but I understood it at last.

Lochiel's wife was jealous of Lochiel's daughter. *You bore me,* I said inwardly. *How can you envy the child you yourself bore?*

But her power was negligible. She was Lochiel's

wife, while I was his *daughter*. Her value therefore was finished; she had borne him a single girl-child and could bear him no more. Now the value passed to the daughter who would, if married wisely, insure the downfall of the Cheysuli.

It was what she lived for. Despite that she was the bastard daughter of the Cheysuli warrior who sat upon the Lion in the Great Hall of Homana-Mujhar.

"What is this?" She touched his chest. "A knife wound, and deep."

I could not see his body because of the way she held the blankets, but I did not need to look. I knew what was there. The Bluetooth is cruel. "He should have bled to death, but the river sealed it. When he warms, it will bleed anew. We shall have to be ready."

She studied him avidly, marking the shape of his battered nose, the muddying of his jawline by swollen bruises, the mutilated left ear. Even his mouth, as if she measured its shape against the way she might desire it to fit her own.

I drew in a sharp breath. It sickened me to see her behave so.

She looked on him, and smiled. Then she looked at me. Something dark moved in her eyes. "*You* may have him."

It stopped the breath in my chest. That she could *suggest* such a thing was monstrous. She would give me my bridegroom because he was so badly hurt as to make him unattractive, and therefore unworthy of her interest.

Revulsion filled me. I looked at the man in the bed, so battered, bruised, and broken. *I hope you are handsome. And I hope she chokes on it!*

"Now," she said, "I will order the women in. We will do what we can do . . . I must make certain my daughter does not lose the man before the

bedding." She said a single word, very quietly—
she is, after all, Ihlini—and women came into the
chamber.

They stripped him of bedclothes and began to
clean his body, swabbing gouges and scrapes,
cleaning the knife wound. He made no sound or
movement until they touched his leg, and then he
roused.

The indrawn hiss was hardly audible in the fuss
around his bed, but I heard it. The tendons in his
neck stood up, hard and rigid, beneath pale flesh.

My mother put her hand on his brow, pushing
away stiffened hair. It was black as my own, and
thick, but lacking luster. Sand crusted the pillow.

"Fever," she said crisply. "*Malenna* root, then."

I looked at her sharply. "It will leave him too
weak!"

"You see how he fights the pain. I need him
weak, and compliant, so the root may do its
work."

So you can assert your control. But I did not say
it.

With no word spoken, the women melted against
the walls, faces downturned. I knew, without looking, my father had come. " 'Sore hurt,' I was told."
He walked through the door. "The leg must be
set."

"You could heal it," I blurted, then wished I had
said nothing; one does not suggest to my father
what he can or cannot do.

My father smiled. "We do not yet know who
he is. He could well be Homanan—why waste the
Seker's gift on a man who is unworthy?" He gestured. "I will set it by conventional means."

That meant splints and linen. They were
brought, and my father motioned for the women
to hold him down. He clasped the bruised ankle,
then pulled the bone straight.

I watched the man who might be Devin, and therefore meant for me. Eyes rolled beneath pale, vein-threaded lids. His head thrashed until one of the woman caught it between her hands and stopped its movement. The tendons stood up again, warping his neck; the battered mouth opened. It split the lip again so that it bled, running down his chin to drip against his neck. It spilled into the creases and stained the pillow.

Brilliant crimson against the pallor of fragile flesh. Devin's flesh?

I felt a frisson of nervous anticipation. If he *were* Devin, he was to be, with me, a means to destroy the prophecy. I could not help but hope he was indeed Devin so that our plans could continue; we were close, too close, my father said, to losing the battle. Kellin, Prince of Homana, need only sire a son and the thing was done.

But I smiled as I thought of it. Indeed, he need only sire a son upon a particular woman—but Kellin had proved all too selfish with respect to his conduct. For years my father had laughed to hear of the prince's exploits, saying that so long as Kellin behaved in such a wayward manner he actually *aided* us, but I knew it could not last. He would have to die, so that we could be certain.

It seemed a simple task. Kill Kellin of Homana—and produce an Ihlini child blessed by the Seker so we need never concern ourselves with the prophecy ever again.

The blood ran freely from the split lip. My mother made a sound of disgust. I wanted very badly to take up a clean cloth and blot away the blood, to press it against his lip so he would not lose more, but I dared not be so intimate before my father.

"There." My father placed the splints on either side of his leg, then bound it tightly with linen.

The mouth went slack again. His struggle had done more then reopen his lip; now blood flowed sluggishly from his swollen nose.

My mother smiled to see it. "A most unfortunate accident."

My father's gaze was on her, steady and unflinching. I could not discern his thoughts. "He will recover," he said, "provided Asar-Suti desires him to." He looked now at me. "I will certainly request it. We need this man."

I stiffened. "Is it Devin?"

"They have searched his baggage more closely. A pouch contained the ring you sent last year, a cache of ward-stones, and the eagle claw charm against *lir* intrusion. And—this." He held it up in the light. It was a gold ring set with a deep blood-red stone, nearly black; in its heart light stirred as if roused from sleep. My father smiled. "It knows me."

"A lifestone!" my mother said, then looked more closely at the man in the bed.

I shut my teeth together. *It makes a difference, does it? You look again to see if he might present a different face.*

"Devin would have one, of course; he is sworn to the Seker." My father's pale brown eyes looked at me over the glinting lifestone. "Unless this man is a thief who stole from Devin, then fell into the water, I think it unlikely he is anyone else."

My mother frowned. "It is set in a ring. Why would he not wear it?"

His gaze dwelled on her face. "Solinde is not entirely ours, anymore. Even in High Crags, men honor the shapechanger who holds court in Lestra. An Ihlini sworn to the god cannot move so freely now without taking precautions. He was wise to put it away."

My mother's carmined lips compressed. "That

will be changed. *We* shall rule again, as in the days of Tynstar and Bellam."

Lochiel laughed. "Did you know them personally?"

Color flared in her cheeks; she, as I, heard the irony. "I know as much of our history as anyone, Lochiel. Despite my Cheysuli blood!"

"Ah, but my blood is *theirs*." He smiled. "Tynstar was my grandsire."

It silenced her at once. Even among the Ihlini, who understood his power, Lochiel was different. It was easy to forget how old he was, and how long-lived his ancestors.

I smiled to myself. *Tynstar, Strahan, Lochiel—and now Ginevra. I am their legacy.* It was more than she claimed, and Melusine knew it.

"Shall we see if he is Devin?" My father held the ring in such a way that the light sparked from it. "If he is an opportunist who decides, upon awakening, he would benefit from our care, we can take steps now to present him with the lie."

I looked at the ring. Light moved within it sluggishly. Indeed, it did know my father; the blood of the god ran in his veins, as it did in the veins of all those sworn to Asar-Suti. I as yet claimed none of it outside of my natural inheritance; I was to drink the cup at my wedding, to seal my service forever to the Seker.

"Will it kill him?" my mother asked.

Lochiel smiled at her. "If he is not Devin, assuredly." He held the ring. "My gift to you, Melusine—adjudicate this man."

"Wait!" I blurted, and regretted it at once as my father turned to me.

Carmined lips stretched back to display my mother's white teeth. "No," she said venomously. "He gives you everything—this he gives to *me*!" She snatched the ring, bent over the unconscious man, grasped his left hand and pushed the ring onto his forefinger. "Burn," Melusine said. "If you are not Devin, let the *godfire* devour you!"

"You *want* it to!" I cried. "By the god himself, I think—" But my accusation died as *godfire* flared up from the ring, a clean and livid purple. I fell back a step even as my mother did, who laughed.

"You see?" she said. "Not Devin at all!"

But the burst of flame died. The hand was unblemished. Light glowed brilliantly deep in the lifestone's heart.

"Ah," Lochiel said. "A premature assumption."

"Then—it is he?" I looked at the ring upon the hand. "This is Devin."

"It appears so. A lifestone is linked to an Ihlini as a *lir* is linked to a Cheysuli." For a brief moment he frowned, looking at Devin. "It is but another parallel . . ." But he let it go. "We will have confirmation when he awakens."

I drew in a breath and asked it carefully. "Then why not heal him instead of relying on normal means?"

Lochiel smiled. "Because even Devin must learn that he is solely dependent on me for such paltry things as his life." He extended his hand. My mother took it. "Nurse him well, Ginevra. There is no better way to judge a man than from the depths of pain. It is difficult to lie when your world is afire."

He led my mother from the room. They would go to bed, I knew. It made my face burn; I did not understand what need it was they answered, save there was one, only that they seemed to be, in all ways such private things are measured, particularly well suited.

One of the women blotted away the blood on Devin's face. Another came forward with a cup. *Malenna* root, I knew, mixed in with water. I wanted to protest it, but did not; it was true he needed the fever purged. If it weakened him too much, I would prevail upon my father to make certain he survived.

My father wanted a child. An heir to Valgaard, and the legacy of the Ihlini. If I did not marry Devin, we would have to find someone else whose blood was proper. Why waste the time? The man was right here.

I sat down on a stool and stared at him. *Live*, I told him. *There is much for you to learn.*

And as much for me.

I had seen my parents' marriage. I was not so certain I desired the same for myself.

I sighed. *The Seker grant me the knowledge I need to make my way in this. I want to serve my father— but I want to serve me also!*

Two

The fever broke before dawn. The *malenna* root did its work, purging his body of impurities so that the sweat ran upon his flesh. The worst was done, I thought; now could come the healing. It would take much time because of the severity of his injuries, but I believed he would survive.

The women my mother had left to tend him slid sidelong glances at me as they cleaned him. They dared say nothing to me, though I knew they felt it improper for me to remain in attendance. But he was my bridegroom; how could they believe I would *not* be interested in whether he lived or died?

I sat upon a stool close to his side. He fascinated me. I wanted to study him covertly so he need never know. A man awake is too aware of his pride and the manner of his appearance; I wanted to know *him* without such impediments.

His breathing sounded heavy in his chest. The wad of bandage pressed over the knife wound came away soiled with blood and fluid, but seemed clean enough. It did not stink of infection. It was a simple wound, if deep; with care he would recover.

He stirred and moaned, twisting his head against the pillow. The oozing of the scrapes on his face had stopped and his skin had begun to dry, puckering the flesh into a crusted film. The hollows beneath his eyes were darkened by bruising. Eyelids flickered. His lashes were as long as mine, and as thick.

Incongruous thought; I banished it. Then summoned it back again as I studied the fit of his swollen nose into the space between his eyes, beneath arched black eyebrows. He was badly bruised, aye, but I thought my mother was blind. She could not see beyond the wreckage wrought by the river to the good bones beneath.

I think when you are healed, you might surprise us all. I drew in a breath. "Devin?"

Lids flickered again, then opened. His eyes were a clear brilliant green, but glazed with weakness. *Malenna* root, I knew; it would rob him of his wits for longer than I preferred. I wanted them back.

I scraped my stool closer, so he could see me. His lips were badly swollen and crusted with dried blood. He moved them, winced, then took more care as he shaped the words. They—*it*—was malformed, but clear enough. "Who—?"

I smiled. "Ginevra."

I waited. I expected him to respond at once that he was Devin, or to make some indication he knew who I was. Instead, he touched his mangled bottom lip with an exploratory tongue tip, felt its state, and withdrew the tongue. Lids closed a moment, then lifted again.

"Your name?" I persisted, desiring verbal confirmation in addition to the lifestone.

A faint frown puckered his forehead. With the hair swept back I could see it was unmarred; the river had spared him her savagery there, at least. "My leg . . ." A hand moved atop the furred coverlet, as if it would pull the blanket aside.

"No." I stopped the hand with my own. "Your leg is broken, but it has been set." The hand stilled. I removed mine. "Do you recall what happened?"

The forehead puckered again. "What place is this?"

"Valgaard."

There was no change of expression in his eyes. What I saw there was a puzzled blankness.

It had to be the *malenna*. "Valgaard," I repeated.

He moved his mouth carefully. His words were imprecise. "What is—Valgaard?"

It astounded me. I turned sharply to one of the women. "How much *malenna* was he given?"

She paled. "No more than usual, Lady."

"Too much," I declared. "No more—do you hear?"

"Aye, Lady." She stared hard at the floor.

He moved slightly, and I looked back at once. "Why am I here?" he asked.

"This is where you are supposed to be. But you were hurt. There was a fight—you fell into the river." Or was pushed; how better to hide a body?

"The river?"

Indeed, too much root. "The Bluetooth." I studied him more closely, marking the dullness of his eyes. More black than green in reflection of the root. "Do you truly recall none of it? Not even the man who stabbed you?"

"I remember—being *cold*—" He paused. "—heavy." The eyes closed, then opened. Their clarity was improved, but not their knowledge. "No more . . ." He stirred. "—head hurts."

"The Bluetooth," I repeated, beginning to understand. If he had struck his head, which was entirely likely in the river, he would likely be confused for a day or two. Combined with the root, it was fortunate he was conscious at all. "It will come back on its own," I promised. "You will know where you are, and that you are safe . . ." I paused. "Devin."

"Is that—I am Devin?"

I grinned. "Tell me when *you* are certain."

He looked at me more closely. "Who are you?"

Your bride, I answered, but could not say it aloud. "Ginevra."

He repeated it after me, rolling the soft, sibilant first syllable between his teeth an extra moment. His accent was odd, more Homanan than Solindish, but Devin is a High Crags man, from high up on the border between the two lands. I had heard the speech before. "How long—?"

"You were brought yesterday. My father sent out a search party since you were so late." I smiled wryly. "You are valuable. It was of some concern."

"Why?" The struggle was in his eyes. "I remember none of it—"

"Hush." I leaned forward. "Do not tax yourself . . . it will come."

"I should remember." Dampness glistened on his forehead. He made more sense as consciousness solidified. "Who am I, that my tardiness is worth a search party?"

"Devin of High Crags." I hope it might light the snuffed candle of his mind.

He tried. "No . . ."

No help for it. It was best simply to say it. "We are meant to be wed."

The candle within lighted, blazing in his eyes, but the knowledge was not increased. "Wed! When?" His mouth taxed him badly. "I remember *nothing*—"

I sighed. "Know this, then, so you need not remain in ignorance. I am Ginevra of the Ihlini, daughter of Lochiel—and we are meant to wed so we can bring down the Cheysuli." I stopped short,

seeing the expression in his eyes. "The Cheysuli,"
I repeated. "Do you recall nothing of them?"

"—a *word*—"

"A bad word." I sighed. "Let it go, Devin. It will
come back, and all will be remembered."

"Who am I?"

"Devin of High Crags." I smiled. "Like me, you
are Ihlini." It was a bond stronger than any, and
he would know it once his mind was restored.

He sighed. "Ihlini, Cheysuli . . . nothing but
words to me. I could be either and never know it."

I laughed. "You would know," I told him. "Be
certain you would know, when you went before
the god."

His eyes snapped open. "The god?"

"Asar-Suti." He knew all of it, but I would tell
him regardless. "My father will take you before
the Seker. The god requires your oath. You are to
wed Lochiel's daughter, and Lochiel is the Seker's
most beloved servant. It is necessary." I smiled.
"There is no need for you to worry. You are Ihlini.
The Seker will know it, just as your lifestone
does."

He followed the line of my gaze and saw the
ring upon his hand. He lifted the hand into the air
to study the stone, saw how his fingers trembled
and lowered it again. "I—have no memory of this
ring."

That was of concern. He was indeed badly damaged in his mind if he forgot what a lifestone was.
But I dared not tell him that. "It will come to
you."

His eyes were slitted. "You—will have to teach
me. I have forgotten it all."

"But surely not *this*." I drew a rune in the air.
It was only a small one; it lacked the intricacy of
my mother's handiwork, but was impressive
enough if you have never seen it—or if one has

forgotten what *godfire* looks like. It glowed livid purple.

He stared at it, transfixed. His fingers trembled upon the fur. "Can I—do that?"

"Once, you must have. It is the first one we ever learn." I left the rune glowing so he would have a model. "Try it."

He lifted his hand and I saw how badly it shook. Awkwardly he attempted to sketch the rune, but his fingers refused to follow the pattern. It was if they had never learned it.

The hand dropped to the bed. He was exhausted. "If I knew it once, I have forgotten."

I dismissed my own rune. It was somewhat discomfiting to discover an Ihlini who could not even form the simplest rune, but not surprising. He would recall it. For the moment his mind was empty of power, of the knowledge of his magic, like a young child. "It will come again." I paused. "If it does not, be certain I will teach you."

The lips moved faintly, as if to form a smile. But his eyelids dropped closed. The root was reasserting its control.

I rose quietly. He looked very young and vulnerable. Against his hand the lifestone was black.

Black, not red.

"It will come back," I said.

At the door, as I lifted the latch, I heard a sound. I turned back and saw the faint glint of green eyes. "Ginevra," he said, as if to try out the fit of my name within his mouth.

I smiled. "Aye."

The lids closed again. "Beautiful," he whispered.

Nonplussed, I did not answer. I did not know if he meant my name, or the woman who bore it.

Then I thought of my mother. I could not help but smile. *You gave him to me*, I thought. *Now let you see what comes of it.*

*   *   *

I went at once to my father. With him was my mother, who sat upon a window seat in my father's tower chamber and gazed down upon the smoky bestiary before the gates. I thought she was very like the fortress, strong, proud, and fierce. I wished I could like her, but that had died. I knew her heart now, and the knowledge bruised my own.

"He remembers nothing," I told them. "Not even his name."

My father stood before a burning tripod brazier. It turned his eyes bronze. He waited.

"I told him. I told him mine as well, and that we are to wed. I told him where he is. But he recalls none of it . . . not even that he is Ihlini."

That brought my mother's head around. Bells tinkled in her hair. "He forgets *that*?"

I refused to flinch beneath the contempt. "He has been badly injured. It will come back."

"Did you test him?" my father asked.

I flattened my palms against my skirts and held my hands very still. "What magic he knew is forgotten. Even *bel'sha'a*. He is a child, my lord father—an infant empty of power." I took a careful breath, knowing what I said was incredibly important. "If you sought a tool, you could not find a better one. He has nothing on which to rely save what we give him. There are no preconceptions. How better to teach the man how to serve the master than by replacing the old memories with the new?"

Only the faintest glint in his eyes betrayed his interest. I knew I had caught him. Now there was no need for subtlety.

My father smiled. I saw him glance at my mother who watched him with narrowed eyes. Hers, too, are pale brown, though not like his; hers are almost golden except when the light hits them fully, and then the Cheysuli shows.

"He shall be mine," Lochiel said.

I put up my chin. It was time I declared myself lest she do it first. "But you will share him with me."

My father laughed. "I shall do better than that. He shall be your charge until I believe the time is right . . . you may have the training of him. In all things."

I could not help the burst of pride in my chest. Never had he bestowed upon me such a gift. It was a mark of his acknowledgment of my blood. He was giving me the opportunity to serve my heritage.

Still, I hesitated. "Are you sure I am worthy?"

He laughed. "You need not fear that you might tarnish the vessel. I will be here for you . . . I will see what you do. He is meant for the god, Ginevra, as you are. Do you think I would give him immortality only to have you watch him sicken and die the way others do?"

"Lochiel!" my mother cried. "You promise too much."

"Do I?" His tone was cool. "Do you wish it for you in place of your daughter?"

Color stained her face. "You have never suggested it. Even when I asked—"

He made a subtle gesture with his hand. I had seen it before; I had tried to mimic it desperately because it always silenced my mother. "Melusine," he said, "you live here on my sufferance."

Her red lips trembled, then firmed. "I am your wife."

"That does not make you worthy of the Seker's favor."

Her eyes blazed almost yellow. "You promise it to *her*!"

He stood next to me. His hand was on my shoulder. The fingers crept into my hair, which hung loose to my hips, and I felt the warmth of his flesh through the velvet of my gown. "Ginevra is the flesh of my flesh, the blood of my blood, the bone of my bone," he said quietly. "Her mind is mine as well. You are none of these things . . . I used you to get the child, and now I have her."

"Lochiel!"

His other hand rose. I could see it from the corner of my eye. I looked at my mother because I could look nowhere else. "Melusine," he said, "I have cared for you. You bore me a child. You suckled Kellin of Homana when I bid you do it. You have served me well. But you surely must see that you and your daughter are destined for different ends."

"I bore her!" It was her only chance now.

"In blood and pain; I know it. But so do the mares, and the cows, and the ewes . . . and they are not elevated by the honor of the Seker." He paused. "Surely you must see."

Her face was very pale. "You mean me to die, then."

"Not before due time."

"Before *her* time!"

Lochiel sighed. "You are a shrew."

It was incongruous. He was the most powerful sorcerer in the entire world, yet all he did was call my mother a name.

It infuriated her; I saw then what he did. "A shrew! In the name of Asar-Suti, are you mad? A shrew?"

My father laughed. There was something between them I could not understand. "Melusine, do you believe you have displeased me? You are all I could wish for. You suit me."

Her eyes glinted yellow. "Then why do you threaten me?"

"To relieve my boredom." He smoothed my hair, then released it. "She is lovely, our Ginevra . . . and this binding of the bloodlines will insure our survival. But Devin must go before the god. The blessing is required."

My mother was less angry now, but still unsettled. She hated to be used; before, I had not seen it. I was old enough now to begin to understand. "And if the blessing is denied?" She cast me a glance. "What happens to Devin then?"

"He dies," Lochiel said.

My mother looked at me and laughed.

I could not echo her. I knew she hoped he would.

Three

"A fool," I told him.

He ignored me. He sat up anyway and swung his legs over the edge of the bed. I watched not the splinted leg itself, which was at issue, but the face of the man who struggled to redeem himself in the eyes of the woman he was meant to wed.

It meant something to him. It meant a great deal to him. It pleased me to know why; that of all things in the world to come unexpectedly, we would make a match between a man and a woman who loved one another.

His color was much improved. A lock of black hair, now clean and glossy, fell forward over his forehead. The swelling of his face was gone, so that the clean lines of nose and brow formed a perfect melding, complementing the oblique angles of his cheekbones and the clarity of his eyes framed in sooty lashes that rivaled my own.

"A fool," I murmured, applying it to myself though he believed it meant for him. Never had I thought I could love a man the way I loved Devin, and we not even wed yet. We were, as yet, nothing but *intendeds;* but they all knew, everyone, despite our circumspection. It was easier for them to know than for us to admit it. As yet, we said nothing of it.

The ends of the splint tapped down; Devin winced. It would not stop him, I knew; I had

436   **Jennifer Roberson**

learned that much of him in the past few weeks.
A stubborn, intransigent man.

And entirely beautiful, in the way a man can be
who is clearly a man. *Male,* I thought, *Expressly,
completely male, like the cats in the undercroft.*

I wanted to laugh. My mother had lost. It
pleased me intensely that he was as I expected,
as I had dreamed between sleep and wakefulness,
when my body would not be quiet. I understood,
now, what lay between my parents.

"Devin—" I shook my head. "It is not necessary.
I *know* you are not a weakling ... let it heal."

His mouth was compressed in a grim, flat line.
He intended to try again. I sighed and set my
teeth; he would only damage himself.

I made a slight gesture from my chair, so that
the bindings undid themselves and the splints fell
away. Unbound, the leg was ill-suited to standing.

Devin looked at the fallen linen and the wooden
sticks. "*You* did that."

I arched my brows. "I did warn you."

"No—you called me a fool."

"That was my warning."

He scowled. Beneath black brows, his eyes glittered like glass. "I cannot stand without aid."

"No."

He sighed. "The lesson is duly learned. Will you
bind it up again?"

He would not admit it, but the leg hurt. Forgoing magic, because I longed so much to touch him,
I knelt on the ground and bound it up by hand
again. The flesh was flaccid and soft. The bones
inside knit, but the muscles were wasting.

He watched me as I tied the knots. His voice
was hoarse, as if he held back something he longed
to say. "If we Ihlini are truly as powerful as you
say, why leave healing to splints and linen bindings? Why not ensorcell my leg?"

I sat down in my chair again. We spent much time together in the small chamber, as I taught him what he knew already but did not recall. "My father desired you to know limitations."

"Ah." His mouth hooked down.

"And there is another reason. Healing is a Cheysuli gift."

"It would seem a benevolent gift. Perhaps if I had a Cheysuli here ..." He grinned. "I see a storm in your eyes."

"You should. Besides, a Cheysuli here in Valgaard would have no power. It is because of the Gate—the Seker is too strong. The only magic here is that which he makes himself."

Devin's expression was serious. "And when will I see him?"

"When my father wishes you to." I sketched *ori'-neth*. "Try it, Devin."

"I *have* tried."

"Again."

He put his hand into the air. His other was naked of lifestone; he had taken it off because, in losing weight, the ring would not seat itself properly. "Your father has not come to me again. How is he to know when I am ready?"

"Make the rune. He will know."

"Because you will tell him?"

"No one tells Lochiel anything; no one *has* to. My father knows things." I sighed. "Devin—"

He tried. Fingers warped, twisted, mimicking the patterns. Only the barest outline appeared, and then he let his hand drop. "There. You see?"

"You mastered *bel'sha'a*," I reminded him. "*Ori'neth* comes next."

Devin was glum. "I have no aptitude."

I laughed at him outright. "Aptitude! You are Ihlini." I smiled at his disgruntlement. "It was better. This time I could see the air parting. When you can separate the air and put the *godfire* in the seam between air and air, you will have learned the trick." I paused. "You learned *bel'sha'a.*"

"In six weeks," he said. "I will be an old man before I learn the third level, and useless as a husband." He scowled at me. "What use are such tricks, Ginevra? They could not stop a man."

"*These* could not, it is true . . . but these are the first runes, Devin. This is a baby's game, to keep the child occupied." I laughed as the scowl deepened. "But you *are* a baby! I could make *bel'sha'a* when I was three years old. A six-month later I mastered *ori'neth.* I have no doubt it was the same for you—you have only forgotten. The river stole your wits."

"I may never get them back."

He was depressed. I pulled my chair closer, hesitated a moment, then leaned forward and caught his hand. It was an intimacy I would not have dared two weeks before, but something I needed now. I wanted to lessen the pain of his weakness.

And increase your own?

I went on regardless, ignoring my conscience. "An Ihlini does not gain his powers until he reaches adolescence, and even then it takes years to focus all the skills. I am not so well-versed myself." I was, but no need to tell him that; I was Lochiel's daughter, and the blood showed itself. "I am a child leading an infant, but who better to recall the days when a simple trick proved difficult? See this?" I made a gesture and felt the tingling coldness in my fingertips. The *godfire* came as I bid it, luridly purple. It hung in a glowing sheet between Devin and me, but our hands remained linked. "This is—"

He jerked his hand from mine and lifted it as if to shred the *godfire*. I tore it aside before he burned himself; he did not yet know how to ward himself. A sheen of perspiration coated his face. "Ginevra—"

"What is it?" I left my chair and knelt by the bedside. "Devin—what is it?"

"That—*that*—" His eyes were frightened. "I remember. Dimly. Fire—flame . . ." He closed his eyes. His body went slack against the pillows. "Why can I remember no more?"

"It will come," I told him, as I had so many times.

He shifted against the bedclothes. "How can you be certain? How can you *know*? And if I am not able to master such things . . ." The chiseled lips compressed themselves flat, robbing them of shape. "An Ihlini with no arts is hardly fit to be wed to Lochiel's daughter."

I took his hand into my own and pressed it against my mouth. "He will be fit," I said. "I will see to it."

Devin's eyes were black. His breathing was shallow and quick. "Can you do such a thing?"

Against his flesh, I said, "I can do many things."

The hand turned in my own. He caught my fingers, carried my hand to his mouth, and let me feel the hardness of his teeth in the tenderness of his lips. "Show me," he breathed.

I shuddered once. "Not—yet."

"When?"

It was a difficult truth, but he was due it rather than lies. "When my father is convinced you are fit to serve the god."

Devin's breath was warm against my hand as he laughed softly. "Fathers need not always rule their daughters in such matters as this."

"Mine does." I pulled free of his grasp. "If you forget that, even once, it could be your death."

"Ginevra—"

"He is *Lochiel*," I said; I knew it was enough.

The tension in his body fled. His mouth moved faintly into an ironic smile. And then it, too, died, and I saw in its place a harrowing despair. "I have nothing," he said. "I *am* nothing—save what you make me."

It shook me. "You are Devin."

"I am no one," he said, "save what you tell me. I am defined by you." His eyes burned livid as *godfire*, save they were green in place of purple. "You are my sanity."

I petitioned the Seker to lend him the strength to find his own sanity, lest mine prove too weak. And then I left the room. I wanted too badly to give him what he asked.

When the splint at last came off and Devin was able to stand, I learned he was taller than I had expected. He had lost flesh in his illness, but movement and better meals would restore him.

Within the week the crutch was tossed away and he walked freely on his own. With renewed mobility came vigor and curiosity to see where I lived. He walked easily enough, but I saw the trace of tension in his mouth and around his eyes. I wanted him to see all of Valgaard so he would know it as I did; it was to be his home. It was important that he understand the kind of power contained in the fortress, so he would not forget himself—once he had relearned the arts—and wield it improperly.

He progressed at last from *ori'neth* to *li'ri'a*. The rune pattern was roughly worked, but achieved, glowing fitfully in the air. He was most pleased that it smoked and sputtered, shedding bits of *godfire;* I reminded him that control was more important than appearance.

"You require new clothing," I told him as we walked the cobbled courtyard.

"I have clothing. And you have already said appearance is unimportant."

"Not unimportant; *less* important—and that is in wielding magic, not wearing clothing." I cast a sidelong glance. "I want you to have better. These do not fit well enough."

"And if I gain back the weight you say I have lost, the new clothing will not." He touched my cheek. "Let it be, Ginevra. I am content with what I have."

"Then at least wear the ring." I took it from the pouch hanging from my girdle. "Here. I sent it to you last year. The least you can do is wear it in my presence."

He took the emerald from me, studying it. I saw the flattening of his mouth. "Even this I do not recall. Any more than the other ring."

"No matter. Put it on."

He did so. The gold band turned on his finger. I saw the look in his eye.

"Bind it with wool," I said. "When you are well, it will fit."

He was frustrated and angry. "Will I ever be well?"

"Dev—"

He stopped dead in his tracks, capturing my shoulders in hands well recovered from his illness. "*Will* my memory return? Or am I sentenced to spend the rest of my life but half a man, able only to form the rune a child of two could make?"

It hurt me to see him so affected. If I could provide help—

I could. It was up to me to risk it.

I sighed. "I think it is time . . . come with me."

"Where?"

"To my father."

The black in his eyes expanded. "You would shame me before Lochiel?"

"There is no shame in this. My father understands."

He shut up the ring in his hand as it turned on his finger. "Can Lochiel restore me? Or is that healing also, and therefore anathema?"

"Come," I said firmly, putting my hand on his arm. "Ask him instead of me."

The room was empty as we entered. It was a small private chamber tucked up into one of the towers, draped with rune-worked cloth to soften the walls, filled with a jumble of chairs and tables, and candleracks sculpted to new forms by hardened streamers of creamy wax. My father preferred the chamber when he desired to have private discussions; he saw no need for opulence among his family.

Devin was nonetheless impressed. It takes people that way, to witness power incarnate. It lived in the room. It was woven into the very cloth that warded the stone walls.

None of the candles was lighted in my father's absence. I blew a gentle breath that set them all ablaze, laughed at Devin's expression, then threw myself down in a chair and hooked a leg over the arm. An undecorous position, perhaps, but modesty was protected by voluminous skirts; I had, of late, put off hunting trews to wear silks and velvets. Even my hair was tamed; I contained it with a simple silver circlet, so that it did not spring forth from my scalp quite so exuberantly. I knew Devin liked it loose; he watched me most avidly from his sickbed when I combed it out after a washing. It took two days to dry; if I wanted it uncrimped, I had to leave it loose.

Devin heaved a sigh and examined the room. His spine was very rigid. *Nervous—and for what? He will be Lochiel's son.* "Be at ease," I suggested.

"*You* be at ease." Then he grinned at me. "I daresay you would feel as I do were you to face the Cheysuli Mujhar."

"Never." I smiled serenely. "But that is not the case—and you are Ihlini, not Cheysuli. What have you to fear?" I slanted an arch glance at him. "Besides, you say you have no memories. How are you to be nervous when you know nothing of the man?"

Devin jeered, though not unkindly. "You have a ready tongue. You put it to his name often enough . . . 'Lochiel' this—'Lochiel' that. What else am I to feel but unworthy of him?"

"Oh, you *are* unworthy—" I grinned, "—but he will lift that from you. When you face Asar-Suti, Lochiel will no longer seem half so bad as now."

"Ah. I am comforted." He folded his arms. "Are we to wait all day on the chance he might come? Or will you send someone for him?" He paused. "Is he even *in* the fortress?"

"He is here." I tilted my head. "Very much *here*."

And he was, all of a sudden, arriving as he does to impress whoever waits. I wanted to chide him for excess display, but one does not chide Lochiel.

Violet smoke roiled in the center of the chamber. Devin stepped back hastily, mouthing an oath he had learned from me, and stared transfixed as the smoke transformed itself into the shape of a man.

"Close your mouth," I hissed.

Devin acquiesced. My father smiled. "That," he said quietly, "is something *you* should be able to do."

The sun had returned color to Devin's flesh. Now he burned darker. "Perhaps I could, once."

Lochiel, in his youth, did not appear much older than Devin. "Has nothing come back?"

"No memories." He glanced at me. "Ginevra has told me what she could of myself, but the words mean nothing. I must believe whatever she tells me; it is the only truth I know."

My father's gaze was unrelenting. "What are you able to do?"

Devin laughed, though it lacked humor. He put out his hand. He drew *li'ri'a*. It was a child's trick, but he could do no better. I did not wonder at the bitterness of his laughter. "That," he said, and banished it.

My father's voice was gentle. "Do you find it amusing?"

"In no way. I find it pitiful, and myself."

"Ah." Lochiel smiled. "But I know who you are. I know what potential you hold. I would not have chosen you otherwise to sire sons upon my daughter." Briefly he looked at me, and I saw a light in his eyes. "That you have forgotten your power means nothing to me. It will be restored. But first you must acknowledge it, instead of relying on the belief that you have forgotten all."

"But I *have*—"

My father reached out and caught Devin's right wrist. By the look in Devin's eyes I knew the grasp was firm. "Call for it now," Lochiel commanded. "Summon it to you. Let the power fill you completely, and you will see what you must know."

Devin was tense. "I *have* tried—"

"Try again." Lochiel's tone was hard. "Do you forget I am with you?"

I saw the alteration in Devin's eyes. He did indeed reach for it, but clumsily. I held my breath, knowing what my father intended to do.

Devin cried out. Wonder filled his face so that his eyes glowed with it, and then the light was extinguished. He cried out again, this time as if in pain, and fell to his knees even as my father released his wrist. His breathing was loud. "You would have—have me be—*that*—?"

Lochiel looked down upon him. "*That* is what you are. It is what I desire of you: power augmented by service to the god, and a perfect obedience. Not powerlessness, Devin. Never that; more." My father put a hand upon Devin's head. "Together, with that power, we can tear down the House of Homana and destroy the prophecy. Do you think I want a fool? Do you think I desire a child? I need a *man*, Devin, who can augment my own strength. A man to lie with my daughter and sire children for the Seker."

Devin still knelt. His face was drained by the knowledge of what he had felt, of the power in my father. "How can I serve with such blankness within me?"

Lochiel smiled. "You are empty. It will pass. We will see to it you are filled. The god himself will do it." He looked at me and smiled, then stretched out his hand. "Take my daughter. Get a son upon her. The wedding shall follow when I am certain she has conceived." He put our hands together, flesh against flesh.

I could look at no one save Devin. My father's voice became a part of the chamber, like a chair or a hanging; one did not acknowledge such things when Devin was in the room.

His eyes burned brilliant green. His spirit could not contain the avidity of his desire.

No more than I could mine.

"There is no need to wait," Lochiel said. "Much is lost, in waiting. The Wheel of Life is turning; if we do not stop it soon, our own lives will end."

Four

We had blown out the candles and now lay abed, delighting in discovery. Devin's breath warmed my neck. "What did he mean?" His mouth shaped the words against my flesh. "Why do our lives end if the Wheel of Life keeps turning?"

"A Cheysuli thing . . ." I turned my head to kiss his chin; to savor the taste of his flesh. "Must we speak of this now?"

His laughter was soft, as were his fingertips as they cherished my flesh. "Aye. You said you would teach me everything—well, perhaps not *this*."

Indeed not this. It made me blush, to know myself so wanton. "I am not the one to speak—" I caught my breath short and bit into my lip as his hand grew more insistent, "—but—it seems to me—*gods, Devin!*—that with all the wits you have lost, you did not forget *this*." I used his emphasis.

Devin laughed again: a rumble deep in his chest. His hand moved to my breasts, tracing their contours. His flesh was darker than mine—I am Ihlini fair, and his eyes were green in place of my ice-gray—but our bones were similar. We Ihlini breed true.

His voice was vibrant. "A man forgets little in the way a body works in congress with a woman."

"So it would seem." Our hips were sealed together. I turned toward him again, glorying in the feel of his flesh against my own. "The Wheel of

Life is a Cheysuli thing. They speak in images, often: the Wheel, the Loom, and so on. They are, if nothing else, a colorful race." I traced the flesh of his chest, glad I could no longer count his ribs. The muscle was firm again. I avoided the scar left over from the healed knife wound. "This prophecy of theirs bids to end our people by making a new race. The Firstborn. If we keep them from that, if we destroy the prophecy, their Wheel will stop turning, and the world as we know it will continue as it is."

"As it is?"

"Well—as it should be. It will take time to turn them away from their gods. They are ignorant people, all of them."

"The Cheysuli?"

It was difficult to concentrate as I explored his body. "And others. The Homanans. The Ellasians. The island savages." I touched his lips with my fingers. "Even the Solindish must suffer—it is a Cheysuli warrior who holds the throne in Lestra."

"Heresy," he whispered; his tone was amused.

"So it is."

"And if we make a child, we can stop this Wheel?"

"My father is convinced."

He turned then and put his hand on my belly, spreading his fingers. The warmth of his palm was welcome. "Have we made it, then?"

I laughed. "Would it please you so much to be quit of your duty after a single night?"

"Duty? Duty is something you do with no real desire for it." The hand tightened as he bent down to taste my mouth. "*This* is no duty."

Breathlessly, I asked, "And if I have not conceived?"

"Then we will continue with this 'duty.'" His

tongue traced my eyelids. "Do you think I wish to *stop*?"

It was abrupt, the chill in my soul. I could not answer.

He sensed my mood immediately and ceased the slow seduction. "What is it?"

I was reluctant to say it but felt I owed him truth. "There is a—strangeness—in you."

The words were too facile. "When a man knows nothing of his past, strangeness is natural."

"Aye. But—" I broke it off, sighing; this was not a topic I wished to pursue. Now.

He did. "But?"

"I wish—I wish you were whole. I wish you knew yourself. I wish you were all of a piece, so I need not wonder what bits and pieces may yet be missing."

Devin laughed. "I am whole where it counts."

"I am serious."

In that moment, so was he. Seduction and irony fled. He turned onto his back. Our hair mingled, black on black against the pallor of pillows. Strands of mine were wound around his forearm. "Aye, I wish I recalled my past—every day, I wish it, and in the darkness of the nights ... but it is gone. There is *nothing*, save a yawning emptiness."

It hurt to hear him so vulnerable. "I want it to be vanquished."

There was no light, save from the stars beyond the casement. I could see little of his face and nothing of his expression. "I cannot spend my life wondering what I might be if it never is recalled ... the present is what matters. What I am is what you are making me. Ginevra—" But then he laughed softly, banishing solemnity, as if he could not bear to think about his plight. He twisted his head to look at me. "What woman would not desire such a man? You can meld me this way and that, until you have what you want."

My vehemence stunned us both. *"I have what I want."*

He caught his breath a moment; released it slowly. He turned onto a hip, moving to face me, to wind his fingers in my hair. He pulled my face to his even as he leaned to me. "Then we shall have to give your father the grandson *he* desires for the Seker, and then we shall make our own."

He was right. What counted was the *now*, not the yesterday. If the child were not conceived soon, the Wheel might turn far enough so that we were destroyed in place of the Cheysuli.

But I could not tell him what I most feared. That the emptiness in him, the bleakness in his eyes that he would not acknowledge, might rob us of our future.

My father gave us five days and nights together, and then he summoned Devin. It piqued me that he would give us so little time—did he think we could conjure a child with a rune?—but I did not complain. Devin was nervous enough without my poor temper, and I dared make no response to my father.

I told Devin to go, that it was necessary he spend much time with my father, to better prepare him for the role he would assume once he had received the god's blessing. I saw the look in his eye, the tension in his body, and wished I knew a way to banish the concern.

But it, too, was necessary; a man facing Lochiel must understand what he did, lest he forget his proper place in the ordering of the world.

And so I sent him off with a kiss upon his fingers and one upon his mouth, knowing very well my father would test him in ways no one, not even

Lochiel's daughter, could predict. If he were to assume an aspect of power within the hierarchy of the Ihlini, he had to learn the way.

It was late afternoon when I sent Devin to my father; only the Seker and Lochiel knew when I might see him again. I set myself the task of embroidering a runic design into the tunic I made for him—green on black—and tried not to think bleak, empty thoughts about what might happen if my father decided, all on his own, that Devin's missing memory might render him weak in the ways of Ihlini power.

My mother came into our chambers. She wore deep, rich red. Matching color painted her lips. "So."

I gritted my teeth and did not look up, concentrating fiercely on the design beneath my hands. She would say what she had come to say; I would not permit provocation.

The sound of her skirts was loud as she came closer. "So, in all ways my daughter is a woman."

Do not be provoked— I nodded absently, taking immense care with a particularly elaborate rune.

She waited. She expected a response. When I made none, the air between us crackled. So close to the Gate, such anger is personified.

I completed one rune, then began another.

My mother's hand swooped down and snatched the tunic from me. "And did the earth move for you? Did the stars fall from the sky?"

Sparks snapped from my fingers. With effort, I snuffed them out. A single drop of blood welled on a fingertip, where the needle had wounded me as she snatched the tunic away. I looked up and saw her smile; it satisfied her to know she had won the battle of wills.

Or had she?

I shook back my hair and rose from my stool,

folding hands primly in violet skirts. "Indeed," I said, "it did move. And will again, I trust, when he returns to me." I smiled inoffensively. "It should please you to know your daughter is well serviced. I have no complaints of his manhood, or the frequency of our coupling."

Breath hissed as she inhaled. The color in her cheeks vied for preeminence over the paint on her mouth. "I will have no such language from you!"

I laughed at her. "You began it!"

"Ginevra—"

"By the Seker himself," I said, "can you not let me have this? You would take everything else from me, even my father's attention ... what wrong have I done you? I am neither enemy nor rival—I am your *daughter*!"

Her face was white. "He gives you everything. *I* have to beg his attention."

"Surely not. I know otherwise. I *see* otherwise." I kept my hands in skirt folds, so as not to divulge the tension in them. "You are only angry that you misjudged Devin. You looked upon his injuries and dismissed him at once, pleased your daughter would wed an unhandsome man. And now that he is healed and you see he is beautiful, you are angry with yourself. Now that we have bedded and you see I am content, you desire very much to destroy what we have." I lifted my head. "I will not permit it."

Melusine laughed. "He will break," she said. "When he meets the god, or before ... perhaps now, with Lochiel. His head is empty of knowledge, his spirit empty of power. He is no better than a Cheysuli hauled here before the Gate, *lirless* and powerless. Pleasing in bed or no, he is wholly expendable."

I gritted my teeth. "The lifestone knew him. If he had no power, it would have consumed him."

Crimson lips mocked a true smile. "There is another test."

"My father tends to such things."

"*You* should tend to this one; you share a bed with a stranger. What if Lochiel were to discover he is not Devin at all?"

It was a refrain. "The lifestone knew him."

"Test him," she said. "Break it."

"It would kill him!"

"A chip," she said scornfully. "The tiniest chip would divulge the truth."

The air crackled between us. This time it was my doing. "I pity you," I told her. "That you must stoop to this merely because he is a man who prefers the daughter to the mother."

"*What?*"

"I know your ways better than you think. I have seen you at meals, and other times. Do you think I am blind? You court his favor assiduously ... but he gives it all to me."

Red lips writhed. "I challenge you," she said. "Break a chip from the stone. Otherwise you will always wonder if you sleep with Devin of High Crags, or a man of another heritage."

Sparks flew as I pointed at the door. "Go!"

Melusine smiled. She built an elaborate rune in the air between us; before I could build my own to ward away the spell, she breathed upon the rune. It was blown to the bed, where it sank into the coverlet and disappeared. "There," she said. "Let us see what pleasure it brings you when next he *services* you."

"There are other beds," I told her. "And if you ensorcell those, there is always the floor.

Melusine threw down the tunic. In her hands, all the stitching had come undone. My labor was for naught.

I waited until she was gone. Then I went to the

chest and drew out the pouch in which he had put his lifestone. I loosened the thong-snugged mouth and poured the ring into my hand.

In my palm the stone was black. No life moved within it. But I had seen it burn twice; first, at my father's touch; then on Devin's hand.

A lifestone crushed ended an Ihlini's life. To kill a Cheysuli, you kill his *lir;* to kill us, you destroy the lifestone.

If he were not what he seemed and I struck a chip from the stone, nothing at all would happen and we would know the truth. But if he *were* Devin and I broke a piece of the stone, it would injure him.

I shut up the ring in my hand. Gold bit into my flesh. The stone was cool, lifeless. *There must be trust between us. If I doubt, I undermine the foundations we have built.*

At my mother's behest.

I bent and picked up the ruined tunic. With great care I picked out the tattered embroidery, gathered silk thread, then began with deliberation to wind it around the ring. I would have him wear the stone where my mother could see it.

When that was done, I would begin the painstaking spell to undo the binding she had put upon the bed. Kept close in my arms, where the emptiness did not matter, it was his only haven.

Five days later, after a night-long meeting with my father, Devin came to me high of heart just as dawn broke. He woke me with a kiss. The bleakness was replaced with good humor and an unbounded enthusiasm. He showed no effects from staying up all night. "He says the power is building. He can feel it, he says."

I sat upright. "Are you sure?"

He laughed joyously. "*I* cannot—I feel precisely

the same today as I did when I awoke here—but
he assures me it is true. And so I begin to think I
may be of some use after all."

"*Some* use," I agreed. "But no one suggests how
much." I laughed at his feigned heart-blow. "And
what are you planning? I see the look in your eye."

His hand rose in the gesture I knew so well.
Two rings glinted upon it: my emerald, and the
lifestone. There was no hesitation in his manner.
His fingers were steady, assured, and the rune was
more elaborate than any I had seen from him
before.

"*Kir'a'el!*" I cried. "Devin—"

It shimmered in the air. Then it snuffed out the
candles and became the only illumination in the
room, dominating the dawn. It set his eyes aflame.

"Only a trick," he said negligently, but he could
not hide his satisfaction.

"Three months ago you could not bestir the air
to save your soul." I raised my own hand and built
a matching rune. It was the distaff side of *kir'a'el*.
Mine met his; they melted together like wax, then
twined themselves into one. The conjoined rune
glowed with the purest form of *godfire*. I stared
hard at Devin, filled with blazing pride. *This* was
what we were born for. "Together we can make
anything!"

"A child?"

"Not yet." We touched our hands together, let
the new rune bathe our flesh, then bespoke the
word that banished it. "We shall have to try
again."

His eyes were still alight with the acknowledgment of power. "Come out with me now. I have
horses waiting."

"*You* are sure of yourself."

"Then I will go by myself."

"Hah." I arched brows haughtily. "You could

not even get beyond the Field of Beasts, let alone
find the defile."

"I found it before."

"Tied to the back of a horse like so much dead
meat? *Aye,* you found it." I caught his hand and
kissed it. "Let us go, then. I could not bear to have
you lost."

But even as I dressed, having banished him from
the chamber—otherwise I would never progress
beyond the disrobing stage—I was aware of a tiny
flicker of trepidation. For so long he had been
helpless, bereft of Ihlini power, yet now he promised power in full measure. I did not begrudge it—
we are what we are—but I was concerned.

Would he become so consumed by the power
and Lochiel's ambitions that he would neglect
me? Once the child was born, would there be a
need for me? Or would I become as my mother:
valueless in their eyes because my duty was done?

Naked, I shivered. Before me I conjured his eyes,
so avid in tenderness. I felt his arms, his mouth;
knew the answer in a body perfectly attuned to
his.

Lochiel had sired me. Melusine had borne me.
But it was Devin of High Crags who had brought
me to life. Without him, my flame dimmed.

*I will not be defined by the man with whom I
sleep.*

Yet he was defined by me. I was his only water
in a wasteland of emptiness.

Devin took me out of Valgaard into the rocky
canyons. It was all new to him, who had seen none
of it, and I gloried in the telling of our history. He
was fascinated, asking many questions, until the
cat squalled. The noise of it echoed eerily.

He reined his horse in at once. His face was

stark white, bleached of color and substance. Even his lips cried out for my mother's paint.

"Only a cat," I said. "Snow cat, I would wager. They sometimes come into the canyons. Though usually in winter." I frowned. "It is early for it, but—"

The cat screamed again. Devin stared blindly.

I searched for any subject to break his mood. "My father will call for a hunt. Perhaps you would care to go. You could have the pelt for your own . . . or perhaps I could make a coverlet for the cradle—"

He turned to me then and fixed me with a gaze of such brittle intensity I thought he might shatter. His voice was a travesty. "The cat is calling for something."

I shrugged. "Its mate, perhaps. Devin—"

A shudder took him. The tendons stood up in his neck like rope knotted much too tightly. His mouth moved rigidly as if to form words, but no voice issued.

"Devin—"

"Do you hear it?" His eyes were wholly empty. "A lonely, unhappy beast."

"Devin, *wait*—" But he rode on, ignoring me. "Snow cats can be dangerous. If it is sick, or injured . . ." He heard none of it. I turned my own mount and followed, irritated. "Wait for me."

He halted his horse roughly. As I saw the cause, I reined mine in as well. "By the god," I whispered.

Not a snow cat after all, but a black mountain cat. She crouched upon a ledge not far above our heads, keening a wail that echoed throughout the canyon. Great golden eyes glared.

I caught my breath. "Beware—"

But the cat did not spring. She merely held her crouch, staring down at him. Then, as I rode forward, she looked directly at me and screamed.

I reined in abruptly, apologizing inwardly to my

mount. But the spell was broken. The cat turned and ran, leaping up through a wide crack. She was gone almost at once.

I released a breath. "Thanks to Asar-Suti . . ." I rode up to Devin. "I thought she would have you."

He stared after the cat.

"Devin."

His eyes were empty.

"Devin!"

At last, he looked at me. "Lonely," he said. Then, "Let us go home."

I was glad to turn my horse and ride back toward the defile, side by side with Devin. I did not like the pallor of his face, or the bafflement in his eyes.

As if he were incomplete, and now knew it more than ever.

Five

He cried out in his sleep and woke me, so that I sat upright with a hand clutched to my breast to still the lurching of my heart. He was still asleep, but he thrashed; I saw him grasp at his naked hip as if he meant to draw a knife.

"Devin." I put a hand upon his shoulder and felt the rigidity of muscle. "Devin—no." He came awake at once and lunged upward, one hand grasping my throat as if he would kill me. *"Devin!"*

His eyes were wild in the shadows of the chamber. Then sense came back to him, and horror. He knew what he had done. "Gods—"

"I am well," I said at once, seeing the look in his face. "Only somewhat surprised by your ferocity." He seemed no better for all my irony. I dismissed it. "I promise. I am well."

One hand raked hair from his face. Moonlight was gentle, but I could see the scars on his back from where the river had embraced him. His eyes were still full of realization: he had nearly strangled me.

I touched his shoulder and felt it tense. "What did you dream?"

"The cat."

At first I did not understand. Then the memory came. "The mountain cat we saw two weeks ago?"

"No. Another." His eyes were black in the darkness. "It was a lion."

"A lion!" Lions were mythical beasts. "Why would you dream of a lion?"

"It stalks me ..." He let his breath out on a long sigh, and the tension went with it. "Only a dream."

"Then I will chase it away." I caught the fallen forelock in my fingers and stripped it back from his face. "I know what to do."

"No." His hand was on my wrist, pushing it away. "Not—now." He turned back the covers and slid out of the curtained bed. "I need to go out."

I was astonished. "In the middle of the night?"

"I need to walk. Just along the battlements. I need to be alone." He slipped into a linen shirt that glowed in the dimness. "I beg you, understand—there is a demon in me. Let me exorcise it, and I will come back to you."

I reached again for irony, so I would not sound too petty, too clinging, too much in need of him. "By morning? Or is this a *difficult* demon?"

"Difficult." His smile was strained. "But my memory of you will vanquish it."

"Go, then." I yanked the covers back over my breasts. "But do not be surprised if I am fast asleep. It troubles me not at all to have an empty bed."

He knew it for what it was, but the smile did not reach his eyes. He finished dressing, pulled on a fur-lined cloak, and went out of the chamber.

I stared into darkness. Resolution set me afire. "I can banish a lion. I am *Lochiel's* daughter."

He came up hours later. I was not asleep. He knew it instantly and apologized for keeping me awake by his absence.

I held the blankets up so he could climb beneath them. "Do you think I care?" His face was worn and bleak as he stripped out of his clothing; we had but an hour before dawn. "Have you destroyed the demon?"

He climbed in beside me, shivering, and drew me very close. At first he was gentle; then he held me so tightly I thought I might shatter. He shuddered once, twice. "Ginevra—" It was muted against my hair, but a cry nonetheless. *"Gods—"*

I had known it was coming. He had been wound too tightly. Now the wire snapped.

I held him tightly, wrapping arms around his shoulders and legs around *his* legs, until he was cocooned in flesh and hair. "Be still," I whispered. "I am here for you. I will always be here for you."

"I think—I think I am going mad."

"No. No, Devin. There is no madness in you."

"I wake in the night, in the darkness—"

"I know."

"—and there is nothing *there*, nothing at all, save emptiness and anguish . . . and then I recall there is you, always you—Ginevra, *here*, for me. And I know that you are my salvation, my only chance for survival—and I am *afraid*—"

"What do you fear?"

"That—you will go. That I will prove myself unworthy. That I will be turned out of Valgaard. That you will repudiate me because I am not what Lochiel needs me to be."

I stroked hair from his face. "You said he is pleased by your progress. And I have seen it also. There is nothing to fear, Devin. What can come between us?" Then, when he did not answer, "Where did you go?"

He said nothing at first. Then he shifted onto his back, cradling me in one naked arm. My head rested in the hollow of his shoulder. "I went below," he said finally. "To the undercroft."

For the merest moment I believed he meant the Gate. "The cats," I blurted.

"Aye." He was very still. The storm had passed, but the aftermath was as painful to see. His expression was wasted. "They are wild things, Ginevra. They were not made to be caged." His breath gusted softly. "Nor was I."

A hollow fear began to beat in my breast. "They are cats."

"I looked in their eyes," he said. "I saw the truth in them. They know what they have lost. They long for it back."

More desperately, I repeated, "They are *cats*."

"So am I, in my own way. I am very like them. I am caged by ignorance."

I knew it suddenly. "You want to set them free."

His hand settled in my hair, winding it through his fingers. "If we did, he would only replace them with others. Perhaps even the black one we saw in the canyon. I think—I think I could not bear to see more imprisoned then he already has. No. Let them alone. They have known their cages too long."

I drew him closer yet, warming his body as I wished I could warm his spirit. *How long?* I wondered. *How long will you know* your *cage?*

How long would I know mine, in the prison of his arms?

As long as I permitted it. As long as I desired it. Forever is frightening.

The door opened very quietly as I sat before the polished plate and combed my hair. In the reflection I saw Devin's face, peeking around the door, and the expression he wore.

I stopped combing instantly and turned on the stool. "What?"

The set of his brows was comical in dismay. "I wanted to surprise you." But he did not seem so disheartened that the smile left his face.

"What?" I repeated.

He gestured me down as I made to rise. "No. Wait." His expression was serious now, and very intent. His outstretched hand was held palm up. He watched it closely; I watched *him*. I saw the concentration, the effort he used, and then the startled wonder he suppressed instantly so as to hide his childlike pleasure in a task at last accomplished.

In his palm danced a tiny column of pure white flame. Slowly it twisted, knotting itself, then reshaped itself into the aspect of a bird, brilliant as a diamond.

I held my breath. The bird made of flame became a bird in truth.

Devin extended the hand. "For you."

I put out my own hand, took the bird onto a finger, and suppressed the urge to cry. It was a tiny white nightingale, perfect in all respects, and very, very real. It cocked its head, observed me from glittering eyes, then began a jubilant song.

Devin's eyes shone. "Lochiel says it is because of Valgaard. That though I have no recollections of power, the power simply *is*. We are so close to the Gate . . . he says there is power for the taking; that we breathe it every day. A man—or a woman— need only know how to use it. Even a Cheysuli, given enough time, if he claims the Old Blood."

The bird's tiny feet clung to my fingers. I could not look at Devin for fear I would see the change as I gave him the truth not all men would tolerate. "You do know, do you not . . . that I am also Cheysuli?"

He laughed. "Since your mother is a halfling, one would assume so."

I set the nightingale on the edge of my mirror. "The House of Homana and my own House are so thickly intertwined, it is a wonder we keep our identities straight." I looked at him now. "You do not mind?"

He came to me and threaded fingers into my hair. "Cheysuli—Ihlini . . . what difference does it make? What matters is that we have one another."

"It is tainted blood. The Cheysuli desire to destroy us."

"So we will destroy them first." He laughed. "It is a matter of upbringing, not blood. Prejudice and hatred is created, not born. You serve the Ihlini because you know nothing else . . . but had you been raised in Homana you would serve the Cheysuli instead."

"I never could!"

"If you knew no better, of course you would."

"But I *do*—"

"So you do. And so you serve the Seker."

It could not go unasked. "What about you?"

Devin smiled. "I will do what must be done. If the god grants us immortality, it would be a sorry thing to repudiate his grace—and therefore watch forever as our race dies out at the behest of the Cheysuli."

I guided his hands and pressed them against my belly. "We will not die out. Not while the child within me lives."

Wonder engulfed his face. His fingers were gentle as he pressed them against the folds of my skirts. "Here?"

I laughed. "Thereabouts. It is too small for you to feel. But in six months you shall have your son."

He cradled my face in his hands. "Thank you," he said. "You have made it possible for me to be a man."

I found it odd. "But you *are* a man!"

"An incomplete one. Do you understand? Now

we can be wed. Now, at last, I can go before the
god and let him weigh my value."

Against my ear I heard the beating of his heart.
Behind us, the bird stopped singing. When I
looked around, the nightingale was gone.

Illusions are transitory. At least Devin was not.

I had seen the Gate many times, and the cavern
that housed it, but never through Devin's eyes. It
made it new again.

I took his hand as we stepped out of the passageway into the cavern. He did first what everyone
does: tipped his head back to stare up at the
arches, the glasswork ceiling alive with reflected
flame. The symmetry was incomparable. So many
layers of ceilings, so many soaring arches, and
massive twisted columns spiraling from the floor.
We were required to pass through them; at the
end of the colonnade lay the Gate itself.

Devin was puzzled. "Where does the light come
from? I see no torches."

I smiled. "It comes from the Gate. See how it
is reflected time and time again, multiplied one
hundredfold in the columns and the arches?" I
watched his avid eyes. "The Gate itself is in the
ground, but it is open, and its light is uninhibited.
It is *godfire*, Devin—it is the light of truth, so that
the Seker can illuminate the dark corners of your
soul."

The light was in his eyes. I could see no pupil
in them, only a vast empty blackness filled now
with livid *godfire*. "He will see my weakness."

"All men are weak. He will draw it from you
and replace it with strength."

"Is that why you have no fear?"

"I have fear." I touched his hand. "His glory is
terrible. When one looks upon his aspect, one
knows he—or she—is insignificance incarnate." I

closed my fingers on the still flesh of his hand. "The Seker awaits."

"Ginevra!" He drew me back as I turned toward the columns. "Ginevra—wait." His face was graven with lines of tension. "I need you."

I carried his hand to my mouth. I felt his minute trembling; he feared as all men do, who must face Asar-Suti. Against his palm, I said, "I am here for you. Before the god, I swear it: I will always be here for you. We are bound already by the child in my body. Once we share the nuptial cup, we will be bound forever."

His voice was raw. "I am—unworthy."

"Of the god?" I smiled. "Or of me?"

Devin laughed; it was what I had hoped for. "Of both," he said.

I arched haughty brows. "Then neither the god nor I have grounds for discontentment. Things are as they should be." I glanced toward the Gate, then looked back into his face. "Come," I said gently. "There is no sense in delaying the truth."

"Truth," he echoed, "is what I fear."

I held his hand tightly in mine. "Why?"

"I am what you have made me. Ginevra's Devin, whatever—whoever—that is. I know nothing at all of my past ... what if Devin of High Crags is a man who aspires to waste his coin in tavern wagers and his seed in roadhouse whores?"

My laughter echoed throughout the cavern. "Then the greater truth will be that Devin of High Crags is now a changed man." I shook back hair. "And they may spin the tale that it was the god's doing—or lay credit where it is due."

He was suspicious now. "Where?"

I set his hand against my heart. "Here," I said, "deep in my soul. What other truth is there?"

Devin looked beyond me. "Then let us get it

done. Have them bring the nuptial cup. I am very thirsty."

My father waited for us at the Gate of the netherworld, clothed in black that the *godfire* dyed purple. In his hand was a rune-scribed silver goblet; at his feet lay the god himself.

"Where is he?" Devin breathed.

"There." I dipped my head. "Beneath the ground—that pool is the Gate."

I heard vague surprise in the timbre of his tone. "That hole in the ground?"

"His greatness is such that he requires no sepulcher," I said it more tartly than I intended; I expected Devin to be more circumspect in his worship of the Seker. Everyone else was.

Devin stared at the Gate. Light lapped at the edges, and smoke rose up. It wound around my father and clung to the folds of his robe. His gaze was fixed solely on Devin.

"Come," Lochiel said.

Devin's grasp tightened. "What is that?" he whispered.

He meant the pedestal just behind my father. "A chain," I whispered back. "A keepsake from a Cheysuli who thought he could defeat my father."

"It is in two pieces."

"The Cheysuli broke it. He surrendered to my father and broke the chain in half." I squeezed his hand. "Enough. There is a task we must do. Or do you mean to put off the ceremony that will make us one in the eyes of the god?" Devin's smile was fleeting. He stared at the cup.

"Empty," Lochiel said from the other side of the Gate. He held out the goblet. "Fill it, Devin, if you would have my daughter."

The tension spilled out of Devin. He turned to face me, brought my hand to his lips, and kissed my fingers. Then he released my hand and turned to Lochiel. He extended his arm across the maw of the Gate.

So vulnerable, I thought. *The god has only to rise and swallow him whole.*

But the Seker did not do it. Devin accepted the cup from my father's hand, then knelt at the edge of the Gate. Without hesitation, with no sign of fear, he dipped the silver goblet into the pulsing *godfire.*

Illumination engulfed him. Devin laughed, then dipped the cup lower. When it was filled, he rose and inclined his head in tribute to Lochiel, then turned to me. The cup's smoking contents flared, burning more brightly, so that the light stripped bare all shadows from Devin's face, washing the darkness from him. His eyes burned brilliant green.

I placed my hands over his and guided the cup to my mouth. I drank liquid light and let it fill me. Cold fire burned as my blood responded to it.

Gods, but it was sweet. Such a sweet, cold fire . . . I laughed and shook back my hair, then guided the cup to Devin.

He drank. I saw the widening of his eyes in shock; I feared, for a horrible moment, he might sprew it from his mouth. But he swallowed. He shivered once. When I saw the emerald of his eyes replaced with livid black, I knew it was done.

My father's voice was an intrusion. It took effort to listen. "You have shared the blood of the god at the god's own Gate. His blood is yours. There can be no parting you now."

Devin turned. "Is there more?"

"There is always more." Lochiel extended his hands, and Devin placed the goblet in them. My father smiled, then dropped the goblet into the light and smoke. "But you have begun already. Kneel down, Ginevra—here, beside the Gate."

I knew better than to question.

"Remain there. It must be you first, so the child, too, is blessed."

I dared not look at Devin. I knelt there beside the Gate, thinking of my child, and waited for the god.

He came all at once, without warning. I knew only that I was blinded as the light sprang forth, and then it engulfed me. I felt hands touching me, reaching through my clothing to pluck at my flesh, until I feared it might be stripped from my bones. I shuddered once, then stilled. The god's hand was upon me.

I knew only what my father had told me: that the hand of the god, the light of the Seker, would reveal the inner soul. Hidden truths would be uncovered. Small vanities displayed. The insignificant desires of a human would be mocked for what they were, so they could be replaced with perfect service to the god.

My perfect service was to bear the god a child. A son for the Seker, Who Lives and Dwells in Light—

I laughed aloud. "A son!" I cried. "A son to bring down the House of the Cheysuli!"

And the god was gone. I felt him go as abruptly as he had come. I wavered there on the edge, enshrouded in swirling smoke, and then Devin raised me up to keep me from tumbling in. "Ginevra?"

It was vital that I know. I turned my head to look at my father. "Is it done? Is it *done*?"

Lochiel smiled. "The god is well pleased."

I drew back then from Devin. "Kneel," I said.

The blackness lived in his eyes, which once had been clear green, but I saw something more. The emptiness remained though he had drunk of the cup.

"Kneel," I repeated. To mitigate the tone, I touched his face. For him, and only for him, I offered the key. "Release the cat," I whispered, so my father would not hear. "Let him go free from the cage of your fear."

Devin knelt. He crossed his arms against his breast and bent low in homage beside the Gate. The god spewed forth.

I held my breath. *It will only take a moment—*

Devin screamed. He screamed and screamed in a language I did not know, shaping words I could not decipher. His head fell back as he flung out both arms. He hung there on his knees, transfixed by the god. Blackened eyes were wide and blind.

I could not help myself: I shouted a denial. I saw the transformation, the alteration of bone and flesh. From man into cat: the hands became paws, the fingernails claws, the teeth elongated into fangs, and the sound that issued from his throat changed itself in mid-note from the shouting of a man to the scream of an angry cat.

Black as night, he was. Like the one we had seen in the canyon. But the eyes were purest green.

I was rooted to the stone. *Cheysuli—Cheysuli—Cheysuli.*

"Punish him!" Lochiel shouted. "Punish the transgressor!"

God, he was *Cheysuli!*

The god made him a man again, so he would know. I looked very hard for the mark of a Cheysuli, the sign of a demon, but all I saw was Devin.

In one step I reached him. I struck with all my strength, smashing my hand across his face. "How could you do this?" I shouted. "How could you do this to us?"

To us, I said. Not *to me*.

It infuriated me.

"How?" I cried. And then, viciously, "Is this part of your *tahlmorra*? To seduce an Ihlini so she conceives of your child?"

There was no response in his eyes. The god held him immobile, crucified on air; was he deaf as well as blind?

"Step back," my father said. "The god will deal with him."

Trembling, I stepped back. I saw the flicker in green eyes. Then a shudder wracked the Cheysuli.

"Tahlmorra," he gasped, in the tongue I did not know. *"Tahlmorra lujhalla—"*

My father overrode him. "Have you ever wondered," he mused, "what it would be like to be trapped in *lir*-shape forever?"

"—lujhalla me wiccan—cheysu—" And then, "Not Devin—"

The god sprang forth again. In a man's place writhed a cat with eyes the color of emeralds.

All I could think of was the incongruity: *Not yellow at all.*

Lochiel looked at me. "We will turn it loose," he said, "and then we will call a hunt."

Six

Was it like this, I wondered, *that they first brought you here?*

The cat remained senseless, deep in enforced sleep; they had thrown him unresisting on his side across a horse, then tied him to the packframe.

"Ginevra," my father said.

The cat's tongue lolled from a slack-lipped mouth. The eyes were half-lidded, dulled by the touch of the god.

We shared a bed, you and I. We shared our hearts. We shared our souls. And now we share this: a hunt to the death.

"Ginevra."

Lochiel again; I did not tarry longer. I turned my horse away from the cat and rode to the head of the party, letting no one see weakness. I was Lochiel's daughter.

I led them out of Valgaard, across the Field of Beasts, through the narrow defile into the canyon beyond. Then my father stopped us and used his own knife to cut the beast free. The heavy black body fell flopping to the ground. It brought no response; dull green eyes remained slitted and senseless, and the red tongue fell out into the dirt.

"Ginevra." A third time.

I looked at them all; at five of my father's minions; at my mother who watched me with undimin-

ished avidity. Lastly I looked at him, who served
Asar-Suti with an unflagging, perfect service.

"Leave it," I said evenly. "The hunt may commence tomorrow."

My mother raised her voice for the first time
since we had left the fortress. "I wonder," she said,
"that you take no steps to insure he does not flee.
Would it not be wiser to kill him now?"

Lochiel looked at the cat. "Where is he to go?
He is bound to Ginevra, bound by the god. And
bound also, perhaps, by the child in her body."

I could not look at him. I was ashamed, so
ashamed that I had defiled myself. That I had permitted myself to love him.

"No," he shook his head, "our prey will not flee.
He will wait here for us, until we choose to come."

"Sweet revenge," I declared. "When you have
trapped him, will you put him with the others in
the undercroft?"

"There? No. When I decide to take him, it will
be for his pelt. I have a whim to rest my feet in
winter on the hide of a dead Cheysuli."

My mother's carmined mouth gloated.

In Valgaard, I threw back the lids to all the
trunks and pulled the clothing from them, then
piled it on the bed. I took the caskets containing
the gifts I had bestowed and dumped the contents
on top of the clothing. Lastly I dug out the
nightshift I had worn the first night we shared a
bed and tossed it into the pile. Then I summoned
godfire.

"A waste," my mother said, "of a comfortable
bed."

I did not turn. I did not care. Let her stand there
if she would; I wanted nothing more than to watch
all of it burn.

All of it. *All* of it. Every bit of it.

"Will you burn yourself too?"

I swung. The flames were in her eyes. It turned them Cheysuli yellow. "You wanted him," I said viciously. "From the beginning, you wanted him. How does it feel to know he was *Cheysuli*?"

My mother smiled. "So am I. So are you. And aye, I would have bedded him. He was in every way a *man*."

I drew back my lips from my teeth. "Shape-changer!"

The light in her eyes was livid. She looked beyond me to the bed as the *godfire* consumed it. "Which one pleased you most?" she asked. "The warrior—or the cat?"

I wanted to scream at her. I wanted to burn her, too. I wanted to tear the mirror from the wall and hurl it into the fire.

Even as I thought it, the mirror shattered.

Melusine shook her head. "A dangerous thing, when Lochiel's daughter is angry. The very walls are at risk."

"Why have you come?" I cried. "Are you hoping I will cry?"

She wore her hair pinned up. Light glittered off all the gemstones. "Once I wanted your father to care as much for me as Devin does for you. He does not. Once I wanted your father to care as much for me as he does for you. He does not, and never will. And so I am soundly defeated in all patterns of the dances which are danced between men and women—even between fathers and daughters." Her face was very still, but her eyes were livid. "I bore a single living child. I nearly spent myself in the birth, and tore myself so badly I could never bear again."

Behind me the bed burned. So did all of his clothing, the jewels I had given him, the nightshift he had removed with avid tenderness. "You are punishing me."

In her eyes *godfire* dimmed; the bed was nearly consumed. "The child you carry is the child of prophecy."

I touched a hand to my belly.

" 'The Lion shall lie down with the witch,' " my mother quoted. "It is what their madman says, the *shar tahl* who was a prince."

"Aidan," I murmured; I was consumed by realization, by the knowledge of what I was: a vessel for the child that could destroy my race. "I shared a cradle with his son. My father told me."

"As an infant you shared his cradle. As a woman, you shared his bed."

It jerked me out of numbness. "That was *Kellin*? Him? But—he said nothing of it! He made no indication! He was—" I broke it off, then finished it by rote, "—Devin. We all thought he was Devin." I looked at her. "You are punishing me. That is why you have come."

Her eyes were yellow again. "You nearly killed me," she said. "But *you* were what he wanted, once I could not bear again. You were his only hope. I counted as nothing. And then *he* came— and once there was a child, Lochiel gave you both what should have been mine!"

The *godfire* died to ash. I grieved for the woman, that she could be so bitter. I grieved for myself, that I had lost my mother when I most needed her.

And I grieved for the child who was not, after all, the salvation of my race, but the herald of its destruction.

"I will be dead," she said, "but you will live to see it."

When I was certain she was gone, I closed the door and locked it with meticulous care. I put a rune upon the lock so not even my mother could open the door. Only my father might, but he would not come.

Godfire was gone. The bed, the jewelry, the nightshift—all had been consumed. All that remained were charred bits and pieces and a drift of violet ash.

Grief roused itself. Anguish awoke. The terrible anger was stilled.

I knelt. I plunged my hands into the ash and closed them on frosted remnants. They did not burn my flesh. The pain was all inside, where no one could see it.

But I would know.

I would always know.

It burns, such pain. It devours the heart and soul.

When the summons came, I did not shirk it. I did not delay. Clad in the tattered remnants of my pride, I went to the tower chamber and presented myself to him. My deference was plain; there was no latitude, in this, for anything save shame.

He sat upon a tall stool set before a grimoire on a tripod stand. He wore russet hunting leathers, as if he planned already how the chase would commence. With his hair freshly cropped close against his head, I saw the shape of the skull. A beautiful man, my father; but the beauty now was tarnished by the memory of another, who had so indelibly replaced Lochiel as the model, in my mind, of pure masculine beauty.

I hated myself for it, but I could not banish it. I looked at my father, saw my father's face, and superimposed the features of another man.

It was easy to do. I saw in that instant that they were very like.

My lips parted. Color drained. "—true," I blurted. "All of it *true*—"

Winged brows arched. "What is true?"

"I did not see it before—but now . . ." I shivered. "We are, both of us, linked by more than enmity."

Only a few candles shed illumination. Most were unlighted. "Aye," my father said; in smoky light, his eyes were bronze. "For years we denied it; for decades, so did they. We came to accept it sooner than the Cheysuli. Most of them still deny it." His smile was slight. "We are everything they cannot countenance, we who serve the Seker. I think it less taxing to us to admit the truth. After all, we merely desire to destroy them in order to maintain what we have fought so hard to win. Autonomy from gods."

I shivered. "But—the Seker."

"I said, '*gods*.'" He emphasized the plural. "They worship a pantheon of gods, while we comprehend true power lies only with one." He held his silence then, weighing me by expression. "It provides many answers." He rose from the stool and lifted something from the gutter in the pages of the grimoire. Candlelight glinted. A gold ring, set with jet. "It lives again," he said. "It knows my touch."

"But—it knew *his*, too! And he is Cheysuli!"

"Kellin is many things. Kellin of Homana is very nearly a Firstborn himself. He has the Old Blood in abundance, twice and thrice again . . . the earth magic lives in him." The ring sparked deep red. "Our lifestones answer power. This close to the Gate, it does not distinguish. It acknowledged his gifts, no more. But it would not kill him; his blood is very like ours."

"Old Blood," I said. "Ours is older yet."

"No." His tone was thoughtful as he contemplated the ring. "Exactly the same, Ginevra. In all ways, the same. If I were to cut into my left hand

and spill my blood, then cut into Kellin's hand
and spill *his* blood, we would see they were the
same. But until we mixed the blood, until we
clasped hands, nothing could come of it save we
each would bleed to death if the cuts proved too
deep."

The cut inside my heart was very deep indeed.
"Then Devin of High Crags is dead."

"It would seem so." He shut his hand upon the
ring and squeezed. When he opened it again, the
ring was naught but shattered crystal. He blew it
from his palm. "Now, certainly." His eyes were
steady. "Come here, Ginevra."

I shuddered once. Suppressed it.

"Ginevra," he chided. "Do you fear me? Do you
believe I would harm you?"

My lips were stiff. "There is no need," I said. "I
have shamed you. I have dishonored you. You
need do nothing save withhold your regard, and I
am diminished."

"Diminished." He smiled. "Lochiel's daughter
should never be *diminished.*"

"I am. I *am.*" I fell to my knees. "The god will
know my shame each time I go before him. And I
will *know* he knows!"

My father came to me. I bowed my head before
him. He put hands upon my head and cradled it
tenderly. "You are everything I could desire in a
daughter. You have not failed me. You have not
dishonored me. There is no shame in what you
have done; you did it at my behest. If you castigate yourself, you also castigate me."

I turned my face to look up at him. "I would
never—"

"I know." Lochiel smiled. His eyes, in dim light,
were black instead of brown. "In anything we do,
there is no shame. Do you understand? I will have

it no other way. In anything we do, there is no shame."

I nodded, grateful he would do so much to discard my degradation.

"Good." His hands shifted. He lifted me up. Our faces were very close. He studied mine avidly, and then he smiled. "There is your mother in you, also. You are her daughter as well."

"Aye." Though I hated to admit it.

"There is much in Melusine I find most entertaining, especially her passion. Are you the same?"

My face burned against his hands.

"Was the Cheysuli content?"

I began to tremble.

"Did you play kitten to his cat?"

"*God*—" I blurted.

Lochiel smiled. "After the hunt tomorrow, I will come to your bed."

"My *bed*?"

"To destroy the Cheysuli's seed, we will replace it with my own."

In my chamber, alone, where there was no bed, I wondered if he would conjure another fitting for his state.

Could I burn that one, too?

He would simply conjure again.

Did he think I would submit?

Or would he also conjure submission?

I looked at the door. I looked at the latch. No ward I made would prevent Lochiel from entering my chamber. No defense I summoned could prevent him from entering *me*.

After the hunt.

After the cat is dead.

What would my mother say?

I caught back the laugh before it became a sob.

I pressed my hands against my mouth to suppress another lest I shame myself.

There were drugs, I knew. There were all manner of ways.

I did not want the child. I desired the child to die.

There were other ways than this.

"There is your mother in you also."

He wanted it this way to gratify himself.

After he killed the cat.

I unlatched the door and went out of the chamber that no longer contained a bed. I thanked the god I had burned it. What the Cheysuli and I had shared, despite centuries of enmity, was cleaner by far than the union my father proposed.

I went down to the undercroft, to see the caged cats. They greeted me with snarls, with lashings of supple tails, with the fixed stare of the predator as they paced out the dimensions of their lives.

What had he said of them? *"They know what they have lost. They long for it back."*

He had lost humanity in the shaping of his self. Did he know he had lost it? Did he long for it back?

Did he know, in the great gulf of darkness, why he could not leave?

Do you remember my name?

Did he understand what had happened?

Did you remember the truths we discovered in our bed?

Did he recall the god at all, and how he had come to be locked forever in cat-shape?

Do you remember the oath I swore, when you said you needed me?

I remembered it all.

"Cheysuli," I said aloud. The word was alien, shaped of a foreign tongue. Its sibilant hissed.

He had said something as the god revealed the truth. Something about fate. I knew the word for that. The Cheysuli called it *tahlmorra*.

"Fate," I said aloud, "is another word for surrender." It was an Ihlini belief; we make our own fates dependent on our needs.

One of the cats snarled. It thrust a tawny, wide-toed paw through the iron bars and reached toward me, slapping air with half-sheathed claws.

What else had he said? *"Prejudice and hatred is created, not born. You serve the Ihlini because you know nothing else."*

"I *am* Ihlini," I said. "What else would you have me do?"

The cat waved its paw and snarled.

"Do you hate me?" I asked. "Because I am Ihlini?"

His words were in my head. *"Cheysuli—Ihlini . . . what difference does it make? What matters is that we have one another."*

I had sworn him an oath.

I looked at the cat. "Oaths are made to be broken."

He was the father of my child.

The father of the Firstborn.

Anguish welled up. "Let me be free of this!"

It echoed in the undercroft, disturbing all the cats.

They know what they have lost. They long for it back.

" 'Let them alone,' you said. 'They have known their cages too long.' "

He was not caged. He would not *be* caged. My father would kill him, then strip the pelt from his body and use it for a rug.

Would he have us couple on it when he saw I had no bed?

The jaws clenched together. "For that, then," I

said. "I honor my oath that much—and then we are quit of each other."

I knew what I had lost. I longed for it back. But knew I could never have it.

In the hour before dawn I went out of Valgaard, crossed the smoky Field of Beasts, and passed through the defile into the canyon beyond. There I found the cat I had known as man, whose name was Kellin.

I was bundled in a heavy cloak. "You know what you are," I said. "*I* know what you are. According to my father, what you are is what you shall be—until he desires to add a new rug to his floor to keep his feet warm in winter."

The eyes were huge and green. Sense had returned to them. They glared balefully.

"I owe you an oath," I said. "I gave it freely, not knowing what you are, and could in all good conscience claim its meaning forfeit . . . but there are things between us that are not so easily governed." I looked at the female beside him. "Did you tell her there is a child? That the child of the prophecy, so beloved by the Cheysuli, lives here in my body?" I pressed my hand against cloak-swathed belly. "If I suffer this child to live, I bring down my people. I destroy an entire race. That I will not do. But neither will I permit my father to kill you. I have no desire to gaze each winter upon the stones they will put in the sockets that once were your eyes."

The black tail lashed. Green eyes did not blink.

"Then come," I said roughly, angry that I cared. "I will set you free of this shape so you may resume your own. We have fought for centuries, the Ihlini and Cheysuli—I think it will do no harm if we fight a while longer."

If it came, it came. But I would not, as my

mother threatened, live to see it. The god would, in making the bargain, require something to seal it. All I had of value was what he had given me.

Worth giving up, I thought, *so I need not spend the centuries watching the descendants of our races waste lives trying to kill one another in the name of a prophecy.*

Worth giving up so I need not replace my mother in my father's bed for the balance of forever.

Interval

The woman knelt at the Gate, and fire bloomed in her hands. She held them out steadily, reached across the pool, and shaped living *godfire* into a reflection of itself. In her hands the god writhed as he writhed within the Gate.

She parted her hands and drew them apart. Flame surged in her palms, licking from her fingers as each gout of *godfire* stretched toward the other. Then she brought her hands together and joined the halves again. She built of flame a goblet, then fed it on itself. Bloody runes formed on the rim. In the bowl sparks snapped; smoke rose from the contents.

She raised it to her mouth and drank the flame away. The goblet was banished. *Godfire* glowed in her eyes.

She looked at the cat who crouched nearby, beside the rim of the Gate. Tufted ears were flattened. Fire blazed in green eyes as the tail beat basalt.

The woman's mouth opened and smoke issued forth. Her voice was alive with light. Each word was a spark that broke from her lips and formed into a rune. The words she spoke bound themselves into sentences, until the runes formed a necklet that dangled in midair.

"He did not know," she said. "He believed himself Ihlini. He came to you consenting, eager for your touch, eager to serve the Seker. He meant to bind himself to you. What you revealed in his soul was not what he expected."

Viscid liquid boiled. Smoke billowed up. The runes that had been words burned brightly in the darkness.

"I do not question the punishment; he is Cheysuli, and transgressor. But he meant only to serve. His heart was empty of hostility. He meant no sacrilege."

A second necklet was conjoined with the first into a glowing girdle. It moved from the air to bind itself around her hips; to seal her wrists together. Smoke issued from her nostrils. Her eyes wept blood.

"To the god of the netherworld, Who Made and Dwells in Light; who illuminates our souls, I offer this bargain: my immortal life in exchange for his true guise."

The blood she wept was black. It ran down her cheeks to fall into the Gate, where the *godfire* hissed in welcome to itself.

She prostrated herself. Her hair tumbled free of pins and fell down into the Gate, where the *godfire* crept up the strands. It lingered at her hairline, then spilled in a glistening net to sheathe her face in a glowing filigree.

Her breath was made of flames. "Let him go," she begged. "Let him be a man. I will give you my life. I will give you the child."

Godfire gouted forth. It broke in a wave over the cat, bound it in white fire, then dragged it inexorably toward the Gate.

"No!" she cried. "I promised you the child!"

Claws locked into stone. And then the claws were human fingers with bloodied, broken nails digging into smoking rock. "Ginevra!" he shouted, with the voice and mouth of a man. *"Ginevra!"*

She broke free of her bonds and thrust herself
to her knees, hands locked around wrists that were
fleshed in human flesh. She dragged him forth
from the Gate, breaking bonds. He climbed out,
dripping gouts of *godfire*, and was reborn as a
man.

Her grasp on his wrists broke as she fell to her
knees. "Done," she gasped.

The man's breathing was labored. He bared
human teeth in a snarl that was wholly bestial, as
if he had forgotton how to make his mouth form
words.

"Go," she said raggedly. "The bargain is made.
If you linger now, you invite his renewed interest."

The man laughed harshly. He knelt upon the
floor in an aspect of obeisance, but the burning in
his eyes was born of different loyalties. " *The Lion
shall lie down with the witch.'* "

She stared at him. "What?"

"My *jehan* had the right of it. And now we are
wed—Lochiel's daughter and the Prince of Homana." The laughter broke again from a throat
made raw from fire. "How the *shar tahls* will un-
tangle our birthlines I dare not predict; it may
take more decades than either of us has."

Her face spasmed. "Go."

"Not without you."

Her breath halted, then resumed. Color ebbed
in a face of fragile, faceted planes, delicate as the
arches that shattered overhead. "That is finished.
That is over."

Green eyes burned in the clean, sculpted features that were, in their fierceness, in their avidity,
far more feral than human. He was predator to
her prey.

"Go," she said again, as the Gate behind her
blazed. "There is nothing between us now."

He closed his hand around her wrist. "What is

between us now is of an entirely different making than what we shared in bed."

The woman's laughter echoed in basalt, and crystal arches. "Enmity?"

He pulled her from the floor. "His name is Cynric."

PART V

One

Kellin knew it at once. *She does not understand—she has no comprehension of what we did here, in drinking from the cup.*

Ginevra tore free of his grasp. Between them she built a wall of conjoined, blazing runes.

His own shredded it. "I drank of the cup," he told her. "What I know is not forgotten."

Ice-gray eyes were black in comprehension. "What have I done?" she whispered. "What have I wrought?"

Oddly, he wanted to laugh. "I think—peace." His mind moved ahead to means. Kellin turned. "Only one thing remains—"

She saw what he meant to do. "No! Not that—"

He did not heed her but went straight to the glassy basalt pedestal, all twisted upon itself, and snatched up the heavy links. He would take the chain to his father and prove himself worthy of being Aidan's son.

He turned back to Ginevra. Her face was bathed in light, but the shadowed hollows beneath her cheeks underscored the exquisite architecture of her face. *Gods, but she is magnificent. They wrought well when they made her.* Hoarsely, he said, "Now we go."

"No! Not me!"

She was pride incarnate, and beautiful, blazing

489

with determination. Light from the Gate glowed
in her hair. All of it was silver now save for the
pure white frame around her face. She did not
know. She had not comprehended what the god
had stolen from her in addition to what was
offered.

Knowing what she is alters nothing. NOTHING. I
want her as much now as I did before. And—I need
her as badly.

Yet looking at her, knowing what he knew of the
woman who was Ihlini, but also whom he loved,
Kellin was keenly aware of a strange division in
his soul. He, too, had been raised to believe in
certain assurances, in certain absolutes, such as a
conviction that only one race could—and should—
survive. Assumptions were made predicated on
traditional beliefs; he wondered now if perhaps
disservices were done in the name of service.

To the Ihlini, service to the Seker is as binding—
and as honorable—as ours to Cheysuli gods. In that
moment he understood. He comprehended at last
how his father could, in the name of prophecy,
give up a son.

Should *he* not be able to sacrifice something as
well to serve a greater purpose?

He looked at the woman. A small part of him
wanted to say she was Ihlini, and enemy, and
therefore worthy of hatred; but the greater part of
him recalled the other woman. Had he not said it
himself? *"Prejucide and hatred is created, not born."*
He had loved her as an Ihlini, knowing no different; now that he did know, why should all things
change? Ginevra was simply *Ginevra.*

Kellin laughed painfully, cognizant of a truth
that no child could comprehend. *He gave up his*
son's childhood, but will have him in adulthood. I
give up old prejudice so I may have a woman, and
therefore serve the greatest purpose of all.

Ginevra scrambled up as he rounded the Gate. "I gave you your freedom! Now go!"

His hand closed upon her wrist. The other clutched the chain. As she struggled to break free he caught handfuls of her hair, all tangled with bloodied fingers and links of rune-wrought gold. He held her imprisoned skull very still between his palms. "I want—" He could not say it. It filled all of his being, he overflowed with it, but he could not say it.

Her face twisted. "You want the child!"

Lips drew back. He did not mean to snarl, to bare his teeth before her, but much of him recalled what it was to be a cat in place of a man.

She was Lochiel's daughter.

Kellin laughed. He saw the spasm in her face, the anguish in her eyes, and knew he had to explain. If he could but find the words. "Ginevra—" He shut his teeth together. *Why not let her believe it is because of the child? It would be easier.*

But he no longer desired to predicate decisions on what was easiest. "I have— I have lost too much . . ." He would say it; he *would*. "In the past—too many people." His breath stirred her hair, stark white around her face, silver in his hands. *Say the words. Say them so she knows—say them so YOU know.* "If—if it is heresy—" He drew in a hissing breath. "If it is heresy to love Lochiel's daughter, then burn me now."

Her eyes were blackened sockets. Ginevra said nothing.

His breath rushed out of his mouth. "I thought it was a lie. *This* Lion, I swore, would never lie down with the witch." His eyes were avid as he cradled her face. "But he has, and found it good—"

"How can you say that?" she cried. "Knowing what we are—"

"Knowing what we are is *why* I can say it." Kel-

lin clung to her more fiercely, wanting very badly
to find the proper words, but not knowing how.
He was afraid, suddenly. Afraid he could not win.
"Ginevra—"

A gout of *godfire* burst from the Gate. It show-
ered them with sparks. An eerie wailing whistle
accompanied smoke.

Ginevra flinched, then her eyes opened wide.
"He knows—the god *knows*—"

The ground beneath their feet shook. High overhead, one of the arches shattered. Glass rained
down.

"No more time—" Kellin dragged her with him
as he headed toward the colonnade that led from
the Gate to the passageway beyond. More glass
shattered. The chime of its landing was swallowed
by the keening from the Gate. *Godfire* lapped at
the edges, then spilled onto the floor.

She staggered next to him, fighting to regain
balance. "I told you to go *at once*, so he would not
renew his interest! You lingered too long!"

He had, but it was for her. "Then we had best
make haste."

The voice echoed in the cavern, carrying easily
above the keening of the Gate. "Ginevra shall go
nowhere. She is my daughter—and within the
Seker's keeping."

They spun in place. Lochiel stood on the far side
of the Gate. In his outstretched palms danced
crimson runes. His cloak smoked of *godfire*, purl-
ing around his body. The ale-brown eyes, in lurid
light, were molten bronze in their sockets. The
clean architecture of bone, so clear and pure in
line, was visible behind the human mask that hid
perverted purpose.

"She made a mistake," he said, "but it is easily
rectified." The runes in his hand flared higher,
brighter, though the brilliance did not distract

him. They twisted into knots, then broke apart and reformed. "First, there is the child. We cannot permit it to live. Ginevra knows that. You have only to look at her face."

Kellin did not. He knew what he would see there. She was profoundly Ihlini; he did not know if she loved him enough to bear the child whose presence in the world would alter hers forever.

Scalloped arches broke from the ceiling in sheets and fell behind them, shattering against basalt. A splinter cut Kellin's cheek. The floor trembled again. The Gate ran white with fire, bubbling over its edges. Kellin had mastered the art of working *godfire* in order to make runes, but he knew better than to believe he might turn back the flood. Lochiel was *Lochiel;* his arts were more powerful, and his intentions deadly.

Kellin moved back two paces and took Ginevra with him.

Lochiel's eyes were fixed on his daughter. "She knows what must be done."

Color stood high in her face. "I serve the Seker."

"Aye," he said, "you do. In all ways necessary— and in certain sacrifices."

"Wait—" Kellin blurted.

Ginevra cried out, then fell to her knees. Her body shuddered once. Her face was alive with pain as her mouth formed a rictus, then loosened its hideous tension into slack astonishment. "—kill me . . ." she gasped. "—to kill it, you kill *me*—"

"Sufficient punishment." Lochiel's runes blazed more brilliantly. "You made a mistake."

Kellin dragged her up and turned her from the Gate, pushing her onward. "Go on—go . . . get out of the cavern!"

Ginevra screamed. "—inside me—" she gasped. "—so *black*—" She thrust out her hands and clawed at the air. *Godfire* sparked from fingertips.

Her hair, in the light, glowed silver. "My own— father—"

Lochiel said calmly, "I can make other children."

Kellin built his own rune and hurled it across the Gate, bleeding *godfire* as it flew. Lochiel's blazed up, then shattered Kellin's rune into a shower of impotent fragments. "Tricks," the Ihlini said, and looked again at his daughter. "I would kill a thousand Ginevras to destroy the Firstborn."

"You—will not . . . you will *not*—" She reached out to Kellin, clawing. "Take—" She bit deeply into her lip as his fingers closed on hers. "I—will not—permit—"

"What choice have you?" Lochiel asked. "This is your sacrifice. Accept it willingly, so you do not shame me."

"*Shame* you! You?" Ginevra writhed against the pain, laughing breathlessly. She clutched Kellin's hand. "I need make no choice . . . you have made it *for* me—"

Godfire rose up in the Gate, then fell back, splashing, to pool again on the floor.

She clutched his hand more tightly. "*Kellin.*" Her grin was ghastly as she bared it to her father. "You are Lochiel the Ihlini, servant of the Seker— but we—*we*—are more . . . in my body lies the Firstborn. Do you think he will allow you to kill him?"

Lochiel laughed. "It is unborn, Ginevra! And will stay that way."

"No—" She bit again into her lip. Blood ran red, unsullied; she had given up immortality. "He drank . . . and I drank. The child has tasted also. What we are together is more than even you can withstand." She bared her bloodied teeth in the travesty of a smile. "The god, like your cats, is hungry. I think it is time he was fed."

Kellin felt her fingers bite into his own, setting fingernails. He saw then what she meant to do.

"—help—" she gasped. "I cannot do it without you—"

No. Nor could he without her, or the child in her body.

"Earth magic," Kellin murmured. "This is a Gate, like the Womb of the Earth. Here it is perverted, but there is still a stronger power—"

"*Now!*" Ginevra cried, and the walls around them trembled. Archways tumbled down, shattering to fragments against the floor.

Godfire blazed up. At its heart it burned white. In its reflection, as its servant, Lochiel's face was without feature. He was, in that moment, the avatar of the god. "*GINEVRA.*"

"He is hungry!" Ginevra cried. "He cries out for food!"

"*In the name of the Seker, in the name of Asar-Suti—*"

"Aye!" she cried. "In his name always, in all ways. You are his creature; let the god have you!"

Lochiel's eyes were livid. "I will raze this fortress before I permit you to take that child from here!"

Ginevra laughed. "You wanted to kill it! Now you change your mind?"

"As I must," he said. "The Seker's aspect is of *godfire*. I think he would like to be human once again, that he may walk the land freely as he sunders it."

She clung more tightly to Kellin's hand. "If you would give him a body, give him your own!"

"*GINEVRA!*"

"Your own!" she cried. And then, "*Now*, Kellin!"

With their power they burned out his eyes, leaving blackened, melted sockets, and exploded the runes in his hands. His clothing caught fire. The flesh of his face peeled away so the bone exposed itself. A rictus replaced his lips, displaying perfect teeth. Lochiel staggered forward, waving impotent stubs on the ends of blazing arms, then tumbled into the Gate.

The *godfire* within dimmed as if measuring its addition. And then it burst upward in a geyser of naked flame, licking at the jagged remains of shattered crystal arches. The Gate bled *godfire* in Lochiel's immolation.

A shudder wracked Ginevra. She fell to her knees. Silver hair streamed around her, tangling on the floor with steaming *godfire* and melting glass. In the rumbling of the Gate, her sobs went unheard.

"Come." Kellin urged her up. "If Asar-Suti desires a second helping . . ."

She caught great handfuls of god-bleached hair in rigid, trembling hands. Tears shone on her face. "What manner of man sires a child such as *I*, who murders her own father?"

A ripple moved through the floor. It fractured the massive columns that spiraled to the roof. Black glass rained down. With it came more arches, the fretwork of the ceiling, and then the roof itself.

"Ginevra!" Kellin dragged her to her feet one-handed as he tucked the two pieces of chain into his belt.

Cracks appeared in the rim of the Gate. Fissures ran toward them. As the roof fell down, part of it splashed into the Gate, so that *godfire* gouted forth. In its depths, something screamed.

The floor beneath them rolled. From high over their heads, from the bulwark of the fortress, came a keening howl of fury.

"They know," Ginevra said. "The bonds are all broken. Lochiel is dead and so *they* die—and Valgaard is falling." She caught his hand tightly. "I have to find my mother."

As they burst from out of the passageway into the corridor, Melusine was waiting. In her hands was a sword made of livid *godfire*. "What have you done?" she cried. "What have you wrought?"

Ginevra laughed crazily to hear her own words repeated. "Lochiel is dead."

"The walls fall," Melusine said; in her eyes shone the light of madness, yellow as a Cheysuli's. "Valgaard is sundered . . ." She looked at Kellin. "Kinsman," she said, then raised the sword high.

"No!" Ginevra struck before he could, transfixing her mother's breast with a single blazing rune. The sword was snuffed out. "No," Ginevra repeated. Her eyes were anguished. "Go away," she said. "Get out of Valgaard now."

Melusine laughed. "Without Lochiel? You must be mad!"

"Mother—" But the floor between them fissured. A jagged hole appeared. Kellin staggered, righted himself, then caught Ginevra and yanked her back as Melusine, screaming, tumbled in. *"Mother!"*

He did not remonstrate, nor try to explain there was no hope as *godfire* gushed forth and drove them back. Ginevra knew. *"Shansu,"* he whispered, though she would not understand.

She pressed a hand across her face so he would not see her tears.

Kellin did not permit them to stop until they were through the defile on their Valgaard horses and safe within the canyon, where the floor did not split, the walls did not fall down, and the roof above their heads did not collapse upon them. There Sima waited.

He expected the link to be sundered by Ginevra's presence, but Sima's pattern was clear. *You did well*, his *lir* said, *to release my kin.*

He thought of the undercroft, where he had, with his power, torn the doors off their hinges and permitted the cats to escape. *They deserved a better tahlmorra than to die with Lochiel.*

Sima's eyes gleamed golden. Tufted ears slicked. *Do you understand?*

No. I was taught we could not link when an Ihlini was near.

There is some of the god in you. Not only in your magic, but in your tolerance. You are both children of the gods; the time for schism is ending. She glanced at Ginevra. *Tend her first. There will be time for us later.*

He climbed off his horse, hooked its reins over a branch, then went to Ginevra's. "Come down," he said, and reached out a hand.

Ginevra looked down at him from atop her mount. Ash marred her cheek. Silver hair was a tangled tapestry on either side of her face. In her eyes was an anguish of such immensity he feared it might break her.

He could not help herself. *"Meijhana—"*

At the sound of the enemy tongue, spoken so close to sundered Valgaard, Ginevra flinched. Then, with careful deliberation, she unhooked a foot from a stirrup and got off on the other side. It put the horse between them.

She could not have taken a blade and stabbed any deeper. He was eviscerated.

Gods, he prayed, *let this woman never hate me. I could not bear it.*

Ginevra took the horse away to the far side of the canyon. She sat down there upon a broken stump clad in the stormwrack of her soul and stared blindly into shadows with ice-gray eyes glazed black.

With effort, Kellin turned back to his horse. He unbuckled girths, pulled off saddle and blankets, scrubbed down the damp back with a handful of leaves. When he was done, he went to her horse and did the same service. Ginevra said nothing.

Smoke crept into the canyon. It was laden now with odors: burned flesh, the stink of the netherworld, the smell of a world come undone.

"It is gone," Ginevra said.

Kellin turned from her horse.

"Gone." She sketched a rune in the air; he recognized *bal'sha'a* by the movement of her fingers. But nothing came of it. Her fingers moved deftly, yet nothing flared into brilliance in answer to her shaping. "The Gate is closed," she said. The hand, bereft of power, slapped down slackly and lay curled in her lap. "And so now there is no *godfire*." Her eyes were oddly empty. "Everyone I knew is dead. Every*thing* I knew is gone."

His voice shook. "Ginevra—"

Her face was a wasteland. "Lochiel was right. We are truly destroyed."

"No." He drew a slow breath, treading carefully; he desired in no way to be misconstrued, or what they had built between them—that now was in jeopardy—would collapse into ruins. "No, not destroyed." He would not lie to her; would *never* lie to her. "This *aspect* of it, perhaps, but your race survives. Asar-Suti is defeated, but there are Ihlini in the world."

"Good Ihlini?" She smiled, but without amusement; it was a ghastly mockery of the smiles he had won before. "Those who repudiate the Seker will surely survive and be looked upon with favor, but what of—us? Those like my father, and Strahan before him, and Tynstar before *him*." The line of her jaw was blade-sharp as she set her teeth. "What of Ihlini like me?"

"You said it yourself: the Gate is closed."

She did not flinch. "Aye."

"I would like to think that as we end this war, such Ihlini as they were will turn from the dark arts to fashion a new world."

" 'Such Ihlini,' " she echoed. "Like me?"

He said it deliberately: "You are not your father."

"No." Moonlight glinted in hair. "No, so I am not. Or surely I would have killed you there at the Gate." Her mouth warped briefly. "Perhaps I should have."

"Aye," he agreed. "Or left the cat loose so the hunt could commence."

It shook her. It shook her so badly he knew she as much as he comprehended the precipice.

He gave her the truth. "I do not believe Cynric's task is to have the Ihlini killed."

Her tone was harsh. "As we killed my mother and my father?"

My poor meijhana. He went to her, and squatted down before her. "No matter how hard you strike at me, it will not bring them back."

Ginevra laughed harshly. "How can I strike at you? You only did as I asked, there in the cavern. What does it matter to me *how* it was done, or that we used an unborn child for his power?"

He caught her hand. "Do not punish yourself for choosing to live. You did—*we* did—what had to be done."

"All of it? *All* of it?" Her hand shook in his. "My father. My mother. My—home." Tears glazed her eyes as she put a hand against her belly. "So falls the Ihlini race. As according to prophecy—but before he is even born!" Her voice was raw. "Are you pleased by it?"

He put his hand on her hand and let it rest against her belly. "He is Ihlini, also."

She wrenched her hand away and pressed both against her mouth. Fingers trembled minutely. Through them, she said, "How can you love me? I am everything you hate."

"When I was Cheysuli—" He smiled to see her start. "When I was Cheysuli, and knew it, I hated Ihlini. There was no choice. They meant to destroy my House. They had killed people I loved. They would kill *me*, if I gave them the chance to do so." He pulled her hands away and held them in his. "When I was Cheysuli but no longer knew it, I was free to understand that life is much more complex. That the gods, when they act, when they wish to humble a man, wield a weapon of irony."

"*Your* gods!"

"Mine. Yours also." He lifted a strand of her hair. In the sunset, the silver was gilt. "You knew what would happen."

Ginevra stiffened.

"You knew very well. It was what you implied when you came to me here, to fetch me to the Gate so you could win me back my human form." He looked into her eyes. "You grieve for more than their deaths. You grieve because of your guilt. That Lochiel's daughter, bred to serve her people, preserved in the name of love the life of the only man who could destroy her race."

"You shame me," she said.

It shook him. "In what way?"

"The truth. The truth shames me. I have betrayed my race." She put trembling fingers against his mouth. "And I would do it again."

He wanted in that moment, recognizing her truth as an absolute, to give her a truth in return. To admit to her—and to himself as well—what demon had lived in his soul all his adult life.

Before, he had not known. And if someone had told him, if someone had dared, he would have taken solace in ridicule. *I have used weapons in my life, but none so sharp as the blade of honesty. It is time, I think, to use it on myself and lance the canker I have cherished.*

Kellin took her hand away, caught up the other one, then tucked both against his chest so she could feel his heartbeat. "I have been afraid of many things in my life, but none so much as the intimacy of loving a woman. I lay with many, aye, to assuage a physical need in vain attempts to dull the emotional pain, but nothing sufficed. I was always empty, always in despair, despite what I believed. Despite what I yearned for." His fingers warmed hers. He pressed her palms against his heart. "In fear of losing others, I distorted my soul on purpose. I cherished bitterness. I drove people away, even those whom I loved, because I wanted no one to care for me so *I* would not be required to care for them . . . to care was to lose them, and I could not bear it. Not after so many deaths." He carried her hands to his mouth and kissed them. "The river gave me the chance to become another man, perhaps the one I was meant to be all along. What you see before you now is not Kellin of Homana, but Kellin *the man*, of whom Ginevra had the shaping." He set his mouth against her palm. "I am your construct. If you would destroy me now, you need only withdraw your love."

She looked away from him. She gazed over his shoulder. Beyond the defile, beyond the Beasts, Valgaard yet burned. The air was laden with smoke.

He would not release her hands. "What we have shared could transfigure a world. Even this one."

The scent of smoke was thick. Ginevra's mouth

warped briefly. "I have no roof," she said. "It has all fallen down."

Kellin cradled her face in his hands, threading fingers into the shining wealth of her hair. Softly he said, "Homana-Mujhar's still stands."

She flinched visibly; he saw she regretted it at once. "I am Lochiel's daughter."

He pressed his lips against her brow. He kissed it twice, thrice, then moved the great distance between forehead and mouth. *Cynric or no, prophecy or no, how could I even consider giving up this woman?*

He never had. Not once.

The truth seared his soul even as his lips shaped words on hers with careful tenderness. "I need you," he whispered, "as I have needed no one. *You* are my balance."

He knew it was not enough. But it was all he had to give her.

When her hand touched his shoulder, Kellin opened his eyes. It was full night. He had not slept. Neither had she.

He waited. He held his silence, his position. The tension in her fingers, as she touched his shoulder, was a reflection of his own.

The canyon stank of smoke. Valgaard burned. The full moon above them was dyed violet and black.

Her hand withdrew. When she touched him again, her fingers were cool on his face. They touched his mouth and clung.

Kellin sat up. He sat upon his heels even as she sat upon hers; their knees touched, and hands.

Ginevra stared into his face. Her own was shadowed in the shroud of her hair. He saw the angle of a cheekbone, the curve of her brow. Her eyes were pockets of darkness. "If I am your balance, you are my lifestone."

In silence, Kellin waited.

She took one of his hands and carried it to her breast. She cupped his fingers around it. *"Make me feel again."*

Two

Ginevra stopped Kellin at the top of the steps leading into Homana-Mujhar. Rigid hands bit into his forearm as he turned immediately. *"Meij-hana*—what is it?"

Her face was a sculpted mask with burning ice for eyes. "How will you say it?" she asked. "How will you tell them who I am?"

Kellin smiled, moving down a single step so he did not tower so much; she was shorter than he, and delicate, but her stature belied the dominance of her spirit. "Easily. I will say to all of them: 'This lady is Ginevra. This lady is my *cheysula*. You all of you should be pleased the beast is tamed at last.'"

Color bloomed in her cheeks. Fingernails dug through fabric into flesh that was lighter than the norm for a Cheysuli, but darker than hers. "And will they want *me* tamed? The wicked Ihlini?" She had left tears in Solinde; what she gave him now was pride fierce as a Cheysuli's. "At least *you* came to my home without excess display!"

It took effort for him to keep his hands and mouth from her here and now, out of doors, before the palace entrance and all the bailey, and the soldiers from the guardhouse. "I was unconscious," he reminded her. "I have not the slightest idea if there was display, or no. For all I know, you might

505

have hung me from my ankles and dried me over a fire."

Ginevra let go of his arm. "It never would have worked. Your brain was much too soggy!"

"*Meijhana.*" He captured her hand and tucked it into his arm, warming it with his own hand. "I know you too well; you are not the one to hide from a truth, harsh or no. You will tell them yourself."

"Aye," she said, "I will. Just give me the chance!"

Kellin laughed. "Then come into my house."

"Gods—" she blurted, "—*wait*—"

He turned around promptly and sat down upon the steps, hooking arms around upraised knees as Sima sat down beside him. The cat's purr rumbled against his thigh. When Ginevra did not move, he eventually glanced up. "Well?"

Sunlight glinted on silver; he had loved her mass of black hair, but found this as much to his liking. *She could be hairless, and I would love her.* And then he grinned; who would have predicted Kellin of Homana would lose his heart at all, and to an Ihlini?

"What are you doing?" she asked.

"Waiting. You wanted me to." He paused, elated by her presence and the knowledge of what life with her would be; never dull, never quiet. The Prince and Princess of Homana did not harbor timid souls. "Should I have food sent out? If we are to be here so long . . ."

Ginevra's sharp inhalation hissed. New color stained her cheeks. She turned on her heel and marched directly into the palace.

He leaned his weight into Sima, who threatened to collapse his leg. *Contradictory.*

Then you are well-suited.

How could we not be? Was it not prophesied?

Sima's eyes slitted. *Not specifically. The prophecy*

merely said the Lion would lie down with the witch. Even the gods could not predict that you would be so much alike.

He smiled. *By now she may well be in the Great Hall confronting the Mujhar himself.*

Or in your chamber confronting the knowledge of other women.

Kellin sat bolt upright, then got up at once.

Sima relented. *She is in the solar speaking with the Queen. Leave the women to one another—your place is with the Mujhar.*

And you?

Sima's tufted ears flicked. She stared past him into the sunlight, transfixed on a thought he could not decipher. The ears flattened once, then lifted again.

Kellin prodded. *Lir?*

She looked at him. Her stare was level. He felt in that instant she looked beyond the exterior to the soul within, and wondered how she found it. *It is for you to do,* she told him.

Kellin smiled. "He will understand. Once I have explained it. All of them will." He laughed aloud for joy. "Most assuredly my *jehan,* who undoubtedly knew very well what was to become of me!"

The cat's glance was oblique as she shouldered by his knee into the palace. *The Great Hall,* she said, *where the Lion lives.*

He went there at once, pushing open the hammered doors, and saw, as expected, the Mujhar sitting quietly in the belly of the Lion, contemplating his hall.

Kellin paused just inside the doors. It had been half a year since he had been sent away by a man clearly desperate to salvage his only heir. *Well, the heir is salvaged. Homana is preserved.* Kellin's smile was slow, shaped by anticipation. There was much he longed to say, much he meant to share, but especially Ginevra. *I will make him understand. And how could he not? Lochiel is dead. The Wheel of Life still turns.*

Kellin drew in a breath, lifted his head, then walked with steady strides the length of the firepit to pause before the dais. There he lowered his eyes out of respect for the man, and gave him Cheysuli greeting.

The Mujhar did not answer.

Anticipation waned. Kellin's belly tightened. *Does he know already? Has word come before us: "The Prince of Homana has taken to wife an Ihlini witch!"*

The Mujhar offered nothing. When Kellin could no longer stand it, he raised his head at last. "Grandsire—"

He checked. He stood there a long while. He denied it once, and twice. The truth offended him. He longed to discard it and conjure another.

But truth was truth. Magic could not change it.

His spirit withered within.

Kellin climbed the three steps and sank to his knees. His trembling hand, naked of signet, reached out to touch the dark Cheysuli flesh that was still faintly warm.

He looked for Sleeta, but the mountain cat was gone.

Kellin thought of Sima. *She knew. When she sat upon the steps—* But he let it go. He looked into the face of the Cheysuli warrior who had ruled Homana for more than forty years. The body slumped only slightly, tilted slantwise across the back of the throne, as if he merely rested. One gold-freighted arm lay slack, hand upturned against a leather-clad thigh; the other was draped loosely along the armrest, so the dark Cheysuli fingers followed the curve of the claws. On his forefinger the seal ring of Homana glinted dully.

Though the flesh had stilled, the bones as yet defied the truth. Brennan was, even dead, still very much a king.

Kellin's mouth moved stiffly as he managed a smile. He said it as he had told her on the steps before the palace. "The lady is Ginevra. The lady is my *cheysula*. You should be pleased the beast is tamed at last."

In the Lion, silence reigned. The Mujhar had abdicated.

"So much—" his grandson whispered, kneeling before the king. "So much I meant to say."

Mostly *leijhana tu'sai*, for being *jehan* as well as grandsire.

The Mujhar of Homana left the Great Hall and went directly to Aileen, where Ginevra was. He was aware of an odd dispassion, as if someone had wrung him empty of grief, and pain; with effort he put into words the requirements of state.

Then he put into words that which most required telling: that he had loved and honored her *cheysul* far more deeply than he had shown, as he loved and honored her.

In her face he saw his father's: chalk eroding in storm; crumbling beneath the sun. It ate below the layers and bared the granite of her grief, hard and sharp and impenetrable, and ageless as the gods.

Pale lips moved at last. "If this were Erinn, we would take him to the sacred tor and give him to the *cileann*."

But this was not Erinn. They would take him to his tomb and lay him to rest with other Mujhars.

Kellin kissed his granddame. He sent for a servant. He sent for a *shar tahl* and Clankeep's clan-leader.

He sent for his *lir* to bide her time with Ginevra, whose eyes bespoke her empathy, and returned to the Great Hall.

People came. They took away the body. They gave him a ring. They called him "my lord Mujhar." They left him as he desired: alone in the hall as the day shapechanged to dusk.

Kellin felt sick to his stomach. He sat upon the dais and wished the day were different, that he could stop the Wheel of Life from turning and then start it up again, only this time moving backward, *backward, BACKWARD*, so the time was turned up-side down and his grandsire could live again.

He stared into the blazing firepit. *I do not want to be Mujhar.*

He had wanted it all of his life.

I want him back. Grandsire. Let him be Mujhar.

They had trained him from birth to be king in his grandsire's place.

A king must die to let another rule in his place.

Kellin shut his eyes. He heard in the silence all the arguments they had shared, all the rude words he had shouted because his grandsire wanted too much, demanded too much of him; chained his grandson up so he would never know any freedom.

The words were gall in his mouth. "Too much left unsaid."

Behind him crouched the Lion. Its presence was demanding. Kellin heaved himself up and turned to confront it. Gilded eyes glared back.

He moved because he had to; he could no longer sit still. He climbed the dais. Touched the throne. Moved around to the back of it and turned to face the wall. He stared hard at the tapestry while the lions within its folds blurred into shapeless blobs.

He remembered very clearly the day Ian had died. One small hand, not much darker than a Homanan's, and one old hand, bronzed flesh aging into brittle, yellowed flesh.

"Gods," he said aloud, "you should have made a better man than me."

"The gods wrought very well. In time, you will know it. I already do."

Kellin turned. *"Jehan."* He was mostly unsurprised; it seemed to fit perfectly. "You know."

"I know."

"Have you seen the Queen?"

Aidan's eyes were steady. "I did not see your *cheysula.*" He let it register. "But aye, I saw my *jehana.*"

The words were hard to say. "Did you know— before?"

Aidan's face was graven with new lines at eyes and mouth. "I am privileged to know things before others do. It is part of my service."

" 'Privileged' to know your father has died?"

"Privileged to know certain things so I may prepare the way for greater purposes."

Kellin smiled a little. "A true *shar tahl,* couching his words in obscurity."

Aidan smiled back. "I believe it is required."

Kellin nodded. His father walked very steadily toward the dais on which he stood. "How does one know if one is worthy of what he inherits?"

"One never does." Aidan stopped before the dais. *"I* know, Kellin. For now, it is enough."

Kellin swallowed heavily. "Did you come for him?"

"I came for you. I came to bind the Lion."

"Bind . . ." Kellin sighed. He felt very old. "I feared it, once." He stroked away a lock of hair. "The Lion lay down with the witch."

Aidan nodded. "I know."

Kellin wanted to smile, but his face felt old, and empty. "You prophesied for me, that day. You said I would marry."

A glint, purest yellow. "Most princes do."

"But you knew it would be Ginevra."

The glint died. Aidan's eyes were calm. "It seemed a tidy way of achieving what we all of us have worked for."

"The Lion lay down with the witch. And so the prophecy—"

"—continues." Aidan's expression was solemn. "Despite what you may hope, it is not yet complete. There are things we still must do."

"Ah." Kellin put his hands to his belt, then undid the buckle with fingers that felt thick and slow. He slid the links free. "Here. This is yours."

Aidan took the broken chain as Kellin redid his belt. "Sit down, my lord. It is time I chained the Lion."

He was too weary to question the task. He sat down. The Lion's mouth gaped. Kellin touched the wood and felt an echo of ancient power. *Mine?* he wondered. *Or left over from my grandsire?*

Aidan stood before the dais, before the firepit. His eyes burned feral yellow in the umber light of the dying day. In his hands were links. "Shaine," he said, "who began the *qu'mahlin*. His nephew Carillon, who took back Homana and ended the *qu'mahlin*. Then came Donal, son of Ali and Duncan—and after him, Niall, followed by Brennan." Gold chimed on gold. "The next link is broken. Its name was Aidan. I shattered it myself to bargain for my son. To know without a doubt that what I sacrificed would make Homana stronger." He held up the shorter length. "Two more links. One of them is Kellin. The other is named Cynric."

Kellin waited.

Aidan smiled. He turned to the firepit and dropped the two halves into flame.

Kellin started up from the throne, then checked.

Aidan said clearly, "The chain shall bind the Lion."

Their eyes locked. *He does not ask, he TELLS.* And then Kellin laughed. He stood up from the Lion and walked down the dais steps. He knelt beside the firepit with his back to the Lion, and knew what he must do.

Aidan waited.

What is fire, but fire? I have withstood godfire; I have made *godfire. This comes from my jehan— surely its flame is cleaner.* Kellin drew in a breath. He put his hand through flames, then farther into coals.

It burned, but did not consume. Fingers found metal. He sought the shape of the link and could not find it. What he found was something else.

"Free it," Aidan said.

Kellin brought it out of the flame, unsurprised to discover his hand was whole. He opened it. In the palm lay an earring. The head of a mountain cat stared back at him.

"More," Aidan said.

Kellin set the earring onto the rim of the firepit. He reached into the flame again, dug down into coals, and took from the pit two *lir*-bands.

Aidan was patient. "And again."

"Again?" But he set the armbands also on the rim and plunged both hands into the blazing coals.

Aidan smiled. "A king must have a crown."

Kellin drew it forth. A rune-wrought circlet of *lir* gleamed against his palms. Its workmanship was such that no man, looking upon it, could withstand the desire to set it on his brow.

The voice was light and calm, pitched to reach

the dais. "So this is Cheysuli magic." Ginevra's winged brows rose as she walked the length of the hall. "Does all your gold come from fire?"

"No," Aidan answered. "Our gold is merely gold, though blessed by the gods in the Ceremony of Honors. *This* gold, however, is to replace that he lost in misadventure."

"Misadventure." Her gaze dwelled on Kellin. She had tamed the silvered hair by braiding it into quiescence with blood-red cord. "The sort of misadventure that rendered him without memory of name, of rank—of race." She looked now at Aidan. "You are the one my father most feared."

In dying light, Aidan's hair glowed russet. "He never told me so."

"He did fear you. He never told *me* so—my father was not a man to admit to such things as fear—but I think he must have. He spoke of you repeatedly, telling me how it was, in your madness, that you came to him in Valgaard to bargain for your son. I think he did not know what else you might do, and it frightened him."

Kellin clutched the circlet. The gold was warm in his hands. What passed between his father and Ginevra was undivulged even in gesture; he could not decipher it.

Aidan's face was relaxed. "I might have chosen you."

"Aye. And brought me here." She cast a glance at Kellin. "My lord prevails upon me to insist that had I been, I would never once have realized I was anything but Cheysuli."

"But you are," Aidan answered. "You are many things, Ginevra . . . among them Cheysuli. Among them Ihlini."

Her chin firmed. "And the mother of the Firstborn."

Aidan looked at her belly. She did not show

much yet, but her cupped hands divulged the truth. He smiled into her eyes. "You may choose what you will be. The gods give us free will—even to Ihlini."

"Choose?" She glanced sidelong at Kellin, then returned her gaze to Aidan. "In what way do I choose? And what?"

"How you shall be remembered." Aidan rose. "You may be Kellin's *cheysula*. You may be Queen of Homana. You may be merely a mother—or the mother of the Firstborn."

"I was and always will be Lochiel's daughter." Aidan inclined his head.

"And it will mark me," she declared. "*That* is how they will know me!"

"Aye," Aidan agreed, "because it is required." His eyes were very feral in the waning light. Flames turned them molten. "As it concerns you, my prophesying is done."

It startled her. "What?"

"You were the witch. But that is done. When Kellin lies down again, it will be with his *cheysula*. If you mean to be anything more, you yourself will make the choice."

Color stood in her face. "You mean if I choose to remind them I am heir to Lochiel's power." She smiled. "I could. I could do it easily."

"That would depend," Aidan said calmly, "on how you chose to do it."

She stared fixedly at him, then looked at Kellin. She was, in that moment, pride and glory incarnate.

Leijhana tu'sai, he thought, *for giving me the wit—or robbing me of them!—so I might see beyond the wall of our people's enmity to the woman beyond.*

The fire kindled her eyes and melted Ihlini ice. The quality of her tone was pitched now to acknowledgment, and a warmth that left him breathless. "Then I would choose to be the woman who crowned a king. So they would know I want no war. So they would know I am Ginevra, and not merely Lochiel's daughter."

"Then do it," Aidan said.

Ginevra lifted her head. She advanced steadily. Beside the firepit she paused, stared up into the blind, gilded eyes of the Lion Throne of Homana, and smiled a tiny smile. *"Tahlmorra,"* she said dryly. "Is that not what you call this?"

Aidan's voice was quiet. "All men—and all women—have a *tahlmorra.* You were bred of Cheysuli gods as surely as of Ihlini . . . they were—and remain—the same. In their view we are all of us 'Cheysuli.' The word means 'children of the gods.' " His smile was gentle, lacking in threat, lacking in arrogance. "We have a saying, of twins: 'Two blossoms from the same vine.' Though our vine was split and the two halves borne away to separate gardens, the rootstock remains the same. It is time we replanted."

She hesitated. "Asar-Suti? The Seker?"

"We are but aspects of our creators. When there is evil among men, look first at those gods from whom they inherited it."

Kellin's belly clenched. "Then he is not dead."

"The Gate was closed in the destruction of Valgaard. It takes times to build another. While Asar-Suti labors, centuries may pass."

Ginevra's smile was crooked. "Then I had best crown the king before the Gate is rebuilt." She held it out, above his head. Flames glinted off gold. Clearly she said, "In the name of all the gods, even the Seker who is but one among them, I declare you Mujhar of Homana."

Kellin bowed his head. The circlet was cool as she slid it onto his head with trembling fingers. It warmed against his brow.

"Done," Ginevra said.

Aidan smiled. "And so the Lion is chained by the witch with whom he lay."

Kellin picked up the earring. "But this is *lir*-gold! How could *this* chain me?"

"Memories," Aidan answered. "History and heritage, and an ancestry that reaches across centuries. When the Lion roars he must recall what went before, so he will rule the world wisely. Responsibility binds a man; it binds a king more. Do not discount its weight."

"No," Kellin said. "Not ever again, *jehan*."

One of the hammered doors scraped open. A man came in. Kellin got to his feet.

"Already," Aidan murmured.

Kellin stared at his kinsman. Hart's hair was white. His gaunt face was lined with grief. He looked briefly at Aidan and Ginevra, then fastened an unflinching gaze on his twin-born brother's grandson. "I came for Brennan," he said, "but it seems the gods have seen fit to deprive me of my *rujho*."

Mute, Kellin nodded.

Hart looked at Aidan. "It would have been yours, once. Is that why you are come home at last?"

Something moved in Aidan's eyes. "I am come home for many reasons, *su'fali*. I am come to honor my *jehan*, whom the gods have taken; to offer strength to my *jehana;* to pay homage to my son, the Mujhar; to witness the coming of the Firstborn." The yellow eyes were fierce. "But also to grieve. Will you permit me that?"

Abashed, Hart nodded. He looked from Aidan to Aidan's son. "Brennan is gone, and so I come to you, his heir." Anguish blossomed a moment, was damped down with effort. "I had a son once.

Owain. Lochiel murdered him. Now I have no son.
I have come to give you Solinde."

Kellin was astounded. "You have daughters!"

Hart's voice was steady. "Blythe has borne only
girls, and will bear no more. Cluna bore three still-
born children and will not conceive again. Jennet
died in childbed. Dulcie was wed to the High
Prince of Ellas two months ago." Hart's tension
lessened. "She grew tired of waiting for you."

Kellin smiled faintly.

"And so the sons she bears, if she bears sons—
we run to girls, I fear—will be reared Ellasian."

Kellin stood very still. The back of his neck
prickled. He looked sharply at his father and saw
the light in Aidan's eyes. *He said he knows things.
He is "privileged" to know. He knew this would
come.* Realization was a knife plunged deep into
his vitals. *And he knows the others will come.*

He would stop it. He knew the way. He looked
back at his grandsire's brother. "You will not die
so soon. This is unnecessary."

Hart said only, "Brennan died today."

After a stricken moment Kellin turned away and
stared hard at the tapestry of lions. He could not
bear Hart's eyes. He could not bear to see his own
grief in his great-uncle's face.

Three

When at last Ginevra slept, wearied from long labor, Kellin sat beside her with their son in his arms, thinking thoughts of wonder, of pride, of relief; of the prophecy of the Firstborn.

Lochiel's daughter stirred, then slid again into sleep. He put one hand into the glorious hair and stroked it gently from her face. The long eyes were lidded, lost to him in sleep, but he knew what lived behind them: the blazing ice of Ihlini *godfire*, legacy of Lochiel's power.

Women had swaddled his son in countless linen wrappings. The child, he thought, was ugly, far uglier than foal or puppy, but he supposed time would alter the red-faced, wrinkled infant into a human child, and eventually into a man.

Kellin drew in a breath. *What manner of power will you claim? Will you be human at all?*

Sima, at his feet, sent a lazy suggestion through the link that he let the child grow up and discover for himself what his *tahlmorra* was. That a father could, if he watered the clay too much, turn it into sludge so that no one at all could use it.

Kellin smiled. *Is that what I was? Sludge?*

Sima blinked. *Clay with too much grit. You cut the flesh of an unsuspecting potter.*

Ah. He laughed softly. And then he thought of other children who had no father to water them at all. *I will have them come here.*

Sima yawned. *Be wary of asking too much. You gave them to those women; if you mean to take them back, you will do more harm than good.*

They are my children.

Bastards.

He heard the echo of his own arrogance, and knew what Sima intended. He acceded to a greater wisdom than his own; she was, after all, *lir*. "Then I will give them leave to come whenever they like, so they will know their heritage."

And?

He smiled. *And I will go to them, so I will share their lives.*

Better. She lashed her tail once. *What will you do with the others?*

What others? He stiffened. *And there more?*

I mean the ones to come later.

Later! Sima, by all the gods, do you think me a selfish, rutting fool? What man in the world would turn to another woman with this *one in his bed?*

Sima purred more loudly and shut her golden eyes. She offered no comment. Her work was done.

Kellin laughed softly and looked down upon his son. *Where would a warrior be without a lir such as Sima? Or Sleeta? Or Teel? Or Ian's Tasha? Or Blais' Tanni?* He touched his son's brow. *What lir will you have—if you have a lir at all?*

"Kellin."

He glanced up. Hart stood in the doorway. He knew without being told what his kinsman had come to say. "They are here," Kellin said. "Corin. And Keely."

Hart's face spasmed. "Did Aidan forewarn you? Or have you your own measure of his power of prophecy?"

It hurt, but he knew the pain was shared. It goaded all of them. "I have no power at all, save what any of us do. I know only what we all do—

that the Lion shall swallow the lands." He beckoned one of the women, gave her Cynric, and rose.
"You came to give me Solinde. I think we will find
they have come to do the same with their own
realms."

In Hart's eyes was a measure of quiet respect.
"Brennan wrote me of his fears, of his frustrations.
He knew very well what you *could* be, if you permitted yourself to achieve it. I see now he was not
wrong." He nodded slightly. "A fitting legacy for
my *rujho*. He wrought well, did Brennan. And Homana shall prosper for it."

Kellin paused in the doorway; it was Corin he
saw first. The Lord of Atvia stood with his back to
the deep-silled casement. A ruddy fox sat beside
one leg: Kiri. Midday sunlight glinted off *lir*-gold.
The once-tawny hair had faded, intermixed with
silver, and the beard Corin yet wore showed traces
of white, but no sign of age softened the tension
in his body or the pride in his stance. For all he
had none of the color, he was Cheysuli to the bone.

Kellin was aware of them all within an instant
of entering the chamber: Aileen's solar, with Aileen in it, seated on a chair; near Corin stood a
dark-haired woman with eloquent brown eyes he
knew was Glyn, Corin's *cheysula;* a second woman
in a chair with hair a pristine white and eyes like
ice—*Ginevra's eyes*—was Ilsa, Hart's Solindish
queen; and Keely, Corin's twin, seated nearby with
Sean of Erinn at her back. The Erinnish lord was
huge, dominating the chamber. Even in quietude
his presence was of the kind another man, even a
king, could not ignore.

And lastly Aidan, his father, who stood quietly
behind his mother with a raven close at hand,
watching the tableau as if he knew very well what
was to come.

No doubt he does know. Kellin looked back at Corin even as Hart moved by him into the chamber to join Ilsa. He wondered what had passed among his kinfolk as they awaited his arrival. They had spoken of Brennan certainly; a quiet grief lingered in Keely's eyes. Her face was tautly drawn over high, pronounced cheekbones. The stubborn jaw was set. But Kellin saw a softness there that she might not acknowledge; she was, they all said, a very proud woman.

He smiled faintly to see her in skirts. He had heard the stories of her tempestuous youth. *She belongs in jerkin and leggings, with a sword in her hands*. Shona, they said, had been very like Keely. In the face of his granddame, he looked for his mother. In the face of his grandsire, he looked for himself.

But Sean was all Erinnish, bred in the Aerie's mews; Kellin was Cheysuli. *As well as other things, which bring me to this point*.

Sean's rumble broke the silence. "Lad," he said, "we've come for other things, but we owe our respects to the Mujhar of Homana."

"Leijhana tu'sai," Kellin said, and saw the startled speculation in Keely's eyes; had she heard that Brennan's heir repudiated his race? Well, it was time they understood. "In the name of my other grandsire, I welcome you to his home."

"Yours," Keely said softly.

Corin's smile was grim. "I came to speak with Brennan on a matter of some importance. I find instead I must speak to his heir. It may be— difficult."

Kellin nodded. "You none of you know me." He looked at Keely; at Sean. "Not even you, who raised a proud daughter well worthy of my *jehan*. And I, am I fortunate, will be worthy of them." He stepped aside and beckoned Sima in. The cat slid through with a rub against his leg, then padded to a deep-silled casement aglow with midday sun. She leapt up, curled herself, and settled on the sill. "You may have heard nonsense of a young, foolish prince desiring nothing of a *lir* for fear he would lose her, or himself if she were killed. But that man was ignorant. He did not know what manner of gift the gods offered." He looked at Sima and saw they did the same. "In time, he came to see that a warrior without a *lir* is not a man at all ... and wholly unfit to inherit the Lion Throne."

Tension fled Corin's shoulders. His smile widened. "News travels slowly."

"Much more slowly than rumor."

Ruefully, Corin laughed. "I know your birthline as well as my own, as I am in much of it ... I have no quarrel with it. But you are young to be Mujhar."

"I am the age you were when you sailed away to your island."

Corin looked at Keely. "A long time ago, *rujholla.*"

Keely's hair also had begun to silver, altering the gold of younger years. "Much too long, I fear, for either of us to recall the feelings of youth, and why we did what we did." She smiled at her brother, then looked to Kellin. "We are informed there is a new Prince of Homana."

Kellin saw no reason to rely on courtesy, or the traditions of a culture that now would be altered. "More than that," he said easily. "Cynric is the Firstborn."

Tension reinfected the chamber. He wondered if they believed he would not acknowledge such a thing; that he would deny sleeping with an Ihlini despite what it had produced.

Kellin understood; it would be so for years, until old prejudices died. "Her name is Ginevra. Among the Houses in her blood is our own: she is, as am I, a grandchild of Brennan."

The silence was heavy. Keely broke it. "We do not question that. The gods made it clear that one day it would happen, though I admit none of us believed you might *marry* an Ihlini." She slanted a troubled glance at Aidan, who had served as Cynric's prophet. "But it is difficult for me to reconcile her as anything other than *Lochiel's* child. He killed my daughter—"

"—and nearly his own." Kellin saw it register; marked startled attention. "When he learned the child she carried was Cynric, he tried to murder her. Ginevra refused to submit to the sacrifice he and his god required. With my help—and the help of her unborn child—she killed her father. She destroyed him in the Gate of his own god." He looked at each of them, one at a time, until he knew he had them. "We have fought the Ihlini forever. It was Ginevra's choice that this war be ended."

Keely's gaze did not waver. Her smile was bittersweet. "If it is possible for you to care so much for her, then perhaps I should take instruction in the art of forgiveness. I would like to forgive; she is, by marriage, my granddaughter. But such things do not come easy to a childless woman."

"Childless!" Kellin looked at Sean and saw anguished affirmation. "But—you also had a *son*—"

The upstanding veins of Keely's hand knotted. "Sean and Riordan went to Atvia to visit Corin and Glyn. This time, I did not go." A spasm of grief wracked her face. "This *once,* I did not go—"

"Keely." Sean put a big hand upon her shoulder. " 'Twas a storm in the Dragon's Tail. I was injured . . . in saving me, my son risked himself." His eyes glazed abruptly though the voice remained steady. "In Erinn, men rule. There is no one else left of my line."

Kellin drew in a breath. "Will Erinn have me?"

Aileen laughed softly. Grief had deeply marked her, but she was still profoundly Erinnish in coloring and speech. "With *your* eyes, my lad? They'll be needing no *kivarna* ... there's no mistaking your blood! They'll be having themselves an Erinnish lord even if he *is* Mujhar of Homana."

"As for me," Corin said, "I have always known I would go elsewhere for my heir." His hand enfolded Glyn's. "A barren queen is worthless, some men might declare—but I know better. I would trade her for nothing, and no one." He exchanged a smile with the woman who could not speak, and looked back at Kellin. "It seemed natural to me that Brennan be my heir should I predecease him, despite the arguments of our youth. He was withal a supremely compassionate and *competent* man, a man who understood responsibility; he was far better fit to rule than I." For a moment his voice faltered. "That now is moot, but there is another man to whom I might entrust my realm."

Kellin did not immediately answer. He was intensely aware that all of them looked at him expectantly, awaiting his response. He knew what it would be, but he wondered if *they* did; if they understood at all what was about to happen in the ordering of their world.

It has nothing to do with me. But they do not see it; they see only *me, and think of immediacies instead of the future. They have not yet reconciled what it is I have done by siring a son with Ginevra. I am Kellin to them, no more—except perhaps to my jehan, who understands very well.*

He smiled at Aidan and saw the answer in yellow eyes; indeed, his father knew. The *shar tahl*

knew many things. He was, after all, the mouthpiece of the gods.

*One day they will know. They will come to under-
stand. It has nothng to do with me.*

Kellin glanced at Sima. Then he looked back at
the others and gave them their answer. "*I* will
have none of your realms." Their startlement was
palpable in the minute stirring of their bodies, the
intensity in their eyes. "Should you predecease
me, you may be certain I shall respect and cherish
your lands, doing what I must to keep the people
content—but I will name none of them mine. I
will serve only as regent until such a time as my
son comes of age." He looked at his father; Aidan's
smile was content. "The Lion may swallow the
lands, but it is the Firstborn who shall rule them
in the name of ancient gods."

Epilogue

The Lion's claws curled down beneath Kellin's hands. His fingers followed the line, tracing gilt-etched wood. He sought the Lion's strength to carry him through the ceremony that would, in its celebration, herald a new age.

His arms were heavy with *lir*-gold; his brow ablaze with more. The weight at his left ear, after its emptiness, was infinitely reassuring. He was, at last, Cheysuli in all things; a *lir*-blessed warrior who also knew his balance.

Kellin drew in a deep breath, held it a long moment, then released it slowly. He was aware of approval emanating from beside his right leg, snugged between Mujhar and Queen to offer them both support: Sima sat in silence with tail tucked over paws. Great golden eyes were fixed on those gathering to witness the investiture of a new Prince of Homana.

So many people. His kinfolk, of course, grouped near the firepit: Aileen first, wearing the *lir*-torque Brennan had given her decades before. Their son, Aidan, with a raven upon his shoulder and his mother's hand in his. Hart with Rael, and Ilsa; Corin and Kiri with mute Glyn; Keely flanked by Sean. And *lir*, so many *lir*, in rafters and windows and corners.

Others also: the Homanan Council, complete in all regards, and the castle staff; Gavan, clan-leader

of Clankeep, with Burr and other *shar tahls;* plus
the multitudes of warriors, and women with large-
eyed children, from all the keeps of Homana. Ihlini also, from Solinde, who did not honor Asar-
Suti. No one was turned away. Those who could
not fit into the Great Hall gathered in corridors,
in other chambers, in the baileys; even, he had
been told, in the castle kitchens.

The firepit blazed. The sun beyond stained
glass slanted into the crowded hall, glinting off
lir-gold and other ornamentation, tinting into a
likeness the fair Homanan faces and dark Cheysuli ones.

Kellin noted it. He noted everything, but nothing stood out so much as the woman at his side.

She stood quietly at his right, holding linen-
swathed Cynric. She wore a velvet robe of deep
bloodied wine that was, in its folds, in its richness,
very nearly black. At her ears she wore rubies and
jet; her slender neck was weighted with the gold
of his *lir*-torque. Unbound silver hair fell in sheets
to her knees. The white around her face framed
an exquisite, alien beauty even more remarkable
for her pride, for the blazing of her spirit, for the
determination housed in icy Ihlini eyes.

This was *her* son. If it be her task alone, they
would none of them forget it.

Kellin smiled. *They will remember her from this
day. No matter what else may happen, they will
never forget Ginevra.*

He looked out again at the multitude, then rose
from the throne. He extended his right hand. Ginevra put into it her left, as her right arm cradled
Cynric. Two steps only, and they stood at the edge
of the marble dais steps.

Aidan moved out from the throng. His voice was
pitched quietly, but no one in the hall could not
hear what he said. "He is the sword." A shower of

sparks rose up from the firepit. "He is the sword and the bow and the knife. He is darkness and light. He is good and evil. He is the child and the elder; the girl and the boy; the wolf and the lamb."

No one spoke. No child protested, no *lir* ruffled wing.

Aidan's eyes were black. "*I am no one; I am everyone. I am the child of the prophecy; child of darkness and light; of like breeding with like until the blood is one again.*"

Stained glass shattered. Empty casements displayed a sudden darkness: the moon slid across the sun and did not depart. Inside, the hall was black; outside, the world was.

People cried out in fear; Homanans, Kellin knew. Cheysuli feared no gods.

Aidan's voice whispered: "*The sword—and the bow—and the knife.*"

Flames roared up in the firepit. The iron lid that covered the stairway to the Womb was flung back on its hinges, crashing into piled wood. In the flurry of ash and flame came a greater, more complex motion: the rushing torrent of dozens of *lir* issuing from the hole. In the flames they were creamy marble, with blind creamy eyes, but as they burst forth into the light, into the darkness of eclipse, marble shapechanged itself into the clothing of living *lir*.

Ginevra's hand gripped Kellin's. He felt her trembling; sensed the wonder in her heart, and his own, that their son could be the inheritor of so much power.

"*I am Cynric,*" Aidan said, "*and I am Firstborn of those who have returned.*"

Lir upon *lir*, freed of imprisonment, joined brother and sister *lir* in hammer-beamed rafters, in rune-rimmed sills, at the edge of the firepit. Others gathered near the dais.

Firepit flames died. The hall was left in darkness.

"*Cynric,*" Aidan said, "*who will bring light to the darkness so all men may see.*"

The darkness was complete. Silence was loud.

Then Kellin understood. He looked at Ginevra, marking the sheen of silver hair in the dimness of the hall. "Unwrap him."

Her mouth parted as comprehension filled her eyes. Ginevra deftly freed the week-old infant from embroidered linen wrappings. With an avid tenderness she handed him to Kellin, who raised him up, naked, to the multitudes.

Tiny arms waved. In the darkness fire bloomed. A pale, luminous gold born of infant-etched runes, that encompassed the darkness and defeated it. Its heart was livid white.

Upturned faces were illuminated. Kellin heard murmurings, saw groping hands reach out to one another. Homanans and Cheysuli were bound together by awe.

He looked at his kinfolk standing near the dais: Aileen, crying; Hart and Ilsa; Corin and Glyn; Keely and Sean, all clasping hands. Their expressions were rapt.

Aidan raised his hands to encompass everyone. "From among them shall come a *lir* worthy of the Firstborn. Worthy of the child who had united, in peace, four warring realms and two magical races." His voice soared above them. "Cynric, child of prophecy; the Firstborn come again!"

There was a shifting among the crowd as warriors looked at *lir*, and an abrupt apprehension that was palpable. Kellin himself felt it.

He looked sharply at Sima. *What is this? Will we lose the lir after all?*

Sima's eyes were fixed on him in an unwavering

intentness. Pupils were nonexistent. *You have wrought well. Decade after decade, until years became centuries, the Cheysuli have labored well. It is time now for two races to become one; for the power to be fixed as it was once before. From you and Lochiel's daughter will come others, and they in their turn shall sire their own, until the Firstborn as a race is viable again.*

He felt a clutch of trepidation. *What of us? What becomes of the Cheysuli and the Ihlini? Do we die out? Are we replaced?* He cast a harried glance at the gathered *lir*. Desperately he asked, *Have I destroyed my own race to elevate yours?*

The tip of her tail twitched.

Kellin began to tremble. *Sima—am I to lose you after all? To my son?* He could not bear it. He could not bear the idea. *Gods—do not do this! Would you have me be a monster to my people?*

Behold, Sima said.

"Behold!" Aidan cried.

Kellin heard it. At first he was not certain. Then he heard Ginevra's gasp and swung awkwardly, clasping the infant against his shoulder. He could not help himself; he stepped off the dais even as Sima preceded him; even as Ginevra fled.

But he knew. He *knew.* And his doubts spilled away.

He looked at Sima. She was fully grown and magnificent. *You knew all along.*

Golden eyes blinked. *I know many things. I am, after all, lir.*

"Look," Ginevra whispered. "Look what we have done!"

Kellin looked again. Words filled his mind, his mouth; too many words. He could not say them all; could not *think* them all.

In the end, he said the only ones he could manage. *"Leijhana tu'sai—"* he whispered, "for a *lir* such as this."

With meticulous precision, the throne unbent itself. Wood split and peeled away; gilt cracked and was sloughed as dust. The shoulders broke through first, heaving free of imprisonment, and then the head, twisting, as it freed itself from an ancient, rigid roar. The gaping jaws closed. The crouching beast dropped to all fours and shook its heavy mane, spraying chips of wood and gilt.

In the hall, people cried out: Homanan, Cheyuli, Ihlini. Some fell to their knees. Others mouthed petitions to various gods.

Wood cracked and popped. From the tattered prison emerged a male lion full-fleshed and in his prime. Golden eyes gleamed, stripped now of age-soiled gilt to display the soul inside. A flame burned there, kindling into a bonfire as he gazed upon the hall.

The lion shook himself. Wood chips flew into the hall; those that landed in the firepit popped once and hissed into smoke.

The grime of antiquity, the sheen of a thousand hands, was sloughed off with a single shrug of massive, mane-clad shoulders. Littering the dais was the wooden pelt newly shed; what stood before them now was the Lion of Homana as he once was, before a power wholly perverted had shape-changed him to wood.

The massive jaws opened, displaying fearsome teeth. His roar filled the hall. Fragments of glass still clinging to their casements shattered into colored spray.

The roar died. The lion scented, tasting the air, then took note of the tiny infant. Golden eyes sharpened. He padded forth to stand at the edge of the steps, gazing down upon the child who was unafraid of his roar. The rumble deep in his chest was one of abiding contentment, of a *lir* newly bonded.

Ja'hai-na, Kellin thought. *Imprisoned or no, this moment alone, here within the hall, has always been his tahlmorra.*

He looked down at the infant he cradled in his arms. The eyes were not open. The fists were impotent. But Kellin knew his son would never be measured by such things; he was Cynric, and Firstborn; he would measure himself against a personal criteria more demanding than any other.

The lion roared again. The moon moved off the sun. Sunlight filled the Great Hall, where a week-old, naked infant shaped tiny glowing runes.

Ginevra cried in silence. Kellin clasped and kissed her hand, raising it in tribute; he would have everyone know he honored his queen. "*Shansu*," he whispered. "The war is ended."

As the Lion lay down behind them, Kellin turned to the gathering and raised his son once more. "His name is Cynric. In the name of Cheysuli gods, who conceived and bore us all, I ask you to accept him as my heir, the Prince of Homana—and the Firstborn come again!"

He was met at first by silence. Then a murmuring, a rustling of clothing, a clattering of jewelry; and at last the acclamation, wholly unrestrained, echoed in the rafters. The tongues conjoining were two: Homanan and Cheysuli. But the answer was encompassed in single word said twice.

"*Ja'hai-na!*"

"Accepted!"

Aidan came first, followed by Aileen. And Hart, Corin, Keely. Sean, Glyn, and Ilsa. Each of them approached the infant Prince of Homana to offer the kiss of kinfolk; only they could.

And then the others came: one by one by one— Cheysuli, Ihlini, Homanan—to pay homage to the heir, to the son, to the Firstborn, while on the dais behind the child, where Deirdre's tapestry hung, the Lion of Homana guarded his newborn *lir*.

Author's Note

The *"Chronicles of the Cheysuli"* was not originally intended as a series, but a single book only, titled *The Shapechangers*. It was my first foray into *written* fantasy, although I'd been reading it for many years; I'd written other (unpublished) novels, but no fantasy, because I was afraid. I loved the genre too much, and feared I couldn't do it justice.

But my favorite authors—Marion Zimmer Bradley, C.J. Cherryh, Katherine Kurtz, Patricia McKillip, Anne McCaffrey, etc.—simply didn't write fast enough to suit my reading addiction; I decided the only way to survive was to manufacture a "fix" by writing my own novel.

And so I concocted a plot about a race of shapechangers and their animal familiars, and a girl born of a mundane culture being absorbed into a magical one.

But plots always require thickening . . . I added royalty, a prophecy, created the Ihlini. And then one day, immediately following a cultural anthropology class in which we'd spent fifty minutes drawing triangles and circles as a generational exercise, I decided to apply my newfound knowledge to my stand-alone fantasy novel.

A trilogy was born.

More triangles and circles got added to the chart. The trilogy became a seven-book series. And when I realized seven didn't *quite* cover everything, I added another and brought it to eight, whereupon I promised myself to end it. *Finis.*

Twelve years later, it's ended. The prophecy is complete.

No author likes to turn her back on a world and its people after spending so much time creating them; Homana's root, after all, is *home.* But she does it, at least for a while, because to linger longer is to risk creative stagnation.

The *"Chronicles of the Cheysuli"* have covered approximately 100 years in the history of Homana and her races, blessed and unblessed alike. It's my belief Cynric, child of prophecy—the final result of centuries of genetic manipulation—had his own share of adventures. It's also my conceit to wonder about the five undocumented years Finn and Carillon spent in exile; the boyhoods of Duncan and Finn; the adventures facing Keely, Hart, and Corin after leaving Homana; the true account of the love between Hale and Lindir and the events that touched off the *qu'mahlin* (although a "prequel" novelette, "Of Honor and the Lion," appeared in DAW's 1988 anthology, *Spell Singers.*)

In a history so vast, there are stories left to be told. Maybe someday I'll tell them.

—*J.R.*
Chandler, Arizona
1992

CHEYSULI/OLD TONGUE GLOSSARY
(with pronunciation guide)

a'saii (uh-SIGH)—Cheysuli zealots dedicated to pure line of descent.

bu'lasa (boo-LAH-suh)—grandson

bu'sala (boo-SAH-luh)—foster-son

cheysu (chay-SOO)—man/woman; neuter; used within phrases.

cheysul (chay-SOOL)—husband

cheysula (chay-SOO-luh)—wife

cheysuli (chay-SOO-lee)—*(literal translation)*: children of the gods.

Cheysuli i'halla shansu (chay-SOO-lee i-HALLA shan-SOO)—*(lit.)*: May there be Cheysuli peace upon you.

godfire (god-fire)—common manifestation of Ihlini power; cold, lurid flame; purple tones.

harana (huh-RAH-na)—niece

harani (huh-RAH-nee)—nephew

homana (ho-MAH-na)—*(literal translation)*: of all blood.

i'halla (ih-HALL-uh)—upon you: used within phrases.

i'toshaa-ni (ih-tosha-NEE)—Cheysuli cleansing ceremony; atonement ritual.

ja'hai ([French *j*] zshuh-HIGH)—accept

ja'hai-na (zshuh-HIGH-nuh)—accepted

jehan (zsheh-HAHN)—father

jehana (zsheh-HAH-na)—mother

ku'reshtin (koo-RESH-tin)—epithet; name-calling

leijhana tu'sai (lay-HAHN-uh too-SIGH)—(*lit.*): thank you very much.

lir (leer)—magical animal(s) linked to individual Cheysuli; title used indiscriminately between *lir* and warriors.

meijha (MEE-hah)—Cheysuli: light woman; (*lit.*): mistress.

meijhana (mee-HAH-na)—slang: pretty one

Mujhar (moo-HAR)—king

qu'mahlin (koo-MAH-lin)—purge; extermination

Resh'ta-ni (resh-tah-NEE)—(lit.): As you would have it.

rujho (ROO-ho)—slang: brother (diminutive)

rujholla (roo-HALL-uh)—sister (formal)

rujholli (roo-HALL-ee)—brother (formal)

ru'maii (roo-MY-ee)—(*lit.*): in the name of

Ru'shalla-tu (roo-SHAWL-uh TOO)—(*lit.*) May it be so.

Seker (Sek-AIR)—formal title: god of the netherworld.

shansu (shan-SOO)—peace

shar tahl (shar TAHL)—priest-historian; keeper of the prophecy.

shu'maii (shoo-MY-ee)—sponsor

su'fala (soo-FALL-uh)—aunt

su'fali (soo-FALL-ee)—uncle

sul'harai (sool-hah-RYE)—moment of greatest satisfaction in union of man and woman; describes shapechange,

tahlmorra (tall-MORE-uh)—fate; destiny; kismet.

Tahlmorra lujhala mei wiccan, cheysu (tall-MORE-uh loo-HALLA may WICK-un, chay-SOO)—(*lit.*): The fate of a man rests always within the hands of the gods.

tetsu (tet-SOO)—poisonous root given to allay great pain; addictive, eventually fatal.

tu'halla dei (too-HALLA-day-EE)—(*lit.*): Lord to liege man.

usca (OOIS-kuh)—powerful liquor from the Steppes.

y'ja'hai (EE-zshuh-HIGH)—(*lit.*): I accept.

DAW

A note from the publishers concerning:

Children of the Firstborn

You are invited to join "Children of the Firstborn," an organization of readers and fans of the works of Jennifer Roberson.

The club publishes a newletter which includes the latest information on Jennifer's books and appearances, as well as pen-pal addresses, convention news, and other items of interest to her fans.

For more information, please send a self-addressed, stamped envelope to:

> **Children of the Firstborn**
> **610 North Alma School Road**
> **Suite 18—Box #104**
> **Chandler, AZ 85224**

(This notice is inserted gratis as a service to readers. DAW Books is in no way connected with this organization professionally or commercially.)

Mercedes Lackey

These are the novels of Valdemar and of the kingdoms which surround it, tales of the Heralds—men and women gifted with extraordinary mental powers and paired with wondrous Companions—horselike beings whose aid they draw upon to face the many perils and possibilities of magic

THE LAST HERALD-MAGE

VOWS AND HONOR

KEROWYN'S TALE

THE HERALDS OF VALDEMAR

THE MAGE WINDS

DAW

Tad Williams

Memory, Sorrow and Thorn

THE DRAGONBONE CHAIR: Book 1
☐ **Hardcover Edition**   0-8099-003-3—$19.50
☐ **Paperback Edition**   UE2384—$5.99
A war fueled by the dark powers of sorcery is about to engulf the long-peaceful land of Osten Ard—as the Storm King, undead ruler of the elvishlike Sithi, seeks to regain his lost realm through a pact with one of human royal blood. And to Simon, a former castle scullion, will go the task of spearheading the quest that offers the only hope of salvation . . . a quest that will see him fleeing and facing enemies straight out of a legend-maker's worst nightmares!

STONE OF FAREWELL: Book 2
☐ **Hardcover Edition**   UE2435—$21.95
☐ **Paperback Edition**   UE2480—$5.99
As the dark magic and dread minions of the undead Sithi ruler spread their seemingly undefeatable evil across the land, the tattered remnants of a once-proud human army flee in search of a last sanctuary and rallying point, and the last survivors of the League of the Scroll seek to fulfill missions which will take them from the fallen citadels of humans to the secret heartland of the Sithi.

—and coming in March 1993—

TO GREEN ANGEL TOWER: Book 3
☐ **Hardcover Edition**   UE2521—$25.00
In this concluding volume of the best-selling trilogy, the forces of Prince Josua march toward their final confrontation with the dread minions of the undead Storm King, while Simon, Miriamele, and Binabek embark on a desperate mission into evil's stronghold.
